Weeping Willow

Volume Two: A Friend in Deed

by

Geoff Hoff and Steve Mancini

JCP

Joseph Coaler
Publications

Los Angeles, CA
JosephCoaler.com

ISBN-10: 0615699391
ISBN-13: 978-0615699394

Printed in the United States of America

Cover design by Geoff Hoff
Back cover oil painting by Evan G. Peele
Coins by the U.S. Mint

Table of Contents

Dedication

This book is dedicated to our stalwart fans who have ceaselessly harassed us to finally get this volume out. We also dedicate it to all those stalwart women who have carried their unborn children for the six years this book has been "in process" so they could give birth to coincide with the publication. We feel your pain. (Well, we are your pain.)

(Just as an update, we are only about $2,060,000 away from the $2,060,000 we keep asking for. When we get closer to the goal, we will post an attractive and informative thermometer graphic somewhere so you can watch with breathless anticipation as we close in on the goal. If you send us the $2,060,000, we'll send you an actual thermometer and dedicate Volume Three to you. Hell, for that, we'll go back, reprint Volumes One and Two and dedicate them both to you. In capital letters and a fancy font of your choice. As long as it's not Comic Sans.)

Introduction

This book has been six years in the making. It hasn't taken that long to write, that was already completed six years ago. It's just that the authors Geoff Hoff and Steve Mancini kept putting the publishing of it on the back burner. They aren't really sure why. In the ensuing years, Geoff has gained weight, Steve has lost a bit more hair and Lee and Peter have remained exactly the same, as if nothing from the outside world has impinged upon their reality. Not even the passing of Ernest Borgnine, if you can believe that. It's as if they were fiction.

If you haven't yet read Volume One, go back and read Volume One. But if you're too lazy to go back to Volume One, we hereby give you some of what you will need to know to make Volume Two make sense.

Lee Harris needed to get drunk.

A 30 year old box of Wheaties.

Dualit, the Rolls Royce of toasters.

There's a corsage in the freezer. And possibly Walt Disney.

Bubble Gum Alley and Danny Bonaduce.

Cuss Jars.

Abby Holiday.

That's all you need to know. Carry on.

Okay, seriously.

After finding out his wife had fallen in love with another man, Lee Harris, an accountant from Chicago, packed everything he could fit from his 8 year marriage into his SUV and left town. He ended up stranded in an odd town called River Bend and was forced to re-examine everything as he started over.

The story began in a motel room where Lee had been fermenting for three days. He decided a night on the town would lift his spirits, so he found a local watering hole called "The Office". It worked until he was thrown in jail for public intoxication after closing the place down. The next morning, hung over and despondent, he attempted to pull money from an ATM to pay for the taxi back to the motel and discovered his bank account was almost empty. He went to a diner, hoping a bite to eat would clear the cotton from his head, and found out that his credit cards were maxed; his wife had wiped him out. Then his car broke down in front of the diner. (During all of this, *Geoff* and **Steve** interrupted and argued about what should be happening, much to the annoyance of Lee, who really shouldn't have noticed, since he was fiction.)

Twain, the scruffy, unwashed diner owner who has a prom carnation (and possibly Walt Disney) in his freezer, took pity on him and offered work and a room in the attic until he could get back on his feet. Twain also got him to his court date (where they garnished his paltry wages to pay his fines) and helped him fix his car.

Flyers, ads and talk about the Willow Lane Theater bombarded Lee everywhere he turned. He used almost a week's pay to see a show there. Although angry with himself for incurring the expense, the experience of watching the play so overpowered him he decided to volunteer at the theater. There, he befriended Peter, a robust man with no fashion sense and a big laugh, who eats melted cheese when he's depressed. Peter has a cat, named Cliche for reasons you'll just have to imagine, and is, perhaps, the world's worst housekeeper. Except his bathroom. That was always spotless.

Lee also met Stella, who isn't very good at her job as the bookkeeper (her main talents are hair flipping and sarcasm) and Bear, a quiet man's man who is the tech director and likes tools.

Meanwhile, Jim Ackerman, a fairly good-looking but incompetent young private dick from Chicago, came to town. Lee's wife Beverly hired him to find Lee and get his signature so she could sell their house. After some hesitation, Lee decided to sign the papers and be done with her. Then he found out how much she spent on the detective. He sent the detective home without a signature.

Peter convinced Lee to get a small part in a play at the theater. He was too nervous to over act and was actually quite good in the part. After his debt to the court was paid, he wanted to leave town but couldn't because of the play. Then his wife sued for divorce. Lee engaged Andrew, one of his fellow actors, a retired lawyer (who might have three nipples), to be his attorney. Andrew also told Lee that Peter is gay and warned him to be careful because he thought Peter had fallen for him and he didn't want to see Peter get hurt.

During a drunken night playing Scrabble™, Peter told Lee that he was gay and was shocked to discover Lee already knew. Lee assured him that he wasn't gay, won the game using a seven-letter word with a "q" and a "z" in it across two "triple word score" squares, then fell asleep on the couch. While Peter pined for Lee, a very young actress and a very old (but strangely alluring) director named Agnes also pursued him, but he had his eye on Kim, a pretty woman he'd met at the bar that first night on the town. He asked Kim out, but ended up going to a concert with Abby, her big-boned, frizzy-haired friend.

Andrew worked out a deal with Beverly's lawyer, Mr. Washington, where he threatened to demand Excalibur, Beverly's Rat Dog, in order to convince her to split the income from the sale of Beverly's antiques with Lee, even though the thought of actually having the damn dog made Lee squeamish. It was a risky bluff, but somehow, it worked.

Jim came back to town. (Remember Jim? The bad detective?) He had realized just how bad a detective he was and wanted to re-invent himself like Lee had done. He wants to be Lee when he grows up. He beat Lee out for a part at the theater. Which didn't change Lee's mild disdain for him. Jim wanted to try every new thing, what with the whole re-invention thing, so he asked Peter out, much to Peter's dismay. After some clumsy, false starts, Jim and Peter ended up in bed. Peter was very, very, very surprised, but happy. Jim kind of hated it. Peter invited him to Thanksgiving dinner and Jim figured a second date, without the stress of the first one, would confirm or refute his straightness (although he really had no idea what "refute" meant).

Peter prepared an amazing dinner for Jim. Across town, Abby and Lee went to a party at her folks. After dinner, Jim lunged at Peter and they ended up back in bed. After the party, Lee kissed Abby goodnight, a kiss that lasted too long to be friendly, and Lee went home very happy. The next morning, Peter woke to discover Jim, fully dressed, sitting in a chair. Across town, Lee woke feeling good for the first time in months.

See? You didn't really have to read Volume One at all, it's all right here. Of course, it's much funnier in the original. And there is a lot more detail. 220 pages of it. Rich, exciting, transformational pages. With tenting pants and a plasma center. Who knows, that one piece of information that could somehow change your life, make you a better person, bring you money, fame, get you laid, bring you the admiration of millions, may be in that detail that is missing here.

In any case, the story continues in Weeping Willow Volume Two: A Friend in Deed. Turn the page. It's right there.

Up til now: Lee has finally signed the divorce papers; Beverly will sell her Beemer to pay for his half of the value of the antiques in order to save the rat dog. Peter didn't listen very well when Lee told him about it. Lee woke to the feel of Abby's kiss on his lips, Peter woke to the sight of Jim, fully dressed, sitting on the chair. Everyone ate way too much for Thanksgiving. Veronica and Billy are proving to be just literary devices. To see how all of this except the eating too much thing relates to the story at hand, read volume one to catch up. Then come back and read this one.

Installment Sixteen
"A Friend in Deed"

Lee could hear a soft whine as he made his way across the dark stage lit only by the single, bare ghost light. The light made the brightly colored set for The Wiz look like a scene from Eraserhead. Lee refused to shiver. The sound grew louder when he went back into the men's dressing room. For a moment he imagined that the sound was coming from Roger's room, that dark maw to the side that took the space between the men's and women's dressing rooms. He walked quickly past the maw but the sound was still ahead of him. He opened the back door of the dressing room. The sound was clearly coming from the tin shack that stood behind the theater and served as the scene shop.

Bear was standing at the table saw, covered in sawdust. The sound from the saw could be heard for miles and miles and miles and miles. (*Who sang that?* **Yes.** *No, they're on first.*) The room smelled of sweet, scorched wood. It smelled really good, like pipe tobacco in the distance on a cold day. Lee breathed it in. Then he sneezed it back out again with four sharp shakes of his head.

He had to shout three times before Bear heard him. Bear hit the switch and pushed the goggles up into his hairline. (**Isn't Bear almost**

bald? *Yes, the goggles are on the top of his head. Toward the back.* **Why don't you just say he pushed them into his hair line fracture.** *Go play, Steve.*)

"Oh, hi," Bear said, then spit sawdust out of his mouth and rubbed it with the back of his hand, which was covered with sawdust. He spit again. "Grab that parrot."

"Arrr," Lee said.

"I mean that plane. Make the wood look old and gnarly. Plane the edges unevenly and leave some raw edges and burrs. Like that," Bear explained, pointing to a few lengths of wood that, but for the freshly cut surface, looked like they had been taken out of an old barn.

"I'm used to using tools to make bad wood look good."

"Welcome to theater," Bear said as he roughly brushed sawdust off his forearm then started to replace his goggles.

"Yeah," Lee said as he picked up the plane. "About that."

Bear let the goggles stay on the top of his head, and brushed sawdust from his moustache as he waited for Lee to continue. It floated down and rested gently on the hair that protruded from the top of his tee-shirt.

"I've been thinking," Lee said, then waited for dramatic pause. Damn, he thought. I would never have waited for dramatic pause in Chicago. "When we finish this set, I'm going to stop volunteering here."

Bear raised his eyebrows. Both of them. They were both covered in sawdust. Some floated gently down to the bridge of his nose, and he absent-mindedly brushed it away with the tips of his fingers.

"I don't know what I was doing here in the first place. I'm not an actor. I never even saw a play until I came here. Well, there was Chorus Line. I hated it. I've had fun, but I'm kidding myself. I'll never be an actor. And I'm tired of finding myself doing things like waiting for the dramatic pause."

"I'm sorry to hear that," Bear said. "You got a really nice butt."

(*STEVE!!! Bear is not gay.* **He has a moustache.** *He's artistic.* **Like I said.** *I've signed you up for sensitivity training.* **Tried it. I pissed the instructor off too much.** *I'm not surprised.*)

"I'm sorry to hear that. I've enjoyed working with you."

He put his goggles back on and hit the switch. The saw threw fine dust in a gentle, insistent arc like the rooster tail behind a speed boat or the meaning behind a mixed metaphor, and almost half of it landed on Bear. The sound that filled the room comfortably blanketed it and deadened any need for conversation. Lee felt the bond that only straight men can feel when they are in the same room completely ignoring each other.

An hour later, Bear turned the saw off, and Lee leaned the board he was mangling against the growing pile of other mangled boards. Bear sent Lee back to Roger's Room to get a few bags of powdered paint pigment. Lee stopped short and looked at Bear.

"Okay," he said. "I won't be here much longer. I have to know. Is Roger's room haunted?"

"Yes."

The answer was so simple and straightforward that Lee had trouble breathing. He hadn't been sure his question was even serious until he had gotten the answer.

"About twenty-five years ago, I guess, the guy who was artistic director of the theater went in there to stoke the furnace. He'd been working alone and the theater was cold. It was about this time of year, I think. There was a puddle of stove oil on the floor and he skidded on it and fell. His foot slipped under a pipe and he hit his head on the floor. He woke up with a broken leg and started calling for help. They found him the next Monday, frozen stiff with his arm outstretched, his face mangled in a frozen, grotesque grimace, and frozen claw marks on the floor."

"Really?"

"No."

Lee tried to decide how to react to that story. His face must have done something strange, because Bear suddenly started laughing.

"I knew you were joking."

"No, you didn't. You're more gullible than Peter. He thought the Angel for Look Homeward Angel was Roger. Screamed like a little girl."

Lee's face got really red, and he turned to go get the paint. He quickly found the five colors Bear had asked for, then purposefully stood to prove he had known the room wasn't haunted. The theater groaned and he ran very quickly back to the scene shop.

After his shift was over, he stopped by the front office to say hi to Peter. Peter's chair was empty, and cobwebs had covered his desk. A thick layer of dust covered everything on his side of the room.

"Where's Peter?" Lee asked Stella.

"He called in sick this morning."

Cliche waited on the welcome mat, curled in a ball, shivering. Lee knocked on Peter's front door. At first there was no response. Then there was a strange sound like a lump adjusting itself on a couch, then more nothing. Lee knocked again. Then he banged.

"What?"

"It's me," Lee said, then, when there was no response, added, "Lee."

The sound of the lump moving on a couch got closer, then the door opened. Peter looked like hell. Well, maybe purgatory. With overalls. And large pores. Without a word, he lumped back to the couch, leaving the door opened. Cliche followed Lee in warily, making sure Peter didn't throw too much lumpness at him, then ran past and into the bedroom. Lee closed the door behind himself. There was an old, tattered copy of Tajar Tales on the floor in front of where Peter sat, next to a sauce pan full of a turkey carcass. The television was tuned to a frenetic sitcom featuring wacky adults and precocious children being snotty to each other. The sound was, thankfully, very low, so only a constant, insistent rumble underscored by frenetic computer-generated laughter leaked into the room, leaving a puddle on the floor that Lee almost slipped on. He cleared a place on the couch for himself and sat. The room was, somehow, even more chaotic than usual. When Lee noticed, on the coffee table, right next to the tiny metal boot, a bowl that was encrusted with several layers of dried Colby, he knew something must be wrong with Peter. He pointed to it.

"The Dick?"

Peter's mind swirled with possible interpretations of that utterance. None of them made any sense. Lee waited for Peter to process. He was now accustomed to minds having to do that, and resigned to having to wait for it to happen.

"Jim?" he elaborated when he realized Peter's processing wasn't going to settle on any satisfactory conclusion.

Peter sighed and looked like he might cry. Lee was afraid the next question might open the floodgates and he would actually have to deal with a blubbering male person, but Peter was his friend.

"What happened?"

"I woke up Friday morning," Peter said with a small sob in his voice, "and the first thing I saw was the clock, which said six forty-two. The next thing I saw was Jim, fully dressed, sitting in the chair."

Cliche walked back into the room just in time to be hit in the forehead by the flashback. (*Film school?* **Evergreen State.** *That's really obscure.*)

Peter slowly sat up, letting the covers slide down his (*Steve, close your eyes*) naked body. He saw Jim's eyes dart away, and he grasped the edge of the blankets and slowly pulled them back up to his neck (*you can open them again*).

"Good morning," he tried.

Jim breathed in and opened his mouth, stopped, then opened his mouth again.

"I knew I'd be too inexperienced," Peter said. "I knew I'd be too clumsy. I'm so sorry. I knew I'd screw it up."

"No," Jim said. "It's not that. It's not you. It's me."

Peter tried not to cry. He was fairly sure he succeeded. He also tried to not roll his eyes. He wasn't so sure he succeeded with that.

"You're really fun, you cook good," Jim said. It sounded somehow written out and rehearsed. "I guess I'm just hopelessly straight. It's not that I don't want to be with you. I don't want to be with any man. I don't want to be with Brad Pitt. I don't want to be with Antonio Banderas. I don't want to be with Mr. T or Tom Cruise."

"What about Robert Redford?"

"Now or twenty-five years ago?"

Peter was really confused. About the whole conversation, not just the now or twenty-five year thing. He had been so sure that Jim had hated it the first time but Jim had asked him out again. Then he had been so sure he had loved it the second time, but here he was declaring his straightness.

"I needed to be sure," Jim explained.

"So this was kind of like the second Laughing Cow Cheese wedge."

5

"Good & Plenty," Jim said. "They don't look like licorice, you know. I always have to be sure. With both a white one and a pink one. I hate licorice. Tastes like medicine."

Jim shuddered slightly. Which didn't make Peter feel good at all. The blanket began to fall toward his chest during the conversation, but he lifted it securely around his neck like a barber's smock, not wanting to cause any further offense to this handsome young man who had had to suffer through two nights with him.

"I couldn't just leave because you fixed that wonderful dinner last night," Jim said. "It would have seemed so, what is the word?"

"Cruel?"

"I was actually thinking ungrateful."

Jim stood, reached out his hand to shake Peter's. Peter made sure his other hand kept the blanket securely in place. He had never been quite so ashamed of his nakedness before. Or, at least, aware of it. Actually, he realized, he had almost never been naked in front of anyone else. Except in high school gym. And there was that night in Barstow. But that has nothing to do with this flashback. They shook hands and Jim left, assuring him they'd see each other around. Peter slowly let the blanket slide back down his naked body (**Geoff, you didn't warn me.** *Sorry.* **I need a Good & Plenty. White**), and was surprised to discover tears leaking from his eyes. I'm the opposite of Liza Minnelli, he thought. I turn men straight. Or at least I'm the test by which they measure their straightness. He was certain he didn't like being litmus paper. He peeked at his wrist. Yep, blue.

"So you've been eating cheese for four days?" Lee asked.

God, straight men are so insensitive, Peter thought.

"God, straight men are so insensitive," he said, instead. "Yes. The one chance I have in decades, and he's hopelessly, incurably straight."

"Wait," Lee said. "I assumed you two... You know... um... "

"Duh," Peter said.

"Then he's gay."

"No, that's the whole point. He's straight."

"But he had sex with a man," Lee protested, realizing somewhere in the back of his mind that, besides a brief thought about his life with Beverly, that was the first time anyone had said that word in several installments, even though they had all been about that.

6

"Oh, so if I spent a night with a woman, even if I hated it, I'd be straight?" Peter was not happy with the turn of the conversation.

"Okay, so he's bisexual."

"No, Lee. He's straight."

"It's like losing your virginity," Lee said. "Once you do it, you can't go back. If he... "

"Look, if I thought he might even be bisexual, then I'd have to say it was that he didn't like me, not that he didn't like it. He's straight. Leave it at that."

God, gay men are so sensitive, Lee thought. Peter, on the other hand, just thought how bullheaded Lee was being.

"I just don't get bisexuality," Lee said, not leaving it at that. "It just doesn't make sense to me. It's like being both a Republican and a Democrat. Just choose."

Peter was nonplused. "People like both vanilla and chocolate ice cream," he said, pointedly ignoring Whigs, Tories and Libertarians. He wondered what ever happened to Ed Clark. He was getting frustrated. This was supposed to be about me crying on my friend's shoulder, not a philosophical dialogue on human sexuality.

"But they're both ice cream."

"And they're both people. Go take a class."

Peter went into his room and slammed the door. Lee was shocked by that. He looked down at Cliche, who was looking at him with a rather judgmental look.

"What?"

Cliche shook his head, then turned and left the room with his head up and his tail in the air.

"I was just trying to help," Lee said. "Jesus."

He sat for a moment waiting for Peter to get over it and come back into the living room.

"God, gay men are so immature," he said, and stormed out. If there had been a dog there, he would have kicked it. Well, not really. The absence of the dog made him think of kicking one, but if there had actually been a dog, he would have just kept being angry, which is ultimately what he did without the dog. No animals were harmed in the making of this installment. Get over it, PETA. The air was that deep gray with dark yellow at the edges that predicted an overpowering snow. That suited Lee just fine. Stupid gay man.

The Office was quiet. There were only two people at the bar, an Ag student with a 4H hat and a faded Doobie Bros. 1977 World Tour tee-shirt that had part of the left arm-pit missing, and an art teacher whose lipstick matched his shoes. The woman with the fur coat was taking the night off. Abby bought the first round and brought it to the table. She was drinking a Cosmopolitan with orange bitters; refreshingly clear and light maroon. Kim had something pink and blended with a plastic sword spearing a maraschino cherry, pineapple wedge and slice of kiwi. The art teacher had a bourbon straight, and the Ag student drank whatever the special was, which that night was named after a rude act you could perform with something gray and murky.

Kim carefully pulled the fruit off the spear one by one with the tips of her fingernails, and placed them on a napkin in a neat row. She looked up at Abby as she picked up the cherry using the plastic sword like a fork.

"Okay, you've been smiling uncontrollably since you got out of your car," she said as she plucked the stem from the cherry like a small boy would pluck the wing from a fly. "What's going on?"

"I always smile," Abby said and took a petite sip of her drink.

"Not like that you don't," Kim said as she took a bite from the cherry, then set it down on the napkin.

"I'm a happy kind of girl." Her smile got even broader.

Kim speared the pineapple and nibbled at the tip of it instead of responding. Abby felt the edges of her face begin to hurt. She looked down at her drink to see if she could make her mouth behave. Even the forced frown felt like a smile so she gave up. Out of the corner of her eye, she saw her sweatshirt, which said "My other sweatshirt is funnier than this one," and it caused her to give up all pretense.

"Okay," she said. "I kissed someone." (**What, is she in sixth grade?** *No, Steve, you are.* **Eat poop.**)

Kim was eating the kiwi from the edges in. She stopped long enough to ask, "Who? When?"

"Lee. Thanksgiving. In my front yard." Her face had started to calm down, but that was too much for it.

"Lee? Harris? From the diner?"

"I know he asked you out. You didn't seem interested. I hope you don't mind."

8

"God, no," Kim said and set the center part of the kiwi slice where all the seeds were down on the napkin and took a sip of her pink stuff. "Have you seen him since?"

Abby gave Kim a "did you take sensitivity training with Steve" look and told her that they had talked for four hours on the phone Friday after the diner had closed. Again for seventeen minutes Sunday afternoon.

"You haven't seen him since, then. So you haven't slept with him, yet."

"No, Kim," Abby said. "I'm saving myself for Ghandi."

Kim looked at her, bewildered, then finished the other half of the cherry. Abby loved Kim dearly and would do anything or go anywhere for her, but sometimes she wondered where she kept her brains. (**That really hurt, Geoff.** *What, brains?* **No the sensitivity training look thing.** *No, it didn't.* **No. It didn't. I'm trying to be sensitive.** *No, you're not.* **No. I'm not.** *Here's a match.* **Cool!**)

When they got outside, the gray and yellow sky had chameleoned into dark white, and snow seemed to swirl up from the ground in loose spirals. Kim and Abby both huddled closer into their coats and ran to their cars. As they drove home, the snow slowed and stopped, a tease for the kids in town who watched the sky, praying for an avalanche. Kids went to bed disappointed. Except Abby's nephew, who had just finished his first stink bomb and was looking forward to detonating it the next day in the cafeteria.

On Friday, Andrew called Lee into his office because the check from the antiques had come. In the package from Mr. Washington's office were also papers he needed to sign to transfer the deed to the house to Beverly so she could sell it. While he signed the papers, he had the nagging sensation he had seen them before. He sat back in Andrew's leather chair and looked at the check. After expenses, his half of the appraised value of the antiques was seventeen thousand, two hundred fourteen dollars and one cent. He realized he would finally have to open a checking account.

"Aren't you going to ask about the penny?" Andrew asked.

It hadn't occurred to Lee that there was anything odd about the penny.

"But I had a joke all prepared," Andrew said, plaintively.

"Okay. What about the penny?"

"It doesn't work, now."

Lee opened his account in the River Bend Mutual Farm and Home Financial Savings and Loan. When presented with a choice for check design, he looked over the ones with Disney and Warner Bros® characters, with rainbows, with mountain lakes, with Snoopy and Woodstock and cute kittens and puppies©, with lighthouses and gardens. There were flower designs and whales, trees and endangered species. Checks with wheat and checks with rice. He chose the green ones with darker green wavy lines™. Checks should look like checks, he thought.

He called Peter to let him know the check had come. Stella said she'd give him the message. Peter never returned the call. He called Abby. After they talked for twenty-even minutes, Abby asked what he was going to do next.

"Look for a place, I suppose."

She offered to help. They made a date for the next afternoon. She'd bring the newspaper, he'd bring the paint brush and Mazola (*Steve.* **What?** *Never mind*) I mean the stiffy (**You should have stopped me when you had the chance**) lunch.

When Lee put the phone down, he felt Twain looking at him. He turned and Twain was, indeed, looking at him.

"Yes?"

"You're moving out," Twain said.

"I guess so."

"I can't afford to pay you more than the hundred bucks."

"I know," Lee said. "I don't know what I'm going to do, really. I haven't even thought about looking for work, I just decided to look for a place to live. I suppose I can tell you I'll stay till the end of the month at least. I don't know. I have to think about what I'm going to do. I don't know. Now I sound like Peter." Damn gay man, he thought.

Twain nodded and went back into the kitchen. He looked a little hurt, which puzzled Lee. Does he expect me to stay up in the attic my entire life, he thought. Why is everyone being so weird, all of a sudden?

After the Saturday breakfast rush Lee joined Abby at a booth. They sat on the same side, poring over a red plastic basket of french fries and The River Bend Bee. The first ad they saw was for an apartment in Old Town. Lee said they should look at that. Abby looked at him like his head had just turned paisley.

"Old Towns are usually quaint," he said.

"In River Bend, Old Town is just old. Let's keep looking." She looked down again, then stopped. "Let's start at the beginning. What are you looking for?"

"Mr. Goodbar."

"Ha ha."

"I don't know. A place with a bedroom. A place with windows. A place in the sun."

"A room with a view?"

"The house of the seven gables."

"Little house on the prairie?"

"The house of Usher."

"That fell. The house of wax?"

"Harvest home?"

"The longest yard?"

"Citizen Kane?"

They looked at each other, waiting for the other one to laugh.

"Here's one in a fairly good neighborhood," Abby said, finally, when neither one did. "And it doesn't seem too expensive."

They marked three possibilities and climbed into Lee's SUV. They would have marked more, but the River Bend Bee didn't have a very large classified section. The section advertising pornographic movies was seven pages. The obituary section was ten pages but listed everyone who might die in the next month or so in seven counties. And, of course, the police log. Lee played Invention No. 8 by Bach on the steering wheel as he drove. Abby sang along.

Lee loved the first apartment they saw, but Abby thought the lines were all wrong. He finally had to agree with her when he bumped into the kitchen doorway. The second home they looked at smelled like old salad dressing and Depends. They held their breath all the way back to the car. After they shut and locked the doors, they exhaled in unison, then started laughing and tried to come up with the perfect description of the odor. They settled on "icky," and Lee started driving.

"So have you heard from Peter, yet?" Abby asked.

Lee shook his head. He still wasn't sure why Peter wasn't returning his calls. He didn't know why Twain was acting so weird. He didn't know what else to do. He didn't know what he had done. He was glad Abby wasn't mad, at least.

"You should just apologize."

"I didn't do anything wrong," Lee said.

They had to drive through downtown, such as it was, to get to the next place. On the sidewalk outside of Mom's Used Records, the man in the John Deere hat was on the top of a ladder which leaned against a lamp post. He was hanging a silvery garland from a wire that was stretched across the street. It looked like a tinsel boa shaped like a child's drawing of flapping bells. There were already garlands shaped like reindeer, trees, stars, angels and what Lee could only imagine must be tree ornaments hanging on wires that were evenly spaced down the street past Bubble Gum Alley all the way to the end. The man in the John Deere hat climbed down the ladder and moved it to the next light post as Lee turned the corner and left Christmas behind.

Nothing that they looked at that day seemed satisfactory, but Lee wasn't in a hurry. He had a place to stay until the end of the month, at least. Unless Twain got weird. Weirder. They decided to meet again after the breakfast rush the next day. Sunday seemed the perfect day to find a place to land. Lee felt normalcy creeping slowly, wonderfully, enticingly into his veins. He liked the feeling. It made him realize what he had been missing since that fateful day when he had seen the look in Beverly's eyes when she looked at the look in the Jerk's. It was heady and made his feet feel warm. It also made him impatient. When the normalcy had finally filled his circulatory system, he would no longer need to look for ways to reinvent his life. He had, he realized with a shudder, always hated people who reinvented themselves. It seemed like such a redundant, unnecessary, unneeded process.

That night, the storm that had peeked its head over the horizon on Monday descended like the wrath of a vengeful god and buried the town like salve on a hooker. By the time Lee descended the stairs from his lair in the morning, the snowdrift in front of Twain's had already reached the middle of the front window. There would be no customers until the plows had come through. He turned on the batter encrusted radio that sat on the shelf by the stove. The college DJ was in the middle of announcing that the county snow plows were snowed in. Lee heard a strange sound from the front of the diner that sounded like a swishing creak. All he needed was for Roger to want breakfast. He picked up a knife and backed up behind the center prep island. He looked at the knife, put it down and picked up a much larger one. Then he picked up an iron skillet. All he needed was chain mail. Now he really couldn't wait until the normalcy took over. The shuffling, creaking noise seemed to be moving closer, and he backed away and slowly bent his knees until his eyes were level with the top of the island. The apparition that floated into view was pure white and slightly fluffy. It shook, and seemed to dissipate into the room. What was left when it finished dissipating was Twain, holding a shovel.

"Isn't the coffee made, yet?" he said.

Lee set the knife and pan down on the lower shelf of the center island and tried to look as if that had been why he was stooping down there, then he stood slowly, making sure his knees were ready to hold his weight after their redundant bout of fear.

Twain sat at the counter drinking coffee and reading the paper. Lee sat two stools down poring over the classifieds. Every time he circled something, Twain muttered. At around ten, Lee finally had to admit they weren't going out that day to look for a place and called Abby.

"And I had a picnic lunch all packed and ready," Abby said.

Lee laughed. Abby didn't. Lee said he was sorry. Abby laughed. Lee didn't. Abby said she was sorry. Then they both laughed at the same time as they both said they were sorry.

"There's an old Jamaican saying about weather like this," Abby said.

"And that would be?"

"What the hell is all that white stuff all over the ground? Mon."

Lee laughed.

"No. Really," Abby said. "I'm part Jamaican. I should know."

Lee didn't know whether to laugh or not. This was getting ridiculous. Up until then, their humor had been so in sync. So peaches and cream. So tears for fears.

"You're really part Jamaican?"

"Actually, yes."

13

"Okay," he said. "What's the other part?"

Abby breathed in.

"Well. Um... ," she said. "Part Chippewa. That's the cheekbones. Jamaican, the skin. Part Norwegian. Except lightening the Jamaican skin, I have no idea what that part gives me."

"Love of fjords?"

"No, I like Chevies. Maybe that huggable protective outer layer that keeps out the cold. Irish, a sense of dark humor and love of fjords. And my grandma was from Malta so I have Italian and French and Arab. Everybody conquered Malta at one time or other and all of them add mass to the butt and a lovely singing voice. Persian, the hair. Maybe that's the Jamaican, too. Persian must be the lips. And the eyes. We Persians have beautiful eyes. And German. Sales. What are you?"

"White."

Then a bus full of Hooters girls broke down in front of the diner. (*No, Steve. No bus. No hooters. No girls.*)

The town started moving again sometime in the middle of Tuesday. Lee and Abby made a date for Saturday afternoon. On their way to the first house on the list, Abby shouted for Lee to stop. Stopping suddenly on winter streets was problematic, but nothing happened that could have added drama to the story. When Lee calmed down enough to ask why she had requested the departure from the agreed upon schedule, she pointed at the tiny handmade "For Rent" sign stapled to a rickety post in the front yard of a strange, little, pale yellow house with a strange, little, pale green garage that was unattached because it was afraid to commit. Lee wasn't sure. Strange wasn't what he had in mind.

"It's darling," Abby said.

Darling, Lee could live with, so they got out and began to explore. The price listed on the sign was well within Lee's budget. The front door was open. Abby went in, and after a moment of extremely uncomfortable hesitation, Lee followed. The house smelled good, not like grease or old salad dressing or anything. The lines inside were solid. There was a stone fireplace in the front room, and a fairly good-sized kitchen. The bathroom wasn't large but was laid out comfortably. Lee stood in the front doorway and looked out at the neighborhood. The houses on either side were brick and looked solid and steady. The trees in the neighborhood looked well established. A lot of them were willows, which Lee thought might remind him a bit too much of his foray into art, but the back yard was decidedly middle class and predictable. He breathed in the cold air that made the hairs in his nostrils stand on end.

"It's old," Lee said.

"It's established."

"It's drafty."

"It's airy. Breezy," Abby countered. "In the spring you're going to get the smell of all the flowers."

"It's not near anything."

"Everything is near everything in River Bend, Lee. It's not Chicago."

Lee didn't want to admit that he was really beginning to like the place. It did feel steady. When she mentioned that he could set up a workshop in the basement, he shook his head and conceded. He was just going to rent it, after all. How long could the lease be, six months? A year? They took down the number from the sign and drove back to the diner.

Peter and Stella had just finished counting receipts from the weekend. The December show always did well, but The Wiz looked like it might break the records set by last year's holiday production of Equus. Peter was in the hallway on his way to the men's room and saw Lee coming back from the scene shop, covered in brown and pale yellow paint splatters. He tried to decide if there was enough time to duck back into the office, or, perhaps, run to the restroom. The moment of indecision froze him for that moment too long. Lee faltered when he saw him, which Peter noticed, which made him angry with himself for not ducking back into the office or running into the bathroom. Maybe he could have snuck into the script closet, but that would have just been too trite. And he wasn't really very good at snucking.

"Hey, Peter," Lee said, trying unsuccessfully to sound like they weren't mad at each other.

Peter just stared at him, not willing to pretend, but not sure what he could say that wouldn't sound just too bitchy. The result was that his face looked like a small puppy locked behind an accordion gate. Lee stopped, waiting for Peter to get over it and join him in his pretense, and when the puppy look didn't go away, he shook his head and left the theater. Peter could feel the puppy look turn into that of a bull behind an electrified barbed wire fence. He completely forgot that he had to pee. He turned to storm back into the office, but saw Stella standing in the doorway with an odd look on her face, like that of a fly on a wall. He turned to go to the bathroom and saw Jim coming out of the theater, whistling a happy tune. Off key, but happy. The script closet was looking very inviting in oh, so many ways. He sidled toward the men's room. Jim didn't see him, thankfully, because Agnes came out of the theater and caught his attention, giving Peter just enough time to disappear. He closed and locked the stall door, in case Jim was in the hallway headed for his own relief break, but his plumbing refused to co-operate. It was quite frightened that Jim could see behind stall doors. He stood there for several minutes. The door to the bathroom didn't open. He noticed an edge of dirty gray in the corner between the floor and wall. Then he saw a spider. Now he knew he wasn't going to be able to pee.

"Quit looking at me," he said.

Then the spider threw an Ohio Blue Tip at him. (*Different spider, Steve.* **Oh. They're both in the theater, maybe it's a clan thing.** *Sort of like church mice?* **Um. Yeah.**)

The landlord of the house returned Lee's call late Monday afternoon. Lee met him Tuesday afternoon to fill out the application. On Thursday, the landlord called back and said he had the house, and to bring a check by for first, last and a security deposit. It was the first check Lee had written in a very long time and it felt weird. It was a starter check, and that felt weird, like training wheels for an accountant. It also felt weird spending the money from the furnishings to his life with Beverly. There was satisfaction and sadness wrapped up in the pen stroke as he signed his name on the micro-printed signature line. He was taking proceeds from his stable life to stabilize his life. The need to process the reaction was fading, though, so he was pleased.

He wanted to call Abby the minute he signed the papers, but she was out in the field, convincing people that radio was the way to get the word out. Then he thought about calling Peter, but remembered that they were being mad at each other. He called Bear instead.

"Congratulations," Bear said. "Let me help you move in."

"Thanks, but I only have a box of CDs and some tools," Lee said with a laugh. "I don't need help with those. I'm going to go Saturday after work and clean, then carry my boxes from the car to the house. Nothing to it."

"Didn't the landlord clean the place before he put it up for rent?"

Lee was not sure even how to respond to that. Yes, he was sure they did, but only enough to get by. He needed to know it was clean.

"I have to do something," Bear said. "I'll bring some beer and help scrub. We'll make it a party."

"You don't have to do that," Lee said.

"Okay," Bear said. "What time do you want me there?"

Lee sighed, resigned, and told him he and Abby would be there around eight-thirty. Then he called Andrew to thank him for all he had done. He mentioned that Bear was coming by to help clean and Andrew thought that was a wonderful idea and that he'd bring the wife. Lee tried to object, but he had learned early on that Andrew overruled all objections.

On Friday, he called the gas and electric companies. The electricity was already on and just had to be switched to his name. The gas, which was how the house would be heated, wouldn't be turned on until Monday, because someone would have to come out to inspect it before they turned it on. They didn't want his new domicile exploding on his first night there. That would look really bad on their record. Every time Lee made or received a phone call, Twain pursed his lips. Lee had never thought Twain would have been a lip purser. Why was he being so un-Twain-like all of a sudden? He was usually so unfazed.

Saturday morning after brunch, Lee went shopping for basic furniture. Abby would have gone with him, but had to go to a live remote for one of her accounts, the House of Flapjacks™. They were giving away free short stacks of apple cinnamon flapjacks with every purchase of a fifteen-dollar gift certificate. They had roving carolers and a guy dressed up as Santa who did a live interview every half hour to get the kiddies excited. Abby really hated having to go, because shopping for furniture with someone else's money seemed like a lot more fun. She was also afraid Lee was going to go to Ikea and get

17

wrought iron, white pine and muslin. Lee told her she had no faith. Then he threw away the Ikea flyer he had found under his windshield the week before. He had enough time to get a couch, chair, coffee table and lamp before he had to get back for the dinner rush. Twain let him go early, which puzzled him.

"You have to move in," Twain said, then wiped what could have been a tear and could have been a stray fleck of butter from his cheek. Lee hoped it was butter, then just wished he hadn't seen it at all. Twain went in back and came out with the poached egg form thing and handed it to Lee.

"House warming," he said.

He was just getting used to Twain being fazed. Why was everyone being so nice to him all of a sudden?

Lee turned on the hot water in his new bathroom to fill the bucket. It spurted, sputtered, splatted then came out cold, orange and cloudy. The rest of the cleaning supplies were stacked in the living room next to the new furniture. He let the water run for a while, and went into the living room to start planning his cleaning strategy. Abby was standing there with a takeout box filled with a short stack of apple cinnamon flapjacks, looking at the living room furniture. It looked inexpensive, and very conservative, but at least it was solid, not "we include the tools". He hugged her, and they kissed, going right past the friendly into the something more. Then she disengaged and Lee tried to decide where they should start.

"First we have to explore," Abby said. "You have to know what you just got."

There was a door to the basement in the kitchen. In the basement was a work bench, but it would take some doing to make it usable. It was homemade, old, full of holes, lopsided, sloppily covered with faded green paint. There was a huge vice on the corner that had been, at sometime in the distant past, bright red. Now, there were a few flakes of red peeking through the grime and oil on it. It smelled like an old vice. It was perfect. Lee really felt at home. There were cans of rusty nails and screws, bolts and nuts and washers and a coffee tin full of what looked like laundry soap. Abby pointed out the gas hookup for a dryer and the plumbing for a washer next to a basin sink. Next to that was a pile of old newspapers. Once he was settled, he thought with a smile, this was going to be where he would spend most of his time. On the way back up the stairs, Abby pointed out some deep scratches on the outside of the basement door. They had been painted over, but never filled. My first handyman project, he thought. The sense of normalcy was almost complete.

They went from room to room, then Abby said they should check out the garage.

"It's all snowy out there," Lee objected.

"Yeah, but it's warmer than inside."

The garage was simple. It had an aluminum pull door for the car and a wooden side door for the people. It was a simple wood frame building. Inside there were a few old boxes that Lee would have to go through at some time. There was also an old wooden Florida Grapefruit box. Lee went to look into it. It was almost filled with firewood.

"Fire!" he shouted, and after Abby calmed her heart, he had her load his arms with logs. He didn't even mind getting dirty and dusty because flames were in his immediate future.

Abby went down to the basement to get some of the newspaper. Lee carefully arranged the logs and paper in the fireplace, then they realized neither had a match. Not even an Ohio Blue Tip.

"Maybe Bear or Andrew will have one," Lee said.

There was a knock at the door. It was Andrew and his wife. They both stomped their feet and came in.

"My goodness, it's cold in here," Mrs. Divine said.

"No gas til Monday. I have wood, but I need a match for the fire. Either of you have one?"

They both shook their heads regretfully. There was another knock at the door. That must be Bear. It was Peter, who stood in the doorway carrying a potted plant.

"Happy house," he said when Lee opened the door.

Lee was very surprised to see him, and asked how he knew they'd be there.

"Bear told me. I was a little hurt that I heard it from him, then I realized I haven't given you much of a chance to tell me anything, lately."

There was that awkward moment when two male friends had to decide if a hug was appropriate. They both were relieved when Peter just handed Lee the plant.

"You really shouldn't have," Lee said, and he meant it. Peter was angry with him, probably had a right to be angry with him, and here he was being all nice and stuff. Lee was really embarrassed.

"I'm sorry I got mad," Peter said. "It shouldn't have been that important to me. It really was kind of a one night stand. Well, two."

"No, I'm sorry," sorry that he hadn't thought to apologize first. "I should have been more sensitive. You were upset."

They stood awkwardly for another moment.

"Jeez, it's cold in here," Peter said.

Lee explained about the gas and the wood and the match. Peter checked his pockets. There was another knock at the door. That had to be Bear. Did everyone in this town come on the little yellow bus, Lee wondered. Or is this a sixties sitcom where everyone just shows up at the same time because they only have a half hour to tell the story? It was someone standing behind a large armful of packages.

"Party favors," Bear's voice said from behind the packages, and Lee took some of the bundles from him. There was a twelve pack of beer, packs of paper plates, napkins, cups and plastic forks, two pre-cooked chickens (one lemon herb, one with paprika and sage), a package of rolls, a large plastic container of potato salad and another of macaroni and cheese. Lee was now really embarrassed. He hadn't even thought of feeding these people who had come to help him clean and move in to his new house. Bear apologized for being late, which embarrassed Lee even more.

"Jesus, it's cold in here," Bear said. "My nipples are perking."

They all explained about the gas and the wood and paper and no matches. He handed the remaining packages to Peter, reached into his pocket and produced a match book. It had "Jakarta, Indonesia Chamber of Commerce" printed on the cover.

They all stood around in awed appreciation as Lee started the fire. It took three matches to get the paper going which caused a little contrived suspense, but soon the wood was beginning to catch. It was old wood and very dry, so it blazed fairly quickly. Everyone started shedding outer garments. Abby's sweatshirt was orange. Peter looked at the fire, then at Lee.

"I hated that we weren't talking," he said.

"Yeah," Lee said. "Me, too. Oh. Speaking of that, I have a job interview on Tuesday."

"Great. Congratulations. Doing what?"

"Accounting."

"Where?" Peter asked, and his voice started to convey concern.

"There are only a couple of accounting firms in town. I sent my resume to both of them. One of them called me in."

Peter looked at him for a very long time. Something was wrong, and Lee couldn't figure out what it could possibly be.

"I hear you're giving up your career as a Thespian, Lee," Mrs. Divine said. (**Wait, Lee's gay?** *Steve, here's a book. It's a small one. With training wheels.*)

"What?" Peter said.

"I, um... ," Lee said. "Yeah. I was going to tell you that, too. I'm not going to act any more."

"Why?"

Lee shrugged. Andrew started rummaging through the food. Mrs. Divine slapped his hand.

"Cleaning first, Thumbs. That's why we're here."

"Let's put on some tunes," Bear said.

Lee explained that he didn't yet have anything to play music on, and Peter looked like he was going to say something, but shook his head, picked up a rag, a canister of Ajax, a pair of bright yellow Playtex gloves and harrumphed into the bathroom. Mrs. Divine attacked the kitchen, Bear took a screwdriver out of his back pocket and checked all the door hinges.

"Did anyone bring a vacuum?" Abby asked.

Lee explained that he was planning on renting a carpet shampoo machine on Tuesday. Abby questioned the need for that, and Lee reiterated that he was going to rent a carpet shampoo machine on Tuesday. She went into the bedroom to dust. Andrew said that something about the house felt really familiar, then started supervising. Lee generally got in everyone's way.

As they cleaned, they joked and laughed. Except Peter, who just quietly scrubbed the bathroom. Abby broke out into song a few times, which embarrassed Lee, but delighted the rest. Except Peter, who just scrubbed the bathroom. Finally, Mrs. Divine announced that the kitchen was inhabitable, and started setting out the food Bear had brought on the coffee table. Everyone came into the living room, fixed themselves plates and happily ate with the hunger brought on by good, hard work. Except Peter, who kept scrubbing.

"Peter," Abby called down the hallway. "We're eating. You can stop now."

Peter came into the living room, took off the yellow gloves, prepared himself a very small plate of food, sat in the corner and moved his potato salad around on his plate like a small boy playing with his Tonka. (**Hey, you can go blind doing that.** *Steve, have you finished your book?* **I'm having trouble getting the skin off.**) After they ate, they all sat satiated like little Buddhas. Except Peter, who quietly played with his macaroni and cheese. Mrs. Divine announced they had to go, and she and Andrew hugged and kissed Lee goodbye. Then Bear said he should split, and he and Lee didn't hug and kiss goodbye. Peter sat in the corner, playing with his chicken.

"What?" Lee asked, when he could no longer ignore Peter.

Peter looked up at him.

"What the hell are you doing?" he asked.

Lee was completely unsure how to answer and said so.

"You're going back to accounting."

"Yeah," Lee said, incredulously. "It's what I do. It's what I am." Peter just looked at him, so he added, "I can only make a hundred bucks a week at Twain's. I can make eight point three times as much money and work in an office. That doesn't smell like grease."

"You make tips, too."

"Ten dollars a day. What the hell are you talking about?"

"You're supposed to love music, but you don't even have anything to play it on."

"I can't afford the stereo I want, and I don't want a chintzy one."

"Can't afford it? You just got a ton of money. I would have thought playing your music would have been your first expense."

Lee sputtered for a moment trying to sort out which one of the many responses to that was the most important.

"I'll determine my priorities, thank you," he said, acid beginning to boil away at the base of his throat.

"Yeah, like giving up acting. You did that really fast, Lee," Peter said, the words beginning to tumble out faster and faster now that he had started. "You were starting to break out of your shell. You were exploring and trying things. You were being reborn. You were going into a renaissance. I was proud to be part of it. You were reinventing yourself. Now you're recreating your old life right down to the desk with a green lampshade. I'll bet your couch is even facing the same direction it did in Chicago."

"No," Lee said, not noticing that his fingernails were cutting into the flesh of his palms. "In Chicago it faced south."

"That is south, Lee. This isn't Chicago. This isn't your old life. Abby isn't Beverly. Snap out of it."

Lee simply went to the front door and opened it. After a moment, Peter picked up his coat and left. Lee slammed the door, then stood looking at it. Abby put her hand on his shoulder. He jumped, then turned to her.

"You didn't have a lot to say," he said to her.

She shrugged and told him it wasn't her ball game, then asked if he had thought about bedding for the night. He hadn't. Actually, he had just assumed he would go back to Twain's, but there was a fire going and he didn't want to leave that, and he was tired, and angry and just wanted it all to be nice again. Abby said that she had brought sleeping bags, sheets, blankets and pillows. She went out to her car to get it all, then set up a bed with it by the fireplace. Watching her methodically arranging the bedding calmed Lee somewhat, and he asked her what she thought about what Peter had said.

"Do you want the truth or to feel good?"

"Can't I have both?"

"Not this time."

"Oh. Then make me feel good."

She kissed him on the cheek.

"You're staying, aren't you?" Lee asked. His voice sounded to him like a little boy's and he wished that the first time he had asked her that question he could at least have sounded like a college student.

Abby didn't say anything for a long time, then she just shook her head. Lee was surprised and hurt.

"Okay," Abby said, trying to figure it out as she talked. "Peter is scared for you. He loves you and sees you going backwards. I'm scared for me."

"Why?"

"You're still married."

"We're finalizing the divorce."

"You're on the rebound. I got attracted to the adventurer. It seemed thrilling. I like you. A lot. I like what you like, and I like how we are, but I can see what Peter means. You're getting off the path and back on the pavement. You still have feelings for Beverly. You have to put some distance between Chicago and River Bend before we can get any closer."

"It would be a lot easier to do that if we got closer."

"That's the wrong reason.

"I like you, too. A lot." Again, Lee could hear the little boy in his voice, pleading. He wanted to slap the little fucker.

"I can't afford to be intimate with you right now. I can't. You can't, either, Lee."

Lee turned away from her. He might as well sleep on a slimy, green couch the rest of his life and get a pet fish. She turned him back and kissed him again, and that kiss was friendly and understanding. Lee's heart sank, and he wondered just how Peter felt when he saw Jim sitting there all clothed and everything. He put his force field up. The temperature in his body lowered and his heart rate dropped to one. He was used to this feeling. It felt normal.

"Thank you for dropping by, Abigail. I'll get the bedding cleaned and drop it by."

"Stop it, Lee. You don't wear that well," Abby said harshly. "You're more the kilt and bagpipes type."

"All right," Lee said with a weak smile. "I'm just tired. I'll talk to you tomorrow."

They hugged briefly, and she left. Lee stood shivering. It wasn't cold. The fire was still going, although not as strongly as it had been. It was almost just coals, but they gave off a nice, even warmth. The shivering had something to do with the fact that everyone was mad at him, and he was fairly certain that he hadn't done anything wrong. What the hell was wrong with wanting a normal life? What was wrong with wanting a normal job? What was wrong with wanting a normal fucking relationship? Well, fuck them all, he thought, then turned off the lights, kicked off his shoes, dropped his trousers and climbed into the bed Abby had made for him.

He woke to a strange noise.

"Shut up, Excalibur," he said groggily, then remembered where he was. Oh, God, he thought. The neighbors have a dog.

Then he heard the noise again. It wasn't quite a dog. The air was cold and the fire was out, but it was still dark. He couldn't place the noise. When you are in a new place, it takes a while to get used to that place's noises; to the sound of the branch that might be rubbing against the awning. To the settling of the beams and walls. The way traffic movement might make its way into the air of the room. The sound of the axe murderer from Oregon who lived next door sharpening his axe. This might, after all, have been where Roger had lived. When he had lived. If he had lived. The noise happened again. It was like a whine, not a creak. Well, that left Roger out, he liked to creak and moan. Lee sat up and pushed the sheets aside, ready to investigate. Then he remembered that in every meat-movie he had ever seen, the only people who had been viciously killed were the ones who went to investigate the sound, especially if they were in their underwear, so he threw a piece of wood on the embers and curled back up under the covers, hugged one of the pillows and tried to get back to sleep.

In the morning, with the light that glinted off the snow streaming into the room, any thought of axe murderers and bloody co-eds seemed a little foolish. He got up, decided to shower at Twain's because the water there would be hot, and left.

Twain's was a-sparkle in metal decorations. There was an aluminum tree next to the little platform draped with what looked like actual metal tinsel evenly spaced on all the branches, large colored tear-drop shaped bulbs with the pigment cracked and peeling, large round ornaments and popcorn balls wrapped in tinted cellophane that could have been made in any of the last five decades, and probably were. The tree was topped by a silver star with one yellow, tear-dropped light in its center, and the base was hidden by a large, white, felt-like blanket with little sparkly flecks in it. The room was bedecked by silver garlands, candy-canes and paper fold-out angels, bells, snowflakes and Santas. It all made Lee's eyes hurt. He went to the tree, found the plug which was at the end of a cloth-covered cord, was round and had only two identical prongs, and plugged it into the wall. There was a strange colored glow, and when he turned around he saw a slowly turning, four colored wheel with a flood light behind it, being turned by a grinding motor that had served for far too many

Christmases. Lee turned around to make sure he wasn't at his grandparents' house wearing flannel pajamas with little bears on them and a trap at the back. Then he remembered he hadn't yet showered and was still wearing the same clothes from the day before.

Twain sat at his stool and Lee poured him his cup of coffee.
"Why didn't you wait for me to help you decorate?" Lee asked.
Twain looked at him like he might have to wipe butter from his face again.
"You weren't here."
No, Lee thought. I wasn't.

The waiting room to the accounting firm was simply furnished with two simple chairs, a table with Newsweek, Time Magazines and Wall Street Journals arranged in a perfect fan and a painting of a vase with flowers. The place was pristine, almost antiseptic. It felt familiar to Lee. As he sat in the chair waiting for the owner to come out, he felt odd. There was something unsettling about the place that he couldn't put his finger on. Perhaps it was because he hadn't interviewed for a job in a long time, except for a play or two, and they didn't pay. The owner wore a nice, off-the-rack suit and a simple blue tie and a Supercuts do. He came out, shook Lee's hand and led him through a large central room where the associate accountants and the bookkeepers sat at desks with computer screens, adding machines and three ring binders, to his office. Everything was garishly lit with bright flourescent lights. Lee smelled graphite and heard the comforting sound of a hundred ten key keys working over time. The room had one pencil sharpener screwed to the wall. Shaped like a man bending over. Lee felt comfortable for the first time since he got to town, but feeling comfortable felt wrong, somehow. A voice shouted in his ear, "What are you doing?" He told the voice to shut up.

The interview was low-key, as if it were merely a formality. Lee had impressive credentials, he was told, and The Firm would be lucky to have him. An offer was made that was much less than Lee would have accepted in Chicago, but seemed fair for River Bend. The office door opened, and a young man with a silk tie, leather-soled shoes and an entirely too self-satisfied look on his face came in. The owner introduced him to Lee as his son. (**Lee's son?** *No, the owner's son.*

Why would he introduce Lee to his own son? *He didn't, Steve he... you do that on purpose, don't you?*) The interview ended with a handshake and a smile, but as Lee walked back out, he couldn't help feeling he didn't like the place. He really couldn't imagine why, it was perfect. The room was neat, organized, just the way he liked it. The owner seemed dedicated. Even the son fit. It would be a good place to work. So why didn't he like it? When he got into his car and looked out onto the snow piled in the gutter by the sidewalk, it hit him. It wasn't messy enough. He couldn't believe that thought was there, but it was. Solidly. The place smacked too much of Chicago and not enough of Twain's. He was going to have to kill Peter.

The morning of Christmas Eve, Lee came downstairs to find a thin, flat rectangular gift sitting on the counter, wrapped in dime-store wrapping and thin green ribbon with a small, simple, store bought tag that said, simply, "Lee." He kept looking over at it as he set up the kitchen and diner and brewed the coffee. He continued looking at it as he poured Twain's coffee. When he sat down with his own, Twain asked, a little peevishly, if he was going to open it.

"Did you get me this?" Lee asked. When Twain just looked at him, he added, "I didn't get you anything."

Twain shrugged. Lee lifted the gift. It was really heavy. He shook it.

"What are you doing?" Twain asked.

"I'm trying to guess what it is."

"Don't."

Lee carefully removed the ribbon, then, even more carefully, separated the tape from the paper, then carefully folded the paper back. It was a photo framed in nice wood. It was a photo of the Partridge Family. A signed photo of the Partridge Family. Signed by everyone but Danny Bonaduce.

"I thought you were mad at me," Lee said, hoping desperately that he wouldn't cry.

Twain shrugged, again.

"I turned down that other job."

"You can stay on here until you land on your feet."

"Thanks, that'll be nice."

Twain shook Lee's hand and wished him a Merry Christmas. Lee felt very odd about the whole month.

At one thirty-three, Officer Bacon came in with a bag. He pulled three small, oblong packages wrapped in aluminum foil covered with Saran Wrap from it, announced that they were homemade fruit cakes, gave one to Twain, one to Lee and left one to be given to Matt.

"I didn't get you anything," Lee said.

"Merry Christmas," Officer Bacon said, and gave Lee a bear hug, pinning his arms to his sides. Lee could feel the night stick pressing against his belt, and was grateful that the hug didn't last a millisecond longer than was acceptable for hugs from gregarious straight peace officers.

"Congratulations on your new home," he said to Lee. "No more couch."

As Officer Bacon left on his merry rounds, Lee wondered how he knew so much. Then he wondered how everyone in this town knew so much.

Matt came in at around three to start with the Christmas Eve rush, that, Lee was surprised to discover, was traditionally very busy. He came in to the kitchen where Lee was putting pots away, and handed Lee a small, very sloppily wrapped gift, and wished him a Merry Christmas. Lee took it with a combination of awe and embarrassment.

"I didn't get you anything," he said softly, and shook it.

"What are you doing?" Matt asked.

"Trying to guess what it is."

"It's a Walkman," Matt said, with a big, proud, toothy grin.

Lee was completely surprised. He carefully pealed the wrapping off the gift. It was a portable CD player.

"Sorry, I didn't get you any batteries."

Lee grabbed Matt and hugged him. Matt stood stiffly, his arms pinned to his sides, waiting for the hug to end, but very pleased that the gift was so appreciated.

"Do you really like it?" he asked, when the hug finally ended.

Lee assured him he really, really did. Matt bounced out of the kitchen to get to work. He would have floated, but happy straight men's feet had to touch the ground at least once every three yards.

At about five, during the peak of the dinner rush, Peter came in with a long, lopsided package. (*Steve, we have to describe Twain's*

Christmas Eve Dinner Special. **Okay, there was lots of good food.** *Good. What about dessert?* **With pudding.** *Thanks.* **No problem.**) He asked Twain to get Lee from the back, and when Lee came out, he handed him the package. Lee was nonplused.

"I didn't get... "

"Just open it," Peter said.

Lee shook it, and Peter squinted, turned his head and told him that wasn't a good idea. Lee carefully removed the wrapping. It was a package of fireworks. (*Wait, he's not you, Lee wouldn't want fireworks.* **Well, Peter's not you, he'd give fireworks.** *I'd give you fireworks.* **Then why haven't you ever given me fireworks?** *Because you're you.*)

"Shut up, guys," Peter said. "I got him fireworks."

"Yeah," Lee agreed. "Shut up."

Lee looked at Peter for a long time, then shook his head and told him he hadn't taken the job. Peter smiled a warm smile.

"I know. Officer Bacon told me. I'm glad."

"And Matt got me a CD player," Lee said, refusing to comment on the Officer Bacon thing.

Andrew came in a short time later and gave Lee a makeup kit. Lee, really embarrassed, told him he hadn't gotten him anything, then reminded him he'd quit acting. Andrew smiled, told him all sales were final, wished him a happy holiday and left, passing Abby, who had just come in carrying a beautifully wrapped package. This is getting entirely too ridiculous, Lee thought, sincerely hoping that you couldn't die of shame and embarrassment.

"I though you didn't want to see me," Lee said.

"I said I didn't want to stay over."

"I didn't get you anything," he said.

"You still have a day. Saks Fifth Avenue is open until nine."

"There's a Saks in River Bend?"

"You have a car," she said with a smile.

Lee started carefully unwrapping the gift, and Abby grabbed it and tore the paper rudely.

"I hate when people do that!" she said. "My uncle Patrick always does that, and I can't stop him because he's my uncle."

"Thank you," Lee said. "It's perfect."

29

He started to move to hug her, but stopped. She moved to hug him, but stopped. They both moved to hug each other, but stopped.

"We're having dinner tomorrow at around two at my family's house. You're invited."

Lee hemmed, then he hawed, then he smiled and told her he'd be there. She waved quickly and left. A moment later, she ran in, hugged him really hard, but really quickly, then left again. Lee had to go in back with her gift in front of his left pants pocket.

Twain came in back and told Lee there was mail for him. It was a bulging nine-by-twelve inch manila envelope and it was from Beverly. I didn't get you anything, he thought as he shook it to try to figure out what it might be. It felt like a shirt. Or a book. Maybe Tajar Tales. Or maybe a well-padded CD. He opened it, wondering if he could ever live down the year he didn't get anybody anything.

The envelope was filled with smaller, window envelopes. Just what he always wanted. From credit card companies. He opened one. It was ninety days past due.

"Beverly!" he shouted.

Will Beverly ever get over her viciousness?
Will Lee ever get over Beverly's viciousness?
Will Lee ever get over Beverly?
Will Peter ever get over the rainbow?
Will Lee and Peter stop bickering like school children?
Will Roger ever show his ugly face?
What rude act can you perform with something gray and murky?
What was Andrew's joke about the penny?
What did Abby get Lee?
What will Lee get Abby?
Does redundant mean repetitive or simply unnecessary?
How does everyone know so much about Lee?
Will anyone eat Officer Bacon's fruit cake?
Will Lee ever act again again?
Will he ever get some?
Will he?
Huh?

To find the answers to these and other predictable peculiarities, tune into our next installment: "Woofers and Tweeters and Bear, Oh, My"

(*We interrupted this installment a lot.* **That's okay, it's over eleven thousand words long.** *No wonder my feet hurt.*)

This installment first published September 21, 2002

Geoff Hoff and Steve Mancini

Up till this moment: Bear scared Lee with a silly ghost story. Lee quit the theater. Peter got mad at Lee, then Lee got mad at Peter. Abby told Kim about kissing Lee. Peter is still not over the dick. Abby just wants to be friends, but invited Lee to spend Christmas with her family. Twain got miffed at Lee for leaving the diner, but let him stay when Lee didn't take the job. Everyone gave Lee Christmas gifts, but he didn't get anyone anything. Beverly sent all her bills as her gift to him. And Lee finally got his own place. Stuff happened. Then there was a lull, then more stuff happened. Read the previous installments. Sheesh.

(I bet I can work Yoko into this installment. *Do you really want to, Steve?* Never mind.)

Installment Seventeen
"Woofers and Tweeters and Bear, Oh, My"

Lee wondered why whoever decided those things decided that the year in western culture should start in the middle of the coldest time of the year. He picked up the top firework in the pile and squinted, trying to read the label. Spring would make so much more sense. The new year didn't even start on a season change like an equinox or solstice, for goodness sake. It started in the middle of nothing. Cold nothing. He held the rocket up to the light that seeped into his back yard from the house and tried to stop breathing so the steam didn't obscure the name. Ah. Weeping Willow.

"What a stupid name for a firework," he said.

He walked out across the crunchy snow and inserted the stick at the end of the rocket into the empty, quart New Coke™ bottle that was anchored firmly in the snow in the exact center of his back yard, tilted slightly so that the rockets wouldn't hit the northern ash tree at the back border of the yard. He knew it was in the exact center because he measured it. Things like that are important.

He removed his right glove and took an Ohio Blue Tip from his right coat pocket. He glanced at his watch before striking the match. Eight fifty-nine. Beverly was probably sliding a pair of dark stockings up her adulterous calves in preparation for an evening of Champagne and sex with the Jerk. He struck the match on his jacket zipper and watched it flare and calm. Good old Ohio Blue Tips. Light on anything. Says so on the carton. Except Beef Wellington. And New Coke™. And water. And snow. Okay, so they didn't light on very much at all, but they did light on zippers. If the zipper didn't pull all the burny stuff off the wood of the match. He touched the now calm flame against the fuse of the Weeping Willow, and when it started to sputter and sizzle with the unmistakable sound of a lighted fuse and smell of wonderful sulphur, he ran like a little girl back to his small porch while putting his right glove back on.

He picked up the Flintstones glass of brandy from the step and took a sip from it as he turned to watch the Weeping Willow take off with a fwoosh. It spiraled a little on its path and knocked several small branches from the northern ash. It exploded in a cascade of golden-orange sparks that made the ash look like a Christmas tree. Of course, he thought, the year has to start in January. It's the first month of the year.

He had spent Christmas evening with Abby and her clan, which seemed to have grown since Thanksgiving, although he hadn't noticed any new faces. The dinner had been loud and delicious and raucous and confusing and she had a wonderful family who seemed to like him and he liked them even if they were all a little loud and raucous and he had spent the final twenty minutes of it standing in front of their house shivering and watching the steam from his mouth intermingle with the steam from Abby's as they talked and he tried to decide just how much permission he had to lean over and kiss the life out of her. The whole evening had been confusing like that. He wanted to kiss her, but didn't want to cross the line and look like a jerk. But if she wanted him to kiss her he would look like a jerk.

She had tried to explain to him that he needed time because he still wasn't over Beverly.

"I'm over Beverly. Look what she did with my credit. I spent my whole life building perfect credit and in one day she ruined it."

"It took her almost three months," Abby said with that smile that made Lee want to wipe her face with his mouth. "Look, you left a message for Andrew. He'll take care of it."

"Abby," he said, not letting it go, "It takes a hundred years to grow a tree and ten minutes to chop it down."

"It takes longer than that if it's a good-sized tree," Abby said, and Lee gave her a "shut up, you know what I mean" look. "And anyway," she added, "perfect credit doesn't mean much."

"Who are you?"

Abby laughed. "You know, we missed The Wiz. Last night was the last night."

He wanted to hug her or leave. He wanted to know what she wanted him to do. He wanted her to pull some mistletoe out of her pocket and hold it over her head. Instead, she put her hands in her pocket and left them there. He wanted her to make the first move.

"Thank you for the charm bracelet," she said instead, lifting her arm up and shaking it with a pleasant tinkle that landed gently on his ear. "Now do I have to get myself some charm?"

"You're welcome," Lee answered. "How could I not after you got me that huge thing."

"I know you needed one."

Finally she had leaned in and gently kissed him on the cheek. Her perfume was intoxicating in a way that Stella's had never been and Veronica's couldn't be. It was simple, more peppery than sweet, perhaps even a little dark.

"Nice perfume," he said.

"It's 'I Know You Want Me Bad' by Roseanne."

He took his right glove off and removed a snake pellet from the little red box with yellow writing and set it on the step. He lit another Ohio Blue Tip and was about to ignite the pellet, but realized that it would leave a mark. A dirty mess. He moved the pellet to a rock by the porch and lit it. The black ash snaked out from the glowing orange ring on the top of the pellet, looking like poop coming out of a (*Steve!*)...

They hadn't kissed and the following week had passed as if he had skipped over it. As if he hadn't even touched ground. A gay man's leap, not a straight man's leap. He decided that he needed to have New Year's Eve by himself because he hadn't really spent any quality time alone in his new place and he did need to sort things out and had informed both Abby, Peter and Andrew and Bear and Matt and Twain of that and was happy with the decision until about three-thirty that afternoon when he'd picked up his phone to call Abby or Peter. Or Andrew or Bear or Matt. But he realized that would seem just too sad and desperate, so he pulled Peter's gift out and set up in anticipation of a fiery celebration of his own. And anyway, they were all probably at the same party drinking Champagne with Jim, who was almost as much of a jerk as the Jerk.

The next firework in the pile was a Piccolo Pete. He set that down because it would be too loud, then remembered it was New Year's Eve for God's sake, and for God's sake, if you couldn't make a little noise by yourself in your own back yard on New Year's Eve, When Could You? He picked it back up and stuck the stick in the spout of the charred New Coke bottle. Stupid soft drink. Stupid gay man. (*Hey, where'd that come from?* **It's New Year's.** *Oh. Wait.* **Quiet, he's about to light more fire.**) He had spent many wonderful New Year's Eves with Beverly. Well, five. They had gone to parties and danced. Well, she had danced. He stood so she wouldn't have to dance alone. Or with someone. He lit the fuse and trotted back for another sip of brandy. He was about to sip and it went off. It was louder than he thought.

"Oh, fuck," he said and tried to cover his ears to keep the shrill knife of sound from piercing through his ear drums all the way to his medulla oblongata, then added, "fuck, it's New Year's Eve," and toasted the air.

He was about to sip, but felt something watching him. Maybe it was Roger. Or cops. Or the two neighbor kids who, when he turned his head he noticed, now, had their faces pressed against the glass of their dining room window. He could just see the back of their house in the space between the back of his and his garage. He raised the glass to them, then drained the brandy. He went back inside for the bottle, and when he came back out, there was a third nose pressed against the glass. Their father, he assumed by the height of it. Fuck, he thought.

He's going to call the cops. Or Roger. Fuck it, it's New Year's Eve. He defiantly picked up the next firework and didn't even look to see what it was called. It was big and that's all that mattered. He strutted like a bull elk out to the Coke bottle. Fuck him. Fuck Beverly. Fuck the Jerk. Fuck Jim. Fuck Abby for thinking I still want to fuck Beverly. Fuck 'em all. He took a slug from the brandy bottle. Fireworks and liquor. Great combination. And snow. Life is good. Life is beautiful. Il Postino.

"Here's to me," he said boldly, defiantly, and took another drink, then went to take his right glove off but it was missing, so he just lit a match and touched it to the fuse.

He turned to get back to the stoop and his left foot hit a smooth patch in the snow and his left knee dropped into the crunchy snow and stuck.

"Oh, shit," he said and turned his head just as the thing went off only a few feet from his face with a sound like a bull elk farting. The fire from the rocket reflected in the frozen snow around his knees, making it look like he was kneeling in a carnival on the Riviera, then faded as it soared.

He watched it ascend, then explode in a shower of bright colors that reflected in the frost in the trees, the snow on the roofs, the glass of the windows and the brandy bottle. That reminded him of brandy and he took another sip and struggled up. There was a sound of awe from the next yard, and when he got back to the porch he could see two young kids, a boy and a girl, all bundled up, standing on their back porch, smiling in appreciation. They must have been the first two noses. The father, still pressed against the dining room window, nodded, then leaned back long enough to take a sip from his beer, then waited patiently for the next assault. Lee remembered his own father, who, when Lee had wanted to set off Roman Candles in their back yard, would give him the obligatory speech about the cops but wouldn't tell him not to. He would then stand at the back window watching with the fire-lust that Lee had inherited bright on his face.

Now he had an audience. Now he had to perform. Stupid town. Of course, he didn't have to audition for this part. If he had, Jim would be setting off his stupid fireworks. Stupid town. Stupid neighbors. Nice kids, though. They liked fireworks. Of course, so did the dad. Nice dad. Wonder where the mom is. Probably sleeping with

37

the Jerk. Stupid mom. Sorry, kids. Sorry, Dad. Sorry, Mom. He looked at his bounty and tried to estimate how long it would take. He looked at his watch. Nine thirty-six. Did he have enough stamina to last till midnight? No. He had about a half-hour left. Of both fireworks and stamina. He set aside a few of the bigger ones for the grand finale, took a swig of brandy, and chose the next victim.

Before he had left the Holiday's house on Christmas, he and Abby had made a date to see Of Mice and Men when it opened. He really didn't want to because Jim Ackerman would be in it. And he wouldn't. The only reason he had agreed was that Abby had asked, "But what if he's really bad?" and he didn't want to miss that. He still had a couple of weeks to back out. But maybe Abby would let him kiss her goodnight after a play.

Several crisp pops in the cold air later, Lee noticed another small nose pressed against a window of the house on the other side of his yard. It was an albino dwarf. (*No, it wasn't, Steve, it was a small child.* **Same thing.** *You are a fool.* **Happy New Year.**) He raised the brandy bottle to the new nose, then put another rocket stick in the pop bottle, which was now quite discolored and stinky. The still air in his back yard was a thick cloud of pale gray smoke that smelled of gunpowder and burned hair. He breathed in deeply, then smiled and lit the fuse.

He found himself standing on his back porch holding a half-eaten stick of beef jerky. He remembered the tub of it he'd bought and went back inside for more, then came out to ignite the finale. It took ten minutes to arrange the rockets, twist the fuses together, gauge the angle, stand in a sprinter's stance and strike a match. He lit and ran. When he got back to the porch he had just enough time to notice that the father was now also outside with his arms around his children, looking up at the sky. Lee also looked up just in time to see the multiple explosion. The golden and crimson tinted gray shadows from the trees and garage quickly changed directions, shape, focus and intensity in a macabre, schizophrenic dance on the snowy yard as the multiple war head ignited. The sky was afraid and hid behind the moon. Everything stood still as the last of the flakes of ash gently descended and the luminescent smoke slowly dissipated. He looked at his watch. Ten oh-three. Now he had an hour and fifty-seven minutes before he could turn in. He looked over at the father and kids just as they turned to go inside. The nose at the window on the other side was also gone. The sky breathed a sigh of relief. Lee noticed one box of snake pellets that had fallen to the side of the stairs. He emptied the whole thing on the step, crushed them all up, formed a neat little pile of snake pellet dust and set a match to it. He knew he'd hate himself in the morning.

Lee fell asleep on the couch and missed midnight altogether.

Besides Lee, there were six guys helping Bear load the set for Of Mice and Men into the theatre. Lee was once again amazed at how many people they could get to work so hard for free. No one made any money at a community theatre, it seemed, except the Artistic Director and the people in the front office. That meant Bear, Peter and Stella. And they didn't make much. Except Stella, who kept the books. And she said she didn't make much just to sound like one of the guys. The shed smelled of burned coffee, stale cigarette smoke, old sawdust and that horrible mucilage stuff that held the paint together. It had begun to be a familiar odor to Lee, and today it was intensified by the odor of eight men who ate too much cabbage. He was surprised to realize he would miss it.

"You missed a hell of a party," Bear said as he and Lee stopped for a sip of old coffee. "Kim Anderson danced naked."

"Really?"

"No."

Lee shook his head and tried not to smile. He would miss working here.

"I set off fireworks."

"Cool," Bear said as they set their mugs down. He watched to make sure the guys that were carrying the back wall of the bunk house didn't torque it too much as they maneuvered it out of the shed. "Agnes danced naked?"

They both laughed, then shuddered, then started loud power tools to scramble the image out of their heads. And they turned away from each other in case their pants tented.

"What were we talking about?" Lee asked when he turned his power tool off.

"Coffee."

"Oh. No," Lee said. "Agnes."

They turned on their power tools again.

Lee and Bear picked up the stage right wall of the bunk house and expertly maneuvered it out of the shed, through the open back wall of the women's dressing room and out onto the stage. Bear liked working with Lee because he knew he didn't need to supervise him. The moment they set the wall down and put the pin through the brace into the stage floor, Lee turned and tripped over the pin.

"Fuck," he said quietly, then he and Bear returned to the shed.

"You like this, don't you?" Bear asked as they stacked the bunk pieces. Lee asked what he meant and he said, "This. Building sets. Theatre. This. You like this."

Lee had to agree and Bear gently reminded him that they were having auditions the next week for The Odd Couple . Lee assured Bear that he was through with all that, all the while not sure at all himself.

"Agnes is directing it."

Lee turned on a power tool.

They brought the bunk pieces to the stage and Bear showed a couple of the guys how to put them together, then they went back to the shed. Bear did a little dance and Lee asked if he was hung over. He laughed and assured him he wasn't, and Lee asked if he had gotten laid. He laughed even louder and nodded.

"By Agnes?"

Bear turned on his tool. One of the volunteers brought an old coffee can with the words "Leaveth Cussing to the Groundlings" neatly painted on the side in a fancy Algerian-style font and handed it to Lee.

"What's that for?" Lee asked.

"You said the 'f' word," the guy said. "Before. Really quietly, but I heard you. Right after you tripped."

Lee gladly dropped a quarter into the can. Just then, Jim came into the shed and asked if he could do anything. Lee quietly seethed. He put five more quarters into the can.

"What are you doing?" the guy asked.

"This is me seething," Lee said, and seethed again.

Jim arrived at the theatre for his volunteer stint and the first thing he saw was a bunch of guys on the stage putting bunk pieces together for his play. Maybe today he'd forgo scrubbing the bathrooms this once and help move set stuff out to the stage. He made his way back to the shed and asked if they needed any help, then saw Mr. Harris out of the corner of his eye dropping quarters into a bucket. Even the simple act of dropping coins seemed somehow sinister and a thrill ran up Jim's spine and exploded at the base of his skull. Right at the medulla oblongata. If he were given to analyzing his reactions to things he would probably have realized that he actually enjoyed being frightened by this strange man. As he wasn't given to analyzing things, he simply observed what Lee was wearing and catalogued it away for his own future clothing purchases, then turned to get his gear to scrub the restrooms in the theatre.

He was holding a bucket of hot, soapy water for the men's room floor, and just as he opened the door, an oddly alluring voice called out, "Young man." He turned and saw an older woman coming out of the office with some scripts in her hand, looking at him. "You're new," she said. "We haven't been introduced. I'm Agnes Livingstone."

"Jim," Jim responded as she sashayed toward him. He had never seen an older woman sashay. Actually, he'd never seen any woman sashay. Except Rip Taylor. He wasn't sure if he liked it or not. "Jim Ackerman. Yeah, my father liked... "

"How nice to meet you," she said and put out her hand. He shook it. It was soft. "You seem like a strong young man," she said and gently touched his bicep. "I have a rather inconveniently bulky couch that I would like on the other side of my living room. No, that would be asking too much."

"No," Jim said reflexively, "I'd be glad to."

"You'd help an old lady?"

"Oh," Jim said. Reflexively. "You're not old."

She brushed his cheek with the back of her hand and told him he was sweet, then told him he would, of course, be compensated. He told her that wouldn't be necessary, that he'd be glad to help. She insisted on compensation and gave him her card. They agreed he'd be there at eight, and she walked away. Jim was leaning against the open door of the men's room, still holding the bucket, staring at her as she sashayed away. Her dress clung to her back and draped nicely off her hips. A man who had tried being gay noticed these things. He turned back to the men's room and sloshed hot, soapy water on the floor when the door closed behind him. He stared at it for a moment, frothing there on the tiles, before he remembered why he was here. If he were given to analyzing his reactions to things, he would still be confused.

Agnes walked out of the theatre with the scripts for The Odd Couple, thinking that had been just too easy.

Lee called Peter with his new phone and told him he had to come visit after work. When Peter knocked on the door, the first thing he heard was footsteps. The next thing he heard was the Blue Note Sessions blasting through the closed door. Blasting loudly. Rattling the windows and front stoop. The door opened and Lee stood there with a big grin.

"You bought a stereo."

"A sound system," Lee corrected him loudly, and led him in.

"Good," Peter said over the sound. "I'm impressed. It sounds good. Can you turn it down, now?"

Lee smiled and obliged. Then he turned it back up again just to show that he could.

"You're a very strange man," Peter said when he turned it back down with a smile.

They looked at each other for a moment, then Lee asked Peter how he was doing.

"Fine," he said. "I sat in on a rehearsal."

"For what?" Lee asked, then he remembered who Peter would be sitting in on a rehearsal to watch. "You're just a little bit of a masochist."

"Yeah," Peter said.

"Um," Lee said. "Is he any... Um. How did... Did he remember his lines?"

"You, too?"

"Me too what?"

"Yes, he's actually doing an okay job," Peter said, diplomatically not pointing out the obvious fact that Lee was also being a little bit of a masochist. (**You mean like we're doing, Geoff?** *Exactly.* **I mean pointing out the obvious?** *Precisely.* **Think anyone will get this?** *No.*)

Lee nodded thoughtfully, then told Peter he needed to show him something and led him through the kitchen to the basement. As he opened the basement door, he pointed at the freshly-dried wood putty in the scratches on the door.

"My first project," he gleamed.

"You need to sand it," Peter said.

"Thanks. Should I paint it, too, Mr. Vila?"

"Okay, so I'm talking to Power Tool Man, here."

When they got to the bottom of the steps, Lee stopped and waited for Peter to notice. Peter looked at the work bench.

"Oh, you got your tools out," Peter said, then noticed that, next to the router and the variable speed drill was a propane torch and a tube of welding rods.

"You already bought a torch?"

"No, I brought it with me."

Then Peter noticed the axe. It was huge.

"And you brought that, too?" Peter asked. It had tar on the blade and sweaty dirt from Lee's hands and he wondered how it could get so much use in Chicago. Maybe he inherited it. I hope.

"Yeah... ," Lee said, still waiting for Peter to notice.

Okay, so it wasn't tools. He looked around and noticed the dart board on the wall and pointed at that.

Lee shook his head. He was still waiting. He must have brought that with him, also. Okay. On the shelf under the work bench was a small can of putty, a number ten can of nails and...

"A gas mask?"

Lee nodded in way that let Peter know he hadn't yet noticed.

"You brought a gas mask with you?"

Lee nodded again, still waiting, but not nearly as patiently.

"From Chicago?" Peter asked, and Lee just stared. "Why did you bring a gas mask?"

Lee sighed exasperatedly and pointedly pointed at the small, heavy-duty speakers that were hanging on brackets in the corner of the wall and ceiling above the workbench.

"Cool," Peter said. "Speakers. In the basement."

Lee, even more exasperatedly, leaned over to the little knob on the wall above the bench and turned it. To eleven. The Blue Note Sessions blasted again. It hurt Peter's teeth.

"Wow," Peter yelled. "How can so much noise come out of such small speakers?"

Lee gave Peter a look and turned it back down.

"I mean music. How can so much music come out of such small speakers? Such beautiful music. Such interesting, unusual, beautiful music. Such... "

Lee gave him an "I get it, asshole" look and Peter smiled. They looked at each other again, and, before the look could pass beyond the appropriate number of seconds for straight comfort, Lee asked Peter if he was still mad at him. Peter shook his head.

"I'm sorry," Peter said, and Lee cocked his head like the little dog on the old record player ads. "About yelling at you. You just scared me. I thought we were losing you to Chicago. I didn't mean you shouldn't take that job. I mean, I probably did mean it, but I shouldn't have. I mean, I'm sorry I told you not to take... "

"I didn't not take that job because of you," Lee said. "Stupid gay man."

All the creatures on the earth stopped. Big and small. Like Burgess Meredith in The Twilight Zone. No, more like a Morgan Stanley Dean Witter commercial. (**Wasn't that Merrill Lynch, Pierce, Fenner and Smith, Incorporated?** *Um. Sure.*) Lee wondered if he had gone too far too soon. Stupid gay man. So sensitive. Then Peter laughed the really loud, rumbling, full, robust laugh he hadn't laughed since installment six, and Lee happily joined him. With a laugh that had a little more Chicago-accountant-like reserve. Well, with a chuckle. Well, a broad smile. They were friends again, past all that deep stuff that so puzzled and annoyed Lee.

"Hey," Peter said, looking around the room again, his eyes getting wide. "Party."

"Party?"

"You have to throw a house warming party."

Lee had a definite "I don't throw parties" look, but Peter was already seeing it. He said it would officially make it Lee's place. People. Food. A couple of spilled drinks. When Lee's face went all pale at that thought, Peter laughed and said that he, of course, meant down here in the basement. On the cement floor. And anyway, he could wet vac it after. The thought of having a reason to buy a wet vac made the color return to Lee's cheeks and forehead.

"Will people break things?" he said like an excited child.

Peter was about to insist that no one would, but noticed the work bench and the small dilation of Lee's pupils and nodded enthusiastically.

"Probably," he said.

"When Beverly threw parties, I was just in charge of liquor and music."

"That's fine. Okay. Cool. Let me think. I'll call Abby. I'm sure she'll be glad to help. Oh. Are you still seeing Abby?"

"Um," Lee said. "Yeah. I think so. Sort of. Yeah. I hope. Maybe."

"Good. I'll call her. It'll be a good chance to get to know her. And we can talk about you behind your back."

He looked at the gas mask again. Then at the axe.

"You're a very strange man. Are you sure you're an accountant?"

Lee smiled. Peter shook his head.

"Okay," he said. "This weekend is tech for Mice and Men, next week is hell week. Opening is next weekend. We'll have it the Saturday after that. In three weeks. It's settled."

He rubbed his hands in wonderful anticipation, and Lee had the strange feeling he had just been sold a Brooklyn Bridge or two, spanning some ocean-front property in Nebraska with proof of huge oil reserves under it. He leaned over and turned the knob on the wall and the music swelled, indicating the end of the scene. (*On-line satirical serial film school, Steve?* **Hey, Lee did it, not me.** *Um. Sure.*)

On Thursday, Lee couldn't stand it any longer and drove over to Andrew's house.

"What's going on with my credit?" he asked the moment Andrew opened the door.

"Hi. Come on in. We don't talk law in the front room."

Andrew led Lee to his office. Lee waited for Andrew to sit before repeating his question. Andrew offered him a cigar. Lee asked if he was playing with him, and Andrew smiled.

"I can probably get them to pay the bills. It won't be hard to prove they were her charges."

"What about my credit?"

"You don't especially need good credit right now. Don't get your panties in a bunch."

"My panties aren't in a bunch. My panties never bunch. I don't wear panties."

"What color are they?"

"Plaid," Lee said. "I've had perfect credit my whole life. My student loan was paid off before there was any interest due. I've never had a late payment. On anything. Ever. The only reason I even know what a late payment is is because of my clients. I usually pay the full amount each month so there are no charges at all. I always pay more than the minimum. I even paid my Columbia House Record Club bills as soon as the records got there. Every time. What the fuck do you mean I don't need good credit?"

"You are not your credit, Lee."

"I what?"

Andrew smiled and leaned back in his chair. He put on his best "I understand your neurosis" look and assured Lee that he was working on it, that he was on top of it, that he had a trick or two up his sleeve, that his butt looked big in those pants, that worrying wouldn't make any difference.

"I'm good, remember? You said so yourself."

Lee stopped hyperventilating long enough to concede that Andrew was, indeed, good. Then Andrew said he'd need a little retainer up front, seeing as how bad his credit was. Lee got the point and took one of the cigars.

"Well, I might as well get something for my money," he said, and Andrew lit it.

"Are you smoking again, Thumbs?" Mrs. Divine shouted from the kitchen.

"She could be in Gary, Indiana and know. She has the nose of a vintner."

"Why Gary?'

"If you can smell anything in Gary, Indiana besides Gary, Indiana, you have a great nose."

"No, I mean why would she be in Gary?"

Mrs. Divine showed up in the doorway to the den. Andrew handed her the cigars and she took one, cut the end, lit it and went back to her household tasks.

46

Twain, as always, went to the opening night and gave Lee Saturday night off to see the play. Abby met Lee at his place because he now had a place for her to meet him. When he opened the door, she gave him a kiss on the cheek and said they should hurry. As he got his coat, he talked to her in his mind, telling her that, if she had agreed to meet him at his house a little earlier, they would have had time to smooch on couch before going. He had that conversation right up until he got back into the front room and led her out to his car.

Their theatre seats were much better than he was used to. As he chatted with Abby amiably, waiting for the play to start, he wondered if all they were ever going to have were unofficial dates. Or was this an official one? He wasn't sure. They had set a time, day and place which is another way of saying "date" so it was a date in the "let's set a time, day and place" sense, but did that make it a date in the "are we on a date" sense? Officially? He wanted to skip the play and just go back and smooch on the couch. He wanted to skip the play in any case.

There was a curtain draped in front of the stage this time. It was gold and sparkling and had two spot lights pointing at it at oblique angles. Lee liked seeing the set right away better, it gave him more of a sense of what was to come. Now that he was a veteran theatre patron of more than one play, he could decide what he liked. The house lights went down, then the two curtain spots dimmed and went out. It wasn't nearly as thrilling as the opening moment of The Effect of Gamma Rays on Man-in-the-Moon Marigolds. He was all set to hate this play. The lights came back up almost immediately, but they were odd. They only lit the edge of the stage, in front of the curtain and a little off to one side, but the curtain was now just a black nothing. The lights suggested the sandy edge of a river surrounded by trees at sunset. There were no set pieces, just lights, but he could swear he saw the water and the trees. Willows. The familiar thrill ran up his spine. How the hell do they do that, Lee thought, and lost himself to the play. There was a call of a sparrow, and the sound of distant ranch dogs barking. A quail call turned into a warning, then a flock taking wing, and two men entered carrying bed rolls.

As the two men, Lennie and George, finished their scene in the almost complete darkness of night, the curtain slowly opened to the bunk house at morning. Another thrill went up Lee's spine and down his arms. He was really beginning to love this theatre thing. The bunkhouse was empty until George and Lennie were led in by an old man. Lee completely forgot that he wanted to hate the play for the next thirteen minutes, until Carlson came in. Carlson, played by Jim. Jim Ackerman. Whose father liked the Rockford Files. A different kind of something went up Lee's spine and he squirmed in his seat. Abby put her hand on his arm. Lee had trouble losing himself, now. He watched every single movement that every single muscle on Jim's body made. He had watched women that closely before, but it hadn't felt the same. Carlson was supposed to be big. Strong. A ranch hand. It looked like they had one of the Beach Boys playing him, for God's sake. Jim couldn't be a big, strong, ranch hand if he tried. It never occurred to Lee to think that he wasn't any bigger or stronger or more like a ranch hand than Jim or a Beach Boy. Except the dead one, of course. Lee didn't watch Jim's muscles for long, though, because a minute later the act ended.

Shortly after Act II started, Carlson convinced Candy to let him take the old dog out and kill him. The whole scene was so wrenching that Lee was again lost in the play and Jim was already off stage with the dog by the time Lee remembered to hate him. By the time Carlson came back in and started cleaning his gun, Lee had given up hating him in favor of just watching the damn play, fully intending to lambast Jim's performance to anyone and everyone who would listen for the rest of his life.

After it was all over, Lee was sullen as he and Abby walked back to the car.

"Actually," Abby said when they were settled in, but before Lee had started it, "he was kind of good."

"I thought you were my friend."

"He was, you know."

"Of course he was," Lee said miserably, trying to find a way to get to all the lambasting he had planned. "He played the guy who killed the dog!"

Abby laughed understandingly, then crossed her arms.

"Some dawgs need killin'," she said, and Lee laughed in spite of himself and started the car.

When they got to his house, Abby kissed him lightly on the lips then went to her car and drove off. Lee went into the house thinking that at least it was progress. Not much progress, but progress.

Peter and Abby had agreed to get to Lee's house by eleven to set up for the party. Abby got to the house about thirteen minutes before Peter did. Lee was sitting on his couch in a pair of Dockers and a crisp white tee shirt, listening to ABBA. When Abby came in, he hurried over to change it.

"No," Abby said as she set the two big bags she was carrying down. "I like ABBA."

"I was just listening to it because I could," Lee said. "Wait, you like ABBA?"

"When I was a little girl, I thought they were named after me and just couldn't spell very well," she said, and handed Lee a receipt. "There's another bag in the car. Oh, and a box. Cool stereo."

Abby took off her coat and rolled up the sleeves of her rust-colored sweat shirt. On the front was a picture of a star field and on the back it said "Shatner and Nemoy - 1971 World Tour".

"Sound system," Lee said as he put on a coat and pair of boots. "After Christmas sale."

Abby started taking party favors out of the bags and stacking them on all available surfaces. Lee came in with the box and set it down. Abby reached in, pulled out the receipt and handed it to him before he went back out for the bag. He set the bag down and started to take off his coat when Abby remembered the folding chairs in the trunk. When he opened the door, Peter was there, trying to get a hand free to knock. Lee took one of the bags from his arms and they set them in the kitchen.

Lee went out for the chairs and Peter followed him for the rest of his bags.

"Sorry I'm late," Peter said as he took off his coat. "I was watching Sesame Street."

"Elmo," Abby said. "Love him."

Peter went into the bedroom to put the coat on the bed.

"Who's Elmo?" Lee asked.

Peter came back into the kitchen to start taking foodstuffs out of the bags. Abby was putting streamer rolls in strategic places around the living room and kitchen.

"Bert and Ernie's love child," she said.

"Did those guys live together?" Lee said, and started to help Peter take things out of the bags.

"Yeah, they were roommates," Peter said, and put three of the things Lee had just taken out back into the bag. "They go in the fridge for later."

"Oh," Lee said, picked up a streamer roll, a blue one, and undid the little piece of tape that held it together. "I thought they lived in a garbage can."

"No, that was Oscar," Peter said as he folded the bag he had just emptied. "The Grouch®."

Abby gathered up the streamer that Lee had let fall all over the floor and took the end that he still had in his hand gently from him, as a mother would take her grandparents fine china from a poorly-trained orangutan. Lee went back into the kitchen to help Peter again.

"I only watched Sesame Street enough to know one-two-three-four-five-six-seven-eight - niiiine, ten©," Lee said and started taking more stuff from bags.

"I watched it from the very beginning," Peter said. "I love it. You know the actor who played the shop owner died and they actually dealt with death on the show instead of just having a different actor do it."

Peter took the loaf of bread out of Lee's hand and set it back down on the counter.

"Was it funny?" Lee said as he opened the refrigerator door and started putting things he thought should go in there in there.

Abby came back into the kitchen with one of her bags and started taking out paper plates, napkins, plastic spoons, forks and cabbage. "No, it was for children," she said. "They don't start making death funny until it's for teenagers."

Peter took the packet of cheese from Lee's hand, closed the refrigerator door and handed Lee a receipt.

"I wonder if this is tax deductible," Lee said, wistfully. "Let me get my checkbook."

"Don't take anything but cash, Peter," Abby said. "We know about his credit rating."

"Damn Beverly!" Lee shouted.

"Hey, calm down," Abby said, and stroked his hair. "I didn't mean to upset you. I wouldn't want you to go to the hospital on a slab on the day of your housewarming. How would that look?"

"Thanks," Lee said, and glanced out the window. "Why are they towing your car?"

"Ono!" Abby shouted and started running for the door, then saw Lee's smile. "Cute."

"I'm going to make dip," Peter said. "Please take your little game into the other room."

"No, don't make him come help me," Abby said as she went into the living room, hoping Lee wouldn't follow. "Isn't there someplace you need to be?"

"Yeah," Peter said. "Aren't you going to the auditions for Odd Couple? It starts in an hour."

Lee let them know in very specific terms that he was done with all that. Abby said he should just go watch the auditions, then. Or go to work. Or go watch Twain work. Or go to the park and watch for snow. Peter came into the living room and looked around.

"You moved the lamp," he said. "You didn't move the couch, but you moved the lamp."

"I like the couch there," Lee said. "I tried it several places, and I like it there best. It's not because that's where it was in Chicago. It's my place. Leave me alone."

"I didn't say anything. It's none of my business."

"Don't you have dip to make?"

"Yes," Peter said. "I do. But my point is that you can't fool me about being done with all that."

"I can't audition. I haven't read the play, yet."

Who do you think you're fooling, straight man, Peter thought. He would have said it out loud if Abby wasn't there. "I saw it on your bed stand," he said instead.

"What the hell were you doing in my bedroom?" Lee said. He would have added Gay Man, but Peter was there.

"He was putting his coat on the bed, Lee," Abby said. "And you'd make a wonderful Pigeon Sister."

"It's a comedy about divorce."

51

"Then," Abby said, while putting her arm around his shoulder and breathing lightly on his cheek, "you should be perfect."

"Fine. Okay. I'll go audition. I hope you're happy. I'll be Felix just to spite you both. And I'll be good. Then you'll be sorry you were so mean to me."

He went into the bedroom to get a shirt and put on socks and plaid panties, donned his coat and boots and shuffled to the door.

"Um," he said, and turned back to them with that look of a puppy dog on his face that they both so loved and were so annoyed by. "When can I come back home?"

"Three," Peter said.

"Four," Abby corrected.

"Thirty," Peter agreed.

When Lee finally left, Abby turned to Peter.

"We're good," she said.

Peter agreed.

Agnes ran her auditions much differently from the guy who directed Of Mice and Men. Lee walked in thinking he knew what to expect and was greeted by an assistant sitting at a long table in front of the closed door to the theatre instead. The assistant handed him the sign-in sheet. First, he scanned the names on it to make sure no on was named Jim. No one was. Then he scanned it to see if Andrew was there. He wasn't. As he filled in his name he told her he really was done with all this, that he was just there to make a friend of his shut up. She seemed unimpressed as she glanced at the part he had listed.

"Felix," she said. "Really."

Without saying a word, Lee took the sheet back, crossed out Felix and wrote in Murray, then added The Cop, just to make sure she knew that he knew enough about the play to know that Murray was a cop. She handed him a couple of photocopied™ pieces of paper that were stapled together.

"Your sides," she said.

"My huh?"

She just pointed at the papers, which were of a scene from the play with Murray in it. Lee pulled his copy of the play out of his jacket pocket and told her he didn't need it. She was momentarily impressed. Then she asked him if his copy was marked with where they wanted the scene to start and where they wanted it to end. He shook his head no in bewilderment and took the sides. He glanced at where the markings were on the pages and handed it back to her. She waved him away, so he took his script and wandered around the lobby of the theatre. There were several other actors and a few actresses there, all wandering around reading sides and gesticulating to themselves. Lee was relieved that none of them were Jim. And disappointed that none were Andrew.

"Oh," a voice behind him said. "Hi."

He turned and saw Veronica standing there in her loose-fitting splendor, smelling of wildflowers. Lee was relieved to discover that nothing stirred but discomfort.

"Hi," he said.

"Auditioning?"

"Yeah. Well. I'm really done with all this. I'm only here because they kicked me out of my house."

She looked at him very oddly so he added that Peter was throwing him a house warming party, and she nodded knowingly.

"Yeah," she said. "Tonight. Well. Break-a-leg."

"Oh. Um. Yeah. Thanks. You, too."

As she walked away, a little something stirred but he sternly told it to behave itself.

Lee found a padded bench in the lobby to sit on and watched everyone do all the strange and interesting things they all did to get ready for or avoid thinking about their audition. The theatre door opened and an actor came out, followed shortly by Kim Anderson, carrying a clipboard. Lee was quite surprised to see her, and had a strange impulse to call her Loni. Kim looked at the sign-in sheet, called out a name and another actor gathered his things and followed her in. This happened several times, and Lee continued watching people come and go. When Kim called his name, his heart lurched. He hadn't expected that. He was done with all this, after all. Kim seemed surprised and pleased to see him, and told him she was Agnes's assistant director and would be stage managing.

"It's really good to see you here," she said as she led him in.

"I'm really done with all this, you know," he said to her.

"Do you have your sides?" she asked and he showed her his copy of the script. She nodded and smiled.

"Lee, darling," Agnes said when she looked up and saw him. "How nice to see you."

He told her he was just there because Peter and Abby had kicked him out of the house. Kim laughed.

"The housewarming thing," she said. "Should be fun."

Agnes had him go up on the stage. The gold, sparkly curtain was closed, but didn't seem nearly as sparkly with no spotlights shining on it. There was one old wooden kitchen chair on the stage, and he stood near that looking out at them while they talked. Agnes told him he could sit if he liked, and he did. She chatted with him for a moment about what seemed like nothing in particular, then said she understood he was reading for Murray.

"Yeah," he said. "I guess so."

Agnes had Kim read all the other parts in the scene. Lee didn't want to be there at all. Except that he really did. A lot. That's mostly what he was thinking about when he read the lines. Then Agnes thanked him, and Lee realized it was all over. He had somehow expected so much more. As he climbed off the stage and walked up the aisle, Agnes and Kim talked quietly, but intently, and Kim took notes on her clipboard. Just as he got to the theatre door, Kim looked up and sweetly said that she looked forward to the party.

That was it. His final audition. No fanfare. He hadn't done badly, but hadn't done particularly well. He hadn't skipped over any lines or mangled any words, but had felt kind of like a board member reading someone else's report. In fact, it felt like the whole experience had been an afterthought for Agnes and Kim as much as it had been for him. Well, he could now tell everyone that he really was done with all this and to leave him alone about it all, damn it.

He still had two-and-a-half hours before he would be allowed back into his house. He thought about going to Twain's to help out, but Twain had given him the day off to get ready for his party, and it would be just too embarrassing trying to explain why he was back. He sat in his car with his hands on the wheel, just looking at the snow-covered landscape around Willow Lane. The chill felt good, the sky had a pleasant light gray cast to it and the air smelled of small town comfort. Beverly really doesn't know what she's missing, he thought, and put the key in the ignition. He was surprised to find himself stopping in front of Mom's Used Records, figured his car knew something he didn't and went in to see what trouble he could get in to.

Lee breathed in the smell of damp wood, dry cardboard and conflicting stale incenses, then spent over an hour becoming familiar with everything in the shop. He picked up the Beatles Anthology several times and put it back down, and ended up leaving with a bag full of ninety-nine cent greatest hits of the sixties, seventies and eighties compilations. Not one of them was even from Rhino. Mom was very happy to be rid of them.

Lee was amazed by what Abby and Peter had accomplished. The house was gorgeous. Like a smaller scale version of the Taj Mahal. Well, maybe a smaller scale version of a cocktail lounge at the MGM Grand. Well, maybe the men's room at the Whiskey A-Go-Go. They had done more than he could have imagined possible from a few bags and a box of stuff. He wanted to thank Abby by hugging her. He wanted to thank Peter by giving him a nice plant. The folding chairs that Abby brought were set around the living room, and Lee noticed that they all had "HOLIDAY" stenciled on the back in orange.

The fireplace crackled and popped comfortably. People started shuffling in shortly after seven. Most brought housewarming gifts. Abby told Lee that if he dared tell anyone they shouldn't have or that he hadn't gotten them anything she would move his couch. The house filled quickly with the smell of fireplace smoke, food and the many colognes and perfumes of the people who filled the house quickly. Lee started the party playing cool jazz, but quickly migrated toward medium jazz. After a couple of martinis, he moved up to hot jazz. Every time someone arrived, the living room was filled with a blast of wonderfully cold air that warmed quickly as it mingled with the party goers.

Abby came into the living room looking for Lee and saw him leaning against the wall, just watching the people. He caught her eye and blushed, so she did, too. She crossed the room and leaned on the wall next to him.

"Hi, Harris."

"Hi, Holiday."

"I like where you put the thing," she said.

55

"Yeah," he replied, watching the growing throng, "it works there, doesn't it? Thanks."

They both watched for a while, but Abby had to join in, so she left with a small glance Lee's way.

Bear came in and handed Lee a masculinely wrapped gift. (*Masculinely wrapped gift?* **It was wrapped in muscle, Geoff.** *Have it your way.* **I always do.**) It was a cordless screwdriver. (*Aren't all screwdrivers cordless, Steve? Steve?* **Don't even talk to me.**) He knew what to get a man to make him happy.

"Nice sound system," he said.

"Sound system," Lee corrected. "I mean... um. Thanks."

Lee took him down to the basement to show him his work bench and was amazed to discover that Peter had transformed the workbench into an hors d'oeuvre and drink table. The basement looked like it could have been the entire party. The pounding of the bass and the people dancing to it above them shook the air in the room. Lee felt it charge his bones and invigorate his chest cavity and legs. He leaned over to turn the knob and music joined the bass thrum.

"This place is cool," Bear said.

"With the havoc Beverly wreaked on my credit, I'm surprised I even got it."

"What are you talking about?" Bear said, sipping from his bottle of cold, domestic beer, "they should have given it to you."

Lee looked at him for a very long time, then finally asked what he meant.

"It's haunted."

"Yeah," Lee laughed. "Ha ha. Roger's Room. Slipped on the ice here, too, huh? Fool me once, shame on me."

"No, shame on you. And I'm serious. Some girl, I think. Korean war. Her soldier didn't come home or something."

Lee didn't know what to think, so he went back upstairs. Bear followed. When they got to the kitchen, Bear pointed out the scratches on the bottom of the basement door and told Lee he could fix that for him. Lee stared at it.

"I did fix it."

"Well," Bear said. "You didn't do a very good job."

Bear turned to rejoin the party, but Lee just stood looking at what looked like freshly painted gouges in the bottom of his door. He mimed the motions of puttying and sanding in the air in front of himself, trying to remember if he had just dreamed doing it.

"Everything okay?" Peter asked.

Lee jumped, was about to point out the scratches, then assured Peter everything was fine. Kim swooped into the room, saw Lee and gave him a huge hug. He was startled at first, then hugged her back. Her perfume smelled of allure, obsession and private moments and a little remained on Lee's cheek when she pulled away.

"It was great seeing you today," she said, and he nodded. "Great party," she said, and he nodded again.

Then she hugged him again, and left the room. Lee stood there, very bewildered, then saw Abby standing in the kitchen doorway. He felt strangely guilty. She came over to him and handed him a new martini.

"Having fun?" she asked.

He nodded, then was surprised to see Stella come in the front door, followed by a fresh cold blast and accompanied by her perfume, which was wearing a stylish gown and pearls. Peter saw her and shouted from across the room,

"You did come."

It only tripped Stella up momentarily.

"Yes, Peter. Observant as always. Oh, hi, Lee."

She A-frame hugged Lee, air kissed his cheek. Her perfume didn't stick to his face. Lee saw Abby see that and didn't feel the least bit guilty. Stella handed him a small, wrapped gift. Lee shook it.

"Hand towels," he said. "Turkish. Thanks."

Stella nodded and looked for booze. Lee went into the living room to pump up the tunes. He put on The Cars greatest hits, but there were several loud objections to that, so he replaced it with one of the collections he'd bought that afternoon. The first song on it was "My Best Friend's Girl."

When Andrew and his wife got there, Andrew stopped just inside the door and looked around with an odd expression on his face.

"Hi, Andrew," Peter said. "Everything okay?"

Andrew shut the door, took his coat off and said that the house just felt really familiar, but he couldn't place it. Peter suggested that it was because he had helped clean it that night, but he said it had felt familiar that night too. Peter led them to the food.

Shortly after eleven-thirty, the crowd from Of Mice and Men started arriving. They joined and increased the laughter and chatter and music and mingling and clinking of plastic glasses and beer bottles and the smell of bodies and cosmetics and fun and the kinetic sense of Brownian motion in the air. A final layer of restraint lifted from the crowded room, which seemed to breathe more easily as it filled. The door breezed open and Agnes entered. The quality of the cold air that followed her was, somehow, different. When the door shut, the air didn't. She held what looked like a bird cage draped with a towel. It took a moment for anyone to notice that she was escorted by Jim who was wearing a thick coat and Dockers™ knock-offs and had a very bemused look on his face, like a small rabbit who had just seen his first logging truck. Jim stopped short when he saw Lee, and the look turned to that of the rabbit after the truck passed over it and it realized that it wasn't dead, but that it didn't have to go to the bathroom anymore. Lee was really surprised to see Jim in any state in his living room, and glanced over at Peter, who stared at Jim, then turned away quickly and looked at Stella, who looked back at him, then at Jim, then at the booze.

"Isn't that the guy from the play?" Mrs. Divine asked Andrew. "The one who killed the dog?"

Andrew nodded.

"It looks like he's lost weight," she said.

Peter slumped into a folding chair, then got up and poured himself a large drink. With lots of brown stuff and a little clear stuff. And an ice cube. And a twist of lemon. He went out back and stood on the back stoop breathing deeply and shivering. A moment later the back door opened again, and Stella stood there with a large drink that was more clear stuff than brown stuff. She was also breathing deeply. And shivering.

"Agnes," Peter said, and Stella nodded, nonplused. "He left me for Agnes. I could even understand if he'd left me for you. Sort of. I guess. But Agnes, for God's sake. What's wrong with me?"

"Hey, he left me for you," Stella reminded Peter. "And then when he left you he still didn't come back to me. What's wrong with him?"

"He was never with you."

Stella had to agree. She didn't like it much, though.

"Agnes," she said again, and they stood there bonding in misery. "And what's with that Abby person?"

Peter stopped bonding with her and told her Abby was a very nice person who seemed to make Lee happy. When Lee let her. Stella gave him a "but how can you, of all people, be happy that anyone you know is happy with someone else" look. Peter gave her an "I'm sorry, were you looking at me" look. She changed the subject back to Agnes.

"Agnes," she said.

"And miles to go before I weep."

"Sleep."

"What?"

"And miles to go before I sleep. Walt Whitman."

"I know, but I don't want to sleep," he said. "And it's Robert Frost."

"Wasn't he that British talk show guy?"

Peter gave her a "we already did this in Installment Ten, except it was with Lee, not you, but it was about poetry so stop it. And that was David Frost" look. The door opened and Lee came out, preceded by the sounds of the party and followed by the smell of all those perfumes dancing with all those colognes. And brie.

"Did you invite him?" he asked Peter.

He understood the look Peter gave him perfectly.

"He's lost weight," Peter said, and no one argued with him. "She's not feeding him well."

"Or she is," Stella said, and all three of them shuddered and took a big slug of whatever was in their respective glasses.

Peter leaned against the rail and stared out at the snow which refused to look depressing no matter how much he wanted it to. Lee went back inside and noticed Jim start and hide behind Agnes when he saw him. Agnes handed Lee the thing that looked like a birdcage. He lifted the towel. It was a birdcage. With a bird in it. A sparrow. A yellow one. A stupid bird.

"Um," he said, sincerely, then added, "thanks."

"A bird brings luck to a house," Agnes said and hugged him, then led Jim to the food and fed him a bit of cracker with dip on it. Her perfume checked the union rules and decided it didn't have to work just then.

"There you are," Abby said when she spotted him holding the bird. "Put that down, Twain is here."

"Twain? You mean from Twain's?"

Abby smiled, took the bird and pushed Lee in Twain's direction. Twain was standing just inside the living room, wearing a silly hat, carrying a big pot with steam coming out of it. Matt stood just behind him with a box of Saltines and a big grin. The room stopped again, but this time to take in the new smell, which was a mixture of ground beef, pepper, onion and some secret ingredient.

"Uncle Hubert's Five Alarm Chili," someone said with an edge of awe, and they all crowded around Twain as he brought the chili into the kitchen.

Peter got bowls, and he, Matt and Twain started serving it to everyone. He didn't even mind being upstaged by chili. This batch tasted even better than the one Peter had made the weekend Lee broke the diner. This batch was made with love. Or, rather, with Twain's blood, sweat and tears. It was really made with blood, sweat and tears. O negative. When everyone was served, Lee, who was strangely thrilled to have Twain in his house, offered him a tour.

They started with the bathroom, which wasn't much besides a bathroom. Twain looked around, seeming sort of unimpressed. Lee pointed out the picture of the Partridge Family that Twain had given him which he had hung over the john. Twain cocked his head a little to the left and nodded once.

"Shirley Jones," he said. "She's a dish."

The second bedroom was empty except for the people standing in it drinking and laughing and a little yellow sparrow in a cage. Twain looked the room over with the same level of enthusiasm with which he had looked over the bathroom. Lee started to worry that nothing in his house would impress Twain. The main bedroom, with the bed full of coats and purses, received little acknowledgment from, nor stirred any emotion in Twain.

They went out to the garage, which was very quiet and dark after the happy throng in the house. Twain wandered around, looking at boxes, unimpressed. Lee was strangely disappointed, then strangely embarrassed that he felt disappointed that Twain wasn't impressed with his garage. Lee wasn't even impressed with his garage, except that he actually had one. He shivered and suggested they go back inside. Peter was still on the back porch, shivering and commiserating with Meg Foster. Her wonderful blue eyes were colder than the snow and matched his mood perfectly.

When Lee and Twain climbed the stoop, Twain pointed down at the burn mark on the step.

"Snake pellets," Twain said.

Lee was sorry he had embarked on this whole tour thing. Now that he had started, however, he had to finish and take Twain down into the basement, it would seem odd not to, but he would be really upset if the only thing that caused any perturbations in Twain's calm were Shirley Jones and a snake-stained stoop. They traveled through the living room. It was filled with more people than Lee thought could possibly fit in his entire house and a little yellow sparrow in a cage and Lee suddenly thought of an old Chinese man with seven faces.

The wife of the man who played Charley and the doctor was standing in the doorway to the stairs to the basement with her bejeweled hand pressed against her chest and an odd look on her face. (**Uncle Hubert?** *No, Steve.*)

"What's the matter?" her husband asked.

"I don't know," she said. "I just feel sad."

She stepped down to the first stair.

"I'm better now," she said, and continued blithely on to the basement.

Twain looked around the crowded basement with the same unperturbed demeanor and Lee was about to just give up. Twain wasn't even moved by the dart board and the dart that just missed him as he moved toward the workbench, upon which was sitting the bird cage with the little yellow sparrow in it. Then Twain glanced under the food and cage bedecked workbench. On the lower shelf, just visible under the table cloth, was the gas mask. His pupils dilated and his pants tented. In the back.

"M17A2," he said.

"No," Lee said. "It's an M95."

Twain nodded once and almost smiled. A chorus of angels sang. Two straight men bonded. Twain didn't even have to ask about the axe. Lee was, at last, happy.

When he got back upstairs, Abby was again looking for him. She handed him a drink and told him there was a policeman at the door. It was Officer Bacon.

"Oh, hello," Lee said. "I'm sorry, are we making too much noise?"

"Oh, good heavens no. It's only twelve-thirty. It's winter. Everyone's windows are closed. There are trees separating your house from your neighbors. You could be getting murdered and no one would know. No, I just brought you this," he said and handed Lee a box with a bow on it.

Lee shook it, then opened it. It was a nice, stone bust of Franz Liszt, with the dates of his birth and death on the base.

"What's this?"

"Franz Liszt," Officer Bacon said. "Arguably the greatest pianist of all time. Not a great composer, but he did write some fairly nifty tunes. When you get a piano, this will go nicely on it. Happy house warming."

Lee smiled, shook his head and thanked him. They shook hands, and Officer Bacon nodded.

"Oh, by the way," he said over his shoulder as he turned to leave. "Fireworks are illegal within the city limits."

He nodded again, smiled and continued on his beat. Lee turned back to the room in time to see Agnes slow-dancing with Jim in the middle of the living room to Earth Wind and Fire's "September". Someone next to Lee shuddered. It was Bear, who then smiled and said that Jim was great dark theatre. Lee said that he usually liked dark theatre, but not when it was happening to him. Bear laughed and re-entered the fray. Lee wasn't joking, and stayed on the edge.

"Oh, there you are," Abby said and put her arm around Lee's back. Lee showed her the bust.

"Helluva pianist," she said.

"Couldn't sing worth a lick," Lee said.

Finally, the throng started to thin. Just like Steve's hair. (**Hey! That's getting personal.** *Okay, I'll take it out.* **Thanks.** *No problem.*) Lee was in the kitchen fixing himself a prosciuto on Triscuit with mayo, cream cheese and an olive with no pimento hors d'oeuvre. The little yellow sparrow glared at him from inside its cage. Lee had the brief thought that he was being judged, and not kindly. He turned his back on the dreadful thing. Then he felt guilty and dropped some cracker crumbs from the counter into the cage. The bird just glared. Lee turned his back again.

"Oh, there you are," Abby said and gave him a little hug. "Agnes is leaving and wants to say goodbye."

Lee suffered through shaking Jim's hand while muttering something about him not sucking in the play.

"Thanks," Jim said, his eyes wide, his stance straight and tall for the first time all night. "That means so much... "

Lee gave him a "I was just being polite, idiot, this is not open for discussion" look and glared at him. He looked like the little yellow sparrow without the cage. Jim stooped and seemed to fade behind Agnes. Lee kissed Agnes on the cheek and they left. When he kissed the wife of the guy who played Charley and the doctor on the cheek, he left a vug in her makeup.

There were only a few people left in the living room, and the lights seemed, somehow, too bright, like a bar at last call. The living room also looked a little tired, like it had been holding the entire population of Jakarta, Indonesia and two guys from Butte for a few hours too long. When Kim left, she gave Lee a huge, full-bodied hug and a gentle kiss. Over her shoulder, Lee noticed Abby notice.

Finally, Abby, Peter and Lee sat, alone, on the couch, exhausted, but happy. Lee looked at Peter, wondering if they could fit a few more commas into the sentence.

"How are you doing?" he said, and when Peter didn't understand he added, "About Jim."

"It's only a one slice of cheese crisis," Peter said with a small sigh, then looked around the living room. "What A Dump," he said.

"I'm going to start cleaning up," Abby said and lurched off the couch.

Lee and Peter also lurched and headed toward the kitchen to start in there.

"It's okay, Peter," Abby said. "I'll take care of it."

Peter was about to object, then saw a strange, confused look on Lee's face. Then he saw the strange, shy look on Abby's.

"Oh," he said, his heart pounding with embarrassment. "I completely forgot. I have to feed Cliche. He's probably already killed a rat by now. And I'm really tired. And I forgot to set the VCR for The English Patient. And and and... "

"It's okay, Peter," Abby said. "We can take care of it."

"I'm so sorry to leave it all to you."

"It's all right. Really. We've got it taken care of. Go feed Cliche."

"Thanks for the party," Lee said. He looked like he really wanted to put his arm around Abby, and if Peter didn't leave very soon, might have to do it right in front of him.

Peter got his coat, and ducked into the kitchen quickly to pick up a slice of Swiss cheese and put it in his pocket. Then he picked up a few more, just in case, and left without looking back.

Abby and Lee stood staring into the fading fire, a few inches from each other. Abby looked up at Lee. He looked back at her.

"I really just kind of... ," Lee said. "Um."

"What?"

He shrugged, and she put her hand on his elbow and asked him again. He leaned over and kissed her very gently on the lips, then pulled back, flush and flustered.

"I'm sorry," he said. "I just... it's really... "

She looked at his eyes for what seemed like a whole lot of seconds when, really, it was only a small portion of a whole lot of seconds. Then she grabbed him around the waist, pulled him to her and kissed him back. He stood stiff and frozen for what seemed like a whole lot of seconds and really was a whole lot of seconds, then realized she meant it and put his arms around her. A whole lot of seconds later, he pulled away and looked at her face.

"Um," he said. "Maybe we can clean up in the morning."

She seemed to agree. But first, Lee picked up a few empty glasses and set them in the kitchen.

Abby woke up with a start. The room was dark with a few streaks of moonlight shining through the window onto the towel that covered the birdcage on the bedside table, and Lee's arms were still around her. He stirred and his eyes fluttered open groggily.

"You okay?" he asked. At least that's what he hoped he had asked. To his ears it sounded sort of like "uuu way?"

"Did you hear that?"

He hadn't.

"Do your neighbors have a baby?"

"I think one of them has a dog," Lee said and played with her hair. His mouth was beginning to work better. "I hear it sometimes."

"No, it sounded like crying. Like a young girl."

"The house settling," he explained. "I'm getting used to it."

"That's weird settling," she said, and he shrugged. Then he kissed her gently, and cocked his head to the side. She asked what was wrong.

"Nothing," he said. "Just... Um. What changed your mind?"

She smiled and recounted the moment when he had told her that her car was being towed.

"It was the first time I didn't hear Beverly in your voice," she said, and leaned in toward him.

Across town, a train went into a tunnel. In a pasture near Veronica Park, nocturnal bees flitted from winter flower to flower, night-time birds flew from tree to tree and a lone skater glided across the ice on the pond in graceful arcs. The River Bend Symphony timpanist practiced his part in Rossini's 1812 Overture. Bolero blared from the little, batter-encrusted radio in Twain's kitchen. An earthquake rumbled in Southern Japan, a volcano in Fiji blew steam, smoke, ash and molten stone into the sky and an iceberg in Antarctica broke in two and slid into the ocean.

The hum of a street sweeper lulled the animals in the San Diego Zoo to sleep.

On Sunday, after they had cleaned up and Abby had left, Lee fixed the scratches in the door to the basement again, then headed for Twain's to work.

On Monday afternoon, Lee called the theatre from Twain's to see if he'd been cast.

"Not that I care, really," he said. "I'm really done with all that."

"Uh huh," Stella said. "Yeah, you got the part."

"Murray?" He didn't want to sound excited.

"Murray? No, Lee. Roy."

"Roy? The accountant?"

"Quite a stretch. Think you can handle it?"

Lee said he would try. Stella gave him the time, date and place of the first rehearsal and he hung up. Twain looked at him again. He'd been doing that all day. Lee didn't mind at all.

The first rehearsal was in Agnes's living room. There was a big fold-out banquet table set up, and Agnes and a few other actors were already sitting at it when Lee arrived. Kim handed him a script. He told her he already had his own, but she said he might as well use that one. He sat down and started to introduce himself to another actor when Jim came in from the hallway. Jim flinched when he saw Lee, and slumped a little. Oh, God, Lee thought. I hope he's not going to be sitting in on the rehearsals. Jim sat at the table as far away from Lee as he could. Then he moved his chair back a few inches. Then he took his script out of his pocket and opened it.

What's Jim doing in The Odd Couple?
Will Veronica play one of the Pigeon sisters in The Odd Couple?
Will Jim kill a dog in The Odd Couple?
Will Lee kill Jim in The Odd Couple?
Will Agnes and Jim remain the odd couple?
Will Lee ever learn that the spotlights shining on the curtains at the beginnings of plays are called "curtain warmers"?
Will that have been our longest question ever?
Will Bear tell any more ghost stories?
Will anyone know that it was E.F. Hutton that people listen to when he talks?
Will anyone get the Seven Faces of Dr. Lao reference?
Will we ever find out what Abby got Lee for Christmas?
Will Lee get over having bad credit?
Can Andrew fix Lee's credit?
Can Abby come over and play, again?
Can Can?
Or Gigi?

To find the answers to these and other microscopic meanderings, tune into our next installment:
"When Words Collide"

(Wait. Peter's gay?)

This installment first published November 2, 2002

Geoff Hoff and Steve Mancini

The story so far: Lee was beat out of a role in a play by the same man who tried to get his signature on a document so that his ex-wife could sell the house they'd lived in together for many years. Peter and Abby threw a housewarming party for Lee and that same guy showed up as the escort of Agnes, an old, but oddly alluring woman. Agnes also brought a small, yellow bird and left it in Lee's care. Lee and Abby finally know if the other one snores. That guy that stalked Lee and took his part is also now in the cast of Lee's second chance at a life in the theatre, which is being directed by Agnes, the old, but oddly alluring woman who brought the guy and the bird to the party. And Twain made chili. To find out how all of this ties together with all of that, read the previous installments. You get them all at once. Read them slowly. The people who have been around from the beginning have had to wait for each one. Sheesh.

(*If we do it tastefully, Steve, can we have a maudlin moment in this installment?* **Only if Ferrante & Teicher play the background music.** *Never mind, then. Sigh.*)

Installment Eighteen
"When Words Collide"

Agnes's house looked pretty much like Lee expected Agnes's house to look. It was pleasantly upper-middle-class in a pleasantly upper-middle class neighborhood. All the houses in the neighborhood were one or two-stories with brick or stone below aluminum or wood siding. Hers was a one-story ranch house, brick on the bottom with aluminum siding above that and powder-blue shingles peeking out from under the snow. It had an attached two car garage. They all had chimneys with wisps of smoke rising from them and several still had tasteful Christmas lights trimming their eaves that twinkled through the icicles in the chilly post-Christmas air. One still had a pumpkin on its porch, but that has nothing to do with this story. There were a few evergreens dotting the front and back yards, but mostly bare trees blanketed by snow, waiting for the warmth of spring. Or Godot. The street was curved and winding in a pleasant way. Upper-middle class pleasant. It all reminded Lee, somehow, of a Monkee's song. It all felt attractive in a way Lee had never thought middle-class living would be to him. He had lived an upper middle-class life with Beverly. At least, looking back on it, that's what it seemed to have been, but he hadn't thought about it in those terms at all. It was just life. And it seemed so long ago.

Agnes's front door opened to a small ante-room with benches to sit on while you removed your boots. (**But I'm not wearing boots.** *Then remove your feet and leave me alone.*) That opened to a large, airy living room that was bright and clean and polished in a pleasant upper middle-class way. The main things that differentiated her living room from the rest of the living rooms in the neighborhood were the framed theatrical posters on the walls and the baby grand piano in the corner by the French doors that opened to the snowy, pleasant upper-middle class back yard with bare, snow-covered fruit trees and a nice attached deck that was also covered with pleasant snow. Lee was very proud of his new home, but wandering around Agnes's living room made him feel, somehow, a little ashamed of being proud of an old rental, and ashamed even more of being ashamed of an old rental. And even more ashamed of having read Emily Dickinson. And not for a class. He didn't want to think about it.

Around the corner from the living room was a bright, spacious kitchen with tile floors, lots of Formica counter space and plenty of windows. On one counter, next to the big, old, solid, dark-green enameled mixer, was a professional quality silver coffee urn brewing pleasantly aromatic coffee. The enticingly pleasant fumes emanating from the urn wafted through the kitchen, into the living room and down the hallway from which Jim had appeared and on into the three bedrooms and the common bathroom. Lee tried to wrap himself up in the pleasantness of it all in order to avoid looking at Jim or wondering what he was doing at the rehearsal table with a script in his hand, but that made him think about the pleasant middle-classness of the smell of good coffee and how different that was from the faint odor of Twain's kitchen that seemed to cling to everything he had in his own place and flick him in the nose every once in a while when he wasn't looking.

Lee let his mind wander, hoping it would wander to something pleasant but unrelated to comparing his former life with his current life. He reigned it in when it wandered, quite unbidden, to the bills his ex-wife had sent him for Christmas. Damn her. After reigning in his mind, it proved more independent than he would have given it credit for by tallying up what he was spending and what he was taking in and coming up with the thought, completely against his will, that he would have to find other work if he didn't plan on going through the entire settlement from Beverly's antiques in a very short time. He was going to try to reign it in again, perhaps force it to think about I Am Curious, Yellow, when Agnes stood up, welcomed them all to the first rehearsal of the Willow Lane production of The Odd Couple by Neil Simon and introduced everyone at the table. Including Jim. Who was there to play Vinnie. Who was supposed to be one of Roy's best friends. Roy. Who was going to be played by Lee. Lee felt his elbow tremble. Damn Beverly.

Agnes had Kim hand out photocopied rehearsal schedules, and said that if anyone had any problems on any of the dates they were scheduled to be there, they should say so right away so adjustments could be made. She also told the poker-playing group that all of their scenes had been scheduled around the performance schedule for Of Mice and Men. It took Lee a moment to register that that was because of Jim. Jim was not only going to be at every rehearsal that Lee would be at, Lee had to bend to Jim's schedule. He was liking this whole thing less and less. But at least it wasn't middle-class, upper or otherwise.

Agnes talked for several minutes about the story of the play, admonished the actors to take their time, that the performances were a long way off, told them that Kim would read all the action and then had them read the first act. Lee actually kind of enjoyed it. The play was really funny. And he got to be snotty. And Vinnie, the guy Jim was playing, was kind of stupid. And even though he and Jim were always in scenes together, he didn't have to talk to him much. But he had felt Jim looking at him through the entire act except for those few moments when he happened to glance Jim's way and catch Jim's eyes dart away. And he felt a strange, unpleasant thrill in his stomach at how many lines he had. He wondered how in hell he was going to memorize all of them. How did people play roles like Hamlet or Stanley Kowalski or Godot? He wondered how horrible it would be if he just sat there in front of an audience on opening night staring blankly at Jim, who blithely remembered every stupid word. He began to picture the front page review in the Bee: "Good Play Ruined by Transient with Police Record". It didn't help that he knew the reviews were always way in the back, under the ads for face cream and River Bend's four adult theaters.

They took a break after finishing the first act and Kim and Agnes went into the kitchen to get coffee and snacks. Lee got up to stretch his legs and calm his gut. He started looking at the objet d'art in the room. (*Don't even start, Steve, Agnes would have objet d'art all over the place.* **I didn't say anything**. *Well, don't... What's wrong? Steve? You didn't say anything.* **You told me not to**. *We can't continue until you say something. We have a rhythm.* **What should I say**? *You always say "poop."* **I want a new word**. *Like what?* **Stool**? *Okay, now we can continue.* **Poop**.) There was a brass urn on the mantle piece. Engraved on it was the name "Dr. Ronald Howard Livingstone" and two dates about fifty-five years apart. That wasn't really middle class. And looking at it distracted Lee from the ball of nerve endings growing like entwining snakes gathering at the crest of his stomach for a light dinner and drinks. He had the urge to reach out and touch the urn, and was very surprised and slightly disgusted by the urge. As he stood resisting it, Agnes came up behind him and offered him coffee.

"My husband," she said as he picked up a cup from the tray. "We were supposed to grow old together."

Someone was tinkling at the piano. Someone else was playing it. Lee was glad for the cup in his hand. It would keep his hand from straying up to the urn. But the coffee smelled unpleasantly pleasant. It didn't taste nearly as good as the coffee Twain served in the diner, and that calmed and disturbed Lee. The guys who played the rest of the poker-playing foursome were gathered near him, talking.

"I have fifty-eight lines," one of them said.

"I have ninety-eight," Jim answered.

The guy with fifty-eight lines scowled at Jim.

"Maybe I'll speak mine really slowly," he said.

"But your character's name is Speed," the third actor said.

"Right. Make interesting choices," the guy with fifty-eight lines said.

Lee had never known one should know how many lines one had. You learn something about theater every day, one thought. So you should know exactly how many lines there were to forget on opening night. Exactly how many opportunities you had to drag the whole production into perdition.

"How do you count lines?" he asked. "Just the lines printed on a page?"

"No," the guy with fifty-eight lines said. "I just count a whole speech."

"What about monologues?" Lee wanted to get it right. It seemed important. "Is that just one big line?"

"I don't know. I've never had any of those. I guess that's still just one line. Sure. Have to be."

"I just count from a capital letter to a period," the third actor said, rather superiorly. "Unless it's 'Mr.' or something."

"That's not a line, that's a sentence," the guy who counted speeches said.

"Isn't the definition of a line the shortest distance between two points?" the guy who counted from capital to period said.

"No," Lee said. "That's a line segment. A line has no beginning and no end."

"Isn't that a ray?"

"No, they have a beginning, just no end."

"A circle has no beginning and no end," the guy who counted speeches countered.

"Okay, smart guy," Lee said, "how many circles do you have?"

They all laughed and simultaneously took sips of coffee. Except Jim, who shook his head and wandered off with a look of complete bewilderment on his face. **(Where else would a look of bewilderment be, Geoff, on his pants?** *That's where you have yours.* **Shut up.)**

"He obviously never took geometry," one of the actors said as they watched Jim wander toward Agnes.

One of the ladies playing one of the Pigeon Sisters joined them. Actors could smell gossip as if it were the scent of a Siren's song. The only thing they liked more than gossip was talking about it. She leaned against the mantle and watched Jim.

"Yeah, and he can't count," the other actor said, then shook his head. "She's gotta be twice his age."

"How many times does twenty something go into sixty something?" The Pigeon Sister cooed.

"Three something," Lee said. He couldn't resist answering a math question. It was a reflex.

They all shuddered, and Lee wished he had a power tool to turn on.

"Okay, so she's three times his age," the actor who said she was two times his age said. "I hope he's using protection. I would hate to see Agnes's children."

Something about that made Lee's heart stop. Which made the snakes writhe a little less casually. Which made his heart start again, but run at double time with a nice polka lilt.

"I don't know," the other guy said. "I'll bet she was a looker in her day. And he's not bad. For a guy. I mean from what I'm told a good looking guy must look like. From my wife. My beautiful wife, who bore me three wonderful children. When does the break end?"

Lee realized what it was that had made his heart stop. The group continued gossiping about Agnes and Jim and disparaging their ancestors and prospective progeny, and talking about the steadily decreasing age of the men Agnes dated, but Lee's entire mind, even the part that had insisted up until that moment on thinking about finances, and the part that was trying to count his lines, and the part that was being annoyed by Jim, started trying to avoid admitting that he hadn't used protection with Abby. And he had no idea if she was using any. And he had no idea how to ask her. Now the snakes let loose and gleefully jitterbugged all over the inside of his abdominal cavity. If he had any mind parts left, he would have wondered what an urn full of his ashes would look like, but, thankfully, they were all occupied.

The second and third acts were a bit of a blur for Lee. Every time he opened his mouth to speak a line, his first thought was that he could never remember the last one, much less that one. His second thought was that he wished he could go back in time and slap himself silly for diving into a drunken night of rumpled sheets without proper planning.

His third thought was to wonder what the fuck Jim kept staring at him for. The humor of the final two acts was fairly lost on him.

The End

(*Steve, it's not the end.* **Sure it is.** *No. It's not.* **Okay, then something has to happen. Someone has to die or something.**)

After rehearsal, Lee had to wait to pull out from the curb because a funeral procession was passing by, but that has nothing to do with this story. (*Happy?* **Sort of, I guess.**)

The End - Part II

Is this really the end or is Steve pulling Geoff's leg again?
Will we ever really get to the end?
Will we ever get the $2,060,000.00 we've been
asking for for two years?
What will the questions be when and if we get to
the end if there is one?
Will any of our readers stick around long enough to find out?
Would they have more of a chance if we got back to the story?
Have we interrupted this installment too much all ready?
Do any of our readers still remember what the story is?
Do we?
Who discovered helium?

Napoleon sat on his horse on the small hill and looked down at his troops. The air was brisk, with a slight hint of the smell of blood and burning flesh, but even in the chill he sat tall in his saddle for such a little man. I mean, Lee sat in Andrew's study waiting for Andrew to come back from the bathroom where he'd gone almost the moment Lee sat down to find out the progress of his case. (Hey, who are you calling a little man? Shut up, Napoleon.) He was distracted. (**Who, Napoleon?** *No, Lee.* **Why would Napoleon be distracted?** *No, Steve, Lee is distracted, not Napoleon. Napoleon has nothing to do with this story.* **Was it because of the horse?** *Yes, Steve, it was the horse.* **What horse?**) The sounds of C-SPAN filtered in from the living room where Mrs. Divine was folding the delicates. Lee had spent the night churning about several things which got all jumbled together until he finally fell asleep to strange dreams of a theater full of little Abbys and Lees throwing tomatoes and asking him for money and calling him "Daddy" while he was trying to write a play for Jim to star in. And pie.

There was a low rumble in the wall that signified a flushing toilet, then the squeal and rapid pounding of pipes complaining that they were tired and didn't want to help someone wash their hands. A few moments later, Andrew came in wiping water off his shirt front with a small towel.

"Okay, where were we?" he said as he sat in his Jello-mold chair. "You may have to chill your heels a little with the sale of your house. Might not happen until as late as April or May. No one wants to buy a house in a snow storm. But they're responsible for the mortgage. And you have your share of the antiques which should last you for a while. If you're watching the spending. And you're an accountant, so you're watching your spending."

Lee didn't respond, so Andrew assumed it was because he was correct in his assumption instead of that Lee wasn't paying very close attention. Instead, he was thinking about a horse. I mean Abby. The jumble had finally coalesced and gelled into the firm, barely conscious sensation of what consequences he might have to face from one thoughtless event. Well, two events, one evening. His whole body participated in trying to resist the sensation. His whole body failed rather miserably.

"And they're paying those bills," Andrew continued. "And I've written to the reporting agencies giving them proof that they were all Beverly's purchases and to reflect them on her credit report, not yours."

"Oh," Lee said, hoping that the sound of his voice didn't vibrate strangely. "Thanks."

"Thanks? A week ago you were about to lose a lung over those bills and your credit rating and I work a miracle and now it's just 'thanks'?"

"Thanks a lot?"

He would have apologized for his distraction and shouted that he had had unprotected relations with a woman and didn't know how to ask her if she were still regular if it wouldn't have opened up so many private subjects that he couldn't open up even if he hadn't had unprotected relations with a woman. And didn't know how to ask her if she were still regular. And besides, he hadn't had any sleep. He couldn't even tell Andrew about that, because he would then have to explain why he hadn't had any sleep and the whole "so many private subjects" thing would start all over right from the beginning.

"Um," he said instead. "I got a lot on my mind."

"The play?"

"Yeah, the play," glad of the change of subject. But that made the snakes come back. "And now I have a pet."

"The bird?"

"Yeah, the bird. I've never had a pet."

"It's not a pet, it's a bird."

"What would you call it, then?"

"A bird."

"So," Lee said. "I have a hundred and three lines in the play."

He had counted them as soon as he'd gotten home. He might as well talk about one of the things that was distracting him. Andrew's face did something strange that Lee had never seen it do. He had a great deal of trouble trying to interpret the flow of expressions. He thought he detected surprise, but that was quickly followed by what looked like might be disgust, which was covered rapidly with a studied neutrality. Which slowly melted into amusement.

"A hundred and three, huh?" Andrew said, and the amusement gave way to an impish grin, which was replaced with a little of what looked like anger. Or gas.

"Um," Lee said. His head hurt watching Andrew's facial muscles. "Yeah. Why? Is that bad? I only had two or three the first time. I don't know because I didn't count them. I didn't know I was supposed to."

"Well, dear boy," Andrew said and his face finally settled on a professorial superiority, "counting your lines is a really stupid waste of time participated in by actors who wish to inflate their importance, their talent, or assuage their deep feelings of inferiority and insecurity. It is really the most ineffective way to assess the merits of a role. If there was even any point in assessing a role's merits once you already had the role. Did you know that the best acting job Jackie Gleason ever did was in a movie called Gigot where he didn't utter a single word? Do you think he counted his lines? Do you think he would have given up the part if he had? Are you a better actor than Joe Smith because you have six more lines of dialogue then he does, or is it, perhaps, that you were cast in the role that only had a total of six lines of dialogue because the director thought you were the only one who would bring something organic, original, and, perhaps, innovative to it? Counting your lines. Sheesh."

"Who's Joe Smith?" Lee asked weakly and determined then and there not to say how happy he was that he had more lines than Jim. Or how scared he was that Jim would remember his better then he would. He wished he'd chosen the "so many private subjects" topic. It would have been easier.

"Oh," Andrew said, "I finally figured out why your house felt so familiar to me."

Lee was glad of the change of subject. Confused by it, but glad of it. He wouldn't even mind if they got into a middle-class vs. upper middle-class conversation. Andrew told him that he had been in that house once in the fifties.

"In high school. I had this crush on a girl who lived there. I didn't really know her, but I have been in that house. I knew I had."

"Yeah," Lee said. "Bear said she died of love for some soldier and is haunting my house."

Andrew looked puzzled.

"She never seemed to me the kind who would have died for love," he said. "Killed for it, maybe. Anyways, I think she actually went to Korea as a nurse or something, so if she died for love for a soldier, she'd be haunting some hut in Seoul. Sort of a soul lost in Seoul, huh?"

He waited for Lee to laugh. Lee just looked at him, distracted.

"Their name was Gardner." Andrew continued, his eyes focused somewhere above and behind Lee as he began to put details back in place. "Evelyn Gardner. Had the most amazing black hair. And her laugh sounded like a cross between Lauren Bacall and Mel Torme. Her room was in the basement, I seem to remember. We all thought that was really hip. Weird, but hip. Okay, weird. But she was good looking. So it was hip. How's Abby?"

Lee almost shouted "Pregnant" but stopped himself just in time. The vibration in his chest made his head hurt.

"Fine, I guess. I don't know. How should I know? I don't know how she is. Fine. I guess. I don't know."

Andrew had stopped being surprised by Lee's strange outbursts and invited him to stay for a sandwich.

"You like head cheese, don't you?"

The diner chilled briefly when the bells slapped against the door with their bell slapping sound. Lee looked up to see Abby and Kim come in. It woke the snakes up and they yawned, stretched, and started looking around for something to eat. Abby waved, and Lee stepped out from behind the counter. He returned her hug a little stiffly, and she looked at him, puzzled.

"Hi, there, Lee," Kim said and hugged him, also. He seemed to return hers very fondly. "The play should be really fun."

"Yeah," Lee said, and had a brief image of the stage floor rapidly approaching his head as he fell face first in front of a full house of critics and Libertarians.

He gave Abby a peck on the cheek and told them he'd go get them menus. They took off their coats, scarves, mittens, hats and bras. I mean mufflers. When they sat, Abby stared at Kim for a long time with an inscrutable look on her face. (*What is the exact definition of "inscrutable"*? **Unable to scrute.**)

Lee brought them water, coffee and menus, pepper, ketchup, Worcestershire Sauce, napkins, A-1, mustard, sesame oil, malt vinegar, half-and-half, spoons, knives, forks, toothpicks, tea-light candles, wasabi and handy-wipes then went back for salt®. The warm air in the diner carried the usual scent of coffee, burgers, old grease and that morning's bacon, which the patrons bundled around their conversations like the coats and scarves that lay across the backs of the booths and on the coat hooks. The scratchy sound from the old, batter-encrusted radio by the stove in the kitchen leaked out on the smells with what could have been Bach, The Replacements, or Bob Marley. Lee refreshed the coffee cup of the man with the John Deere™ hat, then wiped the spilled cream off the counter in front of the man from Butte, who was pouring sesame oil on his french fries. Having Abby right there on the other side of the room made his abdomen queasy.

He really didn't like having a queasy stomach about Abby. He would much rather feel the other sensations he'd had around her, which he'd taken entirely too much for granted while he was having them. And which had gotten him in all this turmoil in the first place.

Peter came in and sat at the counter.

"Hey, Peter," Lee said as he set water and a coffee cup in front of him, then pointed toward Abby and Kim with his chin. The queasiness turned upside down for a moment.

"Afternoon," Peter said to Lee, then turned and waved.

Peter studied the menu while Lee went for Abby and Kim's order. Lee didn't notice the chilled air around their booth. He was too busy not paying attention to the queasiness. Kim noticed it, but wasn't sure what it signified. Abby ordered an open faced meatloaf sandwich and a Fresca.

Matt came in with a cute young girl and grandly led her to a booth. Lee brought them menus, glad to be focused on a different part of the room.

"Hello, Matt. No school today?"

"Hello, Mr. Harris. Lunchtime," he said then presented his companion, who looked like she wasn't quite one of the smart girls and wasn't quite one of the popular girls, and probably played the oboe in band. "This is Jan."

"Yeah," Jan said. "My father liked the Rockford... " (*Steve*! **The Brady Bunch**? *No, Steve, her father is dead and they can't afford a TV.* **Ow.**)

"Hello, Jan," Lee asked, steadfastly refusing to realize that Matt was desperately trying to impress his young friend. "Don't you get lunch there?"

"Too many freshmen," Matt said off-handedly.

"Yeah. Darn kids," Lee said, and waited for them to smile at his little joke. When they didn't, he wondered if his support hose were drooping down around his ankles. Then he wondered if Kim would help him out by not having to go to the lady's room so he wouldn't ever be in the position of being able to have a private conversation with Abby. "But you're here all the time. Why didn't you go to American Bun Stand?"

When Matt looked at him, horrified, he added, "What can I get you?"

"She'll have a cheeseburger, no onions, fries and a Coke. I'll have a cheeseburger, no onions, fries and, um... " Matt said, looking at the man with the John Deere™ hat pour sugar into his coffee and stir it with the handle of his spoon, "... coffee."

He beamed proudly at Lee.

"Ah. The usual," Lee said, finally letting the whole high-schoolness of the situation filter in. He remembered trying to impress a girl once. He had done it by ordering tea with lemon. It hadn't worked. He rubbed the sudden rheumatoidal pain in his shoulder and went to fill their order.

Abby and Kim were eating silently, and Jan was daintily dipping the end of a french fry into a small dollop of ketchup. She ate like a bird. A small yellow one. A sparrow.

"My bird doesn't eat," Lee said to Peter.

(**Nice segue, Geoff.** *Thank you.*)

"What?" Peter said, not noticing the transition. Damn him.

"My bird. The one Agnes got me for a house warming. It doesn't eat."

"Oh."

"Actually, it doesn't do much of anything. It's a stupid bird."

Peter asked if he had named it, yet, as if that may have had some bearing on its behavior. Lee hadn't. Peter chewed thoughtfully on the edge of a piece of lettuce from his garden salad. He told Lee he once got a puppy for his birthday and the thing always bit him.

"When's your birthday?" Lee asked, grabbing any subject that wasn't Abby.

"The day after Christmas."

Lee looked at him, shocked, almost hurt.

"Why didn't you tell me?"

"Why, so you could make a fuss about not getting me anything for my birthday like you made a fuss about not getting me anything for Christmas?"

"Oh," Lee said, even more hurt. "Um. Thanks for the fireworks. I set them off on New Years. Want a bird?"

Peter laughed out loud, and Lee smiled.

"How old are you?" he asked.

"Ninety-eight."

"I'll get you something when you reach a hundred."

"Okay," Peter said. "When's yours?"

"Birthday? April fifteenth."

Lee refreshed the coffees of all the patrons who had coffee. Except Matt, whose cup was still full, quite cold and quite pale with cream that had begun to congeal on the surface in an unpleasant pattern. When he got back behind the counter, he just leaned on it near Peter, who had finished his garden salad and was on to his iced tea with lemon. Lee's glance kept wandering on its own accord toward Abby and his brow kept furrowing. Peter turned back to look at them. Abby picked at her meatloaf in silence. Kim ate a bit of the crust from her tuna melt. He looked back at Lee.

"Thanks for inviting me over to watch the fireworks with you," he said because he couldn't think of anything else.

"You're welcome," Lee said.

"Okay, what's going on?" Peter asked.

After a moment of painful indecision, Lee asked Peter to go back into the kitchen. Peter looked around for Twain.

"He's out getting filters for the air conditioner," Lee told him.

"Now? In January? He's a strange man."

"They're cheaper, now."

"You're a strange man."

Abby watched them leave, then turned on Kim.

"What the hell are you doing, Kim?"

Kim was so surprised that she stopped separating the tuna from the melted cheese.

"What?" she said and ate a piece of cheese that still had bread on it.

The chill around the booth warmed, then heated, then began melting the Formica on the table top. "You're making a play for Lee," Abby said. "You weren't even interested in him at all until I found out that I liked him and all of a sudden you're all over him."

"All over... What?"

"All over him. Just now. And at the party last Saturday." Her voice grew quieter as she went, as if the force of it caused her throat to constrict until only a small, laser-focused beam escaped past her clenched teeth. "You were chatting him up all night. I watched you. I couldn't quite believe it then, but that hug just now was too much. I finally found someone and you can't stand that. I'm finally with someone and you have to prove you're the good looking one. You've been doing this since high school. I like this guy. Lay off. Kim."

Abby's cheeks were red with the heat, and her forehead was white with pale green edges. Kim's cheeks were white. Her forehead pulsed.

"What the hell are you talking about, Abby?" She also whispered intensely. The kind of whisper designed to keep a conversation private that resulted in everyone within a click knowing your entire life story. "You think I'm making a play for Lee? For LEE? Harris? Lee Harris?"

Abby just stared at her. The sting of that peck on the cheek pulsed with a life of its own, quite separate from the rest of her face. She felt like Lee's lips were still there, burning disinterested acid into her skin. She would never forgive Kim for that peck.

"Okay, Abby." Kim no longer even bothered to whisper. "Just for the record, I was being nice to Lee at the party because I'm thrilled at how happy he seems to be making you. Stupid me, I was thrilled to see you happy. It made me happy. And I hugged him just now because we're in a play together and that's what people in plays together do. They hug. I'd hug Agnes the same way. In fact, I do hug Agnes the same way. Abby."

The red in Abby's cheeks started seeping out to the rest of her face. The peck on her cheek started to itch. All ears in the diner were tuned in to their booth. Even the batter-encrusted radio seemed to stop to listen.

"I can't believe that's what you think of me," Kim said as she stood and put on her coat and scarf. "I thought we were friends."

She reached into a pocket, threw a few dollars on the table, picked up one last bit of crust and left while putting on her gloves.

"Oh," Abby said. "Shit."

She grabbed her stuff, threw some more money on the table and followed Kim out. The radio quickly found a song and joined it in progress. It was Boogie Man by K.C. and the Sunshine Band. The man from Butte nodded his shoulders back and forth to its beat and spilled more cream.

Peter stood by the center prep island and Lee stood on the other side of it. They stared at each other, completely oblivious to the theater out front. Peter waited patiently for Lee to start. Lee didn't know how. Peter waited a little less patiently. He looked around.

"You know," he said. "If Twain finds me back here, I'll be the next special. My goose will be baked. So to speak."

"Um..." Lee said. "You know Saturday? After the party?"

Peter knew that much.

"I mean, you know Abby and I... I mean... You know..."

Peter blanched. He stammered that he had assumed. He hoped Lee hadn't asked him back here to talk about that kind of stuff.

"I, um..." Lee said. "Didn't use anything."

Peter didn't understand at first and was about to ask what he was talking about, then realized that Lee had, indeed, asked him back here to talk about that kind of stuff. Why did straight men always want to talk about that kind of stuff? He really, really, really didn't want to have a conversation with Lee about that kind of stuff. Especially in Twain's kitchen. He looked around to see if he could find a graceful way to extract himself from the conversation, but then realized that Lee really needed to have the conversation for some strange reason, so he thought about it point by point in a logical manner. Or at least in as logical a manner as he could think about Lee in that context. Okay. Lee had spent "time" with Abby. Okay. And he hadn't protected himself. Okay. That meant that he was worried about...

"You're not worried about... catching... something... from..."

"Oh. No. No, no. No. Not that. No. Like what? I mean no. No."

Lee was now sure that this whole coming into the kitchen thing had been a horrible, horrible idea. He could feel the edges of his face close in around his eyes, and he looked around the room to see if he could find a graceful way out of the conversation. But he really needed to talk to someone. And the only people he could think of were Andrew, and he somehow didn't think Andrew would understand, and Bear, and he and Bear had more of a "cool power tool" friendship and he'd like to keep it that way, and Twain, and that would just be weird in too many ways, so Peter was it. And Peter would understand. He was gay, for God's sake. They always talked about that kind of stuff. And shoes.

"Oh," Peter said, trying to see where his logic had gone off track. It would be a lot easier if Lee just came out and said what he was worried about. But that would be really, really, really hard to deal with. I mean, if Lee had gone and knocked up some...

"Oooohhhh," he said, his face burning right through his scraggly beard. "Oh. Is she..."

"I don't know!" Lee shouted. It was drowned out by the strains of Boogie Man, which had just been joined already in progress.

"Oh," Peter said, a sharp pain in his chest bouncing off his ribs and spine as he thought about the ramifications of that dilemma and glad for perhaps the third time in his life that he was gay. "Oh. What are you... going to... do?"

"I don't know! That's why I'm talking to you."

"I don't know what you should do," Peter said. "I'm gay. We worry about other things."

"Like what?"

"I don't know. I wasn't at that meeting."

Lee offered him an Altoid, noting that they were curiously strong©, quite sure, now, that this had been a mistake. A huge one. Peter took one because he could think of nothing else to do. Then he spit it back out into his hand.

"Cinnamon," he said and wished he could wipe his tongue off with something clean. "Cinnamon is a stupid Altoid."

Peter tried to think of something, anything, that he could say to his friend that would make some sort of difference, that wouldn't make his own mind think of Abby and Lee, you know... together, and that would get him the hell out of the room. Lee tried to think of a way that he could go hide his head in a bucket of cold water. Filtered, cold water.

Twain came in, dressed in an old fur coat, carrying a box of air conditioner filters and a small bag of peanut butter Jelly Bellies. Lee looked at Peter, hoping he wouldn't choose that moment to stop being dense and start giving him advice, not now, please, for God's sake, of all times, with Twain right there. Peter stared at Twain, frozen like a small yellow bird, one that did eat, and quite often, staring at the mouth of a hungry alley cat. In a fur coat. His mind raced to find ways to assure Twain he had been nowhere near the recipe box. Twain stared at Lee, wondering why he didn't help with the box of filters.

"I should just," Peter said to Lee. "I was just," he said to Twain. "Oh, God."

85

He put his arms out to be cuffed. Twain offered him a Jelly Belly. Peter ate it. He didn't spit it out, but he did think that peanut butter was a stupid Jelly Belly. He realized that Twain's entrance excused him from all that conversation about all that. If he were a Judy Garland kind of gay man, he would have clicked his heels three times.

"Bye," he said quickly and left.

Twain set the box of filters down on the center island and looked at Lee's face.

"You worry too much," he said.

The two men exchanged candies.

When Lee got back into the dining room, the first thing he noticed was that Abby had left without saying goodbye. When he went to clear their table, the first thing he noticed was the money they left on the table. They had stiffed him for at least half the bill.

Lee and Abby drove together in silence. The Saturday afternoon sun glinted off the frosty trees and washed over the surface of the car. The wonderfully hot air from the car heater played with the cold at the edges of the passenger compartment in what would have been an enticing experience for both of them if Abby hadn't been so preoccupied with what to do with Kim and Lee weren't so preoccupied with what to do with Abby.

Abby sighed deeply, and Lee glanced over at her, not quite willing to look at her face too fully.

"I really blew it," Abby said. Lee didn't respond, so she elaborated. "Kim is my best friend and I really insulted her. But what was I supposed to think?"

Lee shrugged in a noncommital way. Abby looked at him piercingly for some time.

"This is important to me," she said.

"Yes," Lee said. "I know. Kim. Important."

"What's going on?" Abby said.

"Are you..." Lee said after thinking for two more unproductive seconds. "Um. Okay?"

"No," Abby said, certain that she had already quite demonstrated that she wasn't.

This frightened Lee in a way that he never considered a single word could frighten someone. Then some unpredictable, spontaneous synaptic connection made him realize she was talking about Kim. They had had some sort of fight. He would have to deal with that in a moment, but he couldn't stand this tight knot of baby cobras eating his stomach lining, so he decided he may as well just jump in, just head bravely out to the gallows. He breathed in, straightened his back and gripped the wheel.

"Have you..." he said.

Abby turned toward him, frowning.

"You're not..."

"What?" Abby said impatiently.

"Have you... had... your...," he said. "Monthly..."

Abby's glum mood shifted.

"My... ?"

"Monthly... "

"Is that what this is all about?" She said, the confusion and despair about Kim melting and transforming instantly into something quite different. "Is that what this silence all afternoon is all about? Is that what this fucking cold shoulder has been all about all week?"

Lee felt like what a small guppy looks like when it makes that one bold move and ends up on the table top gasping for some reason for it all. He tried to stop his mouth from opening and closing with no sound coming out. When he couldn't achieve that, he decided to simply add sound.

"Cold shoulder?"

It was better than nothing.

"Cold shoulder," Abby said. "You barely pecked me on the cheek at lunch on Thursday. You haven't said peep to me since you picked me up today. You want to know if you knocked me up? Is that it?"

It was something like that, but it sounded, somehow, very different coming out of her mouth. Lee had the good sense not to say anything for a moment. Whatever he said now couldn't possibly be productive. And in any case, Abby seemed to be gathering her own steam without any help from him. He noticed that the sky was a startling blue and was sure that he shouldn't be noticing that at this particular moment.

"You sleep with me one night, you get your kicks, you hang around long enough to make sure I'm not pregnant and bye-bye, Abby? Is that it?"

"No," Lee said. He knew he had to say something. He wasn't sure how it had all gone so wrong and he had to get it back on track before he was consumed from the inside out by vipers. "No, no, no. No. I mean... No, it's just... we... no. I didn't just go... It's just... We didn't... No. I didn't mean... Abby, we didn't... I really..."

"Well, I don't know if I'm pregnant. How about that?"

He had been calling it snakes. Now he realized that it was fear. Pure, simple fear. He had to pull the car to the side of the road. It slid a bit before it came to a complete stop, which seemed, somehow, appropriate. The sky was really, really blue. He couldn't get his hands to unclench from the steering wheel. There had never even been a scare the whole time he had been married to Beverly. Not even that time in Barstow. The panic in his eyes was so complete that Abby was about to open the door and defiantly tromp her way back home, forgoing men for the rest of her life in favor of gardening or target shooting.

Then Lee's face did something strange. The terror remained but was joined by something else that went through several odd transformations that Abby couldn't interpret at all. Then the dread faded and the something else finally settled on simply being that strange puppy dog look, but with a glimmer of a surprised smile. His right hand left the steering wheel and wandered in the direction of her belly, then pulled back and hid in his lap. A small flicker of fear momentarily clouded the childlike flicker in his eyes, but it was a different sort of fear altogether. It was almost endearing, like the fear of a small boy who isn't quite sure that nod you just gave him means he can actually have that fresh cookie right from the oven. His glance darted from her belly to her face and back to her belly. His hand looked like it wanted to wander out again, but wouldn't, or couldn't. And shouldn't. Abby forgot her anger watching the permutations of his movements, then remembered it again with a sudden jolt.

"No," she said, completely embarrassed that she had fucked with him. "I was just trying to give you your macho stuff back to you. You sounded like such a guy. I'm not. I mean I don't think I am. I mean I won't be sure for a week or so, but I'm not. I'm sure of it."

He just looked at her, like a man who might actually end up being a really good father someday. As long as there were no matches lying around.

"Isn't the sky beautiful?" she said, because she could think of nothing else to say. And because she had just noticed that it was a startling shade of blue. It's all good, she thought.

"Drive," she said, and put a cassette tape into the player.

"Where?" Lee said weakly as the piano duets made their way into the warm air of the car.

"Just drive. I'll point the way."

Is this the real end of the installment, officially?

Or is this?

How about now?

Will Lee remember all those lines?

Will he survive rehearsing with Jim?

Will Jim?

Will Peter be given a candy he likes?

Does anyone still know who Ferrante & Teicher are?

Where is Abby taking Lee?

Don't you hate when a couple says "We're pregnant?"

Are Abby and Lee pregnant?

Is Agnes?

Is Peter?

Do Abby and Lee go get an EPT?

Or DNA?

Or BBC?

BB King?

Dig it?

To find the answers to these and other unreliable rebuses,

tune into our next installment:

"Search for Spock"

(*No, Steve.* **How about "Return of the Jedi"?**)

"Rhythm and News"

(Soylent Green is people!)

This installment first published December 22, 2002

Geoff Hoff and Steve Mancini

Previously in Weeping Willow: Lee, fearful that he won't remember his lines in the play, scared that he will run through all the money he has from the preliminary property division with his ex-wife, and terrified that he left Abby, his new girlfriend, in a family way, finally talks to Abby about it all while she is trying to tell him that she may have ruined her oldest and longest friendship. Headline, who is the young, stunning bartender at The Office, got his name by knowing a little about everything. Jim, who is in his late twenties, looks more and more like he bit off more than he could swallow by dating Agnes, who is in her sixties. Peter is once again the confidant of all and is without one himself. Oh, and he's afraid of Twain. Oh, and he's gay. To find out what all of this has to do with Jakarta, Indonesia, read the previous chapters. Some of them are in the previous volume. They're brought to you without commercial interruption. And now a word from our sponsor. (This space for rent.)

(Hey, Geoff. In this installment, can we interrupt every sent... *No, Steve.*)

Installment Nineteen
"Rhythm and News"

Peter Principal, Abby Holiday, Twain Newton, Agnes Livingstone, Kim Anderson, Veronica Park and Danny Bonaduce all needed to get drunk, but that has nothing to do with this installment. Ferrante & Teicher blared from the cassette player as Abby directed Lee to some mysterious destination. During their heart-rending rendition of Paint it Black, the music started to speed up in a queer way.

"Oh, shit," Lee said.

"What?"

"It's eating the tape."

Lee pushed the eject button, but it didn't make that satisfying deep clicking sound that resulted in the cassette jumping suddenly just past the slot edge. (**Just say the goddamn tape didn't come out.**) The goddamn tape didn't come out. (*Happy?* **Hmph.**) Lee kept pushing the button and the car swerved in an unsettling way on the wintery road.

"Drive. I'll take care of the tape."

Abby deftly grabbed it with her fingernails, yanked it out like a robin plucking a worm from the ground, and in one movement opened the windows and tossed the tape out.

"Don't..." Lee said as the cassette arced gracefully out the window with a long, delicately fluttering tail of tape streaming behind it, then landed in a snowdrift next to a frozen and slightly soiled athletic sock with blue and red bands that were turning to gray. "... throw it out the window. Oh, great. Littering."

"Nothing'll happen."

Twirling red and blue lights flashed suddenly in the rear view mirror accompanied by the whoop whoop of the police siren. Lee's stomach shouted "fuck" at his heart which responded by pounding out a conga version of the love theme from Dr. Zhivago. He hadn't had much luck with the police in the last several months. He pulled to a stop while looking accusingly over at Abby who just looked forward, cheerily whistling Paint it Black. Her window was now up and she looked very innocent. With her hands folded in her lap. I hope your baby has two heads, Lee thought. (*Steve!* **Well?** *Even in his thoughts he would never think that. Do you have cloven hooves? I mean really. You should really be ashamed of yourself. I mean, I know you have no shame, but really. Two heads? It's his own baby, for God's sake. I mean if she's pregnant. Really. Sheesh. And don't act all Abby on me, you know you've done wrong.* **Stool.** *That's really obscure, Steve.* **Can I have a beer, now?** *Not until you've redeemed yourself.* **Oh, man, I'll never get one, then.** *Okay, where were we?* **Napoleon.**)

Officer Bacon sidled up to the side of the car and Lee rolled his window down. The cold air struck his face and he wondered if Bacon had been tailing him for some reason. For the past several months. Or if he were the only police officer in town. Or why people mixed peanut butter and bananas and put them in sandwiches.

"Hello, Lee," Officer Bacon said. "Abby."

"Hi, Cuddles," Abby said. (*No, she didn't, Steve. Go home. Watch sports. Abuse yourself.*)

Abby nodded, and Officer Bacon asked for Lee's I.D.

"You know who I am," Lee said.

"Yeah, I know. Procedure. And your registration. And proof of insurance."

Lee opened the glove box and pulled the appropriate papers out. A neatly folded twenty dollar bill fell to the floor. Lee just stared at it dumbly and Abby picked it up and tucked it into her coat pocket. Lee looked at her dumbly and she smiled at him innocently. Officer Bacon cleared his throat. Not because he was impatient; he had just had a banana and peanut butter milkshake at American Bun Stand. But Lee thought it was because he was being impatient, so he stopped looking at Abby dumbly and gave the officer the papers.

"Nice picture."

"Thanks."

Officer Bacon started writing a ticket.

"But Abby threw the tape out the window."

"Yes, but you're driving the car," Officer Bacon said as he handed the ticket to Lee. "She's your responsibility."

"Hear that, Lee," Abby said. Innocently. "I'm your responsibility."

"Besides," Officer Bacon said before Lee could tell Abby to shut up, "I don't blame her. It was Ferrante & Teicher."

Lee looked at the ticket.

"Twenty-six bucks?"

"Yeah," the officer said. "That's not your sock, is it?"

Lee looked back to where Officer Bacon was pointing and saw the poor, abandoned sock laying next to the errant cassette and shook his head.

"Good, because socks are fifty-seven bucks. Each. Of course I've never found two. I found two tennis shoes once hanging from a power line. I don't understand that. I've never seen anyone tie their shoes together and throw them over a power line. We don't have a fine for that. Technically, I guess, it's not littering until it hits the ground. The tape still would have been if it just hung from a guard rail or something, though. I guess it's how close to the ground it gets. Anyway."

"Come on , guys, I'm lactating," Abby said.

"Oh," Officer Bacon said. "Bye."

He got in his car and drove away very quickly.

Lee started forward, also quickly, then he slowed down and looked at her.

"Lactating?"

"You're just too easy," Abby said with a smile.

"Twenty-six bucks. You're paying for this."

Abby pulled a neatly folded twenty dollar bill from her coat pocket and handed it to Lee. Lee put it into the ashtray.

"Let's go tobogganing," Abby said, as if that would be a natural thing for two adults to do on a Saturday afternoon.

"What," Lee said, as if he were a rather staid adult. "Now?"

"No," Abby said. "When it really snows. On Beard's Hill. We go every year."

"Who?"

"Everyone."

"I don't have a toboggan," Lee said.

"I do."

"I don't have boots."

"I'll buy you some."

"I'd need gloves."

"Lee, you just got a ton of money."

"It wasn't a ton."

"Stop being cheap."

"I'm not cheap."

"Then you're scared."

"I'm not scared."

"Then you're cheap."

"Look, I don't toboggan," Lee said, finally, exasperated at having to admit it. He had had an incident as a child. Something involving a toboggan with a hole, a rock and a lot of other children laughing. That's when he'd decided to become an accountant.

"Look, it's a party," Abby said kindly. "It happens every year the first time we have over twelve inches in one storm. Turn here."

"I'll go if it gets to forty-five centimeters," Lee said smugly. He really didn't want to go, but was beginning to know Abby well enough to know that she wouldn't quit unless he said something.

"Seventeen point seven inches, huh?" Abby said. "Give or take. That's a lot of snow."

"How did you convert that so fast?"

"Look, I'll give you the benefit of the doubt. You'll go if it reaches eighteen inches."

"In one day," Lee said. "By the end of the month."

"The end of the month is next weekend."

"Not my problem."

"Fine," Abby said. "Okay. Whatever."

"Uh," Lee said, trying to decide if that was a safe bet. Eighteen inches was a lot of snow for one storm. "Okay."

"Okay. It's a deal. I'll get you some gloves."

Abby smiled and nodded and Lee wondered if he had just been hornswoggled. Then he wondered why he would have thought the word hornswoggled even if he had been. He was about to get into one of his frustrating, circular wondering loops, but Abby told him to turn again. He turned. The pavement was worn, and in the bare spots, old, uneven, dark red brick peeked through. How cool, Lee thought. The streets were made of brick here, once. Or someone had spent a lot of effort making it look that way. Like the wall of a new Italian restaurant trying to look old.

"Park here," she said.

Lee parked and waited. Abby pointed to the store they were parked in front of. It was an old, brick building. The glass in the two small windows appeared wavy from age and had a greenish tint. The name of the establishment was painted directly on the brick in now faded white block letters with faded gray drop shadows.

"Aunt Gladys and Sons Janitorial Supply?" Lee asked, and Abby pointed to the newer sign under that, just next to the door.

"And Condom Emporium," Lee stammered, then thought for a moment, then stammered, "I guess that means we're... um... still... "

A slight reddening spread out across Abby's face, starting at her nose and ending at her earlobes. (Editor's note: At Steve's request, we must say that this is Geoff's line. Editor's note 2: At Geoff's request, we must say that they all are.)

"I... uh...," Abby said. "Thought... I mean, if you still want..."

"But what if you're... Um..."

"Let's go buy a condom," she said. "Some. Condoms."

Lee looked around the gravel parking lot and was relieved that there was only one vehicle in it besides theirs; an old, battered white van with a ladder on top and "Dick's Plumbing" painted on the side. At least he wouldn't be humiliated by too many people. When they entered the store, it smelled like Borkum Riff™ cherry pipe tobacco smoke, which Lee had always found to be a wonderful, mysterious aroma. It took a moment for his eyes to adjust. And his ears. There were lots and lots of people milling around the tightly-packed aisles where little neon signs in strange, conflicting pastel colors announced the different style of wares in the different sized bins hanging from the pegboard. Nobody was smoking pipes, cherry flavored or otherwise. There was also driving techno-pop music playing and Lee noticed one sign shaped like a...

Lee's eyes darted from section to section until he found actual janitorial supplies, and he moved there very quickly, spotting buckets of muriatic acid. He picked one up. It would come in very handy cleaning the black marks that had marred his back stoop since New Year's Eve.

"What are you doing with that?" a voice asked.

"Huh?" Lee asked over his shoulder, and saw Abby, who had kept right up with him. "Oh, it's you. You move fast."

She just looked at him.

"You always need muriatic acid."

"What do you use it for?"

"Removing stains from cement."

"You scare me," Abby said.

"Hey, I'm not the pregnant one," he said.

"Yeah, but your butt looks big in those pants," she said, took him by the hand and led him out past the section whose pale pink and green neon sign said "Young Love", and one whose purple and green sign glowed "Senior Moments" and ended up at a section whose orange and green sign buzzed "Marathon Man©".

"Thanks," he said.

She pushed him into the aisle. There was a couple perusing the aisle who looked like a cross between Bea Arthur and Mel Torme. Lee looked back at Abby for mercy, but she was gone. She did move fast. He walked down the aisle, his face pointedly facing forward, his eyes darting against his will toward the bins where packeted and boxed and individually wrapped packages sat laughing at him with their lurid artwork and garish colors. There were pictures of women that looked like Lady Godiva and men that looked like Mr. Olympia and drawn, graphic instructions complete with anatomically correct...

Oh, my, he thought and hurried down another aisle. On the third aisle he went down, he saw the word "Trojan", sighed, relieved, and quickly grabbed a box, hoping against hope that none of the hundreds and hundreds of people that now seemed no longer to be shopping, seemed to be staring at him like one big eye, knew him.

"Haven't you ever bought condoms?" Abby said.

Lee whipped around. Abby stood just behind him, proudly showing him a packet of "Ribbed for Her Pleasure". Lee turned his head to avoid being sprayed with Brut. (See Installment One.)

"If I turned those inside out would they be ribbed for his pleasure?"

"No, you would just be an idiot," she said. "You never have bought condoms, have you?"

Lee looked around at the throngs who now seemed to have grown one communal ear that was tuned in to them like a huge satellite dish.

"No," he said, very quietly, his head down. "Beverly was on the pill."

"Didn't she ever miss?"

"Yeah," he said, very quietly, trying desperately to hint by his pointed quietness that she should also tone it down. Way down. His chin was so close to his neck that his lower jaw didn't move when he spoke.

"What did you do then?" Abby asked, not taking the hint. She seemed to really want to know.

"We didn't have sex," Lee said.

"Wow."

"Yeah. It was a pain in the ass," Lee said, and when Abby laughed out loud, he wished he could turn invisible. Maybe the muriatic acid would remove him from the store. Abby showed him the triple pack of glow in the dark she had in her other hand. Lee stuffed his free hand in his pocket and shuffled away toward the check out stand. He felt like the little boy whose mother had taken him with her to buy lady's underwear. Except not as good as that.

There was a young man at the register, disinterestedly ringing up small packages with soft-core pornography emblazoned on them. Lee was glad that the kid, at least, treated it like it was a deli counter and he was just another number. On the shelf behind the bored clerk, between a Bon Ami display and bottles of 3-In-One, WD-40 and Astroglide, was a bobble-head doll of Danny Bonaduce that looked as bored as the clerk. Lee kept his eyes focused on the counter, where there were small plates with what looked like small pieces of candy. After a moment, it dawned on him what they were.

"They have samples," he hissed to Abby.

"Of course," she said, and grabbed a pink one with a stick attached.

"Have I mentioned, yet, how much I hate you?" Lee said.

Abby just smiled. Lee put the muriatic acid and the box of Trojans on the counter. Abby added her stash to his.

"Thanks, Timmy, I'm back," a sweet, soft voice said. "Why don't you restock the mop heads?"

Lee watched his bored young man disappear, then slowly, with a great force of will, turned his head to see who had replaced him. He knew his number was up. She was tall, perhaps six foot, give or take an inch, thin, with long thin arms, dressed with a loose-fitting, light beige sweater over a light blue blouse. Her face was kind, but old, her hair silver, and pulled back in a utilitarian way. Her name tag, a small piece of brown plastic with letters cut through to the white plastic beneath it, said "Gladys". And she was anything but disinterested. She was the kind of woman who never got mad and never had a reason to get mad because no one ever dared give her a reason.

"Oh," she said as she rang up one of Abby's particularly unkind choices. "You'll love that flavor. It warms with use."

Lee tried to close his face down as he paid, vowing to get Abby back somehow. This would be really funny if he were watching someone else go through it. Damn her.

"Oh, hi, Abby," Aunt Gladys said. "Going to the hill next weekend?"

"Oh, yeah," Abby said. "We'll be there."

"Don't forget your mittens," Aunt Gladys said as she bagged their purchases, then turned her attention to the next person in line, a man with big thumbs and a hat that said Butte on it.

Lee could barely walk. His mind was racing down two distinct alleyways; one trying to figure out how the heck Aunt Gladys the condom pusher knew Abby so well that they were on a first name basis, the other trying to discern if the hill that Aunt Gladys was talking about was Beard's Hill and why Abby was so sure they would be there. And why Aunt Gladys would be there. And why they thought it would be next weekend. And how Abby knew how many inches were in forty-five centimeters. I need to go watch football, Lee said. And I don't even like football all that much. And how Abby knew Aunt Gladys.

When they got back into the car, Lee realized he hadn't been breathing.

"Was all that completely necessary?" he asked Abby.

She patted his leg and told him that they were even, now, then smiled and said that the embarrassment was for the way he had treated her the last week, but that they did need what they'd bought. Then she sat a moment, watching the look on his face not change. Then she apologized for going overboard. He grinned suddenly, which puzzled her.

"I have five gallons of muriatic acid," he explained.

"You really are a scary man, you know," she said, and he kept grinning like a mad seven year old who had recently lost his two front teeth. "It's kind of exciting."

Lee liked that. Then the grin disappeared, and his mind went right back to wondering how Abby and Aunt Gladys knew each other.

Rehearsals were actually going well. Lee was surprised to discover that he enjoyed rehearsing with Jim. Roy got to be really snotty to Vinnie, so Lee could be snotty to Jim and Jim didn't even get it. In fact, Lee suspected that Jim wouldn't get it even if he weren't being so indirect with his snottiness. It was only the fourth rehearsal he had attended for the play, but he decided it was going to be all right. It still bothered Lee that he occasionally caught Jim just staring at him, but it happened less and less. Well, he is gay, he thought. That made him shudder. He thought of power tools. Which made him think of Agnes. That made him shudder. Which made him think of Agnes and Jim. Which made him shudder. Okay, so he's straight, Lee thought.

Sort of. He thought of painting his shutters. That worked. Stupid bird. Then he noticed Jim staring at him again.

"What?"

"Nice pants," Jim stuttered, then turned away very quickly and looked longingly at Agnes.

Lee shivered. At least I didn't shudder, he thought with a quiver.

He was also surprised to discover that he already had a strong sense of his lines. It was easy to remember the ones he directed to Jim, what with the whole snotty thing, but the poker-playing group was growing on him, so talking to them and joking with them and ribbing them came easily. Rehearsing at Agnes's was also comfortable. It would be a while before they moved into the theatre, but the set was basically a living room, so doing it in a living room made it very easy. They were already beginning to block the play. Agnes had moved the rehearsal table out and brought in a couch and dining set that were to serve as the furniture in Oscar's and Felix's apartment.

There were a couple of things that seemed at odds with the general feeling of comfort Lee felt, though; the entire previous evening, Kim had hardly spoken a word to him. He assumed it had something to do with her and Abby fighting. He would probably have to say something to her, eventually. He hated that. Why couldn't theatre people just repress their emotions and pretend everything was all right like real people? Another thing that was at odds with his comfort was that, at least twice, Agnes snapped at Jim. Once when she was blocking him (**I didn't know Agnes played football.** *Yes, Steve, she was drafted early in the third round in nineteen sixty-three from Clemson by the Browns. Ran the forty in four-two.* **Geoff**? *Can we continue, now?* **Um. Yeah.**) and he didn't understand quite what she meant. It had been sudden and Jim had looked hurt. The other time was during the break. He was walking too closely behind her when she turned and it made her spill a drop of coffee. It was only a drop, but when she snapped "Careful. Shit," the entire room got really quiet for a second, then really noisy when everyone started talking at once to hide the fact that they had noticed Agnes snap and been caught being quiet at her.

The poker-playing group was gathered, as was becoming their custom during breaks, around the fireplace.

"Going to the hill this weekend?" the guy playing Speed asked, his eye still on Agnes and Jim, not wanting to miss any of the action.

The others nodded, except Lee, who was beginning to really hate this incestuous town again. He wondered why everyone thought it would snow enough by this weekend for the tobogganing thing, and if he was actually going to have to go. Is everyone I've met going to be there? And how does Abby know Aunt Gladys, and does everyone I've ever met know her, too? He was going to ask out loud, but really didn't want to open up that whole "I was tricked into going into a condom store because I thought I might have made Abby pregnant" conversation. Then he blushed, and figured it was a good time to talk to Kim.

"Hi, Kim," he said as he sidled up to her.

"Lee," she said, sounding noncommital.

"Um," Lee said. It seemed the thing to say, so he said it again. "Um."

Kim just looked at him. Maybe it wasn't such a good time to talk to her, but now he was committed.

"Abby says you guys had a fight."

Kim just stared at him.

"She really feels bad about it."

"Good," Kim said. "She should feel bad about it. She really hurt my feelings. We've been friends a long time, but I never realized what she thought about me. I mean, I guess it's a good thing because now I know what she thinks I am. I mean, I trusted her. I always wanted her to be happy. But she never trusted me, you know? I mean never. How could she think I wanted to take you away from her? I mean, you? You know? I mean, even if I were attracted to someone, I would never try to take them away from someone. I mean, I wouldn't try to take them away from her, she's my best friend. Was. My best friend."

"Well, she," Lee said when he was sure Kim had stopped.

"I mean, how dare she? What else does she think I do? Shoplift? I mean there was that one time in high school, but that's beside the point. I was there when her parents split up."

"Her parents are still together."

"Yeah, but they split up when she was in high school. Her mom wanted to find herself. Abby was a mess."

"She never told me that."

"Well," Kim said. "She tells me everything. She's my best friend."

Kim started crying. Lee was really confused. He never imagined that Kim, with her fashionable jeans and smart casual tops, could cry in public. In private, maybe. With her best friend. He wondered if he should hold her, but the whole thing was about Abby being jealous, so that was out. No one had ever been jealous about him. And even if it hadn't been about jealousy, he would never just hold someone in public. Especially someone with fashionable jeans and smart tops. He didn't have a hanky to offer her. Who would carry a hanky? Those things were a breeding ground for germs. The thought made him shudder. Maybe if he put his hand on her shoulder. But that was too much like holding her. He would just wait. Eventually, she would have to run out of tears. It's physics. Sure enough, she did. Eventually.

"I'm sorry," Kim said.

"No, it's okay," Lee said, grateful that he wouldn't have to hold her. "She really does feel bad."

"She should feel bad," Kim said angrily (**She already said that, Geoff. We're going around in circles, here.** *That's how people talk, Steve.* **I don't.** *You're not people.* **Hey, wanna talk about football?** *No.*) and stormed off.

"What the hell did you say to my assistant?"

Agnes had appeared without any warning, and Lee had to spin around to talk to her.

"Nothing," he said. "She..."

Agnes didn't wait to hear his explanation. Jim, again close behind Agnes, smiled, relieved that Agnes was snapping at someone else.

"What are you smiling at?" Lee asked him.

"Um," Jim said. "Nice pants? Big Guy?"

"Jim!" Agnes said. "Come away from there. Okay, everybody, let's get started again."

As Jim walked away, Lee heard him muttering. He couldn't be sure, but it sounded something like "I used to be a private eye." For the first time, Lee had a glimmer of sympathy for the poor sap. A glimmer. If he had heard him correctly.

Jim wasn't sure why Agnes decided that they should go to The Office that night. He wasn't even sure why Agnes wanted to go there at all, but it was after rehearsal, late, when most of the people there would be college kids, so it made even less sense. But she was being nice to him again, and that should be enough. When she asked him to take her there after the last of the cast had said goodbye and driven off, he'd jumped at the opportunity. She seemed excited to go, which excited him in ways he was becoming accustomed to, which in itself was exciting. But going out in public wasn't usually what Agnes wanted to do with him. Jim had an impulse to be confused, but resisted it.

The neon sign out front said "Cocktails". Jim had seen that before, of course, with Peter and back when he was investigating Lee, but the neon seemed brighter in the cold, cold air. Wondering why didn't occur to him. In the parking lot, Agnes took him by the hand and led him toward the door. Agnes wasn't the hand-holding type. He almost questioned that.

The young, carefree voices that mingled with the smells of grilled burgers and fries drew Agnes closer to the door and she drew Jim in with her to the room. The crowd was young. That night's specials, listed on the chalkboard that hung on the post behind the bar, were lemon drop shooters and buck shots for a dollar each. And it was Dollar Draft night. There was a television on, a show with sweaty young people dancing to pulsating music, and there were young people all over the room, flirting and drinking and playing pool and Asteroids©, hormones raging. Agnes stopped short, and Jim bumped into her. For a moment, she was glad she was holding his hand. The beat of the air filled her blood in a way that felt forbidden. She hadn't realized she would need to cling to Jim. Maybe this had been a really bad idea, she thought. Then she noticed the bartender. Thick, dark, shiny hair and sparkling blue eyes.

Jim felt Agnes's hand tighten on his. He just went with it. Agnes was showing him off. And she didn't seem to be her usual confident self. She seemed like a deer in headlights, a fish out of water, a snow storm in July, a horse with no name. He would protect her. He felt so masculine, which confused him right through his resistance. I thought I was masculine, he thought. But feeling it made him realize he hadn't felt it in a while. Which confused him. A couple left a table and Jim started toward it, but it was covered with beer mugs, pitchers, spilled beer and french fry baskets. He hesitated, knowing that Agnes wouldn't like to sit there until it was cleaned up. The moment he took to look for someone to take care of it was the moment a group of girls descended upon it with an outburst of giggles. He looked around, lost. There were two stools at the bar and he started toward them, but stopped.

He was about to try to figure out what to do, but his head started to hurt, his eyes started to burn, his ears felt hot and the skin on his fingertips tingled. My father liked the Rockford Files, he thought, and that familiar refrain calmed him somewhat.

Agnes looked at Jim and noticed his face was turning red. He's trying to think, again, she thought. Poor dear.

"It's okay, Honey," Agnes said. "We can rough it."

She led him to the two empty stools.

"What'll you have?" the bartender asked.

"Beer," Jim said quickly, like a man. Which he was. Always had been.

"No, Dear," Agnes said, squeezing his hand one more time before letting it go. "I don't think beer would agree with me."

Jim felt the world disappear with her hand.

"Oh, um," he said. "Of course. That's for me. Um. The... um... lady... would like..."

Agnes removed her fur coat and set it in her lap. She was wearing a black cashmere sweater and Jim couldn't help noticing the figure she cut. What a dame, he thought as her perfume wafted out from the fibers of the sweater and brushed him seductively under the chin.

"What would the lady like?" the bartender asked the lady, leaning in over the bar and speaking loudly over the tumult in the room.

His cologne wasn't in the same social class as Agnes's perfume, but carried itself well, seemed almost a counterpoint to hers. Private eyes weren't supposed to notice that sort of thing, Jim thought, and shook his head in an attempt to regain the feeling of being Agnes's protector.

"Do you have a wine list?" Agnes asked.

Headline chuckled politely, pointing to the faux wine cask with taps protruding from it.

"White and Rosé," he said to her. "You'd probably be better off with the beer."

"Oh," Agnes purred, "dear."

"Let me make you something special."

"I'll have one, too," Jim said.

"You'd probably be better off with the beer, Champ," the bartender said kindly, giving him a manly tap on the arm with the side of his fist.

"Yeah," Jim said, not feeling manly at all, all of a sudden. "Chief."

Agnes patted Jim on the thigh and leaned in to let him know she was going to freshen up. Jim's pants tented. The bartender brought Jim's beer, then nodded toward Agnes.

"That's Agnes Livingstone, isn't it?" he said with a look in his eye that could be described as impressed.

Jim nodded, a little surprised.

"Billy is a friend of mine," the bartender said, a look in his eye that could be categorized as conspiratorial.

Jim didn't know who Billy was, but went along.

"Are the stories true?" the bartender asked, and his look was definitely inquiring.

Jim had no idea how to react to that. He was sure he was blushing, which embarrassed him. The bartender extended his hand.

"Headline," he said.

"Jim," Jim stammered. He was about to add "Ackerman," but it didn't seem prudent.

"I remember you," Headline said. "Boilermakers. Lots of them."

He winked and turned to start the special drink.

"Hey, Stud," he continued over his shoulder, "I can get anybody I want, but I want what I've heard she has."

He's just a kid, Jim thought.

"How old are you?" he asked.

"Twenty-three. You?"

"Twenty-eight," Jim said like an older brother. A much more worldly older brother. Whose father liked the Rockford Files. He thought about puffing out his chest. This guy's father probably liked Full House. Or that show with the two guys and the twins. What was it called?

Jim wanted to put all the facts from this conversation into some pattern he could then use to deduce some sort of point, but his mind-o-meter pointed to the red and he could only watch as Headline pulled out a small snifter and poured hot water from a coffee pot into it and set it down. Then he reached really high to pull down a bottle of expensive brandy, dust it off, and set it next to the steaming snifter. When he did, his shirt pulled loose from the side of his pants, revealing a small patch of bartender skin. Jim caught himself looking and quickly turned his head. Then he slowly turned his head back, his eyes following a moment behind. Headline reached under the counter to pull out a clear blue bottle of expensive vodka shaped like a double helix, dusted it off, and set it by the brandy. The shirt tail was still out, but the skin was sufficiently covered. Then Headline pulled a bottle of clear apple liqueur from the front shelf and set that down.

"Don't worry, Chief," Headline said over his other shoulder, "I'll charge you well prices."

He winked again, then poured the water out of the snifter and quickly wiped it out before the glass could cool. He deftly filled it three-quarters full with the brandy. He poured a small dash of the vodka on that, and a smaller dash of the liqueur on that. He gave the glass one quick twirl, then set it down and grated nutmeg from a fresh nut on top with a flourish. Then he picked the flourish out with the tip of his pinky.

He poured more hot water into a small highball glass and set that at Agnes's place. Just as Agnes sat back down, he gently set the bowl of the snifter in the mouth of the glass. The steam from the glass lifted out around the snifter, enveloping it, almost obscuring the pale cinnamon-colored liquid within, and sensuously welcomed Agnes back.

"What have we here?" she asked, and the question completely ignored Jim.

She picked it up and swirled it. The thick, aromatic vapors escaped from the snifter and pleasantly stung her nostrils. The liqueur and brandy raced up and around, then clung to the sides of the glass, slowly draining back in a thin, clear, uneven, delightful film like an old window. She sipped it daintily and found it charming. Her nipples shot holes right through the sweater, poking Headline in his shiny blue eyes. (*Steve, you just ruined a perfectly good scene.* **We can fix it***. No. We can't. And besides, his eyes are sparkly, it's his hair that's shiny.* **Yep, you're gay.**)

"I could tell you what was in it," Headline said with a mischievous grin, "but then I'd have to kill you."

Jim was about to say he'd seen the whole thing, and knew exactly what was in it, then realized, somehow, that that would be intruding, then laughed inappropriately in an attempt to join the party. Agnes was looking down with a coy, embarrassed grin. Jim didn't imagine coy was even in Agnes's vocabulary. It certainly wasn't in his. He really had no idea what was happening and just wished they could go back to her house so she could teach him something new that would erase the image of her being coy from his mind.

Eventually, they did, but her heart didn't seem to be in it.

Twain was also looking at Lee oddly, lately. Lee stood at the sink washing pots, and the steam, surrounding him like a cloud of smoke at a Rotary Club meeting, caused perspiration to bead on his face and gather in the small of his back. The suds were so thick his arms were submerged from the elbow to just above the wrist before he even touched the hot, hot water, and they billowed out over the top of the stainless steel sink. The apron he wore was wet with suds and splashed water that soaked through, drenching the front of his shirt and trousers. Sometimes work was wonderful. Until he felt Twain enter the kitchen. And then he felt Twain stop for a moment and look at him oddly. Lee knew he was being looked at oddly. (**Enough with the "oddly" stuff, Geoff. I let you get away with that with the whole "pleasant upper middle class" thing in Installment Eighteen, and look what happened then. It took six months to get another one out.** *Sorry.* **Enough.** *Sorry.* **I mean it, Geoff.** *Sorry.* **Art is knowing when to stop.** *I get it, Steve.*) He could feel it in the sweat on the back of his shirt. He refused to look around, because, if he did, he knew he would have to ask Twain why he was looking at him oddly, (**Geoff...** *Just checking*) and the whole Kim and Jim thing was all too fresh.

He concentrated on scouring the crusted meatloaf from the pan in his hand. He couldn't see the pan through all the suds, but he could feel the crust. Then he sensed Twain open the refrigerator, take out a bowl of butter, shut it, look at him once more, then leave. He realized he hadn't really been breathing, and breathed in really hard. And a dollop of suds chose that moment to dislodge from its fellows and waft toward his face. It went right up his nose and covered his eyes. He started coughing and sneezing which made him drop the meatloaf pan in the hot, hot water, which splashed all the way through all the suds, up to the apron, through the apron to his shirt which was cold with water, making it suddenly very hot with water just as he lifted his suds encrusted arm to wipe the suds from his eyes, which caused his eyes to burn in a completely different way from the way his shirt, and now pants, were burning.

He slammed his fist down in the sudsy water, making it splash and burn him again.

"FUUUUCK!" he shouted, slapping the water again and again, sounding like a cross between Joe E. Brown and Mel Torme.

Everything, including The Fifty-Ninth Street Bridge Song (Feeling Groovy) that was playing on the batter encrusted radio tuned to the local college station, came to a momentary, embarrassed stop. Lee frantically shook his hands and arms to rid them of suds, then, trusting they were sufficiently suds free, frantically felt around the counter top by the sink for a towel to remove the suds from his face. He found one, but when he brought it to his face, realized by the smell that it wasn't one of the clean ones. He froze, trying to decide if he should use it or not, when another towel magically appeared in his hand.

It smelled clean, so he wiped his face with it, then opened his eyes.

"Thanks," he said to Matt, who offered him a Gummy Bear®.

He shook his head, no, then noticed that Matt was standing a few inches beyond arm's length, and his hand was shaking. He's not going to start looking at me odd... I mean strangely, too, is he? Lee thought, then half heartedly accepted the Gummy Bear® by way of apology for scaring the poor kid. I gotta get a real job, Lee thought. Then Twain came in, stopped long enough to look at him, then offered him a Mentos. Lee shook his head. Then Twain handed him the Cuss Jar. Lee reached into his very wet pocket, and, after fighting with the clinging cloth that was quickly cooling, produced a very shiny, damp quarter and deposited it in the jar. It hit with a clink. His wet pocket hung limply by the side of his pants and his keys, Chapstick, vitamins, two pogs, Trojans and the CD of the Cars Greatest Hits hit the floor with a clatter.

Twain looked at him again.

"What?" Lee said, and the word had the full force of a soaking shirt and pants, burning nose and eyes and frustrated heart.

Twain looked at him a moment longer.

"Be free," Twain said, then turned and left the kitchen.

Lee watched him leave. Matt left quickly, pulled along in Twain's wake. Lee heard the phone ring, and a moment later, Twain called back saying Abby was calling. Again? Lee thought as he took off his apron, collected his spilled stuff, then tried vainly to dry his shirt and pants, and went out front. She had already called him twice that day, just to give him a weather report. At ten, she informed him it was snowing. At noon, she advised him it was still snowing. This time she simply said it was already up to ten inches, then laughed and hung up. Lee looked at Twain, who was still looking at him.

"Sorry about all the personal calls," Lee said, knowing how much Twain hated that.

Twain smiled a strange half-smile and sucked on his Mentos, and Lee had the distinct impression he was being guerilla theatre for Twain, again. He hated that.

He stepped behind the counter and the man in the John Deere™ hat offered him a Zagnut Bar. He declined and refreshed the man's coffee. The man wearing the Fedora offered him a Necco Wafer. A licorice one. He politely refused and wiped the counter in front of him. The Girl from Ipanema offered him a sheet of Dots. He turned them down, and only took one step before the woman from Venus offered him a coffee high colonic, which he accepted. (*Steve!* **Espresso high colonic?** *No.* **Decaf?** *No. No colonic. People are eating.* **Not any more.** *Just stop.* **Wanna talk about football?** *Okay. Brian Piccolo is dead.* **That's cold, man.**)

The phone rang again, and Twain answered it.

"For you," Twain said, this time effectively communicating to Lee with the two words that he was receiving way too many personal calls.

It was Andrew.

"You're calling me in every installment," Lee said.

"Got the papers from Illinois today," Andrew said to him. "The divorce is final."

Lee didn't know how to react to that and was trying to see if anything occurred to him when Andrew added that there was also an offer on the house.

"But you said no one would want to buy it in winter," Lee said.

"I'm not God, okay? Anyways, the offer was for a hundred sixty. Beverly wants to accept it."

"We agreed on one seventy-five," Lee said, quickly calculating how much less his share would be with this offer. Seventy-five hundred, minus commission and fees. He was about to object when Andrew said he'd be responsible for the mortgage if he didn't accept.

"Can they do that?"

"Look, let me drop by your house after work," Andrew said. "We'll talk about it then."

"It's snowing," Lee said, really upset at himself for having to admit it. "I'll come to your place."

"No. I wanted to talk to you about something else, anyways. I'll see you, what, around six-thirty?"

"Okay," Lee said, not wanting to admit that he didn't know why talking about something else had to be done at his house.

Lee hung up. Just then the front door bells clanged and a burst of cold air and snow swirled into the room, followed by Peter, who sat down at the counter.

"Did you hear the news, today?" Peter said, shaking the snow out of his hair.

"Why, what happened?"

"Nothing. Absolutely nothing. Nothing happened today. Nothing. Going to the hill tonight?"

"What is it with this town?" Lee exploded. "Do you know Aunt Gladys, too?"

"Yeah," Peter said, confused by the outburst. "She runs the janitorial supply house out on Bell Road. That's where I get my muriatic acid. Why?"

Then Peter noticed the water all over Lee.

"Nice pants," he said, and Lee had a whole new reason to be upset, what with the whole Jim and the staring and the nice pants thing.

"Is this some type of gay thing?"

Peter just shook his head.

"Did I just ask that out loud?"

"What?" Peter said.

"About being a..." Lee said. "Never mind."

The scene ended with a close up on Peter's reaction, then faded to commercial. (*Making it easier for the network miniseries, Steve?* **Always thinking ahead.** *Keep it up. Nice pants.* **Thanks.**)

Lee stomped the snow off his shoes at his door step, shook it off his coat, and opened the door. He looked around the living room. Piece by piece, the house was becoming a home. It had the faint odor of fireplace smoke and grandma's panties. (*Art is knowing when to stop, Steve.* **Hey, get your own line.**) He looked at the stupid yellow bird in its cage that was sitting on an end table, not moving.

"Hello, bird," he said.

Maybe I'll call it Charlie Parker, Lee thought, and tried it out.

"Hello, Charlie."

The bird cheeped once. Lee considered that. Stupid bird, he thought, and took off his coat.

Shortly after Andrew arrived, the phone rang.

"Fourteen-and-a-half inches," Abby said gleefully, then hung up.

Andrew was sitting on the couch. He pulled the packet of papers from his briefcase and handed it to Lee, who was beginning to be a little frightened by Abby's persistence. Or by the snow. Okay, he was frightened about the strong possibility that he may have to go tobogganing. He thumbed through the papers, noticing the signatures and court stamps in red and green, with dates in blue and black. He set them down.

"So that's it, huh?" he asked, weakly.

"Yup. Except for the house, that's it. I brought Champagne and sparkling apple juice. Which'll you have?"

"A beer," Lee said, getting up to go get it.

"Got one for me, too?"

When Lee returned with the two bottles, he asked again if Beverly really could make him be responsible for the mortgage if he didn't accept the offer.

"Yeah," Andrew said. "She can. It's a fair offer, and they could argue that you were obstructing the deal if you didn't accept it. And she needs the money. And so do you."

Lee nodded. Eighty thousand would come in handy. Minus fees and commissions. And the bank loan. Hell, thirty-six seven could last him a couple of years in this town. Even if he stayed working at Twain's. Which he didn't plan on doing. For much longer.

"Okay," he said, finally. "What else did you want to talk about?"

The phone rang.

"Fifteen and three quarters," Abby said. Lee could hear the gleeful grin all the way over the phone line.

"What was that?" Andrew asked, noticing the fear peek out from under Lee's eyebrows like the brick under Bell Road.

"What else did you want to talk about?"

Andrew sat back with a huge smile, intertwined his fingers and set his hands on his stomach.

"Your house," he said.

"My...?"

Andrew had been doing research. The Gardners had built the house Lee was renting in the early thirties, and their daughter, Evelyn, had been born shortly after that. Andrew remembered that she had a dog.

"Big thing. Called him Gable," Andrew said.

Andrew intertwined his own memories with the research he'd done. Lee was beginning to think Andrew was a dangerously obsessive man. Then Lee excused himself to wash his hands. Twice. When he came back, he got two more beers, and Andrew continued his story. After high school, she'd gone to Korea in the nurse's corps where she was killed by friendly fire.

"I knew she wasn't the type to die for love," Andrew said, proudly. "So it can't be her ghost haunting your place."

The family had lived there for another three years after she died, then moved out of town. They moved to Chicago and never came back. Andrew had checked on all the other owners. No one had ever died there. It had become a rental sometime in the mid seventies, and it was a little harder to get the facts, but someone dying there would have been reported in the Bee. He was about to go into a detailed account of everything he'd found in the Bee about the house when there was a knock at the door.

"Knock, knock," the door said.

"Eighteen," Abby said as soon as Lee opened it. She was holding a pair of new, dark brown leather gloves.

"No," Lee said. "It can't be."

Abby flicked on the Kensington transistor radio she was holding in her other hand.

"... Eighteen inches since this morning," the radio said in a moment entirely too reminiscent of Bullwinkle for Lee's taste.

Abby clicked it off.

"Hey, Abby," Andrew said. "Taking our boy to the hill?"

"Oh, yeah," Abby said with palpable glee.

"Oh," Lee said very weakly. He clicked his heels, but no one transported him back to Kansas.

Will Lee go tobogganing?
Will he get hurt if he does?
Will people laugh at him?
Especially children?
Is Abby in a family way?
Over how many installments will Geoff and Steve drag that subplot out?
How does Abby know Aunt Gladys?
How does Aunt Gladys know Abby?
Will Kim forgive Abby?
Does Kim know Aunt Gladys?
Is Gladys just another name for Happy Butt?
Can you say Happy Butt without smiling?
Is Jim too old for Agnes?
Who's haunting Lee's house?
Does Lee have nice pants?

To find the answers to these and other Unsolved Mysteries©,
tune into our next installment:
"There's Snow Business like Show Business"

(I can't believe you said Brian Piccolo's dead. *He is.* **You're going to Hell. Can I have a beer, now?)**

This installment first published June 7, 2003

Geoff Hoff and Steve Mancini

The story thus far: Lee Harris has been bamboozled into going tobogganing by his new girlfriend, Abby, who may or may not be pregnant. Young Jim Ackerman, who has been learning life in strange and wonderful new ways from his sixty-year-old girlfriend, Agnes, has been replaced by a stunning younger man. Matt and his girlfriend, Jan, think of themselves as better than the freshman at the high school because they're juniors. Andrew's wife calls him "Thumbs" for reasons we will probably never know. Stella and Peter are just friends because a.) they work together at the theatre, and b.) Peter is gay and Stella is bitchy. And Twain is annoyed that Lee gets so many phone calls at the diner. To get all the dirt, read the previous installments. Start with one. We dare you. That's in Volume One, which is a whole other book.

(Can we make a reference to the Beatles in this installment? *That certainly won't be a challenge.* How about James Polk? *Why, Steve?* Because he's my favorite president. *Why, Steve?* Because his name is Polk. *I should have guessed.* Polk.)

Installment Twenty
"There's Snow Business Like Show Business"

The annual sledding party at Beard's Hill was the great equalizer. Everyone had a common goal - to get drunk and slide down a hill. The hill was already there. All it needed were people and booze. And snow. And booze. The snow came, followed closely by the people and booze. (*Okay, Steve, you would never let me get away with a paragraph like that.* What? It's art. And besides, I'm funny.) Beard's Hill was a twisting fifteen mile drive out of town, and there wasn't a house in sight of it. The hill was wide, one end was very steep and the other much less so, gradually leveling off to a wooded area. No one sledded or tobogganed near the trees, but lights from snowmobiles could occasionally be seen weaving in and around them like fireflies, and the faint humming sound of their high-revving engines could be heard if the atmospheric conditions were just right and the car radios paused for a moment. The cars parked at the top, off the road that would have been dirt if it weren't covered with snow, slush and ice. Actually, at this point, most of them were trucks, which helped cut the grooves in the snow-covered road for everyone else.

When Peter arrived in the early evening, the blizzard was losing most of its intensity. The next morning, though, kids all over town would look out of their bedroom windows and cheer. There was one small fire going at the other end of the hill, and a small group of what looked like college-aged kids were building a snowman with exaggerated breasts. Okay, a snow woman. But it had a huge carrot for a (**careful**) dong (**thank you**), so it was a snow evangelist.

He stood at the edge of the parking area, surveying the hill. Booze was already being shared by the cold tobogganers in those forty or fifty feet between the area where people parked and the edge of the hill, and the folks that were already there were already laughing and screaming and throwing snowballs at each other. He had almost not come this year. He was tired of going places alone, and right up until the last moment had defiantly sat on his couch determined not to venture out. Determined instead to stay home. Alone. He knew people who liked being alone. They usually complained about never getting any time to themselves. Well, he'd give them his time if he could. (**Is it "tobogganers" or "toboggananians"?** *What are you off on now, Steve?* **You know, I'm from Michigan and some people call us Michiganians and some say Michiganders.** *Go back to Michigania, Steve.*)

Finally, after sitting on the couch being Peter for several hours, going back and forth in his head between staying home feeling sorry for himself or going to the party and feeling sorry for himself, between berating himself for feeling like he needed to go to the party and chastising himself for not wanting to fulfill his obligation to go to the party, between equivocating and vacillating, he determined that it was time, finally, to make a change. He needed to find a friend. Okay, so he had friends. Lee was his friend, but Lee was now ensconced with Abby. And good for him. Peter wanted to be ensconced. Not in that way, of course. He figured he probably wouldn't ever be ensconced in that way, but in a real friendship. One with someone who he could laugh with and cook for and talk about books with and take care of and be taken care of by. If he was going to find himself someone like that, he needed to pull himself out of his shell. Somehow. God, that sounded like something Dr. Joyce Brothers would suggest. Hearing himself think it almost made him stay home again, but he got up off the couch, got his things together and left, proud and thrilled at the new direction his life might take. He thought of thinking that it was the first day of the rest of his life and that a journey of a thousand miles started with the first step, but anything that came to his mind sounded too much like something on a colorful poster found on a teenaged girl's bedroom wall in the seventies.

A few of the vehicles in the parking area had their lights on, illuminating the gathering through the gentle, steady stream of big snow flakes, and a few others had their doors open and their radios, tuned to the same station, blaring out high energy party music. The wind had died down, and you could see misted breath which sometimes came out in bursts with laughter. Peter watched the groups and couples that had gathered and wondered if any of them would be the one. The friend. He'd have to wait until one separated from the pack to find out. He sat in the center of his tractor wheel inner tube and started down the hill. Very quicky the tube turned backwards, and Peter screamed with pleasure and fear the rest of the way down. At the bottom, he struggled to a standing position, which was difficult because of the packed snow, the slippery tube and his strange center of gravity. Once standing, he brushed the snow from his beard with the end of his knitted scarf, and brushed it off his butt with his tattered mittens.

"I wanna rock and roll all day," Peter shouted toward the top of the hill in his robust baritone voice, shaking his mittened fist in the air, "and party ev-er-ry night!"

"Rock and roll all night," a kid who had just landed near him at the bottom of the hill on a Radio Flyer said. "Party ev-er-ry day."

"What?"

"Rock and roll is all night. Party is ev-er-ry day," the kid repeated. "Kiss."

"I know," Peter said to him, "but it's night, now. And you're too young to know Kiss."

"My dad has the album," the kid said as he picked up his Radio Flyer. "He's such a geek."

The kid effortlessly sprinted up the hill. Peter's knees hurt. One down. He considered singing Joni Mitchell's Songs to Aging Children Come, but decided instead to re-confirm his decision and started whistling It's a Small World©, picked up his tube and trudged back up the hill. Once there, he dropped the tube, poured hot mulled wine from a gingham-colored Thermos™ bottle into the red, plastic Thermos™ bottle cap, and let it warm him from the stomach out. Then he plopped down into his tube, poured another cap full and scouted the party goers, eagle-eyed, for a possible conquest candidate. He was still breathing hard from the trip down and the trek back up, but laughter and shouting and scratchy car radios, combined with the warm, spicy alcohol, exertion and the exceptional opportunity for companionship made him want to hug the world.

There were people of all ages who came to slide down this hill, but the majority of them would be college kids and high school juniors and seniors who had their own cars. A green nineteen seventy-two Impala drove up and parked. Twain got out, slammed the driver's side door, opened the trunk and pulled out Walt Disney (*Steve!*) a long, beat up folding table made from textured aluminum, carried it by the handle and set it up very close to the edge of the hill. He went back and pulled out a long, beat up, rectangular stainless steel chafing dish, set it up on the table, and lit two cans of Sterno. Under its cover were two pans, one full of melted nacho cheese and the other full of thick, sweet, steaming Sloppy Joe mix. Kids were already gathering when he went back for the industrial sized bag of tortilla chips and huge garbage bag filled with hamburger and hot dog buns. As soon as Twain put the table out, Peter struggled back up, went to his car and, in two trips, brought the two industrial coffee urns and set them on the table.

"Peter," Twain said as Peter put the sign that said "Hot Hard Apple Cider" on one urn.

"Twain," Peter said as he put the sign that said "Hot Mulled Wine" on the other one.

Twain pulled a beat up aluminum military canteen out of the camouflage-colored canvas attached to his belt. He uncapped it and let the cap swing free on the chain while he took a healthy swig. Peter poured the last of the mulled wine from his Thermos and toasted

Twain. (**Eeew.** **Toasted Twain.** **What would that smell like?** *Eeew.*)

"Whiskey?" Peter asked after he swallowed a gulp of wine.

"Gin," Twain said.

"Eeew. Gordon's?" Peter asked.

"Gilbey's," Twain said with a look that seemed to imply that Peter should have known better. "In the frosted bottle."

"How can you drink that lamp oil straight?" Peter asked. Twain didn't point out that no one was sampling his wine or cider. Peter didn't point out back that it usually started going when the theater crowd got there after the performance. Twain didn't point out that that wasn't something to be proud of.

After another snort, Twain went back to his car and pulled out a very beat up steel snow disk. It had once been metallic green, but was now only green in some of the deeper dents and near the handles, which were braided rope that had long since replaced the original leather. He brought it to the edge, set a beat up square foam rubber pillow covered in plastic with a barely recognizable emblem on it that could have been a bear, could have been a cougar, could have been a badger, could have been a raccoon, could have been a llama, could have been a yak, could have been a marmoset, could have been a (*Steve. Stop. It's just a pillow*) red devil silk-screened on it. (*Sheesh.*) He sat on that and stoically slid down the hill. The disk didn't spin at all. It didn't dare.

Peter was fascinated by Twain's self-reliance. He was fascinated by Twain in any case. He realized, watching him slide down the hill, that he knew almost nothing about this guy who he saw almost every day of his life. Probably no one did. Not even Twain. Nobody ever really questions him. If they did, what would they ask? What would Peter ask him? He obviously has some sort of answer, look at him. Maybe he could be the friend. That would be really interesting. Or scary. And anyway, Twain would probably not even consider being his new friend. No, it couldn't be him. Realizing he was beginning to sound like a high school girl again, Peter took a healthy swig of cider and went back down the hill on his tube.

The first ambulance came shortly after Peter got back to the top. He took a small amount of pleasure to notice that the person on the stretcher was the kid whose father had a Kiss album. Several revelers saluted the kid with bottles of wine, vodka, Wild Turkey, sloe gin, beer, brandy and any and everything sweet by Hiram Walker. Peter, comfortably sitting again in his tube, saluted him with a refreshed cup of hot wine, then took a healthy swig. The warmth it gave to the inside of his cheeks conflicted delightfully with their wind-chaffed surface, making them rosier than usual. He breathed out another small sigh. It had been an eventful week, and sitting bundled in his overalls which were over longjohns and under his old, bulky coat on a cold night surrounded by a snow party was just what he needed after all. There had been a knock on his door late Wednesday night. (**Is this a flashback, Geoff**? *Yes*. **Pretty abrupt, isn't it**? *I was waiting for your film school genius*. **I'm not playing any more. You wouldn't let me say ermine**. *You're such a child. Go ahead*. **Could have been an ermine**. *Happy?*) A placard appeared that said "Late Last Wednesday, at Peter's." (*Thank you*.)

Peter pulled the last tissue from the box and used it to mark his place in his book then looked at the door for a moment before answering.

"Who is it?"

"Me. Jim."

Peter sat up from his slumped position. He looked around the room, wondering if he should do the dishes, vacuum and straighten up before answering.

"Just a sec," he said, instead, and brushed some water cracker crumbs from the coffee table to the floor, got up and opened the door.

Peter had never imagined that Jim could look that sad. He had never imagined that Jim could look sad at all unless he'd just lost a tooth or a basketball game. Even then, sad probably wouldn't be what Jim would look. Jim stood for a moment, then enveloped Peter in a huge grief-hug. I have an iota of a chance, Peter thought, then chastised himself soundly for the thought. Peter had no choice but to hug him back and pat him on the shoulder, but was frozen stiff while doing it. It felt like Jim might actually cry.

"What's wrong?" Peter asked, thinking the worst.

"Agnes is dumping me," Jim said.

"Is," Peter said, "dumping you?"

Jim untangled himself from Peter, for which Peter was both grateful and disappointed. *How dare he come to me to tell me he was being dumped. By an older woman, yet. By an old woman. But I'm so glad it's my shoulder he came to cry on. It'd better be my shoulder. But how dare he? Am I some sort of hanky to be pulled out of the drawer at his convenience, then tossed aside again? God, he smells good. I need cheese.*

He led Jim to the couch, then went in search of a tissue. There was a box on his bed stand. *Don't ask why.* He gave the box to Jim, then sat next to him, making sure he was the appropriate "concerned friend" distance away. Then he moved an inch closer, to adjust for whatever. *You know.* Then he moved three inches away to adjust for the incredible attraction he suddenly realized he still felt.

"Tell me."

"We went to The Office last night."

"Did you fight?"

"That young good-looking guy was bartending."

"Who, Headline? Oh. Headline."

Peter understood, despite the irony of Jim calling someone else "young". He moved two inches closer in order to put his arm around Jim's shoulder understandingly, then didn't put his arm around the shoulder. Then he clasped his hands in his lap in case he might accidentally put his arm around the shoulder.

"Then tonight," Jim continued, "after rehearsal, she suggested I should go home because she was tired."

He's being dumped, all right, Peter thought. Jim's eyes were actually glistening. Peter really didn't know what to do or say.

"Have you eaten?"

"Sure, I wouldn't have made it to twenty-eight if I hadn't." (*Steve! You have no compassion.* **It's fiction, Ishmail**. *Get your own line.*)

Jim just shook his head. Peter went into the kitchen to fix him a snack. Two minutes later, he brought out a sandwich made with crusty Italian bread, slices of home-cooked roast beef, two slices of Colby cheese, lettuce, tomato, horseradish mayonnaise and a hint of Dijon mustard. There were two crisp dill pickle spears and a handful of chips on the plate. He also brought out a glass of cold beer and some paper towels. Jim ate and drank silently, appreciatively, nodding occasionally. When he was done, he wiped his mouth with a square of paper towel, and sat back. He breathed heavily for a moment, then looked at Peter.

"Thanks," Jim said sadly. "Mind if I crash here tonight?"

Yes I mind, Peter's mind shouted at Jim. No, his mind shouted at himself. Then he got really angry, then really flushed, then really confused, then really angry again. How dare he ask that, he thought. After everything. Then he looked at him again. Is he planning on trying to be gay every time something goes wrong in his personal life? I'm not a yo-yo, I'm a human being. What a sad, wet puppy, Peter thought, angry at himself for always having to be the mother, for being so desperate for contact that he'd take care of anybody. Why can't I just once be a regular guy and say get the fuck out of here, you asshole? It would feel so good to be able to do that. Just once.

Peter got up to get bedding for the couch, which, he was sure, wasn't what Jim had meant. Or, maybe it was. Maybe he just didn't want to drive. But Peter didn't want to know if it was or wasn't, and if it wasn't, it would be too exciting, and too painful, so he got the bedding for the couch.

While Peter was gone, Jim looked around the room. There was a book called "My Head's Too Big to Box with God" by Anne Boleyn on the coffee table with a tissue hanging out of it. How can he read that shit, he thought. He looked up at the wall and noticed for the first time the autographed picture there of some old lady with a striped nurse's scarf on her head. "To Peter," it said. "Rock on. Mother Theresa - '78"

Jim took off his shoes and socks and lay down. He was asleep almost instantly. Damn him. Peter went into his room and went to bed. He lay under the covers staring out at the darkness. He had never noticed how loud the refrigerator was, with the clicking on and hum of the motor. And he could hear the soft snore from the living room of that stupid, handsome young man. He tried counting the breaths like sheep, but that didn't help at all. Finally, he threw the covers back and quietly went into the kitchen. He got a bowl, but realized, as soon as he opened the refrigerator, that he had used the last of his cheese in Jim's sandwich. Damn him. He remembered the can of aerosol cheese product he had bought on a whim years ago, and carefully closed the refrigerator door. Before he found the can, he found a box of Kraft Macaroni and Cheese food product that he had bought on the same whim. What was I drinking that night, he thought, then set them both on the counter and stared at them. I can either melt that shit, or mix this shit. Or go to the store. Just then, Jim grumbled and turned in his sleep. Oh, God, I need some cheese. He sprayed the canned shit into a bowl and put that into the microwave. Thirty seconds later, it dinged. He jumped and opened the door quickly so it wouldn't ring again and wake Jim. The shit was bubbling and looked like melted plastic. He stared at it, trying to decide if he were really that desperate. He tasted a tip of a spoonful. This is bad, he thought.

He pulled out a pan, put water in it and put it on the stove. When it started to form small bubbles, he opened the cheese food product powder packet, sprinkled that in and mixed it, then tasted a tip of a spoonful. This is worse, he thought. Then he mixed the reconstituted powdered cheese into the melted aerosol cheese and tried that. This is awful, he thought, gave up and went back to bed.

There was a shout that snapped Peter's attention back to the cold night on the hill. There were a few more fires going, and a lot more cars. The music from them was throbbing in the snowy air and several kids were unloading firewood, blankets and booze from their trunks. He surveyed the fresh potentials with a swig of cider that had cooled in his Thermos cap, somehow making it taste way too sweet. Lee's SUV drove up and slid to a stop. Peter felt relieved to see him and struggled out of his inner tube. Lee just sat looking toward the edge of the hill, and Abby sat looking expectantly at Lee. When Peter knocked on the window, Lee rolled it down without taking his eyes from the crowd gathered in packs all along the hill.

"You're here," Abby said to Lee. "You might as well get out of the car. Hi, Peter."

"Hi, Peter," Lee said, then looked at him with eyes begging for salvation.

Peter laughed and opened the door. The song filtering out of Lee's car caused a strange dissonance in the air. Several people who were just parking and unloading their stuff nearby stopped what they were doing and stared. Lee could feel the stare all the way through Peter's body, but didn't understand it.

"Otter," Peter said.

"Huh?"

"Turn it to the Otter. One-oh-four point six. Eff-em."

Lee was still bewildered, so Abby reached over and turned the tuner on his radio until his car was in harmony with the cold, vibrant air around the hill. Lee felt that small dismay from someone touching his knob. The feeling of stares turned to a wave of satisfied approval as the new arrivals joined the party, secure in the knowledge that the atmosphere wouldn't be ruined by some old fart. Lee finally stepped from the car and Abby rushed to the back, opened the rear door, pulled out a long, wooden toboggan, grabbed it by the rope secured to the curly end, then stood waiting like a puppy that really had to go pee. Lee sighed and looked at the crowd. They were all so young. Then Twain appeared at the edge, carrying a snow disk. Even he looked younger than Lee. Twain saw Lee, set his disk down, walked over to the SUV and presented his canteen.

Lee's mind did back flips. It didn't have the capacity to process the amount of decisions he had to make before he could even begin to decide to take a swig of whatever Twain was offering him, so he had to list them in some handleable order. First - what is it? Probably whiskey. Safe enough. Second - would a shot of good whiskey help him deal with impending tobogganing? Definitely. Third - was it good whiskey? Doubtful, but possible. Fourth - has Twain already had some? Probably yes. Fifth - did Twain's lips touch the canteen in any place when he'd had some? Probably, definitely yes. Sixth - would Twain forgive him if he refused? Probably not. Seventh - would Abby forgive him if he accepted? Probably yes, she hadn't seen Twain's dirty under... things. Eighth - would he forgive himself? He had seen them. Only if the whiskey were very, very strong. Very. Ninth - could it be strong enough to kill Twain germs? Probably not. Definitely not. Oh, God. I'm going to die on the hill, anyway, he thought, grabbed the thing and took a huge swig. A small swig wouldn't kill enough brain cells. Or germs. It would only maim them so they would survive, mutate and kill another day.

His face twisted into itself as soon as the alcohol hit the back of his tongue. He didn't spit it out, but really, really wanted to. He swallowed it quickly, closing off the front of his mouth and his nostrils so the cold air wouldn't activate his taste buds, but it was useless. His tongue tasted like he had just eaten a pine tree. When he was brave enough to open his mouth again, he wanted to say any number of things, but only one thing could come out.

"It's gin."

"Gilbey's," Twain said as if Lee should have known better. "In the frosted bottle."

Twain took his Chapstick from his back pocked, used it, then offered it to Lee. (*Steve!* **His comb?** *No.* **Panty liners***? Sure.* **Really***? No.*)

Abby pulled the toboggan and Lee toward the gaping maw that was the edge of the hill. He stopped by Twain's table and tried to serve himself some Nachos, but Abby continued to pull. Quickly reading the signs on the coffee urns, looking for any excuse, he told her he wanted some mulled wine. She laughed, told him he could have some when they got back to the top, then reminded him he was straight.

"But I'm in theater," he protested.

It wasn't good enough. Lee looked around for help, but all he saw were the toboggans, the cardboard boxes, the sleds, the tubes, the stupid roll-up plastic things, and some brave soul's body surfing down the hill. It all sent an extra chill up his spine. Abby sighed with exaggerated patience and pulled him to the far end near the trees. The hill wasn't very high there, and wasn't steep at all. She was embarrassed to be going there, it was the wee-wee end where moms took the little kids bundled up like stuffed bears on Saturday afternoons, and she hadn't been a little kid in a long, long time, and had never had to go down the wee-wee end even then. This wasn't tobogganing, it was sliding down a slope. A slight slope. A silly, safe, slight slope. Sheesh.

The way she got past her embarrassment was to convince herself that, because the wee-wee end was closer to the trees, which you could careen off and break a limb or two, it was much more dangerous than the other end, where you could actually toboggan. She wouldn't share that thought with Lee, of course, the whole idea was to get him down the damn hill. There was a drone of internal combustion engines and a slight sweet smell of burned oil in the air here that surprised her, until she looked into the forest and saw the swiftly moving forms of snowmobiles slicing in and around the trees. Because she had never been on this end of the hill, she had never noticed them before. You couldn't get me on one of those things if you paid me, she thought. You can really get hurt on one of those.

Abby carefully positioned the toboggan at the edge and placed herself at the front, looking expectantly back at Lee who suddenly looked very, very old.

"I promise not to laugh at you," she said reassuringly. "Even if you hit a rock."

"Thanks a lot," he said, not reassured at all, and forced himself down onto the flat, thin piece of demon-wood that would be the only thing between him and certain death for his immediate future. The thin, fragile piece of weathered, splintered wood. I'm going to hurt myself, he thought, and I'm going to look stupid doing it.

Peter watched them in the distance. My God, he thought. They're going down the wee-wee end. Is Abby that scared? No, she had dragged Lee here. It was for him. Lee was afraid of something. Peter started whistling Coward of the County. (**That's what I always do.** *What, whistle Kenny Rogers songs?* **No, walk away from trouble.** *No, you don't.* **Sometimes I do. Sometimes I walk right toward it.** *Mostly you create it and just stand back and watch.*)

The moment his butt hit the wood, Abby pushed off and started screaming. Their screams filtered through the snow and cold and party noise and thumping music and fire all the way to Peter's ears and he breathed a small sigh, then went to the table to pour himself some hot wine. Matt was at the table serving up two Sloppy Joes. He handed one to Jan, then saw Peter.

"Hello, Mr. Principal," he said, then introduced Jan, who looked to Peter to be one of those high school girls who did well in both history and Home Ec. Did they still teach Home Ec, he wondered. They had two small inner tubes tied together with a length of rough rope. "We'll race you down."

Jan giggled, and Peter laughed out loud. That would take his mind off the search. The rumble of his laugh was infectious, and several nearby people joined him. He struggled to his feet, told them they were on, warned them he had ballast in his favor, and picked up his tube. Matt and Jan set their Joes down and scrambled into theirs. Several nearby college students saw the impending contest and appointed themselves judges. One bent down behind Jan and held her tube, one behind Matt, and two behind Peter. A fifth raised his fifth to signal the start of the race.

"On your mark," he shouted, then took a swig. "Get set," he said and took another swig.

"Come on, Jason," one of the guys behind Peter said. "I'm all bent over, here."

"Hang on, you wienie. Go!"

They all pushed the tubes, then fell on their faces when the tubes sped away. They cheered the race all the way down. All three of the competitors laughed and screamed hysterically. Peter was slightly behind when Jan's tube turned a little and pulled Matt's back. Then Peter was ahead a little when he turned around backwards and slowed. Then Matt and Jan got a bit tangled in each other and Peter pulled ahead for good. There was a huge cheer from the top of the hill, and the guy who had started the race declared the big guy with the beard and overalls the official winner and they all drank to the race. Twice.

"The thrill of victory," Peter shouted as he stood, just as Matt and Jan came to a stop against his tube, knocking him back down. He pointed at them and added loudly, "And the agony of losing!"

"You mean 'defeat'," Jan said.

"A rose by any other name," Peter said, and purposefully didn't finish the quote.

"Race you to the top," Matt said with a laugh.

"Okay."

Matt and Jan sprinted up the hill.

"You win," Peter said proudly, not moving.

When Jan and Matt got to the top, Matt leaned in toward Jan. At first she pulled away, startled, then realized what he was doing and leaned toward him. It took a moment for them to figure out how to position their faces, but they finally kissed. A small grin spread across Peter's face watching them. It was so charming. It looked like their first kiss together. Maybe even their first kiss ever. It was really sweet and a little funny, more a peck than a kiss, and even with only that, Matt seemed a little light-headed when it was over. On his way up the hill, Peter continued smiling, but there was an odd sadness in his gut. When he got back to the top, he saw Lee position the toboggan at the edge of the hill, several yards closer to the steep end. It was still the wee-wee end, but not as much. Lee helped Abby down onto the toboggan, sat down, and pushed off. It was so easy for some people. Peter served himself a cup of hot cider and tipped it back in one gulp then poured himself some mulled wine.

After that trip down, Lee decided that, even though he was beginning to enjoy himself, he needed fortification, so they left the toboggan and went over to the table. That's when the second ambulance came. Lee was about to serve himself some cider when he saw the red lights flashing off the snow and trees. He froze, then very slowly, very much against his own will, turned toward the source of it.

"There's um... " he said. "An ambulance."

"Of course," Abby said. "Someone got hurt. Is that the first?"

"Second," Peter said.

"Ah. Anyone we know?"

"Some smart-ass kid whose father likes Kiss," Peter said and plopped back down into his tube to rest.

This one was a young adult who had been run down by a wayward sled. He seemed to have hurt his face on the fall. Probably a busted nose. He was saluted on his way. As the paramedic pressed dressing against him and put him in the back of the ambulance he waved and shouted that he'd be back in an hour. The ambulance driver hurried over and poured himself a cup of hard cider before his trip back to the hospital.

"Hey, Peter," he said.

"How's it going, Pete?" Peter said, proud that someone wanted his refreshment, then ashamed that he needed that reassurance from a relative stranger, then alert at the possibility of this being the one. After all, he said "hi" to me. Of course, he sort of had to, he was taking my cider. But he was taking my cider, he might want to be my friend. By the time he worked up the courage to start a conversation, Pete was already back in the ambulance and pulling away. Peter noticed the music, One is the Loneliest Number. That startled him because it really didn't sound like something the Otter would be playing. Especially that night. When he listened again, he realized the song was actually Dude Looks Like a Lady.

Lee's head closed in on himself, and a wave of nausea erupted from his gut. He had to hold on to the table, which wasn't very steady without a wobbly man leaning against it. Peter ran over to counter balance it so the nachos, Sloppy Joes, mulled wine and cider didn't become the next casualties of the night.

"You okay?" Abby asked.

"That's an ambulance," Lee repeated, rather stupidly.

"Yeah," Abby repeated in kind. "People get hurt. It's part of the party. They usually come back and continue drinking after they're patched up. No big deal."

Lee didn't have the energy to figure out all the things wrong with that. Instead, he poured himself a mulled wine and swigged it. It was warm and surprisingly good. I am in theater, the thought.

Peter watched Abby trying to convince Lee to get back on the toboggan, and thought about the day the week before when she had appeared at the theater looking for Kim. He'd said he hadn't seen her, and her face had fallen.

"We had a fight," she'd said and started to cry.

Peter immediately went into care taker mode. He led her into the office, sat her down and hurried off to look for something for her to wipe her eyes. And nose. He found a roll of theatrical tissue, brought it to her, sat in Stella's seat and leaned in to make sure she was okay.

"What happened?" he asked.

"I accused her of trying to steal Lee," Abby asked.

Peter thought there were at least three things wrong with that. One, Lee would never cheat on anyone. Two, from what he knew about Kim, she went for a much younger type. And three... Okay, he could only think of two. He didn't really know what to do for her. He didn't even really know her. He thought of offering her something to eat, but he only had his sack lunch and somehow didn't think that would do. Why did everyone like Lee so much, he thought. He's just an accountant. Why do I like Lee so much? Okay, so he can speak French and play the piano. And he's a helluva Scrabble player. How the hell does anyone just happen to know quetzals? Especially when he's been drinking. And he is, after all, a really good man. But I would never try to steal him away from someone. Even if I could. I hope she doesn't think I would.

Peter's heart started to beat inappropriately, so he focused on her. She really was in pain. Peter put his arm around Abby and she sobbed and put her head on his shoulder. When she finished, she pulled a bunch of theatrical tissue from the roll, dried her eyes, blew her nose, and used the rest to blot her bum. (*No blotting, Steve.* **There's just something very British sounding about that. Have a serviette. Take the lift. Turn on the telly. Blot your bum.** *Who are you?* **Pete Best.**)

She apologized, said she couldn't wait any longer, and left, taking the roll with her. A few minutes later, Kim came in to bring some of Agnes's notes about the set to Bear. Peter told her that Abby had just been there.

"What did she want?" Kim asked, coldly.

"She was looking for you. She really feels bad."

"She should feel bad," Kim said.

"She cried on my shoulder and we don't even know each other very well," Peter said. "You guys have been friends forever."

Kim's eyes welled up, then let loose. Peter pulled her to him, and she buried her face in his shoulder and wailed. At least it was the other shoulder. Now he wouldn't walk with a list. This is who I am, he thought, while stroking her back soothingly. The comforting shoulder. I really am good at it. He was surprised at the feeling of pride that overtook him at the thought. When she finally removed herself from him and walked away, the feeling of pride faded some and his arms felt strangely vacant. Everyone thinks I'm a Kleenex.

There was a huge bonfire blazing, and people were bringing more fire wood and broken Ikea furniture from their cars and trucks to feed it. The sparks and smoke flew up into the clouds and the wonderful, heavy smell of burned wood permeated everything. The light from the fire lit the ground and trees in an orange glow that intertwined frenetically with extreme shadows, and those close to it started sweating and taking off their coats.

Abby and Lee sat on a blanket, away from the fire, bundled up together, sharing a Sloppy Joe and a cup of wine. Abby felt warm pressed against him, and he felt really comfortable against her. Lee was still a little shaky, but had to admit that the last trip down had been a great deal of fun. He hated to admit it, but it had been. It wasn't even at what he had heard someone refer to as the wee-wee end. And he hadn't felt too ridiculous. Perhaps the booze was kicking in. Or the atmosphere. And, no matter what, Abby was a lot of fun. Compared to Beverly, she was like Ringling Bros. Barnum and Bailey's Circus. All three rings. With tigers and clowns. And cotton candy. And the "Giant Rats from Paris". Which had really been rabbits with their ears trimmed. From Butte. How could they do that to a rabbit? And how could they get away with calling them rats? Some people had no ethics. Sheesh. Where was I? Oh, yeah. She was a lot more fun than Beverly.

He had taken off the gloves to eat, and found himself playing with them.

"Oh," he said. "I didn't thank you for these. I didn't curse you for them, either, but I didn't thank you."

"You're welcome."

"Where'd you get them?"

"Goodwill," she said. "You can get a lot of good crap there."

Lee's look communicated that he would never be able to scrub his hands enough or drink enough alcohol to make that okay, and Abby laughed out loud.

"Kidding," she said. "My uncle made them."

"Yeah. Right."

"No, really. My Uncle Patrick. He makes them. It's what he does. That and ballroom dancing."

Lee thought skeptically about hand-tanned leather, then decided that was better than Goodwill. At least they were new.

"They are new, aren't they?" he asked.

"Of course," Abby said. "Now, the condoms are a different story. I recycle."

Lee involuntarily shivered, and Abby laughed.

"Speaking of condoms," Lee said. "How do you know Aunt Gladys so well?"

Abby's face fell in a way that Lee had learned to be wary of.

"What the hell is that supposed to mean? What are you implying?"

"I... Um..." Lee said.

"What do you think I am?"

"I don't know," Lee said, completely sincere, and a little lost.

Abby melted, understanding that she was a handful. A fun handful, but a handful. And Lee was fun, too, in his way. As fun as a night of Parcheesi®, the Royal Game of India. With wine coolers.

And baked potato chips with Imo dip. How the hell could they call that stuff sour cream? It was like calling carob chocolate. It was like calling margarine butter. It was like calling Meg Ryan an actor. Where was I? Oh, yeah. Lee was a lot of fun.

"Aunt Gladys is a substitute teacher."

"What does she teach, sex education?"

"Shop," Abby said, letting Lee know with her look that he was close to shaky ground again. "And seventeenth century Northern Icelandic lit."

"Really?" Lee said, his face brightening. "Did she ever teach the works of..."

Abby gave him a "don't even start with your obscure knowledge of shit no one else knows about, Mr. Know-it-All" look.

"Give me another sip of wine," Lee said, understanding the look and fearful of committing another gaff.

Peter sat in his tube with a cup of cider and watched Lee and Abby snuggle. He was glad that Lee was happy. Only a small, quiet corner of his mind wished for a brief, almost nonexistent moment that he was Abby right now. With a smaller butt. As soon as the quiet thought entered his mind, the rest of his brain told it soundly to be gone like Glenda told the bad witch. Then the rest of his head chastised his brain for coming up with a Wizard of Oz reference and he took another swig of cider. Then Andrew and Mrs. Divine drove up, and Peter struggled to his feet to go greet them. This time, the struggle was more a result of the quantity of mulled wine and hot cider than the center of gravity thing.

After Andrew pulled the sled from their trunk, slung a wine skin over his shoulder and pulled a gallon of jug wine from the back seat, Peter led them to the table and served them both Sloppy Joes. He was very happy to see them. He had a strong impulse to talk about Lee and Abby, and about Jim and Agnes, but, even with the amount of pretentious alcohol in his system, he resisted the impulse. Andrew didn't officially even know he was gay. And he really didn't know Mrs. Divine at all. But you had to start somewhere if you wanted a friend. He served himself some nachos and cheese. It wasn't Colby, but it would have to do. Andrew set the jug wine on the table, and looked around the hill.

"Look at that tree," he said to his wife, pointing at a tall oak that was a little distance away from the rest. "That's a survivor."

She looked at it dutifully, he pointed it out to her every year. She would pretend to hear the story for the first time like she did every year. At least he's consistent, and the story stays the same. The only thing that got bigger was the tree.

"My friends Joe and Frank and I ran over that tree with a sled the first year we came here. I was sixteen. Poor thing was a sapling. Didn't have a chance. They thought it was funny, all bent over and broken. Hell, I did, too, and laughed right along with them. But I felt bad about it, though. I don't know why, but I kept thinking about that tree. The next day I came back with a bunch of left over pieces of baseboard scrap that my dad had thrown away and some twine, and I made a splint and tied it up. And the road here was even rougher than it is now, almost non-existent. I borrowed my dad's truck. Well, I took my dad's truck. I wasn't sure it would live, but look at it now. Old Joe and Frank wouldn't laugh so hard if they ran into it now."

He looked at the tree, his eyes focused on the past, looking as young as the day he repaired the tree. His wife looked at him as if she had never heard the story before. Every year it made her realize in a deeper way why she had married this man.

"I wonder what ever happened to those guys," he finished, like he always did.

"Why don't you call them?" she answered. Like she did every year.

He turned his attention back to the present and the moment was gone. Peter tried to soak up their connection. That was what friendship was.

Shortly after Andrew arrived, as if he were the herald, the theater contingent started showing up. They swarmed around the table, chattering, and gossiping and trying to catch up to the rowdy, happily drunken crowd. One of them pulled a decimated old dresser from the back of his truck, and several people helped him lug it to the fire and throw it on. It stirred the sparks into an undulating frenzy and kids started hooting and removing their shirts. The radios seemed to feel the frenzy and the music changed to reflect it.

The theater crowd poured themselves and each other cider and wine. Peter beamed, and looked at Twain proudly. Twain shook his head, removed the canteen from his belt and lifted it toward Peter before swallowing an amount that would have put a theater person in the hospital. Peter watched him and again wondered how he did it. He didn't even know what it was that Twain did, but he needed to know how. He decided to ask, and moved closer to him. Twain watched him approach. Peter stood there. Twain did, too. Then Peter stammered. Twain didn't. Then Peter coughed, and finally spoke.

"Um...," he said, trying to form the question. "What's..."

Twain waited.

"How..."

Twain took a swig from his canteen and kept his eyes on Peter.

"Do you put cumin in your Sloppy Joe mix?" Peter said. It was the best he would be able to do out loud. In his mind, he was hollering at himself for being so stupid and wasting his one chance, his one question on a stupid cumin question. He knew damn well there wasn't cumin in the stupid stuff, it came from a can. A number 10 can. Now he'd never know. And he'd never even know what he didn't know.

Twain put his hand on Peter's shoulder.

"Food is not the answer," he said and walked away.

The girl who was playing Curley's wife in Of Mice and Men started screaming.

"Oh, oh, oh," she said, and everyone looked at her expectantly, as if she may be hurt or something. "I was looking for a gimmick to move the story along, and I found my old high school memory book."

She ran back to her car to get the book. It was covered with lace and pink cloth and stuffed with notes and papers and old photographs. She opened it up and turned to a section of shots from a Beard's Hill party years ago.

"This was the first year I was able to go. My junior year. Look, here's one of Ben Andrews. What a dream. What ever happened to him?"

"He's a priest."

"Really? Can you do that if you've had sex?" Everyone else laughed, and she turned red.

Kim drove up and got out of her car. The woman who played Curley's wife noticed her and excitedly waved her over.

"Look, here's one of you."

"What?" Kim said, and looked at the photo. It was one of her and Abby, years earlier, their arms around each other, looking longingly at Ben Andrews, who held a bottle of Old Crow in one hand and a Blue Boy in the other. The kid who was standing behind him was bent over barfing. The older couple behind them looked a lot like Burt Reynolds and Sally Field. Behind them was a guy who looked like a cross between Abe Vigoda and Mel Torme looking at the couple that looked like Burt Reynolds and Sally Field. Behind him was a tree, looking at the guy bent over barfing. Behind it was Geoff and Steve, working on Installment Twenty-One, wishing they had time for things like Beard's Hill parties to brighten their otherwise dreary days. (**I'm really sad, now, Geoff.** *Here, have a Space Food Stick©.* **Cool.**)

Peter looked at the photo, then looked at Kim look at the photo. Then he removed the photo from its corner tabs, took Kim by the arm and brought them both to where Lee and Abby were sitting. Abby looked at the photo, and her eyes misted. Kim, who was trying desperately to be firm in her resolution to be mad at Abby for the rest of her life, started to thaw a little.

"I really feel bad," Abby said.

"You should feel bad!" Kim said back.

Peter shot her a glance that could have killed a wild turkey. If you have friends, you should keep them. Abby stood and the two fell into each other's arms, apologizing profusely, promising never to fight again, taking the blame all on themselves. They were silhouetted by the roaring fire in the distance, which cracked and popped loudly as if congratulating them. Lee's pants tented. Peter moved back toward the theater crowd and the mulled wine, his work there done. It wasn't long before Bear knocked head-on into three already piled up sledders and toboggananians and the third ambulance of the evening arrived.

Peter saluted them off, then glanced back at Lee and Abby, who were just then starting a race with Kim who sat on a fuchsia sled. Lee and Abby were rather loose, and would probably win. Peter's eyes lost focus and he started thinking about the day early the last week when Lee had started crying on his shoulder about possibly having made Abby pregnant. (**Okay, Geoff. Enough with the flashbacks of Peter being mother to everyone. We get it. Sheesh.**) He decided to go down the hill rather than dwell on it. (**Thank you, Geoff.** *No problem.* **Can I have some mulled wine, now?** *Have at it, Pal.*

Knock yourself out. Be my guest. You go right ahead. Make yourself at home. **Never mind. Oh, and thanks a lot.** *What*? **I still have Songs of Aging Children going through my head.** *It is a small world, I can't get the smell of toasted Twain out of mine. Eeew.* **You win.**)

There was a flash of bluish light and a brief woop woop. Officer Bacon got out of his cruiser and waved at the few people who had noticed or cared about the greeting. Lee, who waved back weakly, once again wondered if the officer was following him. Officer Bacon spotted Peter and made a bee line toward him. Peter's first thought was, finally. A friend. Officer Bacon asked if he could borrow Peter's inner tube. Peter said sure, and thought, of course. He needs something.

The policeman took Peter's tube to the edge, sat down with as much dignity as was possible by a man in uniform sitting on a big rubber tube in the snow, and took off, cheering like a cowboy in a rodeo. Those close enough and sober enough to notice him cheered him on. After his wild ride, he returned the tube to Peter and gratefully accepted the Sloppy Joe Twain offered. He surveyed the crowd.

"Be careful driving home," he said, waved once again at anyone who cared, got in his car and drove off with a final woop woop.

The guy who played Charlie, the doctor and Candy took a huge swig of Cognac in a Box then bent back, breathed in dramatically, or as dramatically as he could, then started singing at the top of his lungs. He started singing Send In the Clowns. The women who played the Pigeon Sisters joined him. By the end of the song, several of the polker-playing guys from Odd Couple, Andrew and his wife, Veronica and even a few of the drunker college guys had added their voices. The guy whose father had the Kiss album, one arm in a cast, the other hand holding a bottle of Wild Turkey, swayed in drunken time with the music, then fell on his butt. After he made sure he hadn't spilled any of the Turkey, and that he hadn't landed on his broken arm, he started laughing. Lee was standing at the top of the steepest part of the hill. He hadn't joined the singing, but was loose enough to join the laughter. He fell over backwards and slid head first on his back all the way down.

"Oh, my God, oh, my God, oh, my God," Abby screamed, and ran/slid down the hill after him, watching him bouncing and flailing,

Uncle Patrick's glove flying off his left hand, sure that she had made a dreadful mistake bringing him there, that he was, indeed, too old for this, that alcohol and snow didn't mix, that she had finally killed him. "Oh, my God, oh, my God, oh, my God!"

Lee finally slid to a stop at the bottom of the hill, just missing the pointed edge of the runner of an overturned sled. He lay still. Abby's heart beat soundly in her ears as she slipped and slid and ran toward him. He wasn't moving. Oh, my God, she thought.

INTERMISSION

(*Do you have enough popcorn, Steve?* **Sure, thanks.** *Do you have to pee? Now is the time.* **No, I'm fine.** *You don't want to have to leave to pee halfway through the second half, you know.* **I'm fine.** *Good.*)

PART II

All eyes were on Lee. It was so quiet you could hear a fin drop. (*You mean "pin"?*) When Abby got to him, he was laying on his back, staring with wide eyes, and didn't seem to be breathing. A large, gray, triangular piece of a shark fell out of the sky and landed near the top of the hill and everyone's attention turned toward that. (*You mean "fin"?* **I didn't want to point it out.** *You worked so hard for that joke, you can point it out if you want.* **Thanks.**) Fin. Dropped. You could hear it.

A sound formed in Lee's throat that could have been a strangled scream, but, once it formed fully and escaped his mouth, revealed itself to be a huge, gleeful laugh.

"That was so cool!" he shouted.

"Are you okay?" Abby, who had fallen to her knees beside him when she had thought he was dead, asked, nervously.

He nodded vigorously, and Abby sat back onto her legs and punched Lee in the arm.

"I thought you were dead," she said.

"Let's do that again," he said, so she hit him again. "No, the sliding down the hill part."

"This time let's do it on a toboggan."

137

They agreed, she helped him up, and they trudged back to the top. When they got there, they noticed Twain gnawing on a triangular piece of gray fish. Lee insisted on sitting in front this time. He wanted to experience the full rush unhindered. He settled into place and impatiently looked back as Abby got into position. The moment her fanny hit the wood, Lee pushed off. Cold wind and large flakes of snow tore at his face and hair, and he put his head back and yelled hosannas at them. He hadn't felt this much energy in his blood since he had been a small child. Abby could feel his body pulsate all the way through his coat and hers, and she liked it. This had been a good idea. She knew there was a wild animal under there somewhere, and she had finally found a way to release it. Her pants tented.

The toboggan bumped and flew over the uneven ground, causing them to become airborne more than once. Every time they did, Lee's stomach wooshed up into his lungs, then back down into his lowest intestine, a beat behind the rest of his body, and turned the glee up another notch. Then the toboggan lurched in a very unexpected way and threw them high into the air in separate but equal directions. They both landed on their backs. Abby's breath was forced out of her by the pressure of her generous form hitting the ground. She forced herself to pull air back in, and did a quick inventory of her parts to make sure everything was still attached in a reasonable way. After the pain of breathing again subsided and she realized everything was assembled correctly, she sat up and looked for Lee. He was lying on his back about twelve and a quarter feet away, just staring at the sky.

"A rock," he said with disgust.

Abby burst out laughing.

"You promised you wouldn't," Lee said, turning his head to her pitifully, which made her laugh more.

Lee felt childhood tears threaten to well up, and his whole body felt like it might also regress, but he forced the tears back with a stern warning to behave themselves and the rest of his body obeyed as well. He tried to sit up like a fully formed mature adult human man would try to do. He realized he couldn't. The tears started threatening again.

"Um," he said. "A little help. My... um... back."

Abby scrambled over to him.

After the ambulance had been called, a couple of husky boys brought Abby's toboggan over to Lee to transfer him up the hill.

"Don't move him," someone shouted. "It's his back."

"He's in the way."

"Oh. Right. Carry on."

They carefully (as carefully as bellies full of various conflicting drinks would allow them to) maneuvered the toboggan under him and gently (as gently as drunk college boys could) pushed him up the hill.

"There's a rope, why don't you pull him?" the same smart ass guy asked.

They didn't even acknowledge him this time. The smart ass. Sheesh.

Peter lumbered up to Lee and offered him a cup of mulled wine.

"Welcome to River Bend," he said in a voice that communicated effectively that he would also have pounded him on the back in a welcoming way had it not, you know, been a back thing. Several other people congratulated him. Some did pat him on the back. Well, sort of the side. He felt included in a way he hadn't since he had been a very small child.

Lee's first thought, after the tenuous jostling up the hill and all the congratulations, and the feeling included, was how the hell could he work at Twain's with a broken back. He mentioned the concern to Abby, who hadn't left his side. Andrew, who was hovering nearby fretting, stopped fretting when he heard that.

"Twain's?" he said. "What about the play?"

"Oh, my God," Lee said. "What about the play?"

(**I have to go pee, now.** *Steve!* **I really have to.** *Okay, we'll all wait for you. Fear no more the heat o' the sun, Nor the furious winter's rages; Thou thy worldly task hast done, Home art gone, and ta'en thy wages...* **I'm back, what are you doing?** *Nothing.* **I leave for one minute and you start typing crap**. *Guns blazing and tanks?* **Okay, you're redeemed.**)

"They can block around you," the guy who played Charlie, the doctor and Candy said. "Probably. If you can move at all."

"I don't want to look like a scene from Lucy," Lee protested, picturing himself slumped over and shuffling across the stage in a painful way. On her it was funny. On him it would just look fucking stupid. (*That's for Steve's mom.* **Geoff, what the fuck's the matter with you?!**)

"Which one?" Peter asked, a small part of him pleased that Lee couldn't toboggan worth a damn. Something Lee couldn't do. Peter would like to collect things Lee couldn't do, especially things he could do, and this would be a good place to start.

"Which one what?" Lee asked peevishly. His back hurt, and he didn't want the focus to drift.

"Which Lucy show?"

"There were only two," Abby said.

"There were at least four," Peter said, chastising himself silently for being even a little glad that Lee had hurt himself. "Would you look like a scene from The Lucy Show or I Love Lucy?"

"Wasn't one called Here's Lucy?" one of the Pigeon sisters asked. "I remember that one, I think."

Lee felt like the moment was getting away from him. He realized through the throbbing in his tail bone that even after getting injured at Beard's Hill, he would never really fit into this bizarre group of people. Ever.

Peter knew he should probably do something to help Lee be more comfortable, but Abby seemed to be handling it all by herself. He drank mulled wine instead.

"Which one was that?" one of the poker-playing guys asked, and wandered toward Twain's table.

"Wasn't that the one with Mr. Mooney?" another poker-playing guy asked, and followed him.

"No, that was where she was called Lucille Carter and her best friend was a countess."

The entire group was moving toward the table and Twain started serving up Sloppy Joes. Lee was quite sure that he would now die, alone, forgotten, in the slush at the top of Beard's Hill with large, lonely snowflakes falling on his face. Peter joined the group, pointedly not looking back at Lee, allowing himself to feel superior for a moment, and really feeling guilty that he wasn't fussing over Lee. But Lee had enough friends. He had to find his own.

"No, that was Life With Lucy," Andrew's wife said. Then she bit into a Sloppy Joe and its filling burst out around the bun and slid down the sides of her chin.

"No, that's the one where her daughter, Lucy, played her daughter, Lucy," Abby said. She was at the table eating nachos, but still kept an eye on Lee, and wondered if she should bring him something to eat.

"Which one did Ethel play in?" one of the husky, drunken college kids who had pushed Lee up the hill asked. He really seemed to want to know.

As Abby watched Mrs. Divine clean the red, lumpy mixture off her chin and coat front, she thought about the logistics of getting food shoveled into a cold, prone, hurting mouth and decided not to bring Lee anything. Peter drank another cider, then poured himself a mulled wine. It steamed in the chilly air.

"She was in I Love Lucy," the kid whose father liked Kiss answered, and wiped nacho cheese from his mouth with the back of his cast. "Duh."

"No, the other one," the other kid said, "the one where Lucy was called Lucy Carmichael. When Ethel played someone who was younger than Ethel was. Duh yourself."

Lee started to moan quietly. Not necessarily because he was in any more pain, he just wanted to keep himself company. Abby felt guilty for leaving him there on the toboggan all alone and moved toward him. She stopped first, of course, to pour herself some wine.

"That was the one with Mr. Mooney," Peter said, then stood tall like he was trying to imitate someone, looking like anyone but Mr. Mooney, and shouted officially, "'Mrs. Carmichael!'"

"He was also in the one in the eighties where everybody was really old and just shouted all their lines," the actor who played Oscar said. "But he wasn't called Mr. Mooney in that one, he was called Mr. Whipple."

"No, that was the theatrical tissue guy," Peter said, and sat hard onto his tractor tire with a sound of a big body hitting inflated rubber. One person laughed, and Peter tried to focus in on who it might be and tried to decided if they were laughing because of his clever comment, in which case they could be the friend or if they were laughing at the sound of his body hitting his tube. In which case they could still be the friend. Then, through the spiced fog in his brain, he looked at Lee on his back on the bitter cold ground and some cider-stained voice kept trying to get his attention. He told it to be quiet, he didn't want to get up and go take care of Lee. He had Abby and didn't need him.

Besides, he thought. I can toboggan. I can do something he can't. That made him like Lee all the more. He took a swig of cider.

"There were five, okay?" Andrew said, a little peeved that they didn't know. They should have known, for God's sake. It was Lucy. "There was I Love Lucy, The Lucy-Desi Comedy Hour, The Lucille Ball Show, Here's Lucy, and Life with Lucy."

"Who are you?" Lee asked, but the effort to talk interrupted his moaning, so he didn't add anything more.

"And Lucy in the sky," Abby said. "With diamonds."

Andrew was quite disgusted with them all, so he walked away and pulled the wineskin of good Scotch from his shoulder, uncapped it and sampled the smooth Johnny Walker Black Label™, which calmed his annoyance. Another sip brought back his native good will. A third made him downright friendly again, so he walked back. Jan and Matt hung back from the group, watching, amazed. I can't wait to be an adult, Matt thought. Who are these geeks, thought Jan.

"Which one had Mr. Drysdale?" Peter asked.

The music from the cars counterpointed the conversation strangely, a raucous soundtrack that made it hard for people to hear each other, so they had to shout.

"The Beverly Hillbillies, you idiot," Andrew said and needed to walk away again.

"I Love Lucy was the longest running one," one of the Pigeon Sisters said.

"If you count The Lucy-Desi Show as part of it," the other Pigeon Sister said, and the first one agreed vehemently and they both hooked arms and danced a small jig of agreement.

Lee wondered what the longest running sitcom of all time was, then realized that even he was beginning to lose focus and resumed his moaning. He was quite satisfied with the thin timber he was able to achieve with a little effort. His ears felt hot in the cold air, and sound seemed filtered as if through pudding. In the background, the bonfire was now a tribal orgy, feeding on its own energy, no longer a needy baby that had to be tended and fed, no longer even a teen that wanted to consume any and everything that entered its space, it was now a dangerous, fascinating warrior that sought out, found, commandeered and destroyed its own fuel like old ladies at a Blue Light Special. Except not quite as dangerous. Or stinky. A small explosion of sparks erupted when it hit a pocket of sap in one of the greener logs that had been used to stoke it.

"Lucy also used to use the name Diane Belmont," Andrew said as he returned. He figured that, if these dolts didn't know about Lucy, he'd just have to edumicate them. He took another swig of Johnny Walker. Yeah. I said edumicate, he thought defiantly, then had to sit down.

"Was that in the one with the annoying neighbor?" Abby asked. She was now sitting on the ground next to Lee, holding his hand, wishing he'd stop moaning for a moment so she could think. "What's her name, Mary Jane?"

"Oh, God, I hated her," Mrs. Divine said. "She was so whiny."

"So was Lucy most of the time," Andrew said, and took another wig of swiskey.

"Yeah, but she was Lucy," the kid whose father liked Kiss said.

"Yeah," they all said, and bowed their heads.

"And then there's Maude," Andrew said. "Or was that Phyllis?"

"Barney Miller with the goo goo googly eyes," his wife answered, and pulled his left thumb.

Peter couldn't stand it any longer. He lurched from his inner tube throne, stumbled over to Lee and fell, just missing falling on top of him.

"I'm so sorry," he said.

"Huh?" Lee responded.

The ambulance drove up at that moment and a previous casualty climbed out and surveyed the throngs. He had huge white bandaging on his face from the top of his mouth to the bottom of his eyes and almost from ear to ear. It gave him an unnatural smile. Or that could have just been the pain killers they had given him mixing with the schnaps. Pete stumbled out of the driver's seat with an empty cup in his hand and staggered over to the table to refresh it. Lee watched him and remembered that he didn't want to look like a scene from Lucy, but thought better of bringing it up again. Abby climbed into the back of the ambulance with him. She still had a cup of the warm spiced wine.

Someone with a huge truck pulled up and parked. It was, really, more a stereo on wheels, and it singlehandedly tripled the intensity of the sound. The fire liked that.

After Lee was saluted off on his journey to the hospital, Peter decided to have another go at the hill. That would get his mind off himself. And Lee. And cider. And friends. He dragged the inner tube to the edge, took a dainty sip of wine, sat down and pushed off. Halfway down he felt guilty again that he hadn't paid more attention to Lee in his hour of pain. That was so unlike him. He tried to be defiant about it. By the time he got to the bottom, his conveyance conveniently turned toward the hill, he looked up to where he had been, going over and over in his mind what he should have done for Lee. At that very moment, a familiar looking form appeared at the top of the hill, looking young and handsome against the fire-colored sky. The song that was playing on all the radios, incongruously, was Clap for the Wolfman.

"Jim," Peter said softly to himself. His chest constricted a little, and he was about to climb out of the tube to go up to the top of the hill to see if Jim was okay. He had been so sad and lost looking the other night. Maybe he could be my friend, Peter thought. If I can stop being attracted to him. And he can start thinking about someone else besides himself. And grow up a little. And never ask to bunk together again. And stopped smelling so good. Yes. He is my friend. He leaned forward to exit his tube.

Then a bundled up woman approached Jim and handed him a beverage. From the distance, they seemed to be looking longingly into each other's eyes. Oh, my God, Peter thought, and stopped abruptly, then sunk back down. He sure rebounded quickly, Agnes just dumped him a couple of days ago. What an empty, stupid man. Of course, children recover quickly. In high school, you get dumped one day and are already dating the next. Depending on what school you go to. And your complexion. That's not fair, though, Peter thought. One, Jim is in his twenties, and two, maybe I had something to do with his recovery. I am a good caretaker, after all. It's what I do. Go with your strengths. Look at exhibit A. A man recovered. I wonder who this next one is. She was too far away, and turned a little too much for him to be able to tell, but she did seem young and shapely under her winter things. She seemed carefree, like a schoolgirl. Good for him. I can understand that. What the hell. Life is good.

The woman threw back her head and laughed. Then, in slow motion, she flipped her hair. Strand after strand gleefully followed the last in chorus-line precision. Peter's inner tube deflated and his heart simply stopped beating and he felt like he had just been stabbed with an icicle.

"Stella!" he shouted.

Will Peter ever find a friend?
Will he get over Jim and Stella?
Will he get over Jim and Agnes?
Did Lee break his back?
Will he look like Lucy in The Odd Couple?
Was Lucy in The Odd Couple?
Will the tree still be there next year?
Is Abby pregnant?
Will Matt like being an adult?
Will Twain?
Is this our longest installment?
Is it now?
What IS the longest running sitcom of all time?
What is the definition of "Is"?
Is this our longest installment now?
Is a house a home?
Isadora Duncan?

To find the answers to these and other trivial interrogatories,
tune into our next installment:
"Revolution No. 10"
(*We already have two Beatles references, Steve.*)
"With a Little Whelp from My Friends"
(**Notice how I got President Polk in there?** *Yes, very sly.* **Thank you.** *That wasn't a compliment.*)

This installment first published July 27, 2003

Geoff Hoff and Steve Mancini

Previously in Weeping Willow: While zooming down a snowy hill with his girlfriend Abby, Lee Harris encountered a rock and may have broken his back. While drinking high-falutin' hot alcoholic beverages and looking for a friend (but not THAT kind of friend) Peter sees Jim, who has tried to be gay and tried to keep a sixty year old woman satisfied, and Stella, who works in the Willow Lane Theater front office with Peter and competes with him on all fronts, together, and is shocked and upset by it. Andrew, who likes Lucille Ball but finds her annoying and is Lee's lawyer in the matter of his divorce from Beverly who is living with the Jerk in Chicago, has convinced Lee to accept the offer that was made on the house. The house Lee is now renting is probably haunted, (but not by Patrick Swayze, Hamlet Sr. or Wendy) and is inhabited by a stupid, yellow bird, which is worse. And Twain uses canned Sloppy Joe® mix. All of this is relevant. Really. Except the part about Sloppy Joe Cocker®. Read the previous installments. Then read this.

Installment Twenty-One
"With a Little Whelp from My Friends"

Peter threw back his head and shouted, "Stella!"

Just then, something very small attached to something very big hit the left side of his jaw and he was knocked soundly sideways and spun twice in lopsided circles on the snow, then slid slowly to a stop as a large woman scrambled over to him, screaming.

"I'm sorry, I'm sorry, are you okay? I'm so sorry. God, I'm so sorry. Are you okay? Oh, Peter, are you okay?"

Peter shook his head a little, then rubbed the place where her galosh had contacted his face. He was sure she had knocked a couple of fillings loose. He could taste mercury. Or was that blood? Yes, salty iron. Blood. He felt around the inside of his mouth with his

147

tongue to make sure all the teeth were still attached. They were, but there was a knot on the left side of the tongue that was probably the source of the taste. At least the blow had knocked the thought of Jim and Stella out of his head.

"Ahhhh!" he said in anguish.

"Oh, my God," the woman said. "Did I break your jaw? Do you need me to call an ambulance?"

"No," he said and shook his head to punctuate the answer. "It's just Jim."

Peter sat up, carefully avoiding looking up at the top of the hill in case They were still there. Roz sat in the snow next to him and held his back while he finished examining his face with his hand to make sure nothing was broken.

"Damn, Roz, didn't you see me sitting there?"

"Of course I saw you. How could I miss that big head of yours? I couldn't change course. I yelled at you, didn't you hear me?"

"Obviously not," Peter said. His head was slowing down a bit, but the throbbing in his jaw was increasing. He'd have a big bump there in the morning. And his headache would be more than just a hangover headache.

"If you don't want an ambulance at least let me take you home."

Peter tried to stand, and finally managed with Roz's help. When he bent over to pick up his inner tube his head started to spin again, so he froze in a very funny looking half bow. Roz laughed, made him straighten up and picked up the tube for him. The trip up the hill was a scene from a Max Sennett movie. Roz held Peter's tube under one arm and steadied Peter with the other and they slid back several feet several times. Twice Peter landed forward on all fours, and at least three times Roz landed on Peter's tube and had to climb back up to where he was to help him. When they finally got to the top, Roz made him sit in the tube, then went back for her inner tube, which, it seemed, was the snow conveyance of choice for robust people. (**Conveyance, Geoff**? *Sure. You hadn't interrupted yet, so I figured I'd force the issue.* **Actually, I liked it.** *Then why did you question it?* **Because I hadn't interrupted, yet.** *Anyway, it's a legitimate English word. I use the whole English language.* **Use "ergo". Can't fail with ergo: Ergo, I was walking down the street, when, ergo, a car sped by. "Ergo," I said.** *Thanks, Steve. We'll use my word.* **Ermine**? *No, Steve.*) She struggled up the hill with her tube, and plopped down by Peter, winded. No one had offered to help.

"Guys need any help?" one of the college students asked, then swayed dangerously and was escorted away by his friends.

"I haven't seen you since you stood me up for lunch, and you kick me in the face?" Peter said. His words were a little slurred and he wasn't sure if that was generated by alcohol or boot.

"Are you still mad at me for that?" Roz asked.

"No, no," Peter said. "I have so many other things to be mad at."

"I was really sick," she said. "I ate a bad blintz."

Peter laughed, then grabbed his jaw and Roz suggested that she should take him home.

"What about my car?" he asked.

She said they could come back for it the next day.

"What about my urns?" he asked.

She said they could put them in the car before they left.

"They're not empty, yet," he said, and she threatened to kick him in the other jaw.

Fifty-seven minutes later she pulled into his driveway. (**I wonder who had the very first driveway.** *Caesar.* **He had a Ford Probe.** *Now that's just stupid.* **That sounds like Jack Benny.** *Thanks.*)

"Your place is really messy," Roz said when Peter opened his front door.

"Sorry," he said.

She smiled and shrugged. Peter pushed some magazines from the couch and offered her a blintz.

"No," she said. "I'm taking care of you, here."

"Oh," he said, and sat down, not sure how to react to that. It wasn't something that happened often. Not since that night when he'd seen Last Tango in Paris.

"What did you mean when you said 'Jim' after I kicked you in the face?"

"Oh," Peter said. "That."

He really didn't want to go into all that with her. He didn't want to go into all that with anyone. Maybe Lee, but Lee was entwined. Peter's eyes started to tear up.

"What's wrong, Peter?" Roz said, and when he just shook his head, added, "It's okay. How bad can it be? What, did you kill someone?"

He laughed.

"No, I didn't kill anyone," he said. "I just slept with him."

He really hadn't planned on saying that at all, and covered his mouth with his hand. The pain in his jaw completely disappeared and his entire body felt flushed and he tried to figure out a way to take it back, which made his eyes tear up more. Roz pulled him to her and held him, stroking his back, and he was really surprised when he started to cry really hard. She rocked him a little and held him tightly and patted him and smoothed his hair and let him cry without saying anything. He was really embarrassed. Then his nose started to run and he pulled away from her and started laughing and looking for a tissue. The box he'd brought out for Jim the other night was still on the coffee table and Roz pulled several out and handed them to him.

"Thanks," he said, then, after robustly blowing his nose, added, "sorry."

"There's nothing to be sorry about," Roz said. "Who's Jim?"

Peter sighed deeply. He really didn't know how to cry on someone's shoulder. It was entirely the wrong perspective. He didn't know where to start. If he'd been sitting where she was, he'd know exactly what to ask and what to say and what to do and what meal to cook, but nothing was familiar from this vantage point. He decided to just tell her the whole story about Jim. Which, of course, meant telling her the whole story about Lee because of the whole "Jim came to town to find Lee" thing. He had only ever really talked to Lee about Jim and had never talked to anyone about Lee. Not even Stella, although she probably knew how he felt about him. Damn her. Once he started talking, it all kind of came out without any conscious thought or decision on his part. So this is what having a shoulder to cry on felt like. When he got to the part where Jim stayed the night on his couch, then turned up two nights later at Beard's Hill with Stella, of all people, he sputtered to a stop. Then he felt really embarrassed again.

"So," he said. "I'm gay."

"I kind of guessed," she said.

"When?"

"When you told me you slept with Jim, stupid."

"You mean you didn't know all along?"

"How would I know?"

"I don't know."

"I mean, you don't dress like Paul Lynde."

"Paul Lynde was gay?"

"Come on, Peter."

"Well? Did he ever say it?"

"Not to me, but come on."

"So," Peter said. "You don't mind?"

"Why should I mind? We're not sleeping together."

Roz took his hands and looked at him.

"You okay?"

He nodded and thanked her.

"So," she said. "I've always been curious. What don't you like about women?"

Peter had to think about this.

"It's not what I don't like about women," he said finally. "It's more what I do like about men."

"Have you ever been with a woman?"

Peter shook his head.

"I haven't even been with very many men," he said. "I have been curious, of course."

"Really?"

He shrugged. He was really embarrassed, but it felt good to talk about it.

"Sure. But it would have to be the perfect woman and the perfect circumstances."

When she asked what those circumstances would be he said he hadn't ever thought that far, then considered it for a moment.

"I don't know. What are the qualifications for a perfect man?"

"Turgid."

He laughed, then really tried to answer her question honestly.

"I guess she'd have to be really kind and patient. She'd really have to have a sense of humor, obviously. I mean look at me. Intelligent would help, so we could talk after. But not too much. No psychologist, I'm already scarred enough."

They both laughed, and he continued to describe the perfect trial woman. Roz started looking at him funny. She really liked what he

151

was saying. He was describing her perfect man. Actually, with his vulnerability and honesty, he was her perfect man. Except that what he really wanted was the perfect man. He continued talking until he saw the look in her eyes and slowed down, then stopped. They just looked at each other for a very long time.

"Oh," Peter said.

Roz took his hand.

"And... And... She... I... She'd... Um."

Roz leaned in toward him. At first he pulled away, startled, then realized what she was doing and leaned toward her. It took a moment for them to figure out how to position their faces, but they finally kissed. It didn't last long, and when Peter sat back, his head was spinning. Not because it had been a great kiss, but because he had never expected to find himself on his couch late on a Friday night kissing a woman.

"How was that?" Roz asked sheepishly. Peter hadn't imagined Roz could ever sound sheepish.

"Fine," he said and looked at her. "Um. Now, what?"

"I don't know," she said. "Can we go someplace where there's a little more room. I mean, neither of us are a size five."

"You mean like the bedroom?"

She nodded.

"Really?"

She nodded again and stood. He reluctantly stood and she followed him into his bedroom.

"This is even messier," she said, and they stood by the bed looking at each other, not sure what to do.

Cliche, who had been sleeping on the small pile of old tee shirts and socks on the bed, awoke, looked at them, shook his head sadly and left to finish his sleep on the couch. He hated it when Peter drank. You never knew what he might drag in.

"Should we..." Peter said. "Um. Undress or something?"

Roz laughed, unfastened his overall straps, then unbuttoned and removed his flannel shirt. He raised his arms and she took his tee-shirt off, then put her arms out so he could take her blouse off. He very carefully unbuttoned it, pulling at the fabric so he didn't accidentally touch her, and she started to laugh.

"What?"

"You can touch me, Peter," she said.

He laughed, then relaxed a little and got her blouse unbuttoned. They carefully removed the rest of their clothing, then stood looking at each other. (**This is starting to remind me of 9½ Weeks.** *Really, Steve?* **No. Isn't that the movie where the big truck chases the little car?** *Sure, Steve.* **Film school. This scene is what gives Weeping Willow an R rating.** *Have you been to a movie in the last fifteen years, Steve?* **I saw Badlands last night.** *Good. Now shut up.*)

"What do you think?" Roz asked, and Peter started laughing. "Oh, thanks."

"No. Sorry," Peter said. "I just never could figure out why everyone was so interested in those."

"These?" Roz asked, shaking them a little.

"Yeah. I thought it might be different if I saw one live." He studied them a little longer, then laughed again. "I mean, they always just seemed like mounds of fat to me."

"Yeah," she said, "but what fun mounds."

They laughed and fell into the bed together.

Lee was acting insufferably silly, and Abby was having a hard time maneuvering him into his bed. It would have been difficult even if he hadn't been hopped up on booze and pain killers, what with the fractured coccyx and all, but silliness really got in the way. She carefully led him to the edge of the bed, made him carefully lean down to the right butt cheek and roll onto the bed.

"Weeee," he said. "Let's do that again."

"Last time you said that," Abby said as she unbuckled his belt, "you fractured your coccyx."

As she undid his shoes and pulled off his socks, Lee started singing Misty.

"Kitten," he sang loudly. "Up a tree!"

Abby carefully pulled at his pant legs to remove his trousers.

"Come on," Lee said. "Sing with me. Ladies in the back do harmony. Men on the right, bop bop. Come on, I get Misty..."

Abby shook her head and covered him with the blankets and folded the pants.

"You're no fun."

"I'm not on painkillers."

"Want some?"

Abby considered it. Twice. Then she turned the light off instead and went out to sit in the living room. Every now and then, a small phrase from some song floated out of the bedroom, each getting less and less recognizable as music, until the last one became a light snore.

"And I had condoms and everything," Abby said to herself, then chuckled. "Well, I guess it is sort of my fault. I guess. Fractured his coccyx. The dope."

Still chuckling, she got a beer from the refrigerator then settled back down on the couch. She wasn't the least bit tired. She occupied herself for a little while looking around the room. That got boring really fast, and she considered turning on the TV. She reached for the remote and heard a little noise.

"Lee?" she asked.

It was quiet. She got up and looked into the bedroom. Lee was sleeping soundly, snoring lightly, drooling softly, a strange grin on his face. She left the door open a little so she could hear him and went back to the couch and turned on the television. There was some soap opera on about an accountant from Chicago who went to a small town to join a theatre troupe but that seemed just too trite. She flipped past all the white snow channels. The only other show that was on was a documentary about Jakarta, Indonesia. She settled in to watch that. She really enjoyed it, but that has nothing to do with this story.

Then she heard the noise again. It was a little louder and sounded like something scratching at the door. She froze in place and listened really hard. Of course, when you listen that hard, the only thing you can hear is your own heartbeat and your teeth grinding against each other. And your joints crackle. And a tree falling in the woods. She forced herself to relax, told herself not to be stupid, and reached for the remote again to turn down the television. This time, the scratch was joined by a small whimpering that could have been a baby crying. Or it could have been a bear. Or it could have been a cougar. Or it could have been a badger... (*Steve, I have your mom on the phone. She said* *"Fuck."* **She did not. She never has. She never would.** *I just needed you to stop.* **It worked.** *Good. Could have been an ermine.* **Hey!**)

Very slowly, Abby put the remote control down on the couch cushion, then sat very still. The flickering glow from the now quiet television was very disquieting, but turning it off would involve movement, which didn't seem possible right now. The scratch came again, and this time it sounded like it came from the kitchen.

"That's not funny, Lee," she said, hoarsely, but Lee was busy dreaming about typing through a square of correction paper on an old Smith Corona manual typewriter that didn't have any ribbon, while Jimmy Hendrix was in the background playing Misty on a tuba naked while eating Space Food Sticks, so he wasn't any help at all. Those painkillers were good.

Maybe it was the bird.

"Bird?" she said and looked around for it. It was in its cage, near the television, perched on its little perch, just staring at her stupidly. It still had no expression on its stupid little yellow face. She was beginning to understand why Lee hated the thing so much. The kitchen scratched again. The bird hadn't moved.

She forced herself to stand, then stood for a very long time between the couch and the coffee table. When there was no sound for a long time, she started to move out from behind the table just as another scratching sound bounced out of the kitchen. She grabbed the nearest item from the table and froze. Then she forced herself to step one step toward the sound, her entire brain shouting "Don't Go Into the Woods" and "Get Out of the House, Now!" and "Follow the Yellow Brick Road." The step she took made the floor creak and she shrieked, then laughed a weak laugh, then she noticed what she had picked up. It was a roll of paper towels. It had little roses and ivy on the edges. It was double ply. (**Wait, Lee's gay?** *No, Steve, it was on sale. He's an accountant.* **Oh. Okay. Come on, let's go.**)

"What the hell are you going to do with that, smarty?" Abby said to the room. "Wipe them out?"

She started to laugh out loud at that and a whimpering joined her. The jolt that ran up her spine propelled her forward. She dropped the paper towels, roses and all, sprinted to the bedroom and climbed into bed next to Lee. She clung to his back. His completely relaxed, limp body was an extreme contrast to her rigid, shivering one.

"Lee?" she said quietly, hoping her shriek or laughter had roused him. "Lee?"

She prodded him in the back softly, just to make sure. Then she took out a chainsaw and cut off his left arm. No, he was sound asleep.

(*Steve?* **Yes.** *You know she doesn't have a chainsaw there in the bedroom, don't you?* **It's Lee's house. Mr. Tool Guy.** *No chainsaw, Steve.* **An ermine?**) She realized Lee wasn't going to save her from whatever was lurking in the kitchen, but at least she wouldn't die alone. The stupid bird cheeped once, stupidly, and Abby buried her face into Lee's back.

The covers from Peter's bed were in a tangle on the floor, the pillows were soaked and he and Roz were on the floor beside the bed, breathing hard and laughing.

"I'm sorry," Peter said through his laughter.

"About what? That was the most fun I've ever had having sex."

"Technically, we didn't have sex," Peter reminded her.

"Then that was the most fun I've ever had not having sex," she said.

Peter laughed then pushed himself up and stood.

"Hungry?"

"Sure, I could use a snack," she said, and she stood, picked up the tangled blanket and brought it into the living room.

She could hear Peter rattling around in the kitchen, so she put the blanket on the couch and started looking through his video collection. Cliche got off the couch and stumbled back into the bedroom to finish his sleep.

"Wanna watch a movie?" she shouted into the kitchen.

"Anything but The Dresser, I just watched it on Thursday." (*He could watch The Dresser every day for the rest of his life, Steve.* **Then he's as stupid as you are.** *As sophisticated. As erudite. As subtle.* **Like I said, stupid.** *Eventually, you're going to watch that movie.* **I'll watch it when you die. Come on, let's go.**)

On the coffee table there was a plate with bread and chip crumbs, a couple of small, dried pieces of Colby, a small dollop of old, translucent horseradish mayonnaise with a hint of Dijon mustard, two desiccated, half-eaten pickle spears, a stale chip and a used square of paper towel and a glass with what looked like dried beer suds on its side. Roz picked them up and brought them into the kitchen.

Peter was sauteing something in a small pan and the kitchen smelled seductively of browned butter.

"What's that?" Roz asked as she washed the dishes she'd brought in. "I thought you were just making a snack."

"It is a snack."

"What is it?"

"You'll see," Peter said as Roz put the plate and glass in the drainboard. "Now get out of my kitchen and go pick a movie."

"How about Texas Chainsaw Massacre?" She called into the kitchen when she got back to the video collection. (*I said no chainsaws, Steve.* **That was at Lee's.** *No chainsaws anywhere.* **How about A Yank in Ermine?** *That's not really a movie, is it?* **Sure, 1955, Peter M. Thompson, Noelle Middleton, Harold Lloyd Jr. Directed by Gordon Parry. An American guy finds out he's really an earl.** *Wow, I'm impressed.* **Film school.**)

"Part one or two?" Peter asked.

"Very good," Roz laughed, then started screaming. "Hey, hey, hey!"

Peter ran out, frightened, holding a spatula dripping with egg goo, and asked what was wrong.

"You have the Ealing comedies!" she shouted. "All four of them! Alec Guinness is God!"

"The Ealing Studios made more than four comedies," Peter said.

"Not with Alec Guinness in them, you pompous idiot. There's only four of those and they're all that count. And you have them all. And you have egg dripping down your arm."

Peter stopped the flow of dripping goo with his other hand.

"Which one do you want to watch, first?" she asked. "How's your head?"

"My head's fine. Jaw still hurts a little. Wait, first? Oh, my God, you're insane. I don't think even I could sit through four movies in one sitting. Let's start with The Lady Killers and see how we feel after that."

"I just saw that a couple of months ago. It's the only one they play on TV. Let's do that second. How about The Man in the White Suit? Bubble bubble pop squirt. I love that."

"My favorite is The Lavender Hill Mob..." he said. The egg goo was escaping past his hand and trickling off his elbow onto his naked belly.

"Okay, that's good," she said, and pulled a tissue from the box Peter had brought out for Jim and she had used for him earlier that night and wiped the goo off his abdomen, leaving a small trail of tissue encrusted yolk behind in the sparse, course hair.

"... so I watch that a lot," Peter continued, ignoring her. "I haven't seen Kind Hearts and Coronets in forever." (**Okay, Geoff, did you get all four in?** *Yes.* **You sure? You don't want to miss any.** *Yes, they're all there.* **You know it's obvious you're just trying to impress everyone, now, don't you?** *No, I'm not.* **Yes, you are.** *Okay, I am. But they're the Ealing/Alec Guinness comedies.* **Then why don't you own them?** *I have The Dresser.*)

Peter finished cooking and brought in the plates. Omelets with sauteed mushrooms, onions, bell pepper, grated carrots and shallots with melted Camembert, garnished with twisted orange slices, and Texas toast that he had grilled in a pan. He went back in a got the glasses filled with freshly-squeezed orange juice with the pips filtered out.

"Wow," she said.

Peter sat on the couch next to her and they covered their nakedness with the blanket. He picked up the remote and turned on the VCR. The Lady Killers started playing.

"I thought you'd just seen this," he said.

"Oh. My. God!" Roz interrupted around a mouthful of omelet, then chased it with a bite of toast. "This is incredible. You just whipped this up?"

He nodded, pleased.

"Just now," she said. "As a snack."

He nodded again.

"At my place you'd be lucky to get corn flakes."

"Thank God we're not at your place," he said with an impish grin, then added, "of course, I like corn flakes."

She was obviously very impressed with his food, which was the one thing that gave Peter the most pleasure. Certainly more than what they had just tried to do in the other room.

"I beat the eggs and a drop of water with a fork in a cold bowl, then pour it into the browned butter and pull it away from the center of the pan with the fork. Don't stir them. They flatten if you stir. They fluff if you pull."

"I've heard that. Oh, you mean the eggs. I usually just eat left over deli food from work," she said and took another sublime bite. "I'm moving in."

"Deli food is good, too," Peter said, beaming. He tasted his omelet and winced a little. "It isn't as tasty with a half-bitten off tongue, though."

"Ooh," Roz said with an empathetic wince. "Sorry about that."

He waved her off, then looked at her with a strange expression on his face. She felt the stare and looked back at him, questioningly. He just shook his head and laughed a little.

"What's funny?"

"Nothing," he said. "It's just I tried so hard to find a friend and when I gave up one kicked me in the face."

He rubbed his jaw. It was swollen into a nice knot and still hurt. And his head buzzed slightly from booze and concussion and lack of sleep.

"It's fate, I guess," Roz said and brushed some toast crumbs from his beard.

"I don't believe in fate," he said.

"I believe you make your own fate," she said around some sauteed vegetables and a long string of cheese that still went all the way to her plate.

"Then it's not fate, is it?" he said and brushed the crumb she had brushed off his beard off her breast, then broke her cheese string.

"Shut up and watch the movie," she said.

They snuggled in and watch the little old lady show Alec Guinness the room she had for let. Cliche, resigned to his fate, unable to sleep with all the coziness going on in the house, came back in to the living room, jumped up onto the couch, curled up on the blanket between them and watched them eat, wondering once again how they could stomach that horrid stuff that guy made.

Somehow, Abby must have managed to fall asleep, because she found herself waking up when sunlight shown into the room. She stayed in bed curled up next to Lee for a while, but got really bored with that. He was still snoring lightly. Probably dreaming about Jimi Hendrix, the dope. The house didn't seem nearly as threatening in the daylight, and Lee seemed to be knocked out for a while, so she decided to get up. She couldn't just leave Lee there to fend for himself if and when he finally woke up, so she started puttering. That got old very quickly, so she decided to make breakfast. (**Why don't we say she decided to make porridge and have her make porridge?** *Why, Steve?* **Because it's a legitimate English word.** *Okay, I take it back.* **Did you know that porridge was really oatmeal?** *Yes, Steve.* **So, my question is, why don't they just call it oatmeal?** *Because they're English.* **Oh. Hey, I picked up a dead dog today. It peed on me.** *I don't even want to know.*)

She decided to make pancakes. Of course, Lee didn't have any pancake mix. He had flour, but he didn't have eggs and milk so she could make her own pancake mix. Oh, yeah, and he didn't have syrup. Or butter. (**How thick can you make a pancake before its just a cake?** *Steve?* **Yes?** *I don't know. I just don't know. I don't know. Really. And I don't care. Just stop interrupting. You're interrupting way too much. You drink way too much coffee, and all you do is interrupt. All the time. Stop it. Go away. Go home. Have some coffee. It's just too much. Art is knowing when to stop. Stop. Now.* **Geoff?** *Yes?* **You okay?** *Yeah, why?* **Then come on, let's go. Sheesh. Where's Twain?**)

Abby realized Lee would probably sleep long enough for her to run to the store to pick up some provisions. When she returned, Lee was sitting on the edge of the bed, moaning.

The sun was just beginning to come up when the second movie finished. Roz wanted to watch a third movie, but they had been up all night, and had had too much booze before they even started watching movies, and had eaten too much breakfast during the movies, and had expended a lot of energy not having sex, and they couldn't keep their eyes open anymore, so Peter and Roz had just picked up the blanket and stumbled off to snuggle up in bed to sleep.

When Peter's eyes fluttered open in the sun lit room, he glanced at the clock. It was already after one. He could feel Roz snuggled up against his back. It felt good, warm in the chilly room. He carefully turned over and faced her. She didn't wake, but stirred a little, then settled back into place. He looked at her; her round face was nice, her complexion bespoke a bad adolescence which made Peter smile. She looked like a dumpling. Her hair, shoulder-length and slightly wavy, fell across her eyes and was spread out behind her on the pillow. Her eyes opened and she focused, then smiled.

"Morning," she said.

"Afternoon," he said.

She laughed, then snuggled in closer.

"It's chilly," she said, and he nodded. "How's your jaw?"

He rubbed his cheek. The knot was still there, but it didn't hurt as much. She reached out and touched it. He instinctively recoiled a little and she pulled back.

"Sorry," she said.

"No, I'm just being a weinie," he said, and put his arms back around her.

She leaned in and kissed him. He was surprised by his reaction.

"Rosalind," he said.

Downtown, someone got McDonald's™ fries that were hot and fresh. Uptown, a DMV clerk was nice to an ordinary citizen. At the grocery store, a young miscreant with a full cart let an old lady with only one item and a coupon and a check go in front of him at a check out counter. At the cinema, no one talked during the movie. Somewhere out there, a credit card company lowered a customer's interest rate and a telemarketer took someone off their list. There was no line at Space Mountain. A train went through a tunnel, the Eiffel tower still stood, and Peter and Roz did it.

Abby got a glass of water and gave Lee his pills. He'd woken up crabby and didn't get any better when the pills hit. She helped him dress and maneuvered him to the couch, then went in to make breakfast. Actually, by then it was a late lunch, and Lee complained about eating pancakes in the afternoon. Abby threatened to break his other coccyx and he shut up and ate. The stupid little yellow bird chose that moment to break his silence and cheeped one pitiful cheep.

"Shut up, Charlie," Lee said.

"Charlie?"

"I named it Charlie yesterday to see if that made me like it any better."

Abby laughed. "Did it help?"

Lee was too grumpy to even answer. When she cleared the dishes, he stood, stumbled, then painfully followed her into the kitchen. When he got there, he had to lean against the wall, and realized following her into the kitchen had been a very bad idea and that he should have just stayed on the couch. Actually, he should have just stayed on the couch the night before and continued listening to Andrew telling him he had made the right decision to sell the house and spin a stupid tale about hauntings.

"God damn it," he shouted.

"What?" Abby said, startled, concerned.

Lee pointed to the bottom of the door to the cellar, which he had been absent-mindedly staring at because that's the direction his head was pointed while he was leaning against the wall, wishing he had just stayed in bed. Actually, he wished he'd just stayed in Chicago and let his wife have her stupid little affair. At least then he wouldn't be leaning against a wall in this stupid town, in pain from breaking his back while participating in one of the stupid rituals of this stupid town, pointing at the bottom of his door in his stupid house.

"I just fixed that door. Again. For the hundredth time."

The paint at the bottom of the door was covered with deep, fresh scratches, as if some animal had been trying to get it open to go downstairs.

Abby's back tingled, and her head tried to split open from the ears back. She leaned against the counter so she didn't fall and break her own coccyx.

"What did you say?"

"I said I just fixed..."

"I heard you."

"Then why the fuck did you ask me what I said?"

As Abby gathered him up and helped him back to the couch, she told him about the noises she had heard the night before, the noises that sounded like something scratching. In the kitchen. In the dark.

"And don't bite my fucking head off," she added.

"Sorry. I'm in pain. I broke my back."

"You fractured your coccyx, you dope," Abby said, laughing.

"Well, it hurts," Lee said, glumly. "Leave me alone. Okay, so I have mice."

"Those are not mice scratches," Abby said. "If you have mice that big, I'm sure we would have seen more evidence of them than scratches on a door. And I'd never stay over again."

"It's probably that stupid dog," Lee said, even more glumly, and with a touch of sarcasm.

"What stupid dog?"

Lee told her about Andrew's dangerous obsession with his house being haunted, and how the girl who had lived there and used the basement as a bedroom had a dog named Lombard or Gable or something and how she had died in Korea or Viet Nam or somewhere in some war and how the house is haunted but no one had died there. Ever. Which in itself was weird.

"It's probably Gable trying to find his owner," Abby said. "She dies in a foreign country, and the dog dies of grief and haunts the house."

"Come on, Abby, You don't believe that shit, do you?"

Abby started to tell him it was just too weird that she'd heard noises and the scratches that kept coming back and the whole story Andrew told him and everything, when he shouted, "Shit!" again.

"What?" Abby asked, again concerned, but wary this time.

"I'm supposed to be at the diner. Twain'll kill me. What time is it?"

Abby patted him on the knee and called the diner. Twain told her that he'd called Matt in first thing in the morning, and that he would have called to make sure Lee was okay, but didn't want to wake him. He also asked if he'd broken his back, or just fractured his coccyx. **(Come on, Geoff, how the hell would Twain figure that out?** *I don't know.* **You just like typing coccyx, don't you?** *No. Okay, yes.* **Okay, you can type it once more.)** Coccyx. **(Happy?** *Yes. Thanks.* **You're welcome.)**

Then Lee sat forward and was about to shout "Shit" again, but the movement hurt too much and he just winced loudly.

"Now what?" Abby asked, not even a little willing to be concerned. Even with the wince going on over there on Lee's face.

"What about the play?"

"That again," Abby said. "You don't have rehearsal until Monday. If you're still out of commission, they'll have to cope."

"What do you mean, cope? I'm in the cast! They need me!"

"They need you?"

"The show must go on!"

"And a penny saved is a penny earned," Abby said, hoping against all odds that Lee wasn't really serious.

"I'm serious, Abby," Lee said seriously.

"Lee," Abby said, "it's a little part in a community theatre production of a Neil Simon play in fucking River Bend. They can get someone else to do it. Get over yourself."

"Get over myself?" Lee shouted. "I have a hundred and three lines!"

Abby had never seen Lee's cheeks puff out like that and it made her laugh, which made Lee's cheeks puff even more.

"Yes, darling," she said through the giggles. "Get over yourself. This isn't Broadway. And even if it were, they'd still have to cope if you'd broken your back."

"I didn't break my back," Lee said. "You're just jealous."

That made Abby really laugh.

"Jealous? Of what? That you have a hundred and three lines in a play that's been done a million times before?"

"You're jealous because you can't act and I can."

Now, that made her mad. But she realized this was coming from a man who was in pain, so she decided not to let him have it right then. As soon as his back got better, though, she was going to break both his legs.

"Lee," she said with as much control as a part Jamaican, Norwegian, Irish, Maltese, Chippewa, Italian, Persian, French, Arab and German woman could muster, "I have absolutely zero interest in being in a stupid play. Zero."

"Oh, so now it's a stupid play?" Lee said. His cheeks were still puffing, but now Abby found it more annoying than funny.

"No, the play isn't stupid, Lee," she said, giving up any pretense of control. "You are."

"Okay, if I'm being stupid, just leave me alone." Shouting felt good, even if it did make his backside throb. "Go away."

"I will, you know."

"Good!" He winced again, but tried to hide it from her. "I can take care of my self."

"Yeah, you're doing a really good job of it."

"I wouldn't even need any help if you hadn't dragged me to that fucking hill."

"Okay, fine," Abby said as she stood and got her coat and purse. "It's my fault."

She put on the coat and flung the front door open.

"Asshole," she said, and slammed the door behind herself.

Charlie didn't cheep, but looked like he might be smiling. Lee sat fuming, then realized he was in a lot of pain, which made him burn. And he didn't know where the pills were, which made him want to explode. He was seething at Abby, and he was bristling at Andrew, and he was simmering at Beverly and the Jerk and he was smoldering at the stupid bird and he was churning at the ghost dog and he was inflamed at himself. He was just angry. And now he had to go pee. While he was trying to decide how to stand without causing more pain, he realized he had to sneeze. Oh, no. He had to sneeze.

"Abby!"

Will Lee sneeze?
Will it hurt?
Will it make him pee?
Will he get over himself?
Will he get over his coccyx?
Will Steve let Geoff type "coccyx" again?
Will Abby forgive Lee?
Will he forgive her?
Will Charlie?
Will Ferrell?
Wilson Picket?
Woodrow Wilson?
Is the play doomed?
Is the house haunted by a dog?
Is Peter turning over a new leaf?
Is Cliche turning over in his sleep?
Is Roz turning over the keys to the deli counter?
Is anyone going to eat that apple turnover?

To find the answers to these and other pugnacious perturbations,
tune into our next installment:
"Vinnie the Pooh and the Blustery Gay"

Geoff Hoff and Steve Mancini

or
"Cents and Sensibility"
(We're not Bullwinkle, Steve, we only need one title.)
"My Back's in the Saddle Again"?
(Much better.)

This installment first published September 21, 2003

What's gone before: Lee Harris fractured his coccyx after bumping a rock and got good drugs. Peter bruised his jaw after being bumped into by Roz and got good company. Charlie the bird, who used to just be called "Bird", shows no sign of hearing Gable the dog, who used to just be the noises haunting Lee's house. Abby and Lee had an unexpected tiff about acting when Lee's grumpiness at being an invalid got to be just too much to bear. And Abby might be pregnant. Peter and Roz had an unexpected romp when they woke up naked together after watching too many hours of Sir Alec Guinness. And Peter is gay. Bear didn't get hurt when he knocked headlong into several sledders, didn't have a tiff with anyone or a romp with anyone, isn't pregnant or gay, but likes tools. Stella likes Jim, Matt likes Jan, Agnes likes Headline, and Twain likes strange poetry. To catch up on all you would miss by starting with this installment, read the previous installments. Start with One. Go all the way through until you're back here. Then read this. We double dog dare you.

Installment Twenty-Two
"Cents and Sensibility"
(*I thought we agreed on "My Back's in the Saddle Again".*)
"Vinnie the Pooh and the Blustery Gay"
(*Much better.*)

Lee Harris braced himself. The urge to sneeze was gaining force, so he stopped breathing, which put pressure on his bladder, which made his back hurt which made him breathe in sharply which started the whole thing all over again. It would take several minutes to stand and get to the bathroom to release the bladder so he could sneeze without soiling himself unless he hurt himself getting up and running to the bathroom, but he'd hurt himself if he sneezed in any case. His

167

forehead and neck were beginning to sweat. Maybe, if he moved very carefully, he could hold his breath, stand (without hurting his back), walk (without hurting his back) to the bathroom to pee (without hurting his back), and the sneeze would just go away. Because he had fainted from not breathing. Okay, he had to breathe. He let his breath out very slowly through his mouth.

The sneeze reflex took over very loudly. The explosive expulsion startled Charlie, who fluttered in his cage.

"Fuck!" Lee shouted, followed by a stream of pained profanity filtered through clenched teeth that made Charlie flutter more.

Lee was able to tense his legs and stomach quickly enough to avoid embarrassing himself, but that made the sudden sharp pain in his lower back brought on by the sudden sneeze become heavy, dull and constant, as if someone had punched him in the tail bone with a ham-handed fist and then left the fist there, twisting it to bring home the point, whatever it had been.

Now just moving could release the tide, but he didn't have a choice so he stood slowly, which made the fist in his back press harder with an upward thrust. He took two steps around the coffee table and sneezed again.

"Fuck fuck fuck!" he shouted after the new wave of pain subsided enough that the bright, black centered spots sparkling in front of his vision faded.

He'd have to change his sweat pants after he finally made it to the bathroom. He realized that being embarrassed all by himself was sort of pointless, but he kept on being embarrassed anyway, just to spite himself. He'd change into pajamas, take his pain pills if he could find where Abby put them, curl up in bed and hope death came swiftly and with some small amount of dignity. Fuck Abby. Fuck!

"Abby!" he shouted as he took off toward the bathroom.

If he had watched someone else doing the constrained, arrhythmic shuffle that wanted to be a run but couldn't, punctuated with halting, profane shouts, he would have been very amused. Since he wasn't watching it, and it wasn't someone else, he wasn't amused at all. He finally made it, and while he stood there in pain relieving himself, which wasn't much relief at all, he noticed a small wad of Kleenex© on the floor that had missed the waste basket. It sat there, white and fluffy on the pale green flecked Linoleum tile, taunting him. It seemed, even, to be smiling, daring him to pick it up. While he finished peeing and putting himself away, he stared at it. When he was done, he continued staring, willing himself to bend. In his mind, he was Fred Astaire, gracefully sweeping it up, then Magic Johnson, slam dunking it into the waste basket in a flurry of mixed metaphors. His body, however, was a combination of Fred Flintstone© and Mel Torme. There was sound but no movement. He inched his foot forward, opening his toes like claws. Just as he reached the Kleenex©, though, the thought of what the tissue might have been carrying stopped his toe short. Even his toe was fastidious to an absurd degree.

He stood frozen, a stone statue of indecision, trying to figure out a way to properly dispose of the offending, offensive thing without paroxysms of pain or shudders of revulsion. He could shuffle into the kitchen, find a broom, shuffle back and sweep it up. But after all that effort, he'd still have to bend to sweep it into the dustpan. He could strike a match, drop it onto the paper and gleefully watch the horrid thing burn. Ashes seemed more acceptable in an antiseptic sort of way. But he'd still have to sweep them up, which brought back the going to the kitchen, etc., etc. bending thing. He could just move the basket on top of it so he couldn't see it. Well, no he couldn't do that. He wished he had one of those hand grip criss-cross extender things that you used to get cans off of high shelves with or one of those extendable suction cups that you used to change prices on gas station signs or one of those little basket things you used to change light bulbs. He was sure he could order something like that from Hammacher Schlemmer. But he'd probably die, standing there, waiting for it to come in the mail. Finally, he turned and left the bathroom in what would have been a huff if he had been able to do it faster, slammed the door behind himself, and resumed cursing Abby. He cursed her for leaving him alone and in pain to sneeze and wet himself. He cursed her for not being there to pick up the fucking piece of paper. He cursed her for bringing him to the hill in the first place so he couldn't pick it up himself. He cursed her for leaving his car there. His car. How the hell was he going to get his car, damn it?

Peter and Roz lay across their big brass bed. (*No, they didn't, Steve.* **Why not**? *Peter doesn't have a big brass bed.* **Why not**? *He's not Bob Dylan.* **Who is he**? *Peter Principal.* **No, who's Bob**

Dylan? *He's... Okay, that was really cheap humor that we really had to work really hard for.* **That's my favorite kind. We need to have a severed leg in this installment.** *Why, Steve?* **Because I'm hungry.** *I don't think that was cheap, but I'm fairly sure it wasn't humor.* **Poop.**) Peter and Roz (**you said that already**) lay on their backs, glistening. Peter was about to ask Roz if it had been okay, but was saved from the humiliating question when the phone rang.

"You're not going to answer that, are you?" Roz asked.

"This is Peter," he said into the phone.

Roz laughed, then mouthed "This is Peter" into her pinky with her thumb in her ear.

"Oh," Peter said. "Hi, Lee."

Roz stared at him, but he didn't seem to notice. He did seem to be trying to get a word in with Lee. Then he said he'd left his car there also and Roz squinted at him, hoping she was wrong about what was going to happen next. Then he laughed and put his hand on the receiver, and turned to Roz.

"Lee wants to know if I got hurt, too," he said with a laugh, and Roz smiled. "He needs help to go get his van."

Roz's smile disappeared. She'd been right and didn't like it.

"Who's Lee, and why can't he get his own damn van?"

"What about Abby?" Peter said into the phone, listened for a moment, then put his hand on the receiver again and looked at Roz. "They had a fight," he said to her.

Roz didn't seem impressed. Peter took his hand away from the phone and said they'd be right over, but had to shower first because they were both kind of stinky. Then he listened for a brief moment. Then he got really red and said, "Nobody," and hung up.

"You realize, don't you," Roz said, "that you just volunteered me to go with you to get someone else's car."

"Well," Peter said, "we have to go there anyway. You did kick me in the jaw."

Roz sighed and asked for a towel. And she didn't want her boat to be rocked. (*What was that sentence for, Steve?* **We needed a Bob Marley reference in here.** *No. We didn't.* **Okay. I guess you just don't want this scene to be funny, then.** *Why should this scene be different from any other scene?* **I miss Twain. Let's do a scene at Twain's.** *Why?* **I already said I was hungry.** *How will that move* *the story along?* **Non-linear story structure with film noir overtones**. *Can it at least be surreal with deep symbolism of obscure significance?* **Sure**. *Okay.*)

A strong stream of sunlight broke through the window and cut across the counter, highlighting the dark shadows in the diner out of which Matt emerged, his fedora slightly askew, obscuring his eyes. He placed the black and white plate of meatloaf with mashed potatoes and gravy in front of the black and white guy in his multi-gray shaded John Deere hat, then filled the shiny napkin dispenser and straightened the black and white ketchup bottle and salt and pepper shakers. The man in the John Deere hat's cigarette smoke curled up past his eyes, then collected under the bill of his cap. It escaped around the edges, briefly forming the Japanese characters for Matt's birth date before wafting into the shadows. A black bird sang in the dead of night on the wings of a snow white dove. And a tree grew in Brooklyn.

When Peter knocked on Lee's front door, Lee announced that it was unlocked. Peter opened the door and he and Roz walked in. He immediately felt something was amiss. He was surprised to sense that there was a tissue on the floor in the bathroom. Poor Lee, he thought. Oh, well. Lee apologized for not getting up to greet them. He was propped up with bed pillows and had a blanket over his legs. He was wearing Dockers® which looked painful, somehow, and a loose sweater which didn't and he hadn't combed his hair, but had brushed damp fingers through it. If he hadn't looked so much like a complete invalid, he would have looked like a complete geek. Roz noticed the pill bottle and water glass on the coffee table next to the bag of beef jerky and open box of Ritz® crackers.

"Lee," Peter said. "This is Roz. Roz, Lee."

"You can't drive, can you?" Roz greeted.

"Um... Oh. Probably not. Um... I don't know what I have to offer you."

"You've got pills," Roz said.

Lee laughed. Peter shot Roz a strange look. Roz was completely serious.

"I'm completely serious," she said.

"Um..." Lee said, and shrugged. "Sure. I guess. One."

In one motion, she crossed the room, popped open the child-proof cap, dumped a pill into her palm, then popped it into her mouth and took a swig of water from Lee's glass. Peter and Lee were both aghast. Peter because of the pill, Lee because of her lips on his glass. Charlie because of life in a cage.

Roz looked strangely familiar to Lee. She reminded him somehow of thinly sliced salami, which was odd because she obviously wasn't thinly sliced. He asked if they'd met somewhere.

"At Aunt Gladys's Janitorial Supply and Condom Emporium," she said, and Lee turned pink all the way through his pain to the back of his earlobes and shook his head vigorously. "Sure," she said. "You were the one who bought all that muriatic acid. Okay, so if you can't drive, how are we going to do this?"

"What?" Lee asked.

"Hi. Nice to meet you. I'm Roz. How are we going to get your car if you can't drive?"

They all stared at each other while Peter and Lee counted cars and people. If Peter and Roz drove there, they could bring Lee's and Peter's car back, but would then have to leave Roz's car there, or they could bring Roz's and Lee's car back, but then... Lee's mind was starting to feel like a strange puzzle about having three animals that you needed to take across a bridge but you could only bring one at a time but you couldn't leave one with the other. No, that was two animals and some vegetables. No, three coconuts that you could juggle. Fuck it, two goats and an ermine. They would have to leave a car there or take two trips.

"We could take two trips," Peter said helpfully.

"No. We couldn't," Roz said. "We got very little sleep last night. Besides, I get one weekend day off a month, I'm not going to spend the entire day going back and forth to Beard's Hill."

"How else are we going to do it?" Peter said, hoping Lee didn't get the "we" part of didn't get any sleep. Lee seemed still in too much pain to hear an errant "we".

"Call somebody else," Roz said reasonably.

"Who else could we call?" Peter said, then got a bright idea. "What about Abby?"

Lee shot him a "we just talked about this, gay man, Abby and I had a huge fight, it's the whole reason you came over, and I'm the one who's supposed to be in pain and on pain killers, here, so if anyone should forget it's me, do I have to smack you on the side of your big, bearded head and what do you mean 'we'?" glance. Peter realized it hadn't been such a bright idea, gave him an "oops" look and followed it with a "what the hell did you two fight about this time?" gesture. Lee couldn't figure out how to communicate that she told him he was a lousy actor so he just gave him an "I'll drive, damn it" look and tried to stand.

"Uuuuhhhnhnnn..." Lee said out loud at about halfway up, then slowly went a quarter of the way back down and said "Uuuuhhhnhnnn..." again and froze.

"Who else do you know?" Roz asked, completely ignoring the comically painful look on Lee's face and even more comical position.

"Twain?" Peter asked, noticing the look and position and wondering what he could cook to make Lee feel better.

In four little movements, each punctuated by an additional uuuuhhhnhnnn, Lee gingerly settled back down onto the pillows, then breathed quickly in and out several times to get the damn spots out of his vision.

"No," he said after making sure no more movement was necessary, "He's running the diner without me already. And that takes Matt out of the equation, and, uuuuhhhnhnnn, I don't even know if Matt can drive. Uuuhhhnhnnn."

"These are the times when you realize how few friends you have," Peter said as Lee swallowed another pain pill without water and offered one to Roz, who accepted without comment. "Who else do you know?"

"Jim?" Lee said weakly, not noticing the sudden pained look on Peter's face at the mention of that name. But he didn't like Jim any more than Peter did and didn't want him touching his car. "Okay, what about Bear?"

Peter nodded once in emphatic agreement, went directly to the phone and called Bear, who said he'd be right over. He was a friend. A real friend. A true, steadfast friend. A trouper. Someone you'd want in your foxhole when you went into battle. Someone who had your back. Someone who'd drop everything if a you were in need of a friend. Someone who was bored on a late Saturday afternoon, post football season, pre baseball and had just never quite gotten into basketball. He would have to miss Pippi Longstockings, though.

Roz sighed and sat on the couch, causing Lee to uuuuhhhnhnnn again. Peter fretted, which is what he did best.

"Have you eaten, Lee?" he asked.

Lee told him about the pancakes that Abby had made for lunch.

"Pancakes for lunch?" Roz said.

"I know," Lee said and they bonded and he offered her another pill (*STEVE!* **What**? *It's not Valley of the Dolls. Or Fear and Loathing in Las Vegas. Or Easy Rider. Or Fantasia. She's had enough drugs.* **He offers her a beer? Coffee? A lightly-flavored mineral water? Air? Okay, I'll behave.**)

They all agreed that none of them had eaten yet, and Peter set about to make something when there was a knock at the door.

"That was fast," Peter said, and opened it.

Bear strode in.

"Vincent!" Roz shouted, and Bear froze, mid-stride.

"Oh," he said, and forced a nonchalant stance, "hi, Roz."

"Vincent?" Peter said.

Roz, who had finally begun to warm up being there, frosted over again. Lee would have moved away from the chill she radiated all over the couch, but he didn't want to add another uuuuhhhnhnnn to what looked like was going to turn into some sort of very embarrassing social situation. He hated being in the middle of one of those. It was embarrassing. He had already been embarrassed once that day by a drop or two of moisture on the front of his sweat pants, and that would be enough. Of course, if he added an uuuuhhhnhnnn, his pain would be what everyone focused on and then they could go have their embarrassing moment elsewhere where he wouldn't have to sit in the middle of it. But then they'd all be looking at him, and that would be too embarrassing. He took another pill. This time he even washed it down with water. Roz's lips couldn't be that germ ridden, and she hadn't touched the glass in several minutes, and anyway, the last one was still stuck in the back of his throat not killing any pain.

"That's my real name," Bear said. "Vincent."

"I never pictured you as a 'Vincent'," Peter said.

"What did you picture me as?"

"Actually, I don't even picture you as a 'Bear', even. I don't know, Bob or Bill or Dave. Maybe a Chuck or a Don or Paul. Joe or John or Jack or something. Jon, maybe. Or Phil or Carl. Definitely a Carl. Not a Karl. Or Steve or Geoff or Jim. No, not Jim. Maybe James. Or... Chad or Skip or Biff or Donovan or Horatio or Ebenezer or Percival or Ichabod or... (*Steve! That's enough!* **Sorry.**) ... or Ermine. Not Vincent."

(**Geoff?** *What, Steve?* **Why doesn't spell check like "Ichabod"?** *Would you?* **Maybe if he had big thumbs.** *Go have some lightly-flavored mineral water.*)

"Yeah," Lee said, hoping that if he kept this conversation going, whatever that embarrassing social thing that was about to happen between him and Roz could be nicely deflected. "I always wondered why they called you 'Bear'. You're so... wiry. I mean, you're hairy, which makes sense, but most Bears I know are heavy and clumsy and hairy and smelly and have big bushy beards and lots of hair on their head. You know, like a bear. Like Peter. Except he's not hairy. Or smelly. Except that peppery cologne he wears all the time. And you are hairy. Except on top of your head. I'm so confused."

Lee was sorry he had said so much because it made his back hurt. He took another pill.

"They called me Bear," Bear said with a long sigh, "because when I was a kid I used to like to run around naked all the time."

"That would be 'Bare', not 'Bear'," Peter said, trying desperately not to picture Bear running around naked.

"I was a bad speller," Bare said.

"So," Roz said, getting up off the couch.

Suddenly, now that Roz had moved and he wasn't sitting exactly between her and Bear and therefore not directly in the middle of the direct line of fire, and the second and third pill were beginning to hit, Lee realized he was actually looking forward to the embarrassing social situation. Perspective was everything. He took another pill and settled back to watch, completely oblivious to the twinge in his back as he did so.

"Vincent." Roz added, and Lee smiled an inward, expectant smile. "How are you?"

Bear nodded without answering. For once, Lee wished Bear wasn't such a guy.

"How do you two know each other?" he said.

"Um," Peter, who really, really, really didn't like watching other people's lives collide, even if he were really far away from the direct line of fire, said quickly, "shouldn't we get going?"

"We haven't had lunch, yet," Lee said. At least that's what it sounded like inside his head, which was beginning to fill with a really nice liquidy vibration.

He offered Roz another pill. (**Geoff!** *What?* **You wouldn't let me do that**. *Roz doesn't accept this one, so it's okay.*) She didn't accept it.

"How's Dee Dee?" Bear said, with enough social politeness to communicate effectively that he really didn't want to know and would appreciate it if they all just stopped talking and did something with a power tool.

"Who's Dee Dee?" Lee asked, shaking the pill bottle, grinning. Color was coming back to his face and he had a strange, fleeting image of Jimi Hendrix typing on a Smith Corona. Life was good.

"My sister," Roz said at the same time Bear said, "My ex."

"We really should be going," Peter said. He was seriously considering giving them all pills so he could shut them up and get out of this embarrassing social situation.

Lee nodded knowingly, smiling. He waited for act two.

"Yeah," Roz said. "If I'm going to spend an hour trapped in a car with him, let's get it over with."

Peter hesitated. He hadn't considered having to be in an even smaller environment with a socially embarrassing thing, but at least stoned out Lee wouldn't be there stirring it all back up after he had quieted it all down. He opened the door, only momentarily feeling guilty that he hadn't fixed anything for Lee to eat, then thinking it served him right and understanding why Abby had left. Bear whisked out. Roz followed him. Peter stroked her back as she went by him, then looked once back at Lee, blushed and left. Lee watched the door for a long time after they left, feeling disappointed. He wouldn't get his entertainment, after all. A moment later, Peter came back in and asked Lee for his car keys.

"They're on the bed stand," Lee said.

He watched Peter get them, hoping something untoward had happened that Peter would tell him about, then watched Peter leave again. He watched the door feeling more disappointed, and now also a bit confused. It was hard to think about it all through the waves crashing against his eyeballs and ears, and the more he tried, the more nothing was making any sense: Abby was mad at him and it was her that had insulted him. She should be going to get his car, not Bear. And what was with Bear being a Vincent? And who was that Roz person? And was she at Peter's house when he called and woke Peter up at one in the afternoon and they hadn't gotten much sleep? And the sleep they hadn't gotten seemed to be together. And what was that Peter stroking her back, then blushing thing? There should be certain constants in life. Bear was Bear. Abby was his girlfriend. And Peter was gay.

"Nothing makes any sense," Lee said aloud as he scratched Gable's ear. Then he realized through the surf that was trickling down his hairline what he was doing and looked down at his hand, which was stroking the air just above the blanket that had mostly fallen away from his lap. He took another pill.

The conversation for the first ten minutes that they rode away from Lee's house was as boring as Roz's spotless, white Dodge Aries K car, the only interesting part of which was the salt-rust on the underside where the undercoating had worn away. The heater was on, but the air in the car was still bitingly cold. The vinyl seats were even colder. Bear sat in the back with his arms crossed, breathing fog. If Roz hadn't been driving, Peter was sure her arms would have been crossed, also. He tried to start a conversation several times, but the most he could get out of either one of them was a small grunt. His nose hairs stuck to each other. The heater was actually blowing cold air into the car.

Roz seemed to be avoiding looking in her rear view mirror, which, all in all, Peter thought was probably the best plan. Then, about eleven minutes into the drive, Roz did look into the mirror, and her face seemed to twist and color strangely, like the rust on the underside of the car. She looked forward for a moment and Peter tried to believe she wouldn't start something, then she looked back at the mirror. Peter tried desperately to find a cassette tape to pop in, but the only ones he could find were The Best of Bread, Vol. 1 and Black Sabbath's

"Paranoid" and he thought that even the impending socially embarrassing situation would be better than either of those.

"You're a real bastard, you know," Roz said into the mirror.

Peter popped in Black Sabbath.

Bear didn't say anything for another minute or so, and Peter prayed that it would stay that way all the way to the hill. He thought about turning up the volume to assure their cooperation, but War Pigs was playing and he just couldn't make his hand go to the volume dial. Finally, he decided he couldn't take one more minute of Ozzy Osbourne's vocals and popped the tape out. He had planned on popping Bread in very quickly, but Bear chose that brief moment to speak.

"I'm sure she gave you a fair and balanced account of our marriage," he said.

"She told me what it was like to be married to you," Roz said.

"Did she tell you what it was like to be married to her?"

Peter tried to decide how much damage he would do to himself if he just opened the door and took a rolling dive into the next snow bank they passed. One hand still held Paranoid, the other still held Bread. He looked at the Bread hand.

"Did you know that one of the guys on the Baby I'm-a-Want You album also played with the Beach Boys and The Monkees?" Peter said, quickly reading the notes on the back of the cassette cover.

"Okay," Roz said, and Peter had a momentary lapse of reason and thought she was talking to him. "What's your side?"

"Let's just get this done with," Bear said and Peter closed his eyes and willed Roz to agree to just get this done with.

"No," Roz said, and Peter opened his eyes but stopped breathing. "What's your side? I'm all ears."

"I don't need to explain it to you," Bear said. "I wasn't married to you."

"Thank God," Roz said, and took a corner faster than was recommended by the yellow, bullet-hole ridden sign with the squiggly snake-like arrow on it and the Aries K fish-tailed and Peter started hyperventilating. He would have asked her to take it easy, but it didn't seem advisable. He grabbed the armrest instead. "I wouldn't have been so stupid as to marry you."

"I would never have asked you," Bear said with a derisive laugh. "I'm guessing no one else has either."

Roz slammed on the brakes. The car actually stopped after an extended moment of sliding.

"Oh God oh God oh God oh God," Peter said, pounding his temples with the insides of his wrists.

Both of them looked at him and he stopped pounding long enough to notice.

"Did I say that out loud?" Peter said out loud.

"Out," Roz said, turning back to Bear as if Peter wasn't even there. The cold mist coming out of her nostrils made her look like a bull in an animated cartoon, but the image didn't amuse Peter as much as it should have. In fact, it didn't amuse him at all. In fact it scared the hell out of him. Heat was finally coming out of the vents, but it stayed at the edges, also afraid to venture too far into the car.

"Fine," Bear said, and leaned over the seat to get to the door handle.

"Wait, wait, wait, wait," Peter said with a grunt because Bear was pushing the seat forward. "Bear, it's miles back to your car."

"I've walked further," Bear said. "To get away from her sister."

He pointed at Roz, who swatted at his hand. He pulled his hand back and pushed harder on the back of the seat. Roz missed Bear's hand and got Peter right on the swollen bruise.

"Ow!" Peter yelled. "God Damn It! Stop! Just stop! Both of you! Jesus!"

It was such an unexpected outburst that they both did stop. Peter slammed the seat back. The car was starting to warm up a little. Or was that just his head?

"I'm going to throttle you both. Jesus!" He shouted. "Maybe Dee Dee was a bitch. Maybe you treated her like crap. It's ancient history. Jesus!"

Roz was about to say something but Peter rounded on her.

"It was their marriage, Roz. You have no idea what happened. Jesus! She was your sister, but she was an adult. Jesus. I just want to get Lee's car back to him then go home to my cat. I hate people."

They both continued to look at him, then they both looked like they both wanted to say something.

"No!" Peter said. "Shut up."

179

They shut up.

"Drive. Fuck!"

Roz put the car in gear obediently. The car slid a little before it finally caught and moved forward.

"My jaw hurts," Peter said quietly.

"I'm sorry," Roz said.

"Please just drive."

They drove in silence for another ten or fifteen more minutes. Peter didn't even notice that he had stopped shivering. The silence finally got to be too much for him, though, and he popped in Bread.

"I never cheated on her, you know," Bear said a little defensively, melting at the first sappy Bread note that wafted into the back seat with the warming air.

"I never said you did," Roz said a little more defensively.

Peter gave her a "down boy" look and she consciously unfurled her brow, not wanting to cause him to holler at her again.

"She just said you were never home," she said as her final "woof."

"I had a job," Bear said and Peter gave him a look which he ignored. "She never understood that. It was awful to come home after working ten or twelve hours straight and have her complain that I was never home."

Peter turned full around to give him the look with more force.

"Ten or twelve hours?" Roz said, now that Peter wasn't looking at her. "Sometimes you didn't come home til three or four in the morning five or six nights a week."

"Only when a play was going to open," Bear said when Peter turned to give Roz her look.

"You worked in a fucking theatre, for Christ's sake," Roz said, actually beginning to sweat. "Plays are always going to open."

Peter stopped even trying to give them looks and started humming Bread songs to himself. He took off his scarf and mopped his forehead with it.

"And Dee Dee was always going to yell at me whenever I got home."

"Because you always got home at three in the morning!"

"How the fuck do you know?"

The windows were fogging dangerously.

"Because I was the one she called every night, crying, when you weren't there," Roz said. "Jesus."

"Look, I loved her," Bear said.

"I know!" Roz said. "That was the problem. You both loved each other. But you loved your job more!"

"No!" Bear said. "Not more!"

Roz looked at him in the mirror, getting ready to shout at him. He was about to add something to what he just said. Peter was about to turn the tape player up really high. Bear closed his mouth, then opened it again. The movement surprised Roz, and she didn't shout. Peter didn't turn up the volume. Time would have stood still, except that Peter needed to move to wipe the fog off the windshield with his scarf so Roz could see the road.

Bear wasn't in the car anymore, he was in the small house he and Dee Dee had shared. There was a strange loop of film playing in which he and Dee Dee argued over and over, each iteration slightly different. At first all he could see was her shrill face, the way that little vein pulsed at the side of her jaw. He hated that vein. She didn't hear a word he said when that vein pulsed. His stomach recalled the turmoil he had thought he'd forgotten, and he wanted to hit something. All through his marriage he had felt like he had wanted to hit something, and not hitting something had been the hardest thing he had ever done. Slowly, though, his focus shifted. He started to notice himself. He wasn't listening to her either. His whole face pulsed. And she seemed to want to hit something, too. She looked so scared under the anger. So frustrated. So small and frail. And he looked so impassive. So formidable. Cold. That shocked him. Cold was never a word he would have used to describe himself. He tried to swallow, but couldn't.

He closed his mouth in a sort of strange way and turned to look out the window at the dead, snow covered trees. Roz kept a weary eye on him in the mirror as she drove. After a moment of silence, Peter stopped humming. Then, after another moment, he looked back at Bear, whose eyebrows were furrowed in a way that Peter have never seen.

"Bear?" he said.

It looked like Bear's eyes were glistening. Peter never imagined Bear having enough emotions to make his eyes glisten. Vincent, maybe, but not Bear. It didn't feel right at all.

"You okay?" he asked, nervously and looked around for a tissue. (**There's one in Lee's bathroom.** *Damn it, Steve, just once can we have a nice scene? Just once?* **How about Tuesday?** *Tuesdays are our days off.* **Oh, well.**)

Bear shook his head slowly.

"Roz," he said, still looking out the window.

"What?" Roz said a little sharply.

"Could..." Bear said, turning back toward her. "Would you tell Dee Dee that I'm sorry?"

"You tell her," Roz said, still not quite ready to give up.

"I can't talk to her."

"Yes," Roz said. "You can."

Bear didn't say anything for a moment, then he nodded once.

The car was quiet most of the rest of the way to the hill, and Peter didn't even try to start another conversation. He did try to keep the window clear. When the tape came to the end and clicked off, they could see the hill.

The hill was a mess. There were old booze bottles everywhere, black snow radiating out from where the fires had blazed, half-burned logs, frozen blood (for Steve), slush, a moose, a stoat, an ermine, Robert Redford (for Geoff), frozen puke, bits of Sloppy Joes and Nachos, sled runners attached to charred wood. It was really icky. There was a streak of dark gray clouds across the sky, which was nursing a hangover. The air smelled of burned, treated wood, spiced wine, puke and motor oil. It was not a pastoral snowy hillside surrounded by trees at all, but it fit everyone's mood. It took a moment for anyone to notice that there were no cars there, which horrified Peter. What was he going to do without a car? What was he going to tell Lee?

"This is Laird's Hill," Bear said. "Beard's Hill is just over there."

They got back into the car and drove to Beard's Hill. It was a mess. There were old booze bottles everywhere, black snow radiating out from where the fires had blazed, half-burned logs, frozen blood (for Steve), slush, a moose, a stoat, an ermine, Norman Fell (for Geoff), frozen puke, bits of Sloppy Joes and Nachos, sled runners attached to charred wood. Peter stepped out of the car and surveyed the chaos. He felt awful about the carnage and had to do something, so he leaned over and picked up a half-burned cigarette, then looked around, trying to find an appropriate place to dispose of it. He placed it back on the ground exactly where he had found it, then tried to clean the stale, damp cigarette ash off the tips of his fingers with snow.

"Okay," Bear said. "Do you have Lee's key?"

Peter reached into his pocket and produced Lee's key ring. It was a simple chrome ring with three keys. Car. House. Twain's. And a big orange puffy fuzz ball so he could find it in his purse. I mean pants. (**No fuzz ball, Geoff.**) It didn't have any adornment. Peter didn't understand only three keys. He still had keys from his college dorm room on his set, and one for every door at the theatre, several for pad locks he had long since lost and a strange round hollow one for a pop machine. He also had one for a soda machine in case River Bend was west of the Mississippi. He gave the ring to Bear.

"Who has only three keys?" Bear said. His set even had a flash light and a bottle opener. And a chainsaw. Which he used to see if Lee was awake. (**That might be a bit too obscure, Geoff.** *You have no faith.* **Yes, I do. And boy, is my faith red.** *Now, that's just too stupid.* **See? Obscure.**)

Bear stood by Lee's SUV, looking at the destruction on the hill. He wondered vaguely how it got cleaned up every year. Maybe it just melted away with the spring thaw. Roz stood by her car looking at Bear. Peter got into his car quickly in case another round started.

"I still don't like you very much," Roz said.

Bear nodded once and Roz got into her car and backed up. Bear got into Lee's car, started it and backed up. Peter's car groaned twice, then groaned a third time, then clicked several times, then did nothing.

Peter put his head on the steering wheel. His shoulders slumped. The plastic steering wheel began to freeze a strip across his forehead. It felt good against his resignation. There was a tap on his window and he looked up without taking his head off the wheel. It was Bear. Peter opened his window, still without moving his forehead off the wheel.

"Battery," he said. "Dead."

"Oh," Bear said. "Do you have cables?"

Peter shook his head, which was difficult, because it was still attached to the steering wheel, but it seemed easier, somehow, to put the effort into shaking it then it would be to put the effort into lifting it. Roz had stopped backing up when Bear had gotten out of Lee's car. She opened her window and Bear asked if she had jumper cables. She didn't. Bear shook his head, amazed. How could someone not have at least one set of jumper cables? Especially in an area where it snowed. It was like only having three keys on your ring. In an area where there were locks.

"My jumper cables are back at Lee's house," Bear said.

"I am not going to go back to Lee's house to get your jumper cables," Roz said.

"I can take Lee's car back," Peter said.

"Then one of us is going to have to wait here for you to take it back," Roz said. "Or go with you all the way there and all the way back. And it won't be me."

"Wait," Peter said. "Lee."

"What?" Bear said.

"Mr. Tool Guy."

They went to the back of his SUV and opened the back door. There was a big cardboard box filled with road flares and snow chains and a flashlight and assorted tools and spare fuses and a crow bar and spare lug nuts, two cans of Insta-Spare® and an old denim jacket and a plastic tarp and something that looked like bullets and extra batteries and paper towels and rope and motor oil and a bottle of antifreeze and heavy gauge wire and a gun and duct tape and a gas mask and a can of potted meat product and a propane torch and an aroma therapy candle and an earthquake survival kit.

"What the hell does he need that for?" Bear said, pointing at the earthquake kit. "Even I don't have one of those."

Bear pulled the sixteen foot, six gauge deluxe twist-proof jumper cables with heavy-duty yellow insulation and copper parrot clamps insulated with thick, black plastic out of the box. His pants tented. Peter was still trying not to picture him running around naked. Roz was impatient, so they connected Lee's car to Peter's (now, Peter was trying not to picture Lee running around naked) and got him started.

Bear backed up the SUV, turned and started down the hill, followed by Peter, then Roz. Peter followed Bear all the way to Lee's house so he could make sure Lee was okay and had food to eat. At some point on the drive, Roz turned left when they turned right and she disappeared. Bear, alone in Lee's car listening to martial music on the radio, was happy to see her go. Peter, alone in his listening to the Royal Shakespear Company's recording of A Winter's Tale, felt a pang that he didn't understand or like. Roz just thought about James K. Polk and hummed advertising ditties.

That night, alone in her apartment, Abby sat on her couch, rocking back and forth to ease her cramps. There were moments she hated being a woman. Which is something two male writers, gay or otherwise, have no business writing about, so they'll move on. She was trying to decide if she should call Lee and make sure he was all right. Half of her mind was worried about him, but the other half just thought he deserved to spend time with himself and see how he liked it. Which, she thought, was really mean, but, hey, he deserved it. As that thought floated around her head, a rolling cramp floated through her abdomen. She wished she had some pain pills. Lee had pain pills. But he was being entirely too snarky and she just couldn't call him, pain pills or no. She finally decided to just go to bed. Maybe she could dream of Jimi Hendrix. Or Blue Turtles. Or Jeannie.

The next morning her body painfully proved she wasn't pregnant. She spent time making sure she was prepared for the ramifications of that for the rest of the day, which kept her mind off worrying about and being mad at Lee for a while. Finally, she picked up the phone and called him.

"Hi," she said. "How are you doing?"

"Fine."

"Have you eaten?"

"Yeah. Peter came by and fixed me a casserole last night and I had a little just now."

"Oh," Abby said. "We should figure out how to get your car."

"Bear and Peter got it for me yesterday," Lee said. He wasn't going to mention Roz because the whole Roz thing still confused him.

"Oh," Abby said, feeling a bit useless. "Um. I got my period."

"Oh," Lee said, taking a moment to let that sink in. He was both relieved and a little saddened. He was more relieved, though, which relieved him.

"I just didn't notice the symptoms," she said. "Probably because of the all the fun and food and drink on the hill and then the scare and

185

the taking care of you. And you were being such a pill, I just thought it was you."

"Oh, thanks a lot."

"Hey," she said, laughing. "I had Lee-M-S."

There was a pregnant pause, then Lee laughed as much as a broken coccyx and good pain pills would let him. They chatted a little, but Lee didn't feel well enough for small talk, and Abby was still going through the whole not pregnant thing, so she said she'd check in on him a bit later and they hung up.

A few minutes later the phone rang again. Lee smiled, wondering what Abby had forgotten to tell him.

"Hi, Mommy," he said.

"Lee?" a female voice that wasn't Abby's asked.

There was an awkward moment in which Lee considered just putting on a fake accent or hanging up or changing his phone number.

"Yes," he said timidly, instead of any of those very attractive options.

"It's Kim," Kim said. "Anderson. From The Odd Couple. At the theatre."

"Hi, Kim."

"Mommy?"

"I thought you were... an old friend of mine from Chicago," he said with a nervous laugh.

"You call your friends 'Mommy'?"

"What's up?" Lee said, hoping it sounded less abrupt than he meant it.

"Oh, I just wanted to know how you were after your spill on the hill."

"Oh. That's nice of you," he said.

"Yeah. Agnes wants to know if you'll be able to do the part or if we have to replace you."

Lee's stomach tightened and his throat constricted. A strange noise came out that sounded a lot like Gable.

Will Lee be well enough to play Roy?
Will Agnes replace him, anyway?
Will Lee ever stop being confused by Peter and Roz?
Will Peter and Roz see each other again?

Will they watch the rest of the Ealing comedies if they do?
Will they just have sex?
Will Bear call Dee Dee?
Will she hang up on him?
Will she forgive him?
Did Abby forgive Lee?
Did Lee forgive her?
Did God make little green apples?
Did Oswald act alone?
Will he replace Lee in The Odd Couple?
Will power?
Or glory?

To find the answers to these and other pugilistic pursuits,
tune into our next installment:
"Roy, Roy, Roy your Boat"
Or
"I Will Act No More Forever"

(We dedicate this installment to our dear friend Morton Grossman who passed away this week. We will miss you, Morty, you old son-of-a-gun. **He passed away last week, Geoff.** *It was Friday.* **Technically, that was last week.** *It was within a week, so it was this week.* **Fine.** *We'll miss him either way. A lot.* **Yeah.**)

This installment first published November 16, 2003

Geoff Hoff and Steve Mancini

Previously, in Weeping Willow: Lee Harris the accountant was cast as Roy the accountant in the Willow Lane Theatre's production of The Odd Couple, then fractured his coccyx while sledding. Jim, who came to town to investigate Lee at the behest of Lee's ex-wife, and hurt Lee's friend Peter with his unconscious insensitivity, was cast as Vinnie. Stella, who works in the front office of the Willow Lane Theatre with Peter, and flips her hair to show her displeasure, is now dating Jim, who used to date Agnes, the star director at the theatre who is directing The Odd Couple, is in her sixties and is now dating Headline, the young, gorgeous bartender at The Office where everyone gathers on Tuesday nights for Dollar Beer Tuesdays. Andrew, who is an actor that Lee met in his first play at the Willow Lane Theatre, is also a lawyer and is handling Lee's divorce from Beverly, who had hired Jim to investigate Lee, which is why Jim came to town and ended up hurting Peter, getting parts Lee wanted and dating pretty much everyone. Bear, who is the tech director at the Willow Lane Theatre, used to be married to Dee Dee, the sister to Roz who is the deli counter lady at the local grocery store and who spent an evening watching movies and other things with Peter. Abby, who is dating Lee and just found out she isn't pregnant, has no connection to the Willow Lane Theatre unless you count her best friend Kim who is working as the assistant director to Agnes on The Odd Couple. To unravel all this confusion, read the previous installments. You'll get used to our introductions after a few of them.

Installment Twenty-Three
"Roy, Roy, Roy Your Boat"
Or
"I Will Act No More Forever"

The worst thing that could have happened had happened. Well, perhaps not the worst, but it was pretty bad, all things considered. Lee's worst fears had been realized. Well, he had some fears that were worse than this, but he couldn't think of any right at the moment. Kim was on the other end of the line waiting for him to tell her if he would be able to do the part or not. His back felt like hell and he could barely walk. It had taken him a good fifteen minutes to get up, pee and shamble to the couch that morning, which was an improvement over the previous day when most of the afternoon had been taken up in an unsuccessful attempt not to soil himself, but didn't bode well for rehearsing and performing in a play. But he had fought with Abby about this very thing when she had implied that he would be easily replaceable, so not doing the play wasn't an option as far as he was concerned. But if he showed up to rehearsal, if he could actually make it all the way to rehearsal, and wasn't able to move across the stage, or even stand to do his scenes, he'd be holding the whole thing back. But it was his role, damn it. He had a hundred and three lines. Besides, if he didn't do it, that would be the second time Jim would be in a play he wasn't in. Even listening to himself waffle made him feel like a high school girl trying to decide if the taffeta would work for the prom. I mean a high school jock wondering if he should go out for hockey or basketball. It made him feel really immature. He was badly hurt, and logic dictated that he give the role up to someone who could actually walk. Kim was waiting for his answer, and he finally had one.

"Of course I can do it," he said into the phone.

"You sure?" Kim said. "We have to know now if we need to find someone else."

"I'll see you at rehearsal Tuesday night," he said.

She thanked him, called him Daddy and hung up. Now he wondered what the hell he was going to do.

Roz woke up late that morning. She didn't have to go in to work until the afternoon and had needed to catch up on sleep after the weekend. She sat slumped on the end of her couch feeling odd. She liked her life for the most part. The television was on in the background, which wasn't unusual, but it didn't seem to be keeping her much company. She absent-mindedly flipped channels, almost unaware she was doing so. Her living room was very comfortable. She had a fire going, which was odd, since she didn't have a fireplace. The old horsehair couch, which perfectly matched the old horsehair chair, had an Afghan over the back and functional cloth antimacassars on the arms. It was firm and familiar, and smelled like dog, which was odd since she didn't have any pets. There were four different-sized candles on her coffee table that didn't have any scent. There was an oil painting on her wall, framed in thick dark wood, of a violent wave crashing over the jagged rocks in a remote cove. The smoothly painted sky was dark and angry and the water was sea-foam green with light shining through the crested, frothy swells.

(*Steve*? **Yes**? *No fire and no dog.* **Wow, I thought I had gotten away with it.** *Not likely.* **I let you get away with antimacassars.**)

Then a big, big, big, really big bomb blew up and everyone and their dogs vaporized. Her stereo was one of those all-in-one pseudo-modular ones you could get at a warehouse store for under a hundred dollars. Anyone who listened to Bread didn't need a good stereo. The place was comfortable and functional and a little funky and a lot lonely. Like an English kitchen. Or a Dutch date. The ivory-colored Princess phone was where it always was on the end table next to the lamp, taunting her. She looked at it wondering who she could call. Not Peter, of course, although she couldn't come up with an exact reason why not. She didn't know many people in the "just calling to say hi" sense, which is how she thought she liked it, but she had really enjoyed spending the night with Peter and joking with him and cuddling with him and waking up with him. And having sex with him.

That stupid Vincent had implied no one had ever asked her to marry them, the idiot. Well, no one had, but that was her choice. And what's with him being a "Bear" for God's sake? I mean, he's hairy and all, but he's so wiry. And she didn't buy the whole spelling thing. She had thought her life was orderly and consistent and fine, but spending the night with a man, even if it had been a gay one, was making her feel lonely. What was even worse was that she was beginning to realize, looking around the room, that lonely was how she usually felt. She had just never called it that. She had called it Bob. **(Geoff, we had a perfectly good scene going, there, and you had to ruin it.** *You were going to do it, anyway! You always do! I was just heading you off!* **You certainly are an angry person.** *Ermine, damn it!*)

The phone rang and Roz jumped, startled that it really was beckoning her. Then she got over herself and answered it.

"Hi, it's Peter," Peter said.

"Oh," Roz said. "Hi. How's your jaw?"

"Fine. Bruised, a little. The swelling's gone down. Hey, Roz?"

"Yeah?"

"I was just wondering what... I mean do we... are we... after Friday night, I mean Saturday morning... I mean... are we..."

"Oh, for Christ sake, Peter. We had a romp. I'm not interested in marrying and settling down. And I'm pretty sure you're not either. Especially with me."

"Well, um... I've never... Um... I had fun."

"So did I, but get over it. Jesus."

"Okay," Peter said. "I'll talk to you soon. Maybe I can fix you dinner sometime."

"Peter. I don't want to date you. You're gay. Find a nice man."

When they hung up, she looked around her comfortable place with the wave painting and throw rugs and antimacassars and Afghans and big cushions and was surprised when she started crying. (**Well, it serves her right. She shouldn't have been so mean to Peter. He's sensitive.** *Why, because he's gay?* **Don't be so sensitive.**)

Peter got to the theater before everyone else Monday morning and set about opening up. He was back at his desk looking over the reports from the weekend's receipts for Of Mice and Men, which had done pretty well for a January weekend, when he heard Stella come toward the office. At least it should have been Stella, but whoever it was seemed to be humming a jaunty ditty, and if he had ever heard Stella hum, he was sure it had never been any kind of ditty, and if it had been one, it would never have been jaunty. Something about the jauntiness of the ditty really bothered something in the lower half of Peter's stomach. When she came into the office, she flung her coat on the hook on the back of the door, threw her purse onto her desk and flounced into chair.

"Good morning," she said cheerily.

"You're awfully peppy today," Peter said with a trace of bitterness that he didn't even try to hide.

"Oh," Stella said. She flipped her hair, but instead of it being superior, the move seemed soft and sensual, almost girlishly innocent. "Am I?"

Peter couldn't help himself, he pictured her and Jim together. The discomfort in the lower half of his stomach moved up to his chest and fluttered around his heart for a while, snickering.

"You messed up on last week's deposit," he said maliciously, knowing the worst thing he could do to her was impugn her abilities. Especially when there was cause.

"Oh," she said. "I'll go over them again."

She smiled, began humming again, and opened her books. Was it possible, Peter thought, that Stella had never been intimate with a gentleman in the entire time he had known her? No, she had dated Bear for over a year and he couldn't imagine Bear not dallying with someone he was dating for that long. Was Jim really that good? Sad, simple Jim? Or had Agnes taught Jim things that made him be that good? Peter had never thought that the phrase "all she needs is to get laid" had any credence, but here, right in front of him seemed to be irrefutable proof that a good intimate dalliance with someone could change an entire personality over the course of one weekend. And to think he had made Jim sleep on the couch last Wednesday. He had to get out of the room. Her ease was making him feel decidedly uneasy, and he was sure, if he stayed, he'd say more bitchy things to her. And they would simply glide by her like spent shells, impotent and unimpressive.

"I'm going to go check on the progress of the Odd Couple set," he said.

"It's capital 'T'," she said.

"What?"

"It's 'The Odd Couple'."

"No," he said with more than an edge of snottiness, "I'm going to go check on the set for Odd Couple. No capital 't'."

"But the play is actually 'The Odd Couple'."

"I was truncating it. It's what real theater people do with play titles."

"Say 'hi' to Bear," she said, not even taking that bait, and started whistling the jaunty ditty and nodding her head in a disturbingly perky way.

Peter put his coat and mittens on and went back to the shed where Bear was working with a few volunteers. One of which was Jim. Who looked different, somehow. Older. Wiser. Less perky. He was actually a man, now. It was too much for Peter. He stormed back to the office and started speaking before he even got his coat off.

"If you had the cue for passion I had, you would drown the stage in tears!" he said.

"Huh?" Stella said.

"How dare you come in here all..."

"All what?" Stella said, and flipped her hair.

This time it was the old flip, which should have calmed Peter with its familiarity, but each dark strand floating by her face in sensual precision irked him in ways he wasn't aware he could be irked. When her hair made its final bounce and settled back into its job of the soft framing of her head, Peter was ready to pounce.

"Nothing," he said, petulantly.

He wanted to say she was being entirely too pleased with herself. That she wasn't even gloating about having gotten Jim in the sack, she was just being happy about it and that she should be gloating so he would have a reason to be so angry with her. He wanted to rail about how she should be ashamed about how happy she was being all over the place. He wanted to make her feel small and alone and unhappy. He felt awful that he wanted all that and he was angry that she was making him feel awful and he wanted her to feel awful, too. Actually, he wanted her to be her miserable self so he could have someone to talk to about how confused he was about the whole weekend with Roz and Lee and the cars and Bear and Vincent and everything.

"Fine," she said, then smiled pleasantly to herself and set to work on the books.

Peter flounced down into his chair. He had meant to sit down in a heavy huff that made the whole room take notice, but all he achieved was a flounce. Stella looked up from her work.

"Is everything all right, Peter?" she asked. She seemed to really be concerned, which really frosted Peter over.

"No, I'm not all right, Stella, I'm a mess. The last person I dated used me to confirm his straightness then came over to my house last week crying on my shoulder about his affair with a sixty year old sex pot ending and wanted to stay over again just to drive me insane and two days later is happily sleeping with you and making you both into these angelic serene beings and I spent the whole weekend trying to find a friend who wasn't straight or taken and liked fat middle-aged men with scruffy beards and then I had my first wom..." Peter said before he could stop himself, then put his hands on his mouth in case it wanted to say more and make him want to staple it shut and slam his head in a drawer repeatedly until he forgot who he was and could spend the rest of his life happily drooling into his gruel.

"You had what?" Stella said, pointedly glossing over everything he had said all the way up to the "... had my first wom..." part. Damn her.

Peter kept his hands over his mouth.

"You slept with a woman?" Stella asked. "How was it? Who was it? Do I know her? How did you do? How did she do? Did you like it? Was it different than men? Come on, don't stop there, damn it. Be fair."

Peter could feel his entire body flushing. He felt like an old, bearded Charlie Brown. (**Except that Charlie Brown was bald.** *And he wasn't gay, he liked the Little Red Haired Girl.* **She was just a beard.** *Charlie Brown should be off limits.* **Okay. Sorry, Mr. Schultz. May you rest in peace.**) The blood drained from every extremity including his head, then realized it had no place to drain to if it were draining from everywhere and rushed back, making him dark red from head to toe. He gave up and took his hands from his mouth.

"My friend Roz," Peter said with sad resignation. "She took me home after knocking into me at the hill. We started out just watching movies. I'm not really sure even how what happened happened."

"Do I know Roz?"

"I don't know," Peter said. The blood was beginning to go back to its normal circulation pattern. "She works at the grocery store."

"How was it?"

"I don't know!" Peter said. "That's the problem. Fine, I guess. I was tired. My jaw hurt."

"Your jaw hurt?" Stella asked, punctuating it with a strange glint.

"No, you idiot, she kicked me."

"Really?"

"That's where she knocked into me at the hill. Her foot knocked into my jaw. My jaw hurt. Stop thinking that! I'm gay, not kinky, and now I'm very confused."

As soon as he said that he realized that he had never actually said that word to Stella. He knew she knew, they had hinted about Lee and talked about Jim and she called him "bitch" all the time, which isn't something you go around doing to a straight man, but he had never said it out loud to her.

"So you didn't like it," Stella said kindly.

"I guess I liked it fine," he said. "Obviously I liked it better than Jim liked it. I mean... I'm... I..."

"I know what you mean," she said.

Just then, the office door flew open and Jim thrust his young, blond head into the room. It had a huge, silly, endearing grin on it and it stared fondly and longingly at Stella. He was about to say something, probably something insufferably cute, then caught a little movement from the other side of the room and turned his eyes just enough to notice Peter. His pants tented. (*No they didn't.* **Why are pants plural**? *Singular would be a sock. Now shut up and create.*) The grin on his face froze into a strange parody of itself and he withdrew and closed the door, then tip-toed quietly away. Probably tip-toed all the way back to the shed. Both Peter and Stella stared after him. Stella's face softened with a small smile. Peter sighed.

"He has a really good body," Stella said.

"Yeah," Peter agreed. His sock tented.

Lee sat on his couch. He had been doing very little else for the last two-and-a-half days, and was very bored with it. He wanted to go down into the basement and build something, but walking to and from the bathroom was hard enough. Contemplating going down the stairs gave him shivers, even with the thought of power tools at the end of the trek. He had occupied the last forty-seven minutes looking at his watch, counting down the moments when he would have to leave to go to rehearsal. He still didn't know how he was going to get to Agnes's house. He couldn't drive. He briefly thought about asking Abby to take him, but, although they were talking to each other, and she had even stayed over Monday night, he couldn't ask her that. He was afraid to start up the whole argument about the play again. He could call Peter, but he always imposed on Peter, and he didn't want Peter to be only a foul weather friend. In fact, he determined that he would invite Peter over for dinner as soon as he thought he could stand up long enough to cook something. Bear. But Bear had already gone above and beyond getting his car. And Twain and Matt were out because they were already taking up the slack of him not working, and how do you call your boss and say "I know I haven't been at work, but can you take me to rehearsal tonight? Oh, and I won't be at work again tomorrow."

What do other people do? They ride the bus. He knew nothing about buses. And he liked it that way. He could take a cab. It couldn't be that expensive. He lived in town and Agnes was in town. The ride from the police station had only cost him twenty bucks including tip, and that was way over on the edge of town. He picked up the phone book and turned to Taxi Cabs. He expected to see maybe two or three companies. There were thirty-six, starting with AAA Cab Company and ending with Zion Taxi and Condom Emporium. He never used the first name in the book, so he started with Aaron's Livery. The line was disconnected. Well, a livery company in a town like River Bend was doomed to failure. The second company had a recording with the voice of a woman who sounded like she had been drinking Jack and smoking cigars. He didn't leave a message.

On the twenty-third call an actual person answered. He was so surprised he didn't know what to say.

"Oh," he said. "I didn't expect a person."

"What did you expect?"

"Is this a cab company?"

"Yes," the guy said very patiently. "Do you need a cab?"

"Yes, yes I do," Lee said.

There was a pause that sounded expectant, then the guy said, "Where do you live? Where are you going? When do you need to be there?"

Lee told him where he lived, where Agnes lived and that rehearsal started at seven. The guy said he'd be there by six-thirty and hung up. At six twenty-eight there was a knock at the door. Lee had spent the last half hour getting dressed. The shoes had taken most of that time. He hadn't put shoes on since he'd gotten back from the hospital. He could get them on, but couldn't bend to tie them. He had always hated loafers, but was beginning to see their point. He was able to slip the shoes on, finally, but tying them was impossible. After trying everything he could think of, including trying to bend his legs backwards on the bed and tying them behind himself, he resigned himself to going out with untied shoes, and tucked the laces in with a yardstick. (**He just has a yardstick laying around, huh**? *He's Lee, Steve. He would.* **Okay. How about a meterstick**? *No, Steve, he's from Chicago.* **Oh, yeah.**)

He opened the door. The guy standing there looked strangely familiar, but everyone in River Bend looked familiar, it seemed.

"The transient jail-bird," the cabby said. "I never forget a fare."

"Please," Lee said, miserably, wondering if he would ever live down his first week in River Bend. "Call me Lee."

"Do you have money this time?" the cabby said. "Lee?"

"Of course I do," Lee said. "Oh, fuck."

"Don't tell me," the cabby said.

Lee pulled out his wallet. If it had been a cartoon, a moth would have flown out of it. Since it wasn't a cartoon, it was a bat. (*Steve, you can't fit a bat in your wallet.* **You can if you fold them properly**. *Go get bent.*) Abby had used his last twenty of ready cash to get provisions. And never gave him the change. Damn kids.

"There's an ATM right around the corner," Lee said sheepishly.

"I'm a cabby," the cabby said. "I know where they all are. Do you have more then nineteen ninety-nine in there?"

"Yes," Lee said indignantly and started out the door.

The cabby caught him by the arm just in time and helped him. Lee felt like an eighty-year-old invalid and didn't like it. A thirty-seven year old invalid was bad enough. They got to the bank and the cabby helped Lee out and up to the ATM. Lee got his card from his wallet and was about to insert it into the slot when he noticed the little screen.

"Temporarily out of service," it said. It didn't even have the decency to apologize. Or even beep. He started to hyperventilate. Cabbies carried guns, he was sure of it. He never believed the signs in the windows that said "Driver carries less than twenty dollars in cash." How could they give change with only twenty in cash? Do they deposit the money at the cabby place after each fare? That would just be silly. So they carried more than twenty. Probably much more. Which is why they carried guns. He's going to shoot me dead. Lee had a few moments to figure out what to do. The cabby was standing the appropriate ATM distance away, so he hadn't yet seen the out of order sign screaming its out of orderness. I could just make a run for it, Lee thought. Well, I could make a hobble for it.

"What's the matter?" the cabby said when he realized there had been no appreciable movement for far too many seconds.

Lee shakily pointed to the readout. He was going to die right here. With untied shoes. At least he was wearing clean underwear. He would have shouted "It's not my fault" but even in his mind it sounded too much like what the coward would say in the black and white movie while the hero stood there stoically, taking his medicine like a man.

"It's not my fault," he said quietly.

The cabby sighed.

"We'll go to the grocery store," he said.

Lee was confused.

"Where you can buy something and get cash over," the cabby said slowly as if talking to a child. "Come on, Lee."

Lee bowed his head, humbled in the presence of a superior mind. He didn't know why this man was driving a cab. He was probably going to be canonized. The patron saint of cash machines. Or just of cash. The impossible was already taken by Jude.

When they got to the grocery store, they were just locking the doors. (*Steve! That's contrived suspense.* **No it isn't, it's just cruel**. *Well stop it. The grocery store is open later than six- forty-seven.*) The cabby helped Lee out of the cab and into the store.

"I don't need anything," Lee said. He was used to feeling helpless around this man.

"Get a pack of Necco Wafers™."

"Who are you?" Lee asked. "You get something."

"Really?" the cabby said.

"Yeah. Just don't go crazy."

Four to six minutes later they were standing in front of the deli counter.

"Salami," the cabby said to Roz. "Thinly sliced. About six or seven pounds. He's buying."

He winked and Roz laughed. The cabby said just make it a quarter pound, and Lee started breathing again and laughed with them. Roz said hi to Lee and set the slicer. Lee remembered that he hadn't given the cabby a tip the last time and told her to make it a half pound. She got sixty-three slices out of it. Lee noticed that she didn't give the cabby an extra slice. It made him feel special, somehow. Which made him feel really pitiful because the only way he could feel special was that he was once given an extra slice of very, very thinly sliced salami because he had obviously been so poor. What a pathetic man I'm turning out to be, he thought. I'm sure glad my mom's dead. (*Steve!* **Sorry.** *That goes way over the line.* **Sorry**. *His mother's not dead. You apologize this minute.* **Sorry, Mrs. Lee's mom**. *That's better.* **She's in a coma.**)

With the side trips to the bank and the store, the fare came to nineteen dollars. Lee gave the cabby the twenty he had gotten from cash back. The cabby called him a hussy, and Lee called him a tart. The side trips also made him late to rehearsal.

"You're late, Mr. Harris," Agnes said when he came into her living room.

"I'm sorry," Lee said. "I had to take a cab. And we had to stop for cash. Twice. Oh."

"Oh, what?" Agnes said. She didn't like late comers and this absurd conversation was taking even more time.

"I didn't get enough money for a ride back."

"You can deal with that later," she said.

"I'll take you home," Jim said with a smile. "No problem."

"You can deal with that later," Agnes said with a tone of finality that everyone took note of.

Lee shuffled to a chair and carefully sat. Once he was settled, he realized the room was very quiet. Agnes was watching him with a very cold look on her face, and everyone else was watching her, waiting for the drama. Actors were such pains in the butt, Lee thought.

"I'm fine," he said, and to prove it stood and almost fell over, so he sat back down again. "I'm fine."

Agnes shook her head skeptically, but continued with her interrupted rehearsal. Lee was grateful that at least some of the scenes were spent sitting down. Thank goodness he wasn't still doing Look Homeward Angel where he had to almost carry Andrew on to the stage. Maybe he could figure out a way where someone here could help him across the stage. Except it would probably have to be Jim.

With the difficulty moving, Lee found it easy to be sarcastic to everyone, which is mostly what Roy did in The Odd Couple. Of course, it was easy to be sarcastic to Vinnie because Vinnie was being played by Jim. Every time he spoke a sarcastic line to Jim, though, Jim looked at him sort of confused and hurt, which made him want to be sarcastic all over again. Lee had to concentrate hard simply on moving, and the unpleasant thought of being driven home by Jim kept getting in his way, so he wasn't really thinking much about acting, anyway. Jim was watching him even more than usual during the whole rehearsal, though, which made it really hard to concentrate on moving. Of course, tonight everyone seemed to be watching him more than usual, so he couldn't be too annoyed with Jim. But he was, anyway. Especially when he noticed that Jim was wearing the same style of pants he usually wore. Which just felt creepy.

There was a moment where the stage directions required Lee to make a "mad dash" back to his chair. Any dash Lee attempted to make would be mad, so he just did the best he could. There was a lot more running around and back and forth, trying to make sure Felix didn't kill himself all over the place than Lee remembered, and he felt a little like the Keystone Cop who was always three steps behind the rest of the pack. The one whose coccyx really throbbed. The one moment that worried everyone, but that no one was willing to admit they were worried about, was the moment when Felix disappears into the bathroom, and when he comes out Roy is hanging on to him, then a few seconds later he collapses into Roy's arms. When they got to that moment, everyone stopped and Agnes stood still, deep in thought for a very long time. All the actors watched her, expectantly. Except Lee who watched her in muted terror. Almost nothing that came out of that long a contemplation could be good for his back. He was about to be fired, he was sure of it. From a little part in a community theatre production of a Neil Simon play in fucking River Bend. Damn Abby.

When Agnes looked up, she muttered to herself a little then spoke out loud in her best "I'm the director, damn it, listen to me" voice.

"Shit," she said. "It's easy. We'll just have Vinnie do it. Jim, darling, could you hang on to Felix as he comes out of the bathroom? Good. Let's try it. Places everyone."

Lee was right. Nothing good at all came from that contemplation.

During the first break, Jim came up to Lee and started talking about Stella. It seemed to Lee from the words coming out of Jim's mouth that Jim was sleeping with Stella, which confused him a little. Of course, Peter had said that Jim was straight. But wasn't he sleeping with Agnes? Jim also seemed, when talking about Stella, to have less of the annoying puppy dog demeanor. He seemed strangely adult. Lee listened as politely as it was possible to listen to a man wearing matching pants, hoping Jim wouldn't get too personal or descriptive. When it looked like it might go in that direction, he excused himself and hobbled over to Kim to start a conversation with her.

"I spent the afternoon with Abby on Saturday," Kim said. "She was really mad at you."

"Oh," Lee said. "Yeah."

That wasn't what he had wanted to talk about. Actually any subject would have been better than finding out his girlfriend was spreading details of their life together to everyone. Of course, he had told Peter about the fight, but he had a reason. He'd needed a ride to get his car. That was very different. He hadn't picked up the phone just to gossip. Gossip had just happened all on its own, unbidden. He turned to find someone else to talk with, but Kim spoke again.

"And I guess she's not pregnant, either."

"When did you find that out?" Lee heard coming out of his mouth before his brain had time to tell it to shut the fuck up.

"Sunday morning," Kim said with a smile. "She called me, you know, right after. Good news."

Lee turned and found a chair to sit in and spent the rest of the break practicing looking unapproachable. It was easy when he started staring at his shoes and remembered they weren't tied.

When they were done going through all the card playing scenes several times and were all sitting in a circle for notes, Lee was surprised when Agnes told him he was doing a fine job and to keep it up. It made the pounding throb in his butt from all the rushing around almost worth it. When they all got ready to leave, Jim tried to help Lee with his coat.

"I can do it," Lee said sharply, then felt a little ashamed and added, "Thanks."

When they opened the front door and Lee saw the distance they had to go over snow and ice at a dangerous incline to get to Jim's car, he froze. Jim, who had simply bound out the door toward his car, stopped when he realized Lee wasn't right there beside him. He came back and took Lee by the arm. Lee really wanted to tell him he was fine, but he also really needed the help. Having been led around by the cabby was one thing. Being led by Jim was entirely too humiliating. They looked like the Bobbsey Twins with the same color and style

Dockers walking arm-in-arm. And if he were going to look like a twin, he didn't want it to be turn of the century, blond, curly-haired cute little urchin detective ones. It was a relief when he was finally in the car and the door was finally shut. He had a brief moment of respite while Jim bound around the car to climb into the driver's seat.

When Jim started the car, Lee started to give him directions, but he said he remembered where Lee lived. This information didn't please Lee at all. Lee tried to ride in silence, but Jim kept talking about Stella. Then he mentioned how different it was than with Peter. Then he asked if Lee knew he had been with Peter. Then he talked about Stella some more. The only thing that kept Lee from squirming during the whole ride home was the throbbing pain in his rear. In fact, the only thing that kept him from just shouting for Jim to be quiet about his sexual life was the pain in his rear. He wanted to shout that they weren't friends and Jim shouldn't be talking about that stuff with him. Or anyone, for that matter. He wanted to shout that he didn't even talk about that stuff with his closest friends. He wanted to shout that he didn't even talk about that stuff with his girlfriend, but that would be too close to talking about that kind of stuff. He also couldn't shout that stuff because the man was giving him a ride home. He concentrated on not squirming.

The ride itself was surprisingly smooth, though. Even while talking about things no civil person would talk to a relative stranger about, Jim seemed to be driving especially cautiously, very careful not to jostle Lee. When Lee realized this, he felt a little guilty for being so annoyed at Jim. Until Jim described a particularly exotic move that Agnes had taught him. Then Lee wondered how much damage he would do if he just opened the door and flung himself into the next snow drift.

When they got to Lee's house, Jim shut the engine off, which worried Lee, then came around the car and opened Lee's door. Lee really wished he could walk over snow by himself, but let Jim help him out of the car and escort him by the arm up the steps. During the endless walk, Lee determined that the next time he would take a cab both ways. He would buy a cab. He would open one of the many defunct companies he had called that afternoon and have his own cab pick him up and take him home. He would simply walk the whole way. Both ways. He would fly. He would get over himself and have

Abby take him. When they got to the front door, Lee took out his keys. Jim stood there expectantly. He looked disturbingly like a young man on a first date waiting for a sign that he could get a good-night kiss. Lee felt an almost uncontrollable urge to shake Jim's hand. He shuddered and unlocked the door.

"I'd invite you in, but," Lee said. "Um... Thanks."

He opened the door, and with the quickest move he had been able to manage in several days, stepped in and closed the door, then leaned up against it. He could feel Jim hesitate all the way through the heavy door, then heard him turn and walk down the steps and walkway, crunching in the snow and frost with a disappointed gait. Lee waited until he heard the car start and drive off, which seemed to take an unusually long time, as if Jim were sitting in his car waiting for him to change his mind and invite him in. When Lee finally pushed away from the door and moved toward the couch, he realized he was going to pay for the Baryshnikovian move into the house. He sat on the couch with his coat still on and took a pill. He kicked off his shoes and was glad for the first time that night that he hadn't been able to tie them. It took another pill before he could get the image of Jim and Agnes and that exotic move out of his head.

The following Wednesday afternoon, the tin shed was cold. The rotten cheese and burning hair smell of the paint wasn't nearly as overpowering in the cold air, it sort of just stayed underneath the chill, insinuating itself into your nostrils, sidling past the frozen nose hairs and hinting at something dead or evil or both. The only heat in the uninsulated building came from the old, battered, paint-splattered wood-burning stove in the corner which had an old-fashioned, battered, paint-splattered, tin, percolating coffee pot sitting on it. The air around the stove was unbearably hot, but chilled exponentially the further you moved away from it. Bear usually didn't notice the cold, he was usually working too hard to notice, but at that moment he was sitting on a stool, leaning against a workbench staring at a window flat that he had just spattered with texture. Normally, he wouldn't be staring at a recently spattered window flat, he would know it was fine and would move on to the next task, but he was distracted. So distracted that he forgot he was still holding the paintbrush that he had used to spatter the texture onto the flat. Paint dripped off the brush and hit the floor of the shed with an audible bleup. Bear looked toward the sound, then shivered with the cold. He looked around the shed. The only volunteer that was working that day had just left to get some lunch. Bear put the brush down and picked up the phone, which had, at one time, been a black Trimline®. It was still a Trimline®, of course, built solid in the days when the phone company still owned all the phones, but now it was smudged with every color imaginable except for a curious lack of umber. He dialed long distance information.

"In Smith's Creek. Dee Dee Pugh, please."

He waited for a moment.

"Oh. Um... Try her maiden name," he said. "Um... Pitality. Oh, gosh, I don't know. Um. P - I - T - I - no, wait a minute, P - I - no, A - um... P - O - T - no, it is I. P - I - T - T - um... Damn..." **(Geoff!** *What?* **He's not you, he can spell.** *We already said he couldn't.* **Anyway, it's right up there, two sentences ago. Sheesh.)**

"P - I - T - A - L - I - T - Y," he blurted really fast. (*Happey?* **Sure.**) "Okay, thanks."

He dialed the number and waited while it rang.

"Hi, Dee Dee?" he said. "Dee Dee, it's Bear. Vincent."

There was a long pause **(How long, Geoff?** *It doesn't matter.* **Yes it does. Every detail is important.)** There was a two minute, forty-six second pause before Dee Dee said anything, then all she said was "Oh."

"Yeah. I ran into Roz the other day. I got to thinking about everything," he said, not really knowing at all where he was headed with this phone call. In fact he now wished he had just gone and spattered another flat and resisted the whole distraction thing. "I... um... I'm really sorry for everything I put you through."

He could feel the ends of his moustache hairs quiver. He hadn't shaved, and he rubbed his chin, leaving a long streak of paint that counterpointed nicely with the other long streaks of paint in his stubble. Dee Dee was a little flummoxed, obviously, not having expected him to call, and not ever having expected him to apologize if he did happen to call.

"Thank you," she said, finally.

"Sure," he said.

He was about to hang up and pretend for the rest of his life that he had never made this strange and humiliating phone call, when she suggested they might get together for coffee sometime.

"Oh," he said. "Sure. Um... When?"

"I don't know, this week is kind of bad for me. How about sometime next week?"

There was a two minute fifty-two second pause.

"Um, no," he said, and cringed. "There's a play opening next week."

The phone suddenly got colder than that side of the room.

"Thanks for calling," Dee Dee said and hung up.

Bear still sat on the stool, still leaned against the work bench, still held the phone against his ear until it started squealing its piercing, pulsing warning tone, at which point he hung it up very fast and left the shed to go reestablish his masculine stoicism in the men's room.

After his experience with the first rehearsal after the accident, Lee had pointedly arranged rides to and from rehearsals well in advance so that he had an honest excuse every time Jim offered him another ride. His rehearsals had only been twice a week thus far, though, so he had little else to do all day. And doing nothing all day was never something Lee could stand for very long. And doing it sitting down was even worse, so every few days he tried going out, getting in his car, starting it up and driving. There were days when he could drive almost a whole block before the leg movement required to step on the brake became excruciating, and he had to park and wait for the pain to subside so he could get back to his house. There were also days when just stepping down the steps was more than he could manage.

Peter did come by for dinner that Saturday, but it was a boring evening where nothing untoward happened, so we won't impose it on you. By the next Tuesday, Lee found that he could stand for long periods of time, so he figured that he could probably go back to work on a somewhat limited basis. Twain had been very patient, but enough was enough. He would have to find a way there and a way back, of course. Abby said she would take him there in the mornings on her way in to her job, which, of course, would give her more of an excuse to stay over more often, which, of course, they both thought was a good idea. And he could take a cab back.

Abby dropped him off at six-thirty the next morning, about a block from Twain's. (*She's not that mean, Steve.* **Hey, he made her get up early, it serves him right.** *She's not you.* **I know. I have perkier breasts.** *I'm gay and that even scares me.* **Wait, you're gay?**) Lee could stand to wash dishes for about twenty minutes, then he would have to sit, so he would slowly make his way out to the corner booth to clean and fill salt and pepper shakers, napkin holders, sugar dispensers and ketchup bottles. Then he'd get up and wash more dishes. The first day, he lasted three hours, after which Twain sent him home because he was starting to get testy.

The next day, he lasted almost four hours. Just as he was ready to leave, Andrew came in for the Champagne brunch. Twain was out of mimosas, though, so he just had sausages and eggs and a virgin Sex on the Beach. Lee came out from the back, taking his apron off. It was bloody. Today was slaughter day at Twain's. Every day was slaughter day at Twain's. (*Steve.* **Yes?** *Twain buys his beef already slaughtered just like you.* **Nobody mentioned beef.** *No wonder you never invite me over to your place.* **I will after we get that $2,060,000 we keep asking for.**) Andrew motioned for him and he hobbled over.

"Any word from Chicago?" Lee asked after he gingerly lowered himself onto the stool next to Andrew.

"Escrow went through," Andrew said. "It was a clean escrow. There should be no problems. You should be getting your check any day unless something drastic happens."

Lee was flabbergasted. (*Does "flabbergasted" have two "b"s or not two "b"s?* **I'm sorry, what was the question?**) His mind bounced around the inside of his head, trying to land on an appropriate response to that.

"Why didn't you tell me?" he finally said, after his eyes stopped fluttering around in their sockets.

"I just did," Andrew said.

"When?" Lee asked, hoping it was a more intelligent response. "I mean when did you find out? And when did it go through? And when will the check come? And what drastic could happen?"

"Calm down, Lee," Andrew said around a choice bite of sausage. "Can you drive, yet? How are you getting home?"

"Um...," Lee said. "A cab I guess. I want to know about the escrow."

"I'll drive you. It's not out of my way. Very much. And what are you worried about? You've got to still have a little of your settlement from the antiques left. And even if you don't, the check will get here soon. Sooner than either of us thought. The postal service isn't going to go on strike this very minute. The bank will honor the check when it comes. It'll all work out. This isn't fiction."

"Well, I know it's not," Lee said, sort of petulantly, annoyed at being talked to like a child.

"You sound like you think you're living in some satirical soap opera or something where bad things just always happen to you. The Trials and Tribulations of Lee Harris. Get a grip."

The ride home was even more boring than the dinner with Peter.

The third day after Lee came back to work, while he was filling salt shakers, Twain sat on the stool on his little platform in the corner of the dinner.

"The country is growing cold," he said into the microphone. "And in large places, a soft breeze wafts by, whispering doom. Listening to a radio at night will do, I said into my beer. And birds flew by because they can. I would fly, too. A blackbird sang in the dead of night on the wings of a snow white dove."

The whole place gave him a standing ovation. Of course, the only people there were the guy in the John Deere hat, the guy from Butte and a strange old woman in a fur coat with a Hungarian accent, who had ordered the cold borscht and a side of Tang. Lee figured that was his cue to call his cab.

When the cabby came into the diner to gather him up, Lee paid him in advance. It just seemed easier that way. On the way to his house Lee decided that, as he was riding with this guy so often, he should at least know what the guy's name was.

"Cab," the guy said.

"You're kidding," Lee said. "What's your last name, Driver?"

"No," Cab said.

Lee felt very odd not participating in the striking of the Of Mice and Men set the Sunday after closing. Partly because he was now used to being part of that process, and partly because it would erase Jim having gotten a part in it when he didn't. It felt even weirder not helping load the Odd Couple set into the theater. He was beginning to think of himself as a theater person. And it seemed that fractured coccyxs were not conducive to active participation as theater people. (**Shouldn't that be "coccyxi"**? *I don't know, spell check doesn't like either one of them.*)

Describing hell week would have taken entirely too many words and cut into their drinking time, so Steve and Geoff flashed forward to opening night.

The air was brisk with a chilly wind which blew snow up from the drifts in crystalline swirls that glinted and sparkled in the light from the street lamps and car headlights. Veronica Park walked up to the ticket booth, escorted by her roommate Ron, who was wearing a lot more than he had been the last time we saw him, and his date, who had blond hair with brown roots and looked like she might have more tattoos than Ron did under her old coat. Ron seemed like the type of guy who only dated women that looked like Courtney Love™. Veronica picked up their tickets and they went inside. The young woman who stood behind them in line, bundled in a thick, fuzzy coat, told the nice blue-haired lady who was manning the booth that she had ordered a ticket by phone that afternoon.

"And what's your name, Dear?" the blue-haired lady asked, vapidly.

It wasn't easy to make such a simple inquiry sound vapid, but she managed. It was a talent that should be studied by a scholarly group of scientists with a fat research grant, but, as she was completely unaware of her gift, it would always be hidden under its little bushel basket like an obscure biblical reference.

"Dee Dee. Dee Dee Pitality. That's P - I - T - O, no, P - I - T..."

(*Stop. Now.*)

Dee Dee got her ticket, paid for it and went into the lobby, which was wonderfully warm after the cold outside. She felt a little strange, out of place in the room that was beginning to fill with people waiting to see the play.

Headline came in wearing a coat that matched his black hair. The cold air that followed him in matched his ice-blue eyes. He also looked a little out of place. He often served the theater crowd after a rehearsal or performance, but had never been to an actual play. Dating Agnes Livingstone, however, made it seem impossible not to show up to opening night. Dating Agnes Livingstone made it seem impossible not to do lots of things he had never considered doing. He looked around to see if he recognized anybody. He recognized that woman, what was her name, Abby, who came in to The Office lately with that guy who drinks Tanquerey and tonic and got really sloppy that first night when he sat next to Kim Anderson. Lee something. He recognized almost everybody in the lobby, actually, but the context was all wrong, so he kept to himself.

Abby took off her coat. Her sweatshirt said "A Bad Day Fishing Is Better than a Good Day Angling". She'd gotten it at the Everything Less than a Buck Unless Otherwise Marked™ store. It was on sale because it was irregular. Of course, so was she, so it worked out.

More people were gathering. It was going to be a full house. Stella came in, followed closely by Twain who was escorting a stunning woman in her mid forties with salt and pepper hair and mischievous green eyes. Someone opened the doors to the auditorium and a few people went in. Most, however, stayed in the lobby talking and laughing. The sound of people in a theater lobby was distinct from the sound of people in any other environment. It was a happy sound, chaotic and expectant. Bursts of bright laughter punctuated it, laughter that would have sounded too loud or enthusiastic elsewhere, but sounded just right in the light, expansive air there. Dee Dee didn't feel part of the crowd, so she went in and found her seat. It was the second worse seat in the theater.

Backstage, Lee sat in his chair at the makeup counter, looking at his reflection in the mirror, fiddling with a roll of theatrical tissue. His face stared back at him, pale and strained. It had been a bad day, and his back really, really hurt. Peter stepped into the dressing room to wish everyone a good show, then came over to Lee.

"How're you doing?" he asked, concerned, when he saw the expression on Lee's face.

"I don't know, Peter," Lee said. "I don't know how I'm going to get through this. My back really hurts."

Peter put his hand on Lee's shoulder reassuringly and told him he'd be fine.

A few minutes after Peter left, Kim poked her head in.

"Places, everyone," she said.

Lee's heart jumped, which made his back hurt more. Then he sneezed.

Will Lee make it through the play?
Will he ruin opening night?
If he ruins it, what will Agnes do to him?
If he makes it, what will Agnes do to him?
Will Lee let her do it?
Will he like it?
Why is Dee Dee there?
What's Cab's last name?
What was on Crapp's last tape?
How long will Jim and Stella continue being calmed
by each other?
Will they nauseate everyone first?
Even Twain?
Will Twain win a Pulitzer?
How about a Wurlitzer?
How about a Howitzer?
How about a Dancer?
Or a Dasher?
Or a Prancer or a Vixen?
Or a Comet, Cupid, Donner or Blitzen?
Will winter ever end?
Sheesh, guys.

To find the answers to these and other chilling challenges,
tune into our next installment:
"Risk Is Just a Board Game"

This installment first published December 21, 2003

Geoff Hoff and Steve Mancini

What's come before: Lee Harris is having trouble walking because he fractured his coccyx, which has caused some consternation to his fellow cast members in the Willow Lane Theatre's production of The Odd Couple, and he's awaiting the check from the sale of the house he and his ex-wife shared in Chicago. Bear, the tech director of the theater, is having problems dealing with the realization that he wasn't a very good husband to his ex-wife Dee Dee, who showed up unexpectedly at the opening of The Odd Couple. Agnes, the sixty year old director of The Odd Couple, has dated increasingly younger men since her husband died, and is now seeing Headline, the stunningly handsome, twenty-three year old bartender at the local tavern. Peter, who works in the front office of the theater and is Lee's best friend, is having trouble dealing with his sexuality now that he's been with a woman. Stella, who works with Peter, and Jim, who dated Peter, don't seem to be having any problems except that they are annoying everyone with their happiness together. The entire town of River Bend, it seems, has come to the opening night of The Odd Couple, including Twain, who always bathes before coming to opening night. When all this stuff happened, it was hysterically funny. Read the previous installments to get the laughs, then come back here.

Installment Twenty-Four
"Risk is Just a Board Game"

Agnes's house was noisy and festive. Benny Goodman flowed seductively from the speakers in the corners at just the right volume; loud enough to set the mood but not so loud that it made conversation hard. There weren't many guests, yet; the play had ended only a short time before. The cast members needed to get out of costume and makeup and the crew needed to close the theatre before leaving for the opening night party. Agnes had left the theatre as soon as the final curtain fell, after a quick trip back to both dressing rooms to congratulate the cast and say she'd see them all at the party, in order to see that everything was satisfactory at the house before anyone arrived. People began trickling in shortly after she got there; those who had been in the audience, theatre folk who weren't involved in this production, friends and family of those who were and those who knew opening night parties were a good bet for free food and alcohol. Peter had been one of the first to arrive, which was to be expected, but wasn't put immediately to work, which wasn't. Everything was well in hand and Agnes had everything under her control, which is what Agnes did. Peter stood in a corner not knowing how to act at a party where he wasn't put to work. He decided to greet people as they came in. It wasn't real work, but it was something.

Headline came in shortly after Peter, went straight to Agnes and kissed her. Everyone within their immediate vicinity shuddered, but no one turned away. Theatre was theatre wherever you found it. When he was done kissing her, Agnes patted him gently on the shoulder and moved away to greet more guests. Headline stood awkwardly for a moment. He wasn't used to feeling awkward in any situation. He kind of liked it. Finally, he got bored with awkwardness and found the banquet table covered in a fine table cloth and heavily laden with almost as much booze as he kept behind the bar at the Office. He fixed himself a Seven and Seven. He used real Seagram's instead of the well bourbon he used at the bar when making a drink for himself. Then he mingled. Usually, in a crowd, he was behind the bar and any interaction was chatting up customers to get a good tip. He decided he liked mingling. It was turning out to be an interesting night for him: attending an opening night, feeling awkward, mingling and drinking real Seagram's. He hoped this thing with Agnes would last.

A young man wearing a tuxedo with pants shiny from use, shirt front a little dingy and listless and jacket cuffs slightly frayed, was circulating among the guests serving hors d'oeuvres from a tray. His pants were bunched under the belt in back, making his bottom look very odd, and his hair didn't seem to want to stay slicked down around the back of his part, which was crooked. He wore a white glove on his left claw. Peter sampled a stuffed mushroom cap from the tray. It wasn't very good. He would have used brie in the crab stuffing instead of cream cheese and he would have parboiled the mushroom caps then painted them with drawn butter before baking them so they stayed pale and smooth and didn't shrivel in that unsightly way like the legs of a woman too old to wear shorts or a man too hairy to wear Speedos or George Hamilton™. He took two more mushroom caps before the young man moved on, then followed him long enough to take one more.

When the cast began to arrive, the energy and decibel level in the house rose. Jim arrived with Stella. She had her hand daintily placed at his elbow, which was gallantly held slightly away from his side. For a brief moment it looked like he was wearing a driving jacket and gloves and had a handlebar moustache, and she had on an Easter bonnet and they held a parasol above and slightly behind their heads. In the Good Old Summertime floated out from the speakers in the corners. That only lasted a moment, though, before everyone in the room shook their heads and went back to their conversations. He was wearing a knock-off designer jacket and she was wearing a stupid smile and the music was It Don't Mean a Thing (If It Ain't Got That Swing). And it didn't.

Agnes greeted them and welcomed them to her home, which felt very odd to Jim, who had spent many nights there as the king of the castle. Well, maybe the duke. Then Agnes moved away, passing Headline, her hip surreptitiously glancing against his thigh as she did. Jim's eyes glazed over for a brief moment and he pressed his elbow to his side to remind himself of Stella's presence. She breathed in and sighed pleasantly at the movement. Jim calmed and they joined the party.

Abby escorted Lee in by the arm, but they didn't fade to a simpler time. She led him to a chair and deposited him, then went in search of food and drink. Mostly drink. Lee wasn't in a good mood at all and she needed to anesthetize her natural response to that before she popped him a good shot in his tail bone. When Lee lowered himself to the chair, he expressed his bad mood.

"Fuck," he said.

Agnes appeared as if from nowhere and handed him a ceramic bank shaped like an apple, a slit cut in the top near the stem, and the word "Cuss Bank" lettered on the side.

"You're kidding," Lee said.

"Twenty-five cents, Dear," she said.

"But you say 'shit' all the time."

"Not at parties. Fifty cents."

"You said twenty-five."

"That was for the first one."

She smiled sweetly and Lee pulled two damp quarters from his right pant pocket and slid them into the slot with an almost inaudible mutter.

"What, Dear?" Agnes asked.

"I said you're all nuts," Lee said defiantly and tried to find a position to sit where his butt didn't throb like a submarine engine or the lowest note on a baritone saxophone or a throbbing butt. Agnes patted him suggestively on the shoulder and disappeared back to wherever she had appeared from, fifty cents richer.

Lee looked around to see if he could locate Abby. Her hair was hard to miss and he finally spotted it. It had its back to him and was talking to Kim. Lee momentarily wished those two were still fighting so Abby would get a drink to him faster. He felt guilty about it briefly, but then Veronica Park came in, followed by a young man who looked vaguely familiar and a young woman who looked vaguely skanky. Veronica looked briefly in his direction, then her face did something funny and she looked away. Then she seemed to make a decision, turned back with a smile planted on her face, and marched determinedly toward him.

"I really enjoyed what you did tonight," she said, "Mr. Harris."

"Mr. Harris?" Lee blurted, flummoxed.

This woman whom he had kissed, who had brought him to her place and he had almost gone to bed with except that her roommate was noisily going to bed with someone else just a floor away, oh, that's who that guy is, her roommate, he was naked the last time he had seen him, was calling him "Mr. Harris."

"Um..." he added. "Thanks."

Abby appeared as suddenly as Agnes had and thrust a drink into his hand. She seemed to have that special talent that some women have where some trigger on the surface of their skin buzzed when a better looking, younger female was in proximity to their mate. (Insert very funny argument between Geoff and Steve about sensitivity and gender stereotypes with lots of topical references and intellectual allusions here.)

Veronica's own trigger buzzed and she moved on into the party. Lee looked sadly up to Abby.

"She called me 'Mr. Harris'," he said.

Abby smiled and sipped her Fuzzy Navel. Then she sipped her drink. Then Steve hit Geoff and he promised to behave himself. Peter came over with a plate of hors d'oeuvres and handed it to Lee.

"You looked incapacitated and Abby seemed encumbered with your drink," he said. "Don't waste your time with the mushroom caps. Hi, Abby."

"Peter," Abby said.

"Thanks," Lee said.

"You were good tonight," Peter said to Lee.

"Oh," Lee said, confused. "I'm not even sure how I got all of my lines out. Thanks."

Lee sat considering the compliment, then decided Peter was just being nice, so he added, "I had a hundred and three of them, you know."

"Are you okay?" Abby asked Peter.

"Yeah," he said. "I guess. Today a couple of board members came in to the theatre just to feel important and I was up to my armpits clearing a clogged toilet because Stella's volunteer never showed up. Great impression. Ah, well. We had a brilliant opening night, so it all evens out."

Just then Bear and Dee Dee came in.

"Wow," Peter said, and Lee and Abby looked at him for an explanation of the interjection. He noticed them waiting and explained that Bear never came to opening night parties. "He works so hard during hell week, I guess. After he closes the theatre down, he probably just goes home and dies."

Peter bustled over and greeted Bear.

"Hey, Peter," Bear said. "Oh. This is Dee Dee."

Peter's eyes got really wide. He really wanted to say "Roz's sister Dee Dee? Your ex-wife Dee Dee? The reason for all that social discomfort in the car Dee Dee?" but he just said "Hi" and left it at that.

"Dee Dee came to the play tonight," Bear said. His voice was a little odd when he said it.

217

"Oh," Peter said, really confused now. Weren't opening nights why they got divorced? "How... nice."

Just then the energy in the room shifted suddenly into the blue and all the noise slowed and quieted. Every face seemed to be slowly aligning like iron filings that had just discovered a magnet. Peter was one of the last to catch the field, but his face finally lined up properly. A spark of energy like a charged proton accelerated across the room toward a young man that almost no one in the room knew, a thin young man with tattoos on his arms. Those who did know him knew him as Ron.

The proton was Agnes and when she reached him, she attached herself to his arm and the energy from the two particles meeting burst out in a flash and re-animated the room, having diverse effects on the diverse occupants, each a distinct particle with its own properties and relationship to a metaphor stretched far beyond its physical and logical limits: Bear and Lee, across the room from one another, both shuddered and thought of power tools; Peter thought of men using power tools. Then he shook his head and searched the room for Jim, which didn't make much sense to him, but, hey, it was a molecular reaction; Jim watched Agnes pull the young man to the drink table and his stomach felt really fluttery and painful all of a sudden, which confused him. He looked at Stella, with whom he was very happy, hoping that would make his stomach behave. It helped a little. Stella saw the look on his face and her own face started brewing a storm, and Jim's stomach went even more funny.

"You're with me, now," She said coldly.

"What? I know. Of course. What do you mean?" Jim said stupidly.

He leaned over and kissed her, which calmed her slightly, but he kept one eye open and trained on Agnes and Ron.

Veronica had only one reaction.

"Eeeeww," she said.

Ron's skanky girlfriend agreed, grabbed Veronica and planted an open mouth kiss on her, just to make the point.

"Eeeewww," Veronica said again.

Headline caught sight of Billy, who was there as a device, and brought him a drink.

"How about that?" he asked, and Billy agreed. "I never thought I'd be too old for a sixty-year old woman." He thought about that and added, "I never thought I'd say that." He thought about that and added, "Hell, I never thought I'd be with a sixty-year old woman. Even when I'm sixty. Especially when I'm sixty. If I make it to sixty. But that has nothing to do with this party. What was I saying? Agnes. Wow."

"Nice ride while it lasted, though, huh?" Billy said.

Headline agreed, and wondered distractedly if he should be devastated. Billy moved off, waiting for another moment when the writers would need him to get a point across, and Headline checked to see what his reaction really was. Billy had been right, it had been a great ride. He spotted Kim and brought her a drink. It was really convenient being a bartender and knowing what everyone usually ordered. He had the perfect device to mingle. And now that he had been to an opening night and an opening night party he had a whole new perspective on the theatre crowd he had been serving all these years. Being a bartender added to his experience of the party, and now the party was going to add to his experience of work. He could mine this information for greater tips. Life was good. Agnes was already becoming a fond memory.

Lee thought about the moment a long time ago when he had seriously considered dating Agnes. At least sleeping with her. And it was only a few months ago. He shuddered again. He was too old for Veronica, which made some sort of sense, but he was too old for Agnes, which was too much to handle. He would have begun brooding about it like an old man, but Cole Porter's Where Would You Get Your Coat started playing.

"Hey," Abby said. "Our song. Let's dance."

"You've got to be kidding," Lee said. "Of course. It's you. You're kidding."

"No," Abby said. "Actually, I'm not. Step out a little."

"I can barely stand."

"But," Abby said, "you can stand. That's all I need. And you're already moving your toes to the beat, you sneak."

Lee looked down at his feet and discovered that he was, indeed, moving his toes to the beat. Stupid toes.

"And besides," Abby added. "I've seen you dance. Your back won't make a difference."

"Thanks a heap," Lee said and with her help, struggled up.

She led him into the middle of the room, planted him at a position that suited her, grabbed his hand, pulled it up to shoulder height and started twirling and dancing in a convincing jitterbug. Lee started laughing, which felt really good. He was good at being a curmudgeon, but laughing was better.

"You don't even need me," he said.

"No," she said, "but it's nicer with someone. And you're kind of cute in an accountant, old man sort of way."

Lee blushed and Abby spun under his arm.

The front door opened, and the energy in the room changed one more time. The guy playing Felix came in with a stack of newspapers, followed by a satisfying swirl of snow. Lee had learned from Look Homeward Angel that some eager actor was always sent down to the paper on opening night to get copies of the Bee fresh off the press to bring to the opening night party so they could see the review. After the review was read, the party usually broke up and everyone went home, which seemed reasonable, since the paper didn't hit the stands until around four and that was late enough for anyone to stay up who had just gone through opening night. Lee looked at his watch. Three fifty-two. The paper was early that morning.

"Extra, extra," the actor shouted, and everyone gathered around, grabbing copies and fumbling for the arts page. Agnes, with a stunned Ron slightly behind her looking like what a puppy dog must look like if confronted by a weaving cobra, politely took a copy from someone and elegantly found the page.

"Calm down, everyone," she said, cleared her throat, and began reading.

She paused briefly when she saw the headline, which didn't portend good news, then she steeled herself and spoke.

"An Uneven Odd Couple," she said evenly. "By R. Pendleton Smythe."

"Oh, man," someone complained.

"He always pans everything," someone consoled.

"He always tries to be so clever," someone else said, bitterly.

"He should stick to bake sales and the financial page," someone else exclaimed.

"Get your hands off my mushroom cap," someone else interjected.

After they all agreed that the review was useless and that it would be pointless to take anything it said seriously, and why bother even reading it because it was all tripe and trash anyway, they urged Agnes to continue. The first paragraph simply talked about the play, and someone said that he was just outlining the plot, not writing a review.

"Agnes Livingstone directed, and the set and lighting were designed by Bear Pugh..." Agnes continued, then read a list of actors and the parts they played, and someone scoffed that he just listed the actors, but didn't say anything about them, and that it wasn't a review, it was a book report.

"... Jim Ackerman who debuted in Of Mice and Men last month..."

Lee's back stiffened a little, which wouldn't have seemed possible before hearing Jim's name mentioned in a newspaper.

"... and Lee Harris, who was delightfully scathing as Roy, the accountant in the group of poker-playing friends, and is a welcome addition to the River Bend theatre scene, gave this lackluster production a few moments of shining professionalism. He is someone to keep an eye on."

There was a stunned silence and no one seemed to be keeping an eye on Lee. Then Agnes quickly finished reading the review which continued with the address of the theatre, the dates of the play and phone number where tickets could be reserved.

"Now we'll never be able to live with him," Abby said into the silence, and several people laughed, grateful for the break in the tension.

As Lee made his way back to the chair, several people came up to him and congratulated him with what sounded a lot like false enthusiasm. Lee didn't realize that feeling good could feel so awkward and, unlike Headline, he really didn't like feeling awkward. Even the waiter with the bunched pants, who had nothing to do with the play and shouldn't have cared, walked by Lee too quickly and with his tray held too high for Lee to grab even a lemon wedge from it. When Peter came up and congratulated him, though, that felt genuine.

"I told you you did good," Peter said, then looked around at the people pointedly avoiding him. "Don't mind them. Beware of the green-eyed monster, my lord, it mocks the food it feeds on."

"Meat," Lee said.

"What?" Peter asked.

221

"Meat," Lee said. "O, beware, my lord, of jealousy! It is the green-eyed monster which doth mock the meat it feeds on. Othello. Act III."

"I was just trying to be nice," Peter said. "Asshole."

"And then there was one," Abby said with a smirk, and brought Lee his coat.

Lee showed up at Twain's just before the lunch rush on Saturday. There were already three people at the counter, and one booth had a couple drinking coffee and sharing a newspaper. Lee wondered if they were reading his review. He made a strange arc into the room so he could casually glance over their shoulders. The guy was reading the want ads and the woman was reading the obituaries. They were all for men, once again, except for the one woman who, allegedly, had been disposed of by her husband, who then, allegedly, disposed of himself. There was a picture of Judge Darling on the page. He hadn't died, he was promoting a book signing. It was a book by someone else, but he was going to be at Comma, Colon and Dickens signing it. Lee never realized how much you could glean from a casual glance of a newspaper page over someone's shoulder. He had gleaned that more people needed to read his review.

"Hi, Mr. Harris," Matt said when Lee got back to the kitchen. "Who drove you today?"

"I decided to drive myself. It felt good to drive. Now I'm exhausted and need to go home."

Matt laughed. Twain came back just then and asked what was funny, so Matt explained Lee's joke. Twain looked at Lee, trying to decide if it had been a joke. Lee wasn't laughing, after all, and he was already sitting on the stool he had brought into the kitchen for those moments when his back flared up and he didn't want to go out into the diner. Lee sensed the question behind Twain's look.

"Hey," he said with a growl, making fists, bending his arms and swinging them very slightly in front of his transversus abdominis in an absurd parody of a muscle man at a beach or Popeye anywhere or George Hamilton. "I'm a real man."

"With dishwater hands," Twain said.

"Oh," Matt said, "I saw your name in the paper. Congratulations!"

Lee's chest swelled. Then it fell a little while he looked around to make sure none of the other actors from the play were in the kitchen with them. Then it swelled again. It had been a great review, and he had been the only one praised in the whole production. But it would be unseemly to brag about that. But he was the only one they praised.

"Yes," he said. "Thanks. It was a good review, wasn't it? I was the only one they praised in the whole production."

Twain went back out front, not sure if there was enough room for him in the kitchen with Lee's humility rattling the teacups and taking up all the room back there.

"Cool," Matt said, and copied Lee's parody of the strong man with a laugh. "I'm a man!"

Matt went back about his work, very proud at having bonded with Lee. The lunch crowd wasn't very big, for which Lee was thankful. He was able to keep up with the dishes and get all the table paraphernalia filled.

He had to rest before facing the drive home, however. It had been more than he should have attempted. That night backstage, most of the cast members were strangely distant, which really annoyed Lee. He wanted to be able to celebrate his review, but with everyone being distant, any celebration would look like gloating. Everyone except Jim, of course, which was even more annoying. Jim actually congratulated him on the review, and seemed to want to hover while he put on his makeup and costume. Lee had grown fond of having an audience, but not backstage while dressing. It wasn't done. One of the things that made it possible to undress and dress in front of all these guys was that none of them noticed each other doing it. In fact, they made a point of not noticing each other doing it. Lee briefly considered ducking into Roger's Room to change, but just as he considered it, a strange noise fell out of it. It was probably just the furnace rumbling. He wasn't going to be the one to find out.

"Don't you have makeup to get into?" he asked Jim, who seemed to wake up somehow, as if he really had forgotten that he had to get ready, also.

Lee took advantage of the distraction and got changed.

By Wednesday, Lee wasn't afraid of sneezing, tying his shoes was almost no challenge at all and he was able to drive himself to work without troubling his back because Steve was really tired of the whole bad back thing. He was still tentative about getting out of bed in the morning, and very careful about how he sat down and stood back up because Geoff wasn't, yet. He was really looking forward to the time when he could actually take for granted all those things that people who hadn't fractured their coccyx took for granted, just to tie it all up.

During a lull at the diner, Lee called Andrew to see if the check from the house had come, yet. Andrew told him it hadn't and to have patience. He also congratulated Lee on the review.

"Thanks!" Lee said, enthusiastically.

"You should be proud," Andrew continued. "You did do a good job."

Lee's chest, which was already really swelled and had been for so long it was beginning to hurt, swelled a little more. Just then Matt, who had come in with Jan for their lunch hour, walked by and did the strong man thing with a big grin. Lee laughed out loud.

"It might be time to take some acting classes," Andrew added.

"Huh?" Lee's chest imploded.

"You're getting good, you want to get better," Andrew said. "Now comes the work. Anyways, you don't want to be like George Hamilton, do you?"

"Whadayamean?" Lee said defensively, "I loved him in The Man Who Loved Cat Dancing."

"Well, sure," Andrew said. "But then he did Zorro, the Gay Blade. And did you see Godfather III?"

"Oh," Lee said.

"My point exactly. Take a class."

When he got off the phone, Lee asked Twain if the mail had come, yet.

"No," Twain, who had watched Lee while he was talking to Andrew, said. "The postal service is on strike."

"You're kidding!" Lee said, his heart pounding, his brow glistening and his toes curling as if he were living in some satirical soap opera or something where bad things just always happened to him all the time.

Twain just walked away.

Ten minutes later the phone rang, and Twain called back to the kitchen to tell Lee it was for him, letting him know by the tone in his voice that he was spending entirely too much time on the phone.

"The check just came," Andrew said.

Lee said he'd be right over and hung up. Then he looked at Twain, who had heard him say he'd be right over, and asked if he could go run a very important errand. Twain toyed with him for several moments before he scowled and said not to take too long because there had been a lot of dishes piling up while he was on the phone. Although he said it with a lot less words than that.

About forty-six and a half minutes after Lee left, Abby came into the diner for lunch. She sat at the counter and ordered a cheeseburger, fries, Tang™ and a wedge of hot apple pie with a scoop of vanilla ice cream because Geoff is on a diet and has to live vicariously through a fictional straight woman who doesn't watch what she eats. She asked Twain where Lee was and he just gave her one of his looks and filled her water glass.

She was starting on the pie when Lee got back and she got up and gave him a big hug, then stepped back far enough so he could see the sweatshirt she was wearing under her coat. It said "Baby" and had a big arrow under that pointing down.

"Cover that up!" Lee whispered loudly and tried to close her coat front.

Abby laughed and pulled away from him.

"Everyone will think it's true," he said in a desperate whisper, trying to button the coat. "Everyone will think it's me!"

"Is that so bad?" Abby said with a wicked grin and took her coat off.

She laid it on the stool next to hers, sat back down and asked Lee to come around and fill her water glass again.

As he filled it, he looked around to see if anyone had noticed the sweatshirt. No one had. Until, of course, he'd whispered for her to cover it up. He continued to talk to her in a whisper hoping that would make everyone else in the place just fade away. Abby asked him where he'd been.

"Oh," Lee said, still whispering but not quite as much. "The check came. For the house."

"Wow!" Abby said. "Let's see it!"

"I already deposited it," he said, and Abby looked at him funny. "I have a photocopy, though."

Abby looked at him even funnier.

"You make photocopies of your checks?"

"Yeah," Lee said, slightly confused. "And the deposit slips. Don't you?"

Abby shook her head slowly, once again amazed at this strange man she had somehow found herself with.

"So what are you going to do with it?" she asked instead of telling him again how weird he was.

"I've always wanted to invest but I've never been able to except for Beverly's stupid antiques. When I was married, all our money went into those and cars and our lifestyle."

He stopped for a moment to think about that. Their lifestyle. Their stupid, boring, safe lifestyle. He missed it for a moment, then shook his head before thoughts of Beverly and the Jerk could flow in to ruin everything again. Damn her.

"I'm going to find a good broker," he continued, "one who has a good reputation for careful investing and build a nice blue chip portfolio."

"You're really boring," Abby said and smiled.

"What?" he said. "No. I used to be. Now, I'm a delightfully professional actor. I got a review."

"Congrats on getting the check."

She looked at her watch, said she had to get back to it, leaned over the counter to give him a kiss which he accepted with embarrassment, looking around to see if anyone was noticing the public display. Then Abby pointedly put her coat back on and buttoned it all the way up.

Lee went back to attack the dishes that had piled up since the phone call. There weren't that many of them, he thought. Twain didn't have to get all "I'm the boss" on me. He was halfway through the first sink of steaming suds when Twain came back.

"Sorry I got all 'I'm the boss' at you," he said.

Lee thought, Who are you? but didn't say it out loud. He had a feeling Twain understood anyway.

In the late afternoon, Peter came in. A blast of cold air followed him into the diner, which accentuated his foul mood. He sat at the counter and the cold seemed to hover around him. He hunkered into his coat and slumped his shoulders and eyebrows. Twain plopped a menu down in front of him, which he ignored, and poured him a cup of coffee, which he didn't. After putting entirely too much cream into it, then stirring in almost an entire dispenser of sugar so it became sludgy, more like warm coffee-flavored ice cream than hot coffee flavored coffee, he tasted it and found it satisfactory. Twain watched him, thinking, Who are you? Peter didn't notice or care. Instead, he ordered meatloaf. And green beans. And mashed potatoes with gravy and a large salad and side of fried eggs with toast and a strawberry milkshake and a flan.

"Hey, Peter," Lee said when he was about to set the order on the serving window. He brought it out rather than setting it there. "How's it going?"

Peter glared up at him from under his eyebrows and harrumphed.

"My check came," Lee said, then, when it looked like Peter didn't know what check he was talking about, added, "From the house. Beverly and mine. That we just sold."

"So," Peter said, wondering why Lee never seemed to be able to read even the most obvious moods and feeling a small pang of pity for Abby, "you going to buy a Ferrari?"

"What?" Lee said, startled even by the thought. "There's hardly enough for a Ferrari."

"Okay, a Porsche?"

"No, I put it in the bank. I'm going to invest it."

"I thought guys always wanted to buy Ferraris or Porsches when they got a windfall."

"No," Lee replied, confused by almost every part of that statement. "I'm going to invest it."

"God, you're boring."

"Not you, too," Lee said, in his own version of a hurrumph. "You're a guy. Would you buy a Ferrari with it?"

"No, I'd get as far away from the Willow Lane Theatre as I possibly could."

"I thought you loved theatre," Lee said, then finally noticed the slump and scowl and general cold air surrounding Peter. "You okay?"

"No, I'm not okay," Peter exploded.

"Oh." Lee said. Then he realized something was required of him in this situation. See, I can learn, he thought. "What's wrong?"

"Stella," Peter said dramatically, "got a raise."

Peter let that statement hang in the air as if it explained everything and needed no elaboration. Lee had no idea why that piece of information would cause someone to scowl and slump so and be so surrounded by cold. Peter breathed in as if he were about to elaborate, then sort of deflated back into himself.

"I haven't had a raise in three years," he said quietly, almost to himself. "And that was only twenty-five cents. And Stella gets one." And then less quietly, still not quite to Lee, he added, "Because she flips her fucking hair at the board of directors." And then he gave up all pretense of quietness. "The only reason the stupid theatre hasn't folded and imploded into a dark stinking hole in the earth is because I always check her fucking work." Then he noticed Lee standing there listening. "You know. You looked at her books that first day you were there. She's a lousy book keeper. With a glass eye." (*Steve, she doesn't have a glass eye.* **Then what was that I felt?**)

"If you need some money..." Lee said, really trying to help.

"No. No, no, no. No, that's not what I mean. No. How much?"

Lee laughed then said, "I'm serious. If you need anything..."

"No," Peter continued. "Thanks, but no. And anyway, that's completely beside the point. I'm at least worth what Stella makes. I put up with her moods and her arrogance. I fix her mistakes and cover her ass. I put up with her grabbing every volunteer who walks in the door. I do twice the work she does on my own without even doing hers and then I do hers and I never complain about it and then she gets a raise for it and they think her fucking shit doesn't stink."

"Why don't you ask for one, too?" Lee asked in a slight whisper. It seemed like a logical question, but he hoped when Peter answered it, he'd quiet down before he started attracting an audience. It was bad enough with Abby, and he wasn't sleeping with Peter.

"Because I've seen the books!" Peter exploded. "I know how much money we make and how much money it costs to put on a play and how much money it takes to maintain the building and I know we're just scraping by. I should be running that place. The board of directors has no idea what the fuck is going on, they just want to be able to say they support the arts and get a glow in their pants when Stella flips her hair at them."

Peter seemed to run out of steam at that. He couldn't compete there. When it came to getting a group of men to do just what she wanted she had all the tools and he didn't have any of them. In fact, the tools he did have seemed to have just the opposite effect. He glanced over and noticed that Twain was looking at them, sharpening a cleaver, scowling, and the cuss jar had been placed on the counter next to him. Peter dropped several quarters into it. Twain still scowled. Peter dropped a bill into it. He didn't even notice whose picture was on it. Twain gave the cleaver one more swipe with the wet stone, then walked away.

"I'm sorry," Peter said to Lee. "You're at work. I should just eat my fucking meatloaf and green beans and mashed potatoes with gravy and large salad and side of fried eggs with toast and strawberry milkshake and a flan and leave town."

He wanted to shout all that, but the man with the cleaver was still somewhere nearby, so it lost much of its power by coming out in a hushed whisper.

"Why don't you come by tonight," Lee asked. "I'll have some snacks and we'll get bombed."

"Really?"

"Sure. It's been, like, ten installments. You need to drown your sorrows and I want to celebrate. It's perfect."

"Sure," Peter said after a brief moment thinking how good it would feel to just go home and feel sorry for himself all by himself. "Okay. What time?"

"I leave around four-thirty. I'll stop and get some stuff. Be there around six. Mind if Abby's there, too?"

"No, the more the merrier. Misery loves more people."

Lee didn't even try to correct him.

"Thanks, Lee," Peter said. "Oh. And you are at least going to take Abby out for a nice dinner, aren't you?"

"Tonight?"

"No, stupid, with your windfall."

"Oh," Lee said. "Yeah. Of course."

"You hadn't thought of it, had you?"

"No," Lee admitted. "Um... Thanks."

Lee put away groceries and David Byrne's odd, Byzantine voice conga-ed out into the room. Abby bounced slightly to it. She was still wearing the sweatshirt that said "Baby" with an arrow pointing down. Lee disappeared into the bedroom with one of the bags for a moment. When he came back out, he was wearing a tee shirt, which was weird enough, but on it was emblazoned "I'm With Stupid™" with an arrow pointing to the right. Abby burst out laughing. Lee stood on her left so it pointed directly at her for a moment, then went back toward his bedroom.

"Where are you going?"

"To change."

"No, you're not."

"Peter will be here any minute, Abby."

"Exactly," she said and grinned.

They argued good-naturedly for a moment while Lee built the fire. Building fires was what Lee did. It was ablaze in less than five minutes. They finally compromised: He would wear the tee shirt, but would put another shirt over it. That way Abby would be able to know he had stepped out, but he wouldn't have to step out to the point that he embarrassed himself in front of his friend. Lee also tried to get Abby to cover up her sweatshirt, but she simply refused. He would just have to deal with the embarrassment for that. There was only so much compromise available, it seemed.

After he got suitably covered, Lee tossed another log onto the fire and sparks spiraled up towards the flue with angry hissing and popping. He used the fire irons to arrange the logs and looked like a wizard in his lair conjuring some dangerously mythical beast. A spark popped loudly and leapt toward him, but Lee got the screen in place just in time. He laughed demonically.

At six-oh-one, Peter knocked on the front door. Phish was now dripping out of the CD player. Peter's afternoon grump had evolved into an evening numb funk. He moved to the fire as if it had physically pulled him into the room. A spark popped loudly and he jumped.

"Hi, Peter," Abby said as he took off his coat. "See what I brought?"

She held up a Risk game. There was a big green rubber band holding it together that looked like the kind of rubber band on one of those big punching balls. The corners of the cover were all ripped up the seams and the white that surrounded the big red "RISK" on the top had long since faded to a pale ochre. On one side panel someone had scratched out the "er" on both Parker and Brothers, so it said "Park

Broth s", which looked like it was trying hard to mean something but was probably just done by some child like Steve.

"You're kidding," Peter said. "You've obviously never played a board game with Lee."

"Why?"

"He never loses. And what the hell are you wearing?"

Peter laid his coat on the arm of the couch. He was wearing a badly hand-knit sweater made from yarn with alarmingly mismatched colors that bunched in all the wrong places. His cologne smelled of peppercorns.

"I," Abby said, "have never lost a game of Risk in my life. A sweatshirt, why?"

"Well, it should be an interesting evening with neither of you losing."

"Consider the source," Lee said. About the sweatshirt, not the losing thing.

"Here," Peter said to Lee and handed him a card and small gift-wrapped box.

"Consider yourself at home," Abby said.

Lee looked at Peter questioningly, then shook the box next to his ear.

"Just open it," Peter said peevishly. "Sheesh." Then to Abby, said, "consider yourself one of the family."

"We haven't a lot... to spare©," Abby said.

Lee tore the paper off the box. It was a red Matchbox Ferrari.

"Who cares... what... ever we..." Peter continued.

"STOP!" Lee demanded and opened the card.

It said, "Because you won't do anything interesting with all that cash. Congratulations, Peter."

Lee laughed and handed Peter a shot, which he'd already poured. Once he noticed a mood, he knew what to do to help. Especially if helping involved booze. Peter drained it in one gulp.

"Mmmm," he said warmly, "Canadian."

"Crown Royal," Lee corrected him.

Peter handed the shot glass back and Lee poured him another, then poured one for Abby and one for himself.

"To all that money," Abby said, raising the glass high above her head.

"To all that money," they answered, raising their own glasses.

They drank, then Abby added, "Not that you're going to do anything interesting with it."

Lee gave her a look and she smiled innocently.

"To all that money," she said.

Peter raised his glass again and said, "To misery and company!"

They toasted that. The smooth, burning whiskey vapor smelled earthy, like good clean topsoil.

"To err is human," Lee toasted.

"'Er'?" Peter asked. "Isn't it 'ere'?"

"No," Lee said. "It's 'err'. Not 'er' or 'ere'."

"Sounds like you don't know what you're saying," Abby said. "Er... Um... what I meant to say was air."

"Okay," Lee said, changing the subject, "we have snacks."

"We have booze," Peter agreed.

"And we have board games," Abby concluded. "Game."

Lee set out snacks, which Geoff will resist describing so Steve doesn't hit him, and Abby set up the game. She had to move the newspaper clipping of the review preserved in a plastic sheet protector to the end table. Abby and Peter sat on the couch, and Lee brought a chair from the kitchen for himself and sat across from them. Led Zeppelin rang out and circumambulated the room. There was a small movement over by the television which caught Lee's eye. He glanced back in time to see Charlie bobbing his head to the music. He either liked it or was in pain. Stupid bird.

A sudden gust of hungry wind rattled the house. The hollow sound of it made Peter and Abby shiver, but the house braced itself, making the room feel even more warm and secure, more solid. This house was built by someone who was going to live in it.

"How many houses do I get?" Peter asked.

Abby and Lee just looked at him for a very long time.

"What?" Peter wasn't in a mood to be looked at.

"They're armies," Abby said, then she smiled a wicked smile.

"Patsy," Lee added to that, agreeing with her smile.

"Fine," Peter said, "How many armies do I get? Nancy."

"Thirty-five," Abby and Lee said simultaneously. Then they both laughed and said, "Nancy."

"I want the boot," Peter said. They looked at him again and he said, "It was a joke. A joke. Like saying I hope the Raiders win the World Series or I hope George Hamilton wins an Oscar. A joke. What I really want is the wheel barrow. Especially if it's old enough so the little wheel turns."

"How about a shot?" Lee said.

Lee chose green. Abby chose blue. Peter asked what colors there were.

"Mauve, chartreuse, egg shell, off white, white, cream, wheat, cream of wheat, crimson, periwinkle, harvest gold, avocado and plaid," Abby said.

"I'll take brown," Peter said, sounding sort of brown.

"Okay," Lee said. "Do you remember how to play?"

"Um..." Peter said. "Sure. I think. Tell me."

"Well, we each throw one die and the winner goes first, then we put one army on a country in turn until all the countries are occupied. Then, when they're all occupied, we fortify our countries until everyone has placed all thirty-five armies on the board..."

"Then," Abby cut in, "on the first turn we don't get any new armies, but on each other turn you do. You get one for every three countries you have and several for each continent you completely own. You also get some if you turn in cards. When you have three of a kind or one of each kind of card, you can turn them in for armies, but you don't have to turn them in until you have five cards."

"How do you get cards?" Peter asked. He was sure he had already missed something vital. He hoped his eyes hadn't glazed over. He wouldn't want them to think he wasn't paying attention. Which he wasn't. The box top said it was a game of world conquest, and that seemed appropriate, somehow, given his day. They were still talking. He had to focus.

"If you took a country in your turn, you get a card at the end of your turn," Lee explained. "The first person to turn in cards gets four armies, the next gets six, then eight, then ten, twelve, fifteen, twenty, twenty-five, etc. And if you own the country that's on the card, you get two for that, but even if you have more than one card that matches your armies, you only get two extra armies, and you have to put them on that country. Get it?"

Peter was sure he didn't get it, but was also sure that if he said so, they would try to explain it again. He glanced at the box top again. It said for ages 10 to adult. He silently dared any ten year old to understand one word of all that nonsense. He would have dared them out loud, but there weren't any ten year olds present and if there were, they might show him up by actually understanding, and then where would he be? Some wind came down the chimney, stirred up sparks, and blew a little smoke into the room. Peter sipped some whiskey and watched the fire. Then he realized they were still explaining.

"Okay," Abby said, "on the first turn you don't get extra armies, then you fight, then, when you're done fighting, you can move any amount of armies from one country to an adjoining country that you're already occupying to fortify that for your next move and you get your card."

"The attacker uses the red dice," Lee said. "And can use one, two or three, but you can't use more armies than you can lose and still keep your country, and when you win a country, you have to move as many armies to it as how many dice you threw. The defender uses the white dice. Got it so far?"

"Let's just play," Peter said wearily, hoping it would all make sense in process. He ate a chip.

Abby laughed. Lee turned the box top upside down and threw a die into it. It bounced and chattered to a stop and came up six. Peter threw one and it came up one. Abby threw a six and laughed. The contest was on. Peter was already fascinated. Two people who don't lose. He expected fireworks by the end of the evening, and would be greatly disappointed if he didn't get them. Maybe they would add some sparkle to his world view. Of course, tonight that would take a lot of fireworks. Tonight, that would take a lot of friends. Tonight, let it be Lowenbrau.

"Ladies first?" Abby tried.

Lee threw the die again without even commenting. It came up five. Abby's came up three. Lee put an army on Brazil. Abby put one on Eastern Australia. Peter put a house on England. I mean a flat. I mean an army. (**That's why they don't allow gays in the military**. *They let you in.*) As they took their successive turns, Abby began spreading out from the lower right hand corner of the world, Lee from the Western edge, and Peter was all over the fucking place. He had put one on Indonesia thinking that would be a good way to keep Abby from getting a whole continent. She laughed and told him he was just wasting an army. He put one on Peru because Lee seemed determined to have South America, and Lee didn't say anything but looked like he thought Peter was just wasting an army. Abby put an army on Alaska and Peter asked why she laughed at him for Western Australia if she were putting one on Lee's continent and Lee said it was because she just wanted to fuck with him. Abby smiled knowingly.

"So," Abby said after placing an army on East Africa, "You had a bad day at work, I hear."

"Yeah," Peter said. "I guess. It's just a lot of things. Those idiots on the board just don't have a clue. And then, this afternoon when I was driving around avoiding getting back to the theatre, I passed the old Renaissance Inn and it's all boarded up. Did you ever go there?"

"Sure," Abby said as Peter put an army on Iceland. "Dinner and a play for twenty-three bucks. Saw I Do! I Do! It didn't."

The last continent occupied was Asia. Peter took the last country, which was Irkutsk. He had always wondered how they came up with the names in this game. Then the fortification rounds started, and on the next three turns Abby put more armies on Alaska, and each time Lee said, "See?" but Peter didn't see.

Instead, he said, "When I was in college, there was this great old movie house. It was huge, with a great big screen and big cushy seats and lots of gaudy gingerbread everywhere. I saw one movie there my first semester. They broke it down into three screens in November, covering up all the decorations. By my sophomore year, they were only playing dirty pictures there. By the middle of my junior year it was closed. It became a flea market. They kept the theatre front, though, so every time I passed it I'd get upset."

On Lee's first move, he attacked Iceland from Greenland. Peter felt slightly betrayed.

"What movie did you see?" Lee asked.

"Huh?"

"The first semester. At that movie theatre."

"Last Tango in Paris," Peter said, sadly, and put down his Laughing Cow cheese wedge. It had caraway seeds in it anyway, so he probably wouldn't have finished it.

Lee went after several of Abby's countries, but both lost whole battalions before any country fell. On Abby's first move, she attacked Western Australia from Eastern Australia. Peter felt picked on. The dice clattered in the box top. It only took one roll to remove him from her path. He felt like he was a speck of beige lint that had been flicked off a tan shirt. They'd been right, he had just wasted two armies. He ate the cheese wedge. Then Abby went after Lee and the bloody battles intensified. Another gust of wind shook the windows, trying to get in on the game. Even the weather had more interest in it than Peter.

"You have all that money," Peter said when it looked like Abby was going to conquer Brazil. "You could buy a flame thrower and burn all her armies."

"I already have one."

On Peter's first turn, he realized he didn't have one country with more than three armies, and most had only two. He didn't have a lot to fight with. On his first throw, one of the dice bounced out of the box top and on to the floor. Abby picked it up for him and he threw it again. He tried to get Iceland back from Lee by attacking it from Scandinavia. He failed miserably. This promised to become a two player game very quickly. Peter sat very close to the Crown Royal and chips. That was a war he could win.

"If I'd just sold a house in Chicago, I could buy a stealth bomber and get Iceland back," Peter said miserably.

"I'd just buy a couple of politicians and have them stage a bloodless coup," Abby said. "Not nearly as messy."

"Or as fun," Peter said glumly.

"You're both really good at spending my money, here."

"It's all just fantasy. What would you do with it?" Abby asked. "If you hadn't already said you'd invest it in boring stocks?"

"Invest it in boring stocks," Lee said.

"No," Abby said. "It's a game. Play for a minute. Don't be such a blue chip fart."

"Okay, I'd buy fireworks and liquor."

"You've already done that."

"I bought him the fireworks," Peter said and ate a Ritz cracker with Cheddar cheese. Steve hit Geoff for describing the food.

"I'd invest it in boring stocks," Lee insisted defiantly. Peter and Abby gave him one of his own looks. "Okay, how about a howitzer?"

"How about a Wurlitzer?" Abby asked, and decimated Western Europe. "Or a Pulitzer?"

"Real estate," Peter said as he gave up after trying vainly to make a dent in Egypt and ended his turn without getting a card. "A skyscraper."

"A private jet," Lee said and placed twenty-five armies on Brazil.

"A public jet," Abby said, bracing herself for the onslaught with a shot of Crown Royal.

"Proctor and Gamble," Lee said as he started his attack on North Africa.

"The stock?" Abby asked as she fought back with sticks, stones and a flame thrower.

"No, the company," Lee said as he moved his armies onto North Africa.

"Too blue chip," Abby said as Lee rolled to continue his advance into the continent of Africa. "How about Columbia Records?"

"I'd buy a defunct theatre," Peter said.

"Sure," Lee said. "What would you do with that?"

"Put on plays. I'd buy the Renaissance."

"We could do I Do! I Do!," Abby said. She was beating Lee back and regaining ground.

"Hal David and Burt Bacharach," Peter said. He looked at his sad collections of armies scattered piecemeal around the world looking lonely and detached. They were all the little I-Beam armies. Lee and Abby had little III's, V's and X's. Peter imagined the plastic being extruded and cut like pieces of pasta. Then he wondered how interesting it was that simply making pasta into a different shape changed the way it tasted. Then Abby attacked Italy. Well, Southern Europe, but it contained Italy.

"No, that's Promises, Promises," Lee said, allowing himself to take a slight break while Abby systematically removed Peter from Europe. "I Do! I Do! is Tom Jones."

"'THE' Tom Jones?" Abby asked. Europe was hers, except for the forty-three armies Lee had on Iceland.

"Well, certainly 'A' Tom Jones," Peter said, hoping Lee would just finish him off on his next move so he could stop being distracted by this stupid game and just get on with drowning Stella with Crown Royal and cheese dip.

"Tom Jones the singer?" Abby insisted. "I knew he sang My Cup Runneth Over from that show, but I didn't know he wrote it."

"No, Tom Jones the novelist," Peter said. He wasn't paying as much attention as he could be. Lee had just whomped Irkutsk and was advancing on Siberia. After that, all he had left was China, which should mean something with as many people as China had, but his China only had three armies on it and wouldn't last another winter.

"Tom Jones was the novel," Abby said. "The novelist was Thomas Fielding. I had to read it in college."

"Henry Fielding," Lee corrected her. "Tom Jones the playwright. Who wrote I Do! I Do! He also wrote The Fantasticks. Which is where Try To Remember came from. Which is what Tom Jones sang, not My Cup Runneth Over, which Ed Ames sang. And now China is mine and I get all of Peter's cards."

Peter handed him his cards with a touch of sadness, which surprised him. He had been looking forward to getting out of the game so he could just sit in his funk, drink, eat snacks and watch Lee and Abby destroy each other in an obscene, glorious, plastic bloodbath. He sadly gathered up his houses and put them back into their little plastic box. He only felt sad for a moment, though. Then he sat back with his shot glass and thought about spending Lee's money. The scent of burning wood was mingling nicely in his forehead with all that Canadian.

"We could serve food that had to do with the play," he said. "Like doing A Doll's House and serve Swedish food."

"Mmmm. Lutfisk. We'd close before the first act ended," Lee said, then threw three sixes, whooped once and waited grandly while Abby took all her armies off of Yakutsk. When she was done, she leaned over and unbuttoned Lee's shirt. He tried to brush her away halfheartedly while he moved his armies to the newly vacated Yakutsk. The music had moved from Rolling Stones through Benny Goodman and had landed on Leon Redbone. The gravelly voice was grinding into the carpet and scraping the paint off the walls.

"What the hell are you wearing?" Peter asked him.

Lee looked down, then looked at Peter. He seemed to be having trouble focusing and that sweater was making it harder.

"A tee-shirt," he said matter-of-factly.

"What would we call the theatre?" Abby said. "How about Aunt Abby's Playhouse and Condom Emporium?"

"How about Peter's Theatre," Peter said.

He liked it. It had a nice ring. Stupid board of directors. His head was beginning to swim a little. The world was almost evenly divided between blue and green armies. The green armies were neatly arranged on North and South America, most of Europe, and some of Asia. The blue ones were haphazardly piled on Australia, Africa and the rest of Europe and Asia. The border between the two seemed to shift and move, snakelike, but didn't really change substantially for a long time.

"It's my money," Lee said as he collected his card, carefully examined it with the rest of the cards, then neatly placed them all just under the edge of the board. "If we call it anything, we should call it Lee's Theatre. Which we won't because we aren't buying a theatre."

"Let's call it Barbara," Abby said. "And serve only bad hamburgers and cheese fries and put on Aida."

"Yeah, with real elephants in the processional scene," Lee said, swaying his shoulders in uneven syncopation to Frank Sinatra. "But we'll serve ermine under glass."

"Wha'ja say?" Abby asked.

"I said 'we'll serve pheasant under glass'," Lee said. Then he stopped. He wasn't sure what he had said. He wasn't even sure what they were talking about. Something about Ed Ames. "Yeah. 'Pheasant under glass'."

"And how the hell do you know about the processional scene in Aida?" Abby said.

"We could do Hamlet," Lee said. He had read somewhere that every actor wanted to play Hamlet. And he was an actor. Who had gotten the only good review.

"I got a good review," he said, and picked up the clipping in the sheet protector to prove it.

His eye knew exactly where on the page his name was. He pointed toward it to Abby. She nodded patronizingly and threw the dice.

"That play has like a hundred characters," Peter said, ignoring the review thing and hoping Lee would put it down and forget he'd ever gotten it. "It's a dinner theatre. You want everyone to eat while they watch everyone kill everyone? How about Sweeney Todd?"

"It's my dinner theatre, I could put on anything I wanted to. Anyway, death is good for the digestion. I could hire Laurence Olivier to play Hamlet."

"He's dead."

"So is Hamlet. And I have money, damn it, we'll get Laurence Olivier and do Hamlet," Lee said and took a drink. Then he looked at Peter, who had a sort of far away look in his eye and added, "you know we're only goofing around, don't you?"

"Of course," Peter said, sounding kind of disappointed but accepting in a drunken, emotionally numb sort of way. Maybe just being resigned to everything for the rest of his life would help, somehow. Maybe Alka-Seltzer would help. Plop, plop, fizz, fizz. Things go better with Coke. A silly millimeter longer. Okay, we're done. You're soaking in it.

"We could do a tuxedo night," Abby said after whacking Lee in the left shoulder for attacking Egypt again.

"People have to come in tuxedos?" Lee said, and whacked Abby back but not as hard. He was, after all, a gentleman. And she'd probably kick his ass.

"No, we give away a tuxedo with each ticket, like at a ball park."

"Okay, I'll buy a porch," Lee said. "I mean a Porsche. And then I'll spring for a hair transplant for Steve." (**Hey!**)

There was a strange whimpering sound which made the small hairs on the back of Peter's neck stand up and wiggle. He rubbed the back of his neck, leaving four trails of sticky, phosphorescent orange corn curl dust.

"Quiet, Gable," Lee said offhandedly and re-took Brazil, which Abby had re-taken in the last move. Then he advanced on North Africa, which had changed allegiances almost as often as Malta.

It was strangely quiet for a moment. Peter tried to figure out why. The wind was still blowing in syncopated gusts, so it wasn't that. He finally realized there was no music. All the CD's in the changer must have played. He stumbled up from the couch and looked through Lee's collection. He put on The Rite of Spring, but Abby threw a cushion at him, so he took that off and put on Joni Mitchell's Mingus album.

"We don't seem to be making any headway," Abby said. "Should we call it a draw?"

Lee looked at her in utter disbelief.

"You're not getting off that well. I mean easy. I mean nice try," Lee said.

"You're already very drunk," Abby said reasonably.

"He got quetzals when he could barely speak," Peter tried to say as he sat back down.

"What the hell's a quetzals?" Abby asked.

"It's a bird from Central 'Merica," Lee informed her with a slight nod. "Green and red feathers. Plural."

"And it's four hundred poinch," Peter said. "If you put it on a triple letter score. I mean square. You guys are an irresistible object and an immovable object. I mean force. A forceful object and an irr... imm... er... can I have some more Crown Royal? Wait. Who's Gable?"

Peter woke up at five thirty-six, very thirsty, wondering where he was. He was on a couch, covered with a blanket. There was a large glass of water on the coffee table next to the Risk board which still seemed to be in play. There was a weight on his feet that felt like Cliche had gained several pounds. He wondered why he had gone to sleep on his couch. Then he remembered they had played Risk at Lee's. The last time he had played a board game with Lee, it had been at his house and he'd had to tuck Lee in on his couch. Lee had obviously paid him back. Well, probably Abby. Okay, bearings. What day was it? Wednesday night. Actually, it was Thursday morning. He had to go to work in a few hours. Work. Damn it. Well, it's what you do, isn't it, he thought. He'd get over it. So Stella could charm her way into a raise. He knew how important he was to the place even if the board didn't. He pushed the blanket aside and sat up, then was sorry he had because his head kept sitting up long after his body was already there. He drank the water in one long drink and that seemed to help.

He stood, making sure he didn't spin and fall, then made sure he could move relatively normally. He really didn't remember the end of the evening. He hoped he hadn't been rude. He hoped he hadn't been weepy. He hoped his butt didn't look too big in those pants. He

241

wondered if he had slept through the fireworks he had been so looking forward to, but looked at the board and realized there probably hadn't been any. Then he found his coat and put it on. He looked around to see if there was anything else he should take. His keys were on the coffee table, so he took those. And his shoes were on the floor by the couch. He sat back down to put them on. He went quietly into the kitchen to pour himself another glass of water, gulped it, then left, quietly closing Lee's front door behind himself.

Twenty minutes later, Lee sat up in bed very suddenly.

"Fuck!" he shouted.

"What?" Abby said, coming instantly awake. "Is it your back?"

"No!" Lee said. "It's Peter. Him and his damn theatre. I've been thinking about it all night! I can't even get to sleep. Damn it!"

Abby looked at him very strangely.

"You're just drunk," she said. "You'll feel better in the morning."

"No," Lee said. "I won't."

Will Lee feel better in the morning?
Will acting go to his head?
Will he take acting classes?
Will the rest of the cast continue to avoid him?
Will he be the Willow Lane Theatre's new star?
If not, will he go elsewhere?
Then will he put on Hamlet with Laurence Olivier?
Will he put on Oliver with George Hamilton?
Will he put on his game face?
Will he face the music?
When the music's over, will he turn out the lights?
Will Ron escape Agnes's web?
Will he want to?
Willy Wonka?
Will Geoff comment on the glass eye thing?
Will Peter have a hangover?
Will he ask for a raise?
Will he have it out with the board?
Will Lee and Abby finish the board game?
If so, who'll win?

**To find the answers to these and other pernicious puzzles,
tune into our next installment:
"If You Got The Penny, Honey, I Got the Dime"**

(**Wait!** **I'm not gay**. *Took you long enough, Goober. You were never in the military, either.* **Are you sure**? *Yes. And stop taking notes. That's creepy.* **Your mother's middle name was Yolanda, right**? *That ain't funny, man.*)

This installment first published February 15, 2004

Geoff Hoff and Steve Mancini

Thus far: Lee's back didn't hurt as much after he got a glowing review for his performance in the Willow Lane Theatre's production of The Odd Couple, but his good feeling was complicated by the fact that he was the only thing in the production the reviewer liked. Peter's job satisfaction was complicated by the fact that he just found out his office mate Stella got a raise and he didn't. Abby's life is complicated by the fact that she's dating Lee, who can be hard to deal with when he's in pain or drunk or both. Or neither. Bear's status quo was complicated by the fact that his ex-wife showed up at the opening night of The Odd Couple. Twain serves Tang at the diner. Get to know all the glorious complications; read the everything that came first, first. Then you'll be ready for...

Installment Twenty-Five
"If You Got the Penny, Honey, I Got the Dime"

Abby woke up before Lee and stumbled into the living room. The blankets she'd used to cover Peter were rumpled, but he was no longer under them. She thought fleetingly about his inebriation level and wondered distantly if he had been all right going home. She also wondered how she was going to get through a work day. She wasn't in the habit of drinking on a work night, but Lee had just gotten his final settlement check and wanted to celebrate, and Peter had needed a night away from his thoughts, so she had joined them both. The pine tar in her brain told her that next time she would just wish them both well and watch Rhoda reruns by herself in the relative safety of her own apartment. The Risk game was still where she and Lee had left it. She vaguely remembered finally talking him into letting the game be by promising to finish it the next night. If she hurried, she could put it all away and he probably wouldn't even remember. She could even tell him he'd won. No, it would be far more satisfying to tell him she had. She picked up the box to start dismantling the board when Lee came in behind her.

"What are you doing?" he asked in a surly tone.

"Nothing," she said, surprised that her tone was almost as surly as his, and consciously toned it down before adding, "How are you feeling? Dickhead."

"Awful."

"You drank a lot," she said.

"Who cares about that?" he said. "I didn't get a wink of sleep. I kept thinking about buying a theater."

"Oh, that," Abby said. "So buy one."

"I thought you thought my acting was silly."

"Yeah," Abby said as she put the Risk box down and kissed him on the cheek, "but you don't."

She was halfway down the hall to the bathroom when he shouted behind her that he couldn't buy a fucking theater, that it was insane, and that he had to go kill Peter.

"Who'll take care of Cliche if you do that?" she shouted through the closed bathroom door.

She didn't hear what he answered because she was busy splashing her face with cold water to see if that made her feel less like wanting to violently remove her brain, stomach and nervous system and curl up in a ball on some soft, fur covered surface. It didn't. It just made her face wet.

Bear hadn't gotten much sleep either, but for entirely different reasons. He had spent the entire time since Saturday morning thinking about Friday night. It was Thursday, now, and he had to focus because the run through was that evening. He didn't have to be at the theater until early afternoon, though, so he built a fire and sat on the floor of his little bungalow in front of it. The fireplace was something of an anomaly in the old house. Some previous owner had probably put it in to add either class, warmth or both. It barely added either, it was obviously a do-it-yourself job, was barely up to code, or, perhaps, barely below code and Bear was fairly certain that the carbon monoxide levels in the house increased with the smokey air that fell off the fire. He didn't really care much, he didn't require a lot of oxygen.

He picked up his guitar and cradled the bulk of it under his right arm. The psychedelic decal of the Monkees just off the sound hole, which was half covered by the psychedelic decal of Orson Bean, was chipped and faded and Peter Tork's face was completely removed by years of repeated pick scratches. The rounded edges of the cold wood pressed into his bare arm, chest and legs. He was only wearing a pair of plaid boxer shorts and the flat vibrating back warmed from the heat of his body. His fingers absently plucked at the strings and something like [Four Dead in] Ohio rang out of body. It would have been more like [Four Dead in] Ohio if he had actually been thinking about what he was playing. Someone had once said he played okay, but all he knew was white boy music. He never knew why they'd had a problem with that. He was a white boy. With freckles. Under the hair. He scratched at the hair on his chest as a metallic, smokey-wood chord hung in the air then faded toward the Formica tabletop in the next room, and his mind once again replayed the strange events of opening night.

After the review had been read and the party had begun to wind down, he'd given Dee Dee a ride back to her car which she'd left at the theater. On the way there they had begun to talk, and it had been nice. Easy. Unstrained. They'd both avoided dangerous subjects, of course, like family and what had gone wrong with their marriage and cutlery, but when he'd pulled into the parking lot they sat talking in the van with the engine running, and we abruptly changed out of the past perfect tense to indicate that we were now going into a full-fledged flashback. Strunk and White be damned. Dee Dee shivered and Bear said he had an extra coat in back and started to get up.

"I can get it," Dee Dee said.

Under the coat and on top of all the old boxes and clutter of old tools and rusty guy stuff was a new red and yellow box covered in cellophane.

"What the heck is this?"

He looked back, then turned a little red.

"It's... Um... An earthquake survival kit," he said defensively. "You never know."

"In River Bend?" she said with a laugh.

"When there is one, I'll be the only one prepared," he said. He would have added "Me and Lee" but decided to change the subject instead.

They continued talking until Dee Dee pointed out that the sun was coming up. There was a beautiful pink edge to the horizon threatening to turn tangerine and Bear realized that he was really cold even though he had a coat on and the heater had been running the entire time. He really wanted to ask her over but couldn't, somehow. The evening had been really pleasant and he didn't want to do or say the wrong thing. She said she had to go, opened the door, then stopped, turned and kissed him on the cheek. Then she sat looking forward for a moment.

"It's been nice talking," she said. "We never did that."

He nodded. That was safe and he had done really well so far and didn't want to blow it by some errant guy utterance. His mid-section was talking very loudly, though, and he had to concentrate very hard on her mouth in case she said something else. Which made his mid-section talk even louder. She looked at him for another moment before she spoke again. The door was still slightly open and the cold air in the van got colder. The heater gave up and decided to call it a night.

"I'd really like to keep talking, but it's getting really cold here," she said, and Bear stopped breathing while he waited for her to finish. Or to start. Or to say something else. "Is it okay if we go to your place for a little while? You can bring me back to my car later."

He nodded because he was sure his mouth wouldn't work if he tried to say anything, then put the van in gear. He had to be really careful driving because his instinct was to go really fast and it had been a long night after a long day, and he was very tired and there was snow and ice on the street and he'd had one or two beers at the party. Concentrating on driving slowly and carefully also distracted his mid-section some. When they pulled into his drive, the beautiful colors in the sky had turned to a uniform early morning pale gray and the trees were yawning and looking for their cigarettes.

Dee Dee surveyed his bungalow. It was really a small, faded, off-green box with a roof. It had asbestos siding which had been popular on cheap houses back in the late forties when the house had been put up. The yard was just frozen dirt and patches of dirty snow. In the spring it would be damp dirt and weeds. It was surrounded by a chain-link fence with an open gate at the driveway which made the whole fence moot. The rest of the houses in the neighborhood were also boxes with roofs. There were lots of vans and big cars from the eighties parked in the driveways and frozen Big Wheels with cracked and faded plastic, broken swing sets and a few van parts and big eighties engines in the yards. Directly across the street was the one house that tried with all its might and energy to bring the property values up, but that was like putting a BandAid on a severed limb or hanging an air freshener from the rear view mirror of Howard Stern's car or putting a dress on Margaret Thatcher. Bear had never been ashamed of his place, it was perfectly functional and perfectly reasonable and close enough to the theater that he could get there in only a few minutes if something went wrong, and that included splashing water on his face and dressing, but the look on Dee Dee's face made him miss a stride as he walked her toward the door. He had never noticed the line of straggly, frozen weeds peeking up along the cracked walkway, left over from last year's crop.

The house was barely furnished. The only piece of furniture in the living room was a ratty couch that smelled like dog, which was odd because he didn't have a dog. He did, however, have a vicuna. (*No, he didn't, Steve*. **A stoat? A badger? An ermine?** *We've already done that.* **A yak?** *Sure. Why not. It's fiction.* **Say it ain't so!** *Steady, old man.*) The kitchen table had tubular aluminum legs and a ribbed band of aluminum around the top which had rounded corners and was covered with faded, scratched, sky blue Formica with overlapping pink and green boomerangs on it. The vinyl on the backs and seats of the two chairs with tubular aluminum legs matched it perfectly but were split with dark yellow, degrading foam and vicuna fur showing through. The table and counter top, which was pale pink Formica with brown and gray spots, were both clean and empty except for a small pile of mail on the table and a small can of Chock full o'Nuts® coffee with that heavenly flavor and a glass-sided toaster on the counter. The stove was small with only two burners. It was turquoise and had an aluminum percolating coffee pot on it. On the back ledge thingy where the clock, stuck at 8:59, and oven vent were, was a box of Ohio Blue Tip matches used to light the burners.

Dee Dee didn't have a lot of time to make a judgement about it all, though, because they found themselves, somehow, undressed and in his bed, engaging in the completely physical, unthinking, full-on, total body coupling of the entirely exhausted who hadn't done it with anyone for a very long time.

Bear woke the next day in the early afternoon and turned to look at Dee Dee. He had planned on staring fondly at her sleeping face, but there was no sleeping face there to stare at, fondly or otherwise. Only Buddy Hackett's bare bottom. (*Steve! Ew!* **An erm...** *No!* **Sorry.** *Wow, you haven't apologized since Installment Four.* **Sorry.**) Maybe she had gotten up to go to the bathroom. He checked. She was no where in the place. He would have looked in all the nooks and crannies, but the house was too small to have any. He went back into the bedroom to see if she had left a note on the bedside table, which was actually a packing crate with a lamp on it. No note. There was no indication anywhere in the house that she'd been there at all except the strange, empty, pulling energy running from his groin to his abdomen and back. There wasn't even a stray wisp of her perfume hanging in the air. His knees buckled and he sat down hard on the floor of the living room. Nothing looked right in the room, nothing looked familiar. Eventually some impulse of professionalism triggered the muscles in his legs and he got up, showered, dressed and went to the theater to run tech for the second night, but his mind never quite caught up.

Her car was gone from the theater parking lot, so she must have gotten a ride there from his house. He considered calling her to find out what had happened, but that kind of complete disappearance was incomprehensible and felt like a strong communication of some sort if he could just decode it, and he had no idea what to do but calling her didn't seem possible. The pull in his mid-section intensified as the day continued and it took every bit of mental energy he could summon to get the stage ready for the show that night. During the second act, he even missed a light cue. It wasn't very late, but all the actors noticed and Agnes stormed up to the light booth and glared at him through the entire rest of the play, which didn't help his focus much.

He thought of calling Dee Dee all day Sunday, but he didn't know where he stood and was completely afraid to pick up the phone. Every thought he had was filtered through the visceral, muscular memory of their mindless, transcendental physical encounter followed by the complete emptiness of her being gone with no explanation. Sunday night he didn't make any real mistakes, but the timing of every light and sound cue was slightly, almost imperceptibly off.

The rest of the week had been fog and smoke, and we had returned to the past perfect tense to show that we were back to Bear's recollections as he sat semi-naked in front of the fire, plucking absent-mindedly on acoustic guitar strings. When he realized Fire and Rain was pouring from the guitar (**his guitar is pouring fire and rain? That's cool. Special effects.** *No, Steve. It's a James Taylor song. A sad one. Now shut up and eat your chum*), he realized he had to call her or he'd never be able to move again. He'd be sitting alone in his faded, off-green, asbestos-sided bungalow with his hairy, freckled body in his plaid boxers playing white boy music for himself and himself only for the rest of his life. He put the guitar down and crawled to the phone.

"Hello?"

"Hi," he said weakly. "It's Vincent."

Cold silence rattled the earpiece. Finally her voice came through, but it was even colder than the silence.

"You go too fast," she said.

Bear didn't know how to respond to that. It had been her idea to come to the show. It had been her idea to go to the party. It had been her idea to go to his place. He couldn't even remember how they had ended up in bed, and he hadn't objected to it at all, but he was fairly certain that had been her idea, also. He couldn't say any of that, of course, because he knew it would trigger some sort of torrent from her. He couldn't tell her that he had thought of nothing but her since then because that would trigger some sort of deluge from him. He couldn't say how much he had enjoyed seeing her because he was no longer sure "enjoy" would adequately capture the overwhelming drain in his body.

"Oh," he said. "Uh... I'm... Sorry."

There was another silence, but it didn't seem as cold.

"I'll call you sometime, okay?" Dee Dee said.

"Sure," he said, hoping that the word conveyed the complete range of disparate emotions stampeding through his beleaguered carcass, but afraid it probably only sounded weak.

"Bye," she said and hung up.

Dee Dee sat staring at her phone. She had been in a perpetual state of embarrassment since she'd woken up Saturday afternoon in his bed and didn't know if she could ever look directly at her own reflection again. And she really, really, really wanted to sleep with him again.

That night at the run through of The Odd Couple, no one could tell if Bear made any tech mistakes because the whole cast was slightly off balance. Oscar missed several entrances, Felix missed several cues and both of the Pigeon Sisters tripped - one over the couch and the other over Oscar. During scenes that they weren't in, the poker-playing group gathered in the auditorium to watch. Once, Lee leaned in toward the guy who played Murray the Cop and whispered a suggestion on a different way he could deliver one of his lines. The guy who played Murray the Cop stiffened, then slowly turned toward him and stared at him with a look of shock and disbelief.

"What?" Lee whispered.

The guy slowly shook his head then turned back around. A wall seemed to emanate from his back. He turned to one of the other actors and whispered something. The other actor looked past him at Lee with wide eyes, then scowled and added to the wall. None of the actors said another word to him the entire night. Except Jim, who blithely chittered on about something inconsequential all the way out of the theater and through the parking lot. Something about something or other; about this or that; about whosits and whatsies; something Jiministic. (*Did we just coin a word*? **I hope not.**)

By the end of the performance on Friday night, the wall the cast had thrust out between them and Lee was so dense there was barely room for him on the stage. He couldn't figure out what was wrong. He sat at his place at the makeup table idly toying with his pot of foundation, staring through his reflection in the cracked mirror covered with the thin patina of face powder and angst. In the small room there wasn't enough space to make a wide berth around him, but his fellow cast members somehow managed the effect of a berth anyway. Even Jim seemed to be eyeing him strangely. Well, more strangely than he usually did. Lee couldn't believe he was actually wishing Jim would talk to him until he did, then Lee wished he could be in some safe accounting office blithely wasting his life, blissfully ignorant of his God-given talent as an actor. Well, maybe god-given, but it was real talent. R. Pendleton Smythe had said so. And he should know. He wrote for the Bee. Lee put the pot of foundation down, picked up the theatrical tissue and cleaned the makeup off his face.

He was still confused and depressed the next morning as he shuffled around Twain's, starting the coffee and setting the kitchen up for breakfast. Lee picked up the phone and dialed Peter's number. Twain wasn't there, yet, but Lee looked around to make sure, anyway.

"Huh?" Peter answered.

"Hi, Peter," Lee said. "It's Lee."

"Time is it?" Peter asked.

"I don't know, seven-thirteen? I'm sorry, are you with someone?"

"No," Peter said. "Who the hell would I be with?"

"Roz?" Lee offered. "Jim? Buddy Hackett?"

"No," Peter said peevishly. "I'm not with someone. I was just asleep. What's up?"

"Everybody hates me."

"Then don't call them at seven-thirteen on a Saturday morning," Peter said, then felt instantly guilty about it. "Okay, what's wrong?"

"I don't know. You know. I don't know."

"Lee, come on. It's seven-thirteen. My teeth hurt."

"I'm sorry. I'll call you back."

"No, damnit, I'm awake, now. What's wrong?"

Lee didn't say anything for a very long time. Then he actually heard the peevishness all the way across the phone line. Show business was really making him sensitive, it seemed.

"Ever since the review, no one in the cast will talk to me," he said. As it came out it even sounded to him like a fifteen-year-old girl, but he didn't care. People talked to fifteen-year-old girls even when they whined. "I even tried to start a conversation with one of them Thursday night, and he just turned away from me."

"Well," Peter said reasonably, or as reasonably as he could at seven fourteen on a Saturday morning. "What did you say?"

"I don't know, you know. I just offered him a suggestion."

"About what?" Peter said, beginning to worry.

"I don't know. About how to say one of his lines. Something like that."

"You gave him a line-reading?" Peter shouted, and Lee had to pull the phone from his head. "Actors don't give other actors line-readings! Directors don't even give actors line-readings unless the actor is so incompetent nothing else will work or the director is so incompetent he doesn't know any better! Or he's Fellini. And he's Fellini, for God's sake. You don't give line-readings! It just isn't done, man. Sheesh."

"Oh," Lee said, sort of stupidly. "But I have a hundred and three."

There was a long, peevish silence.

"Um... " Lee said. "Well... There's something I want to talk to you about, anyway. Can I come by this afternoon before the show?"

Peter said sure and Lee told him to go back to sleep, then turned and tripped when he saw Twain sitting on his stool at the counter staring at him. Lee poured him his morning coffee, trying to pretend he hadn't tried to sneak in a phone call. Twain looked at him like you would look at someone who was acting entirely unlike himself, and hoping it was just a phase. Like Scientology.

"You're being Jiministic," Twain said.

Good grief, another Twainism, Lee thought, and poured himself some coffee.

The first thing Lee said when he got to Peter's that afternoon was, "Were you really serious about buying a theater?"

"I...," Peter said,"What... ? Um... No. Whadaya mean? No. What?"

"Come on," Lee said as he moved a pile of Newsweeks from the couch and sat, "you hate your job, and no one at the Willow Lane appreciates me."

"I don't hate my job," Peter said. "What makes you think I hate my job? Do you want a snack?"

"Okay, so what would it take to start a theater?"

"Wait," Peter said. "Slow down."

"What would it take?"

"I don't know."

Peter went into the kitchen to gather his thoughts. When he came out he had a platter of water crackers with cheese, salami and smoked salmon slices and a much clearer mind. Lee looked at him like you would look at someone you wanted to make think you were waiting patiently when you weren't being patient at all and just wished they would stop making snacks and answer your fucking question.

"Okay," Peter said, understanding the look all too well.

He moved the slightly scorched Spirograph box aside and set the platter down, then began to detail what would be needed to start a theater, trying the entire time to make it sound even more complicated and difficult than it would actually be, and it would actually be very complicated and difficult. Halfway through the smoked salmon, Lee had several steno pad pages of notes filled with numbers and ideas and a couple of bad drawings of airplanes and trees and what looked like little boxes with circles and triangles in them. He'd found the steno pad under a pile of Time magazines on the floor by the coffee table. The top page on the pad had a list of bills to be paid and the date "October 13, 1986" on it. Lee had wondered briefly if those bills had ever been gotten to as he'd turned to a blank sheet.

"Okay," Lee said. "Look. You know everything about theaters. I know numbers. I have money from the house. Damn Beverly. You run the day to day stuff. I'll take care of the books. And the acting. How hard can it be?"

Peter's head was swimming in Jello Instant Pudding™. Chocolate™. He tried again to make it clear to Lee just how complicated, difficult and hard it could actually be. And at the same time he was trying to figure out how long he would have to wait until he gave notice. And chastising himself for even thinking that he could ever leave the Willow Lane Theatre. It was his life. And thinking that if that was his life, he was a very sad man, indeed. And trying to tell his heart to stop beating so hard, there, in his chest. And thinking about the phone call he had to make on Monday to Dramatists Guild about the rights to Man of La Mancha. Or was that Tams-Witmark? And that he would have to take a real pay cut to start his own theater, and he had just been complaining about not having gotten a raise. And reminding himself that he had always said he wanted his own theater, and that now was his chance. Probably the only chance he would ever have in his life. And reminding himself that he had always said that only because people had to have things they always said, but he couldn't really ever see it happening, and Lee was just talking about it because he was angry and had getting too big for his britches. And if he let Lee convince him and he put in his notice, what would he have to do to Lee if Lee tried to back out of it? And what the hell was he thinking, even imagining he could have his own theater. And wondering if he had enough cheese to last the weekend. Or even the afternoon.

"We'd be partners," Lee said. "You'd like that, wouldn't you?"

Peter had to admit to himself that he would, but instead asked how much he'd have to put up.

"Well," Lee said, "I have thirty-nine thousand, two hundred and fifty dollars I could put in. How much do you have?"

"Well, with what you have," Peter said, embarrassed, "And with what I have, we'd still be shy of forty thousand."

"How shy?"

"Um... ," Peter said. "About five hundred dollars."

Lee's face fell a little, then he brightened.

"Don't worry about that right now," he said.

He did seem determined, which was a look Peter wasn't used to seeing on his face, and he liked it. A lot. And wanted to encourage it. A lot.

"I have my coins," Peter said.

"I don't want you to sell your coin collection," Lee said.

"No," Peter said. "Not a collection. I have a couple of jars of coins. It could bring us closer to forty thousand. A little. Wanna see them?"

"Sure," Lee said, and Peter stood and led them to his bedroom.

He stopped for a moment, remembering what his bedroom looked like, then shrugged. Lee couldn't be too put off by it, he'd seen the living room and kitchen. Lee stopped short when he saw the bedroom, but stifled the shudder that rose reflexively up his spine upon remembering the smell of socks he had noticed on his last peek into that room. He steeled his body and bravely entered. He was a good friend and wouldn't make any rude comments. He also wouldn't touch anything. Peter climbed over a few piles of clothes and one of books and pulled the light cord in the closet. There were clothes packed in very tightly on hangers, which puzzled Lee because he only remembered Peter wearing a few different things, and there were piles of clothes, both clean and dirty, and piles of papers and books on the closet floor. Peter pointed at a large, light tan can with dark brown speckles. It had a dark brown, almost paisley shaped logo that said "Charles Chips" on it. There was a star instead of a dot over the "i". It didn't have a lid and was almost filled to the brim with coins.

Lee almost forgot the smell in the room.

"Oh, my God," he said. "I thought you meant a little mayonnaise jar."

"No," Peter said. "There's a couple more."

He pushed some of the clothes out of the way and revealed another can. That one had a lid.

"Wow," Lee said. "Is that full?"

"Yeah," Peter said, a little frightened by the look on Lee's face. "They all are. Except that one."

"All?" Lee whispered, breathlessly.

Peter pushed more clothes and papers aside.

"Oh, that's where that was," he said as he took out a little, hand held Dust Buster, covered in dust. He tried to turn it on, but it wouldn't cooperate, so he tossed it on the growing pile behind him. Peter with a Dust Buster was about as useful as Margaret Thatcher with a teddy. All tolled, there were nine cans. Some were dark brown with light brown logos that said "Charles Pretzels", but they were all the same size. Lee's pants tented. He had to sit down on the edge of the bed to catch his breath. He didn't even notice the pan of oatmeal and eggs he had to push aside to sit.

"I've been throwing coins in them since college," Peter said nervously. "Every day. The Charles Chip guy used to come by the theater all the time. I used to buy the chips and pretzels and sometimes the white chocolate covered pretzels, but they came in bags. And sometimes I bought the red candy licorice whips, but they're not really licorice, are they, if they're red? They're cherry. I think. I don't think they're strawberry. Maybe they're just red. Once I got the chocolate turtles. I think they came in a bag, too. They were good. He hasn't come in a long time. I don't know what happened to him. I don't even know if the company is still around. I'm on my last can. I don't know what I'm going to do when this one is full."

Peter wound down a little and stood looking at Lee's strange face.

"How much do you think it is?" he asked. "A couple of hundred?"

"Um... " Lee said, after clearing his throat. "More like a couple of thousand. More than a couple of thousand."

Now, Peter had to sit. He landed on one of the piles he had created from pulling piles out of the closet. He didn't even move the Dust Buster.

"How... ," Peter said, then had to start again because it came out more a funny squeak than a word. "How much more than a couple of thousand?"

Lee looked at the nine cans sitting on the floor of Peter's closet for a long time, considering. He breathed in sharply once, let it out slowly and said, "I don't know. I'd say about five thousand, four hundred seventy-five dollars. And seventy-five cents. Roughly."

Peter looked at him for a very long time. His mind was trying to comprehend having five thousand dollars sitting in his closet under his dirty clothes. There was something very surreal about that and part of him was arguing that if it were surreal, it was dreamlike, ipso facto, and if it were dreamlike, it wasn't real. So it couldn't be true. The other part of him was telling that part to just shut up so he could get around to comprehending having five thousand dollars sitting in his closet. A third part was longing for cheese, which it knew would shut up all the other parts.

"Peter?" Lee said, and all the parts of him jumped. "Um... Anything else you have just lying around that I should know about?"

"Just my butt plug."

(*Steve!* **What?** *My dad reads this.* **Oh. Yeah. Sorry. Sorry Geoff's dad.** *Your mom reads this.* **Oh. Yeah. Sorry, Mom. Happy Mother's Day.** *Sheesh. Peter does NOT have one of those.* **Why not?** *I'm not even going to answer that. Sheesh. Butt plug. Man. Now I have to go wash all my senses. How did you ever get like this?* **Jarts.**)

"Okay," Lee said. "Whether or not we go in on a theater, you should roll up these coins and get them in a bank. You can get two percent a year for them. That's about a hundred and nine fifty. Not much, but it's a hundred and nine fifty more than you're getting with it in your bedroom. Besides the room in your closet that you could use for... Um... Whatever."

"More stuff," Peter said.

"Whatever."

"Okay," Peter said. "Should we take it to the coin thingy at the grocery store?"

"No, CoinStar? Are you kidding? They take eight percent. That's like four hundred thirty-eight thirty."

"Like?"

"Well, based on the previous figures," Lee said offhandedly. "Of course, the time it would take you to roll it all would have to be figured in."

"Well, we could make a night of it."

"You keep saying 'we'," Lee said.

"Oh," Peter said. "I thought... I'm sorry. No, I can do it. I just thought you... Um... would you be willing to... I mean maybe you and Abby could... Never mind."

"Abby would not want to roll coins," Lee said. "Maybe you could get Matt. You could order him a pizza."

"Child labor. Isn't it great?"

Lee relented and they decided to count coins on Tuesday night. He was correct about Abby, who didn't want to roll coins, and was afraid even coming over would do to her head what she'd had to deal with after last Wednesday evening and didn't want to risk it twice in one month. Matt, on the other hand, was really excited to have been asked and called his mother right away to find out if it was okay. He sheepishly told Lee he'd have to be home by ten-thirty, but added that he could probably fudge that to eleven or so.

Lee stopped by his bank on Tuesday afternoon. When he asked for five hundred each of quarter, dime, nickle and penny wrappers, the young teller with the blue dress shirt with the straight-out-of-the-package creases on it and the plastic name tag that said "Mike" looked at him really funny for a very long time.

"They come in cases of a thousand each," Mike said and cocked his head the other way to look at Lee funny from that angle.

"Oh," Lee said, trying hard to ignore the look and trying even harder to sound like it was a reasonable request that he made on a daily, or at least weekly basis. "Can I have half a case of each?"

The teller looked at him funny again from the first angle, then went to talk to the bank manager, who was standing by a desk behind the teller windows talking to another bank employee. Lee wondered why managers of banks were always standing by desks behind the teller windows talking. Didn't managing banks require other talents? While Mike was talking to the manager, a tall woman with really high, fragile looking hair and spectacles hanging from a chain around her neck, glanced over his shoulder several times as they talked. Finally, Mike nodded and came back to Lee.

"They're five dollars a case," he said.

"I just deposited almost forty thousand dollars," Lee said indignantly.

The teller went back to talk to the manager again, who glanced over his shoulder at Lee several more times.

"Well," he said when he returned, "then you should be able to afford to pay for the wrappers."

Lee sighed and gave him ten dollars and Mike the teller sighed even more loudly and went in back where they must have kept their coin wrapper cases. He was gone for a long time, then came out with four medium sized boxes and gave them to Lee with what could only be described as an attitude.

"Oh," Mike said, just as Lee was about to decide to hate him for the rest of his life, "I liked you in The Odd Couple."

"Um... ," Lee said. "Thanks."

Matt worked extra fast closing the diner. He was really thrilled he'd been invited to help Mr. Principal and Mr. Harris. He'd been feeling frustrated for two weeks; Jan's parents had gotten her a car and he wasn't allowed to even learn to drive until he was a senior. Well, he may only be a junior, but the grownups were including him. He couldn't wait. He'd have something to tell Jan. While she drove him to school. Darn her. He and Lee arrived at Peter's house at eight fifteen. Peter had tried to drag one of the cans into the living room, but had only gotten it as far as halfway down the hallway, where he had to leave it because his arms felt like they would fall off, and his back was beginning to make strange creaking noises. Charles Chip cans full of coins were really heavy.

"Hi, Mr. Principal," Matt said when Peter opened the door.

Peter welcomed him into his house and apologized for the mess. Cliche was sauntering into the living room. He saw Lee and continued sauntering. Then he saw Matt and turned around and ran. Matt was about to ask what that cat-like streak was, but was too busy noticing that the room was, indeed, a mess. Lee set his boxes half full of wrappers on the couch, then the three of them stood looking at the can on the hallway floor. Matt did the strong man Popeye thing and Lee smiled. Matt laughed, pleased at having gotten a smile out of Mr. Harris, then bent to pick up the can. He was almost able to stand all the way up before he had to put it back down again. Lee did the Popeye thing and didn't try to pick up the can.

"I was going to have them all out here when you got here," Peter apologized.

"Well," Lee said reasonably. "We better go in there and figure out how to move them."

Peter pushed opened his bedroom door. Cliche, who was just getting comfortable on the bed, saw Matt and ran very quickly past him, back out into the hallway. Matt was again going to ask about the cat, but, again, was too busy noticing the incredible mess. He had never seen a room in such disarray. Or smelled one.

"Wow," he said. "I can't wait to get my own place."

He looked around eagerly.

"You eat in bed," he added, astonished, when he noticed the plate with the dried mustard streaks and piece of wilted lettuce nestled in the folds of the rumpled bedspread. "That's so neat."

Matt thought that if the evening went well, and Mr. Harris and Mr. Principal liked him, they might invite him over more often. Maybe to watch a movie or talk politics or play poker. It would be so much better than what he and his friends did. Risk and Scrabble. How lame. He looked around the room, trying to imagine what it would be like to live like that. Like heaven, probably. Peter and Lee watched him and both felt old and a little sad. Then they all turned their attention to the nest of Charles Chip cans gathered on the closet floor.

"Okay," Lee said. "Do you have a hand truck?"

"My mom has one," Matt offered cheerfully.

"I've got a luggage dolly," Peter said.

"When do you travel?" Lee asked. "Barbara."

Peter just shrugged and started to dig in one of the piles in the corner of the closet behind the cans. It wasn't there, so he looked behind the closet door. It wasn't there, so he reached up and felt around on the shelf above the hanging clothes and found it. A stack of papers, an old coat, a full salt shaker and a sleeping bag fell down when he pulled it off the shelf. He pushed them aside, brushed salt from his hair and shoulders, then extracted the flimsy handle from the flimsy dolly frame and put the edge of the lip next to the open can. Lee and Matt tipped the can so he could get the lip under it, then carefully set it against the dolly and tipped it back as Peter eased the dolly to an angle. Peter started pulling it, walking backwards, and almost tripped over the sleeping bag. Lee moved that and went ahead of him to clear a route. The dolly wobbled ominously as the little baby-doll carriage wheels started to splay on the hollow axle. The dolly listed toward the bed, so Peter tipped it the other way, and it started to topple toward the dresser.

Matt grabbed the can, then followed, stooped over, holding it steady so it didn't spill and completely annihilate the poor luggage dolly, further grounding Peter to his cluttered life. Peter backed out of the bedroom, down the hall and into the living room. Matt couldn't wait to tell Jan about all this. She may have a car, but he was already helping grownups do grownup things. Anybody can get a car.

When they got to the living room, Cliche was warily watching them from behind the couch. He moved slyly around the back of the couch, then sneakily around the perimeter of the room so he could once again escape the treacherous Matt. He would have been completely unnoticed in his crafty maneuvers except that his chosen route forced him over several piles of papers, books and stuff, which he hurriedly scaled, causing them to fall as he jumped to the next pile. He finally gave up the pretense of cunning escape and dashed out of the room, almost knocking into Matt's legs.

"You have a cat," Matt said as he, Peter and Lee went back into the bedroom for the next can, then felt really stupid, and hoped Mr. Principal hadn't noticed. "I mean, what's her name?"

"His," Peter corrected automatically as they started getting the next can ready for transport. "Cliche."

(Geoff, can't we just have Bewitched blink the fucking things into the living room?) Then Samantha twitched her nose and all nine cans appeared, as if by magic, on the living room floor just to the side of the coffee table. (*Happy?* **Wow. I should have asked for nice shoes.**) Darren did not approve.

"Cliche is a strange name for a cat," Matt said as he settled down on the floor next to the cans. "My English teacher always writes that on my themes. It might be a good name for a yak, though. Or a stoat. Or a satirical serial writer."

"Are you done, Steve?" Peter asked.

Steve apologized for the interruption, and Lee pulled a strange thing out of one of the boxes of coin wrappers. It was black plastic, vaguely rectangular and had four rounded grooves in it that ran from the top to the bottom of the front, each a different size. When Peter looked at it, puzzled, Lee explained that you stack coins in the slots and when a slot was full, you had a the right amount for a roll.

"You just had one of those lying around?" Peter asked.

"Yeah," Lee said. "I like my coins rolled."

Peter shook his head and looked at Lee in awe, and Matt laughed.

"What?"

"I bet if I asked for a nuclear bomb, you could pull one out of the back of your SUV," Matt said with a grin, "Couldn't you, Mr. Harris?"

"He probably has a side of beef in there."

"No. Those things weigh about four hundred pounds," Lee said.

"How do you just know these things?" Peter asked.

Lee was just puzzled by the question.

"Mr. Harris, you should be on Jeopardy," Matt said. "Shouldn't he, Mr. Principal?"

He could feel a strange heat in his cheeks and he wished he could just shut up. He was trying to make these guys like him, but some strange energy had taken over his brain and was making him stupid. Everything that came out of his mouth sounded like something a high school junior would say.

"You can call me Peter, here, Matt," Peter said.

Matt got bright pink at the suggestion, and Peter decided he'd let him call him whatever he wanted to call him. Ah, to be young and eager, he thought. Matt clamped his teeth tight and pursed his lips so he wouldn't be able to say anything at all. So far, Mr. Principal must not have noticed him be stupid, and he wanted to keep it that way. He had to calm down so he could fit in. He couldn't very well tell Jan he'd spent the evening at Mr. Principal's being stupid. Lee was still trying to understand Peter's question about how he knew these things, so he didn't even notice that Matt insisted on calling him "Mr. Harris" or was being particularly high schoolish. Okay, he wouldn't have noticed even if he were paying attention. He was Lee, for God's sake.

They ordered pizza; pepperoni for Lee, extra cheese for Peter and shark fin for Matt. Peter found a copy of the Bee in one of the piles on the couch and opened it up on the floor next to the cans, then tipped the open can over onto it. The glorious, cascading sound of coins flowing out of the metal container onto the paper rang out into the room, an elongated shushing ching, and all three of them spontaneously grinned and stared at the wonderful pile of tarnished metal disks. A dusty, earthy, coppery metallic scent wafted up from the pile. (**This is really exciting**. *Yeah, I know.*)

Cliche, who had decided he was really a bold animal and that a bold animal wouldn't be quite so frightened of this new guy and that he was going to just boldly march right in and sit in the same room as the guy, darn it, had just slunk around the corner into the room when the ching rang out. He jumped straight up into the air and seemed to hover for several seconds directly above the spot he had been slinking on when the coins fell. When he landed, he stood, frozen, staring at Matt, hoping this crazy human being hadn't noticed him and wouldn't reach out and do something heinous. His fur tented. Then Peter grabbed a handful of coins and at the sound, Cliche sprang straight back up into the air, hovered momentarily and landed again. Matt laughed, and he sprung a third time, the exact same spring, then, upon landing, left the room as quickly as he could, not caring that he did it with absolutely no dignity at all. What was the point after three ignoble sproings.

"Okay," Lee said. "You guys separate them and I'll stack and roll."

"Beer first," Peter said.

"Cool," Matt said.

"Coke for you."

"My mom lets me drink beer," Matt protested.

"No, she doesn't," Peter said.

Matt looked like he was going to argue, then shrugged and grinned. He'd have Coke, but he'd still be there while they had beer, that was something.

"Can I at least smoke a doobie?"

Peter pulled a big fatty out of his pocket at the same time that Lee produced a football sized spliff from his boot. (*Come on, Steve, Lee doesn't wear boots.* **Sorry.**)

Peter came back from the kitchen with two beers, a Coke, a bag of chips, two bowls of fresh dip, one garlic and one not, and a plate of stoat-on-a-stick. (*No.* **Weasel kabobs?** *No.* **Fine. Chips. Boring chips. Dull, boring old chips. Stupid, dull, boring old...**) Ruffles™. (**You're really boring for a gay man. Dull and boring. Stupid,**

dull, old... *Does muriatic acid remove writing partners?* **That's mean.**)

Peter sat on the floor across the newspaper full of coins from Matt and leaned against the couch. Matt opened his Coke and lifted it, toasting to coins. He felt a glow when both adults saluted back.

"Mr. Harris," he said, "should I just make little piles of each kind for you?"

Lee told him sure and he lifted a handful of coins from the pile and started pulling the pennies out and stacking them neatly on the coffee table. Okay, this is cool, he thought, and pulled a little piece of blue-gray lint from the coins in his hand. He rolled the lint between his thumb and forefinger and was about to deposit it on the floor under the coffee table, but stopped mid-deposit; that probably wasn't the best place to put it. Even in Mr. Principal's house. Mr. Principal's cool, indescribably messy house.

"Do you have a trash can?"

"Just put it under the coffee table," Peter said.

Matt really wanted his own place. A place where his mother wouldn't make him pick up after himself. A place to park his car in front of. A place to call his own. A place in the sun. A place where he could go and tell his secrets to. In his room.

When the pizzas arrived, Lee stood and arched his back like a cat, then arced it back like a man arcing his back back. Matt stood and also stretched. Peter suggested they pay with coins, but Lee pulled out a five and told the guy to keep the change. Pizza was cheap in River Bend. Besides, it was Pizza Night. Hungry, yet? Peter cleared a space on the coffee table for the stack of pizza boxes and opened the top one. Matt reached out toward a slice, but noticed his hands. It looked like he had been crumpling carbon paper for the last half hour, not sorting coins. Copper gunk was really messy. He wouldn't have minded a few years ago, but Lee had already gone in to the bathroom to wash his hands, so he followed. When Lee came out, Matt went in. He quickly lathered and rinsed. He was about to leave when he noticed that he had left black, finger shaped smudges on the towel. Then he noticed the darkly tinted lather bubbles on the soap bar and the unsightly black, watery residue splotched all over the sink and counter. Then he noticed how clean the rest of the bathroom was, and was suddenly very confused. Maybe he'd have to rethink the whole my own place thing.

He hated cleaning bathrooms worst of all. Grownups were so baffling. He turned the towel around, splashed some water over the soap and sink, then wiped his hand on the other side of towel. He didn't notice the slightly fainter finger shaped smudges he left on that side of it.

Peter just picked up his piece of pizza with a napkin.

They fell into a rhythm fairly quickly; Matt and Peter piled separated coins on the table, then ate some pizza while Lee stacked the coins in the coin sorter, slid the wrappers over the stacks when they reached the appropriate height, then folded the ends of the wrapper, tapped both ends against the table and put the roll on the growing stack. By the time Matt was on his third Coke, it was a small mountain. The pile of stuff under the coffee table, full of lint and buttons and a couple of keys and paper clips, was the size of a small bundt cake. Lee and Peter seemed to be getting really smiley. Matt liked watching them. It was different from when his parents drank beer. They only had one or two, then fell asleep. Well, his dad. His mother would have a glass of wine. He felt light-headed by proxy.

Lee looked at the growing pile of coin rolls skeptically. He placed a newly finished penny roll on it and the pile slid.

"Peter, do you have something we can put the rolls in?"

Matt suggested the empty Charles Chips cans, but Peter pointed out they'd never be able to carry them to the car and then into the bank. Peter suggested a suitcase, he knew he had one somewhere, which was why he had a luggage dolly, but when he suggested that, Lee just gave him a "how the hell are you going to carry a suitcase full of coins?" look, and Matt didn't feel so bad about the can suggestion.

"I have a bunch of grocery bags with the handles," Peter said. "And I always get paper and plastic both, so they're really sturdy."

Lee estimated that they'd need at least thirty, and that he couldn't possibly have that many. Peter got up clumsily, the final few inches an unsteady freeze that could have ended with success or humiliation, then went into the kitchen. He came out with a huge stack of neatly folded paper within plastic bags and dumped them on the floor in front of Lee. Lee looked at him oddly, then counted them. He couldn't help himself, he had to know how many bags Peter had collected. There were seventy-three.

"Who are you?"

"There are three more piles of them in the kitchen," Peter answered.

While he was up and moving, Peter decided to get another round of beer and Coke, then sat back down and scooped up a handful of coins. Lee opened four bags and Matt helped him separate the rolls of coins into different bags. Lee picked up the steno pad he had used the other night, turned to a clean sheet, drew four columns on it and put tick marks for each roll that was put in the bags. When a bag was about a third full they set it aside and started another. They checked them regularly, of course, to make sure they were liftable. Lee would have to be careful that he didn't fill any too much as the night went on. Whoever took these things to the bank was going to look really funny, Lee thought, and took a sip of beer. Matt sat back down and scooped up a handful of coins.

"Maybe you should get help carrying them," Lee suggested, then glanced at Matt, who was a kid, and kids always looked really funny, so it wouldn't matter. Then he looked at Peter, who was looking at him like a sad puppy, and he realized that it would probably be him helping. Damn it. Why the hell am I always so nice?

Matt noticed Peter put a dime in the penny pile, and moved it to the dime pile when Peter wasn't looking. Once he noticed the first one, he kept part of his concentration on what Peter was doing, just to make sure nothing got put in the wrong wrapper. He didn't want to show Mr. Principal up but he couldn't let it go by. Mr. Harris would think he wasn't paying attention. And the bank might arrest them for fraud. But he could keep them safe. What are friends for? He took a sip of Coke. This felt good. He felt like he understood grownups much better than he understood the kids he went to school with. He had always thought he was more mature than his friends. He realized, now, that he must have been right. He ought to be spending all of his time around adults. Then he could convince his dad to let him have a car and give Jan a ride to school.

He also realized he had to go to the bathroom, but Cliche had, somehow, completely unnoticed, come into the room, sidled up to Matt and fallen asleep with his head against Matt's left thigh, and Matt knew if he stood to go into the other room he would wake him up.

"I had a bunch of coins when I was a kid," Matt said, instead of thinking about waterfalls, "and I used to count them all the time.

Grandpa used to give me some every time he was there, sometimes a whole handful. My mom said that once I heard on the radio that there was a robbery and I hid my coins under the bed. I was just a kid."

"Do you still have them?" Lee asked.

"No. I bought a bike with them. A ten-speed. It cost three hundred dollars. Dad gave me a little to make up the difference."

"How much did he give you?"

"I don't know. Sixty bucks. You could buy a whole car with all this."

That stupid bike. He still had it. He rode it to school in the fall and spring. He used to be so proud of it. He started thinking about what car he would buy when his parents let him. He'd get a cool car. A sedan.

"Or a theater," Lee said and burped.

"I started a coin collection with the cool ones, though," Matt said, not having really heard what Lee had just said. "I have some really cool coins. I have three steel pennies, they're from the war, nineteen forty three, and a lot of real silver dimes and quarters that don't have the copper line in them. You know, the sandwich ones. They stopped making real silver ones in nineteen sixty-four. They aren't worth a whole lot, but I like them. And maybe when I'm really old, like forty or something, they probably will be."

"Yeah," Peter said. "If you live to be that old."

"No, my dad's already forty-three. And my mom is almost as old as he is."

"I used to put my pocket change into a jar on the dresser," Lee said. "But it never accumulated much because Beverly always spent it. Damn her. Sorry, Matt."

"It's okay," Matt said. He knew he had turned a little red. It had startled him a little, but he thought how cool it was to be around adults who swore. His mom never swore, and he his dad only said "shit" once. "My dad swears all the time."

Matt pulled a rumpled piece of paper from the pile of coins on the newspaper now almost completely black from the oxidized copper, and looked at it.

"Is this important?"

Peter took it from him. There was a name and phone number on it. He tried hard to remember who it was, and all of a sudden his eyes got really wide.

"Oh, my God," he said.

"What is it?" Lee asked.

"A phone number."

"Whose?"

"A guy I knew a long time ago. Fred Ogg. We went out once. Saw Last Tango in Paris. Never saw him again."

"You should call him," Lee said. "His name was 'Ogg'? Really? Was it short for anything?"

"I'm not going to call someone I haven't seen or talked to in a hundred years," Peter said, then he saw Matt looking at him oddly and turned bright pink. "Yeah, Oggg. It's a last name, stupid. You don't have a last name be short for something. We called him Og, though. That was short for Ogg."

"Call him," Lee insisted. "You're not seeing anyone."

Peter gave him a "what the hell are you doing, you've already said way too much in front of the kid, straight man, he's already starting to figure it out, he's not a stupid kid, and only you and Abby and Stella knows, and Andrew, and of course Jim, oh, and Roz, but Matt doesn't know and he's just a kid and he doesn't need to know and I don't want him to hate me, so just shut up, stupid straight man" look. Lee glanced back with a "huh? Oh. Sorry" look.

Wait, Matt thought. Mr. Principal's gay? Wow. I had no idea. That's so weird. I didn't know I knew anyone gay, and now I know a gay man, and he's a grown up. Of course, he'd have to be, wouldn't he, or he wouldn't be a gay MAN. I never thought there even were any gay men in River Bend. I never really even thought there were any real gay men anywhere. Not really. But it was kind of a cool thing to know. And no one else knew. He'd have to tell Jan.

He glanced up under his eyebrows to see what a real gay man really looked like and noticed Mr. Principal glance away. Matt unconsciously gave him a "I'm really uncomfortable now, maybe I should change the subject" look.

"So, do you have a butt plug?" he asked, and Geoff hit Steve really hard, but Steve figured it was worth it for the joke. Then Geoff hit him again.

Matt had pulled all but the pennies from the handful he held, so he deposited those on the table. He noticed a dime in the penny pile and a nickel in the quarter pile. When he picked up the nickel, he froze.

"Wow," he said quietly.

"What?" Peter asked.

"A nineteen thirty-seven- D," Matt said.

Lee cocked his head at Matt. He hadn't realized until that moment that everything Matt had said all night was filtered through some need, but that statement was completely unadorned, and the simplicity of it made everything else he'd said all night ring a little strange.

"Does the 'D' mean it was made in December?" Peter asked as he held his hand out to see the coin.

"It's a cup size," Lee said.

"Huh?"

"Nothing," Lee said. A kid and a gay man, he thought. Sheesh.

"No," Matt said, laughing a silly laugh. "It means it was minted in Denver."

"Is it worth anything?" Peter asked, looking really closely at a nickel. "Hey, the buffalo has only three legs."

Matt nodded and got really embarrassed. He wanted to have the coin for his collection, but he knew he could never ask. He knew it was worth a couple hundred dollars, and he could never afford that. Everyone who collected coins needed a nineteen thirty-seven-D three-legged buffalo nickel. And Mr. Principal had one. And he didn't even collect coins. Well, he didn't collect them in that way. He briefly considered asking if he could buy it on an installment plan, but he wasn't sure if people did that and he didn't want to look really stupid if they didn't. He'd looked stupid enough already.

"Yeah," he said, finally with an off-hand shrug. "It's worth a couple of hundred. Dollars. An engraver in Denver noticed some burrs on the die and buffed them out too much. Yeah. Some people try to fake them by sanding the leg off of a good one from that year, but you can tell really easy."

"Wow," Peter said, and Matt nodded in agreement, trying not to look too eager. "Even Lee didn't know that."

Matt let that sink in for a moment, then realized he had just been compared to Lee and his smile broadened, his chest expanded and his face turned bright red. He had to look down quickly so Mr. Principal and Mr. Harris didn't see. He busied himself separating quarters from a handful of coins. He couldn't make his smile muscles calm down, though. He couldn't wait to tell Jan. Cliche yawned and stretched his front leg out and Matt thought he could finally get up to go pee, but Cliche set the paw gently down on his thigh and closed his eyes again, so Matt did a Kegel and concentrated on finding dimes.

Peter, completely unaware of Matt's current dilemma, or any previous dilemmas for that matter, brought beer from the second six-pack for himself and Lee and a fourth Coke for Matt. Lee opened his, took a healthy swig, then sighed deeply. Peter asked him what was wrong, and he shrugged.

"I don't know," he said. "I've never been a really social person, but it feels funny that everyone is ignoring me."

Matt wanted to tell him that he wasn't ignoring him, but kept it to himself.

"People are threatened by you," Peter said with a shrug.

"What?" Lee said. "Really?"

Matt could sort of see how people might be threatened by Lee. Lee was really cool. I mean, I'm not threatened by him, he thought, but I can see how people might be.

"Sure," Peter said. "Some of these guys have been doing this a long time and you breeze in with no experience at all and have natural talent and they resent that."

Matt really liked that they were having a really personal conversation with him in the room. He wanted to join in, but was afraid that if they noticed him and remembered he was there, they'd stop, so he tried to make himself really small and just separate his coins with as little movement as possible. And moving as little as possible also wouldn't disturb Cliche. And it wouldn't reawaken his bladder, which had finally stopped insisting on demanding release and had settled into a dull, throbbing ache. He put some quarters on the table, then reached out and plucked a penny from the dime pile.

Lee only heard one word in Peter's whole speech.

"You really think I'm talented?" he asked. His head was buzzing a little with the thought. And the beer. And the copper fumes.

Peter smiled and nodded kindly, then set the can they had been working from aside, opened another one and spilled it out on the paper. Cliche opened his eyes long enough to give Peter a "you can't get me

271

with that, again" look, then licked his paw a little, stood, stretched and stumbled into the other room. Matt would have gotten up then to go pee, but he didn't want to miss any of the conversation he was being let in on.

In the new pile of coins was a little, white, metal button with a pin on the back. On the front was a black circle with a big black "A" in it. Peter was about to put it on the pile under the coffee table, but looked at it more closely, and started to laugh.

"It seems funny that the symbol for anarchy has stayed the same for the last fifty years," he said, and put the button on the pile and looked at Lee. "Yes, you are. Talented. And you're starting to be a bit of a pain in the ass about it, too, which might be putting people off a bit."

"I'm going to ignore that last comment," Lee said.

"What comment?" Peter said innocently.

"If we do start our own theater, are there any other actors who would act in it?" Lee asked, then took another swig of beer, then wiped his fingers very clean on a sheet of the paper towel roll Peter had gotten out for him, and picked up a piece of now very cold pizza.

"I don't want to think about that," Peter said and shivered. "It's too scary. Can we just count coins, please?"

"Isn't that why we're counting coins?" Lee asked around the cheese and pepperoni.

"No," Peter said and shook his head vigorously. "We're just getting them ready to put into the bank."

Matt held his breath. He suddenly realized he had just heard a really big secret. This was almost as good as having a car. Well, at least as good as knowing how to drive. He hoped his heart would stay quiet so it didn't make them notice him sitting there and stop talking.

"And anyway, what about Twain's?" Peter said.

At the mention of that name, Matt knew it was all over. Both adults suddenly looked over at him as if he had just burst through the front door.

"Um," Lee said. "Kind of keep this all under your hat, okay?"

"Sure," Matt said through the large obstruction in his throat that seemed to have grown there as soon as they looked at him. "Sure. I won't say anything."

"I mean," Lee said. "I like working at Twain's."

"Yeah," Matt said, his throat clearing a little. "He likes you, too."

Lee looked really surprised.

"He does?"

"Sure," Matt said. He had information that Lee didn't have. He liked it. A lot. "He lets you get away with murder."

Lee looked surprised again, but not in nearly as good a way.

"What," Lee asked quietly, "does he let me get away with?"

Matt had a whole list of things, but the obstruction had returned and he wouldn't have been able to say even one of them even if he wanted to, which he didn't. And wouldn't. Ever. And he suddenly really, really, really had to go pee. He excused himself and quickly ran down the hallway. He made it in time, but only barely.

Lee sat looking at the place on the floor where Matt had just been sitting. I've been doing Twain a huge favor, he thought. He barely pays me. What does the kid mean, letting me get away with murder? I hold that place together. Of course, Twain did let me stay there when I didn't have any place to go. And he fixed my car. And he lets me work around my theater schedule. And he let me run the place by myself that time. And I did serve chili. Of course, he also made me do his laundry.

Matt returned and settled back down on the floor. He felt better, but his bladder still hurt, just to remind him that he had made it wait so long. He picked up a pile of coins and started sorting so he wouldn't say any other incredibly stupid thing. He plucked a Rolaid®, still in its ratty foil wrapper with the torn end folded over and almost fused with the lozenge, the exposed part of which was pitted and dusty with lint, and tossed it on the pile under the table.

"Anyway," Lee said to him, "we don't even know if we are going to do this, so keep it to yourself, okay?"

"Sure," Matt said, nodding, but not looking up.

He wouldn't breath a word of it to anyone. Not even Jan. Not even if she let him kiss her. Not even if she let him drive her car. He pulled several dimes and put them on the dime pile on the coffee table, taking two nickels out of the quarter pile for Peter. Lee finished another stack of quarters, rolled it, pounded the ends and placed it carefully in the quarter bag. He lifted the bag experimentally and figured he could get another roll or two in it. It wouldn't be long before they had another one done.

Cliche came back into the room, sat, and watched the movement. He inched closer to the table and watched more closely. Then he slyly stretched one little arm up and bent one little paw and knocked over a pile of dimes. Peter swatted at him and he ran out of the room with his tail in the air. Lee watched him run, amazed. He had never seen him act so cat-like. And he didn't approve.

Matt jumped a little, then looked around for a clock.

"Oh," he said. "What time is it?"

"Oh, yeah," Lee said. "I should get you home."

He looked at his watch and realized it was already after ten-thirty.

"Oops," he said.

"It's okay," Matt assured him. He had a little leeway, but he knew his mother was going to give him heck if he was very late. But he couldn't let them know that. Their mothers didn't give them heck if they were late. He almost cringed when he thought about what his mother would say. "Really. Not a problem." He hoped she wouldn't kill him. "Really."

They had only gone through three-and-a-half cans, and all three of them looked at the other five and a half cans waiting to be opened, spilled, sorted, stacked, rolled and bagged, and their faces sagged. Matt felt like he had let Mr. Principal down. This whole evening had been an almost complete bust. He had said really stupid things, he couldn't tell Jan about the evening, they were never going to invite him back, his mother was going to really holler and they hadn't even finished the job. He didn't think he could feel any worse.

Peter realized he would have something to do while watching television for the next several years. At least it would put off the moment when he would have to confront the decision of wether or not to leave the Willow Lane Theatre. And maybe Lee would have forgotten all about it by then, so he wouldn't ever have to confront it. Before they left, though, he wanted to know how much they had so far. Lee counted up the tick marks and multiplied and added. And divided. And conquered.

"Two thousand, four hundred fifteen dollars and fifty cents," he said. "Not counting the buffalo nickel. Or the lint. Or the shirt buttons. Or the phone number."

Peter, who had gotten up to escort them out, sat back down again heavily.

"I should buy a Ferrari," he said.

"Or a Porsche," Lee agreed.

When they got to the door, Peter reached into his pocket and pulled out the nineteen thirty-seven-D three-legged buffalo nickel and handed it to Matt.

"Thanks for helping, Matt," he said. "'So shines a good deed in a naughty world.'"

"What? Oh. You're welcome. No, wait," Matt said when he realized what Peter was handing him. He was really confused, but really thrilled. The evening hadn't been a waste. Mr. Principal wanted him to have the coin. He had something he could tell Jan about. And they obviously didn't hate him or think he was just a kid. "I can't take this. Really."

"Sure you can. To me it's only worth five cents."

"But you could sell it for a lot more," Matt protested.

"Yeah, but I probably wouldn't."

"So you're saying Matt's help here is only worth five cents?" Lee said and tips of horns began to protrude past his hairline.

"No," Peter said. "No! No, I mean, he wanted to... I mean. No. Matt, I really, really appreciate..."

"Hey, Mr. Harris," Matt said. "Don't blow it for me."

Lee and Peter laughed and Matt joined in, feeling really included and really good. Lee put his arm around Matt's shoulder and they left, purring.

(**Aaaand, cut**! *What are you doing?* **I'm ending it**. *But this isn't the end.* **Oh. Sorry. Roll 'em!**)

Peter turned around and stood looking at the bags of coins. Then he sat on the couch and looked at the amount still left to do. He was trying to remember how much cheese he had. Well, he had enough money to buy more if he needed. Then he noticed the rumpled piece of paper that he had set aside, and picked it up. He looked at the number for a very long time, then picked up the phone and dialed before his rational mind could figure out what he was doing and slap some sense into his head.

"Hello?" a very sleepy voice said.

Who answered the phone?
Will he be Ogg?

If so, will he remember Peter?
Will Peter ever finish rolling all those coins?
Will Steve and Geoff describe the rest of the coin wrapping in numbing detail?
Will they make mention of Peter actually getting a quote entirely correct?
Will Dee Dee ever finish being mad at Bear?
Will Matt tell Jan about the theater?
Will there even be a theater?
Will Lee ever be able to act again if there isn't?
Will anyone at the Willow Lane Theatre ever talk to him again?
Did Abby and Lee finish the Risk game?
Did Peter and Lee think Matt was a fellow grownup?
Did Oswald act alone?
If so, how many lines did he have?

To find the answers to these and other laconic contortions, tune into our next installment:
"Willow Talk"

(Butt plug.   Sheesh.)

This installment first published May 16, 2004

The story so far: Lee has alienated almost everyone at the Willow Lane Theater, so he considers starting his own and talks to Peter about it. Abby and Kim were mad at each other and didn't talk, then weren't mad at each other and did. Bear spent a long week in his underwear thinking about Dee Dee and not talking to anyone. Then he changed and went to the theater. Stella, who just got a raise, is happily dating Jim who was dating Agnes, who was dating Headline and is now dating Ron, which everyone is talking about. Peter discovered that the Charles Chips™ cans full of coins he thought might be worth a couple of hundred dollars might actually be worth several thousand, but only counted half of them, then called an old acquaintance, just to talk. Twain has never dated Agnes or talked about Charles Chips®. And somebody shot J.R.

(Geoff, in this installment, can we make a joke about unbleached flour? *Knock yourself out, Steve.*)

Installment Twenty-Six
"Willow Talk"

Old Paint dragged his hoof across the dry, sandy crust of the plain, causing a small cloud of dirt to join the long trail of dust that marked their arduous journey. It had been nine hours since they had crossed the stream, and he'd only drank enough water for four. The sun was halfway down the sky, but the heat was still almost more than he could bear, and caused clear ripples to rise up from the ground in the distance, obscuring the low hills on the horizon. It was hard to hold his head up, much less move forward with his burden. The rider was slumped in the saddle, oozing blood from the gunshot wound in his shoulder. The poor sap who was lucky enough to win me in a poker game was too stupid to stay out of the way of a bullet, Paint thought wearily. I should be in town eating fescue grass and standing under the shade of the big oak tree in the square in front of the saloon. He's going to get us both killed. Maybe if I really got spooked by a tumbleweed, I could dump the guy and leave him behind. Hell, he's going to die, anyway. But that just wouldn't be right. Damn. I hate having a conscience. Water. Must have water. The rider shifted and grunted. So he's not dead, yet, Paint thought. Damn. (**Geoff**? *Yes*? **What about Peter?**)

"Hello?" a very sleepy voice that sounded like a cross between Mel Torme and Moms Mabley said.

"Og? I mean Fred?," Peter said sheepishly into the phone. "Fred Ogg?"

"It's eleven o'clock at night. Who the hell is this?"

Peter's first reaction was to hang up quickly and pretend he'd never even heard of telephones. His second reaction was to just hang up. His third reaction was to hang up and cut his face off. But he had already woken the poor guy up and it would be rude not to answer his question.

"Oh, um," Peter said. "I'm sorry. It's Peter. Peter Principal. Remember? Last Tango in Paris? I threw up. I'm sorry. Go back to sleep. I'm sorry."

He was about to say he was sorry about five more times, but the person at the other end of the phone hung up, which, Peter thought sadly, was what he should have done before he'd allowed his fingers to dial the fucking number. (**Mom, Geoff said the "fuck" word**. *Tattle tale.*)

He hung up, then sat staring at his hand, which still rested on the receiver looking like it might pick it back up and dial some other number and humiliate him even more. He forced his arm to pull his hand back and place it in his lap where it couldn't do much harm. He breathed in haltingly and looked at the five-and-a-half cans full of coins. He tried to think of all the riches they held, but his mind perversely insisted on imagining how much work would be required of him to finish putting it all in rolls. It had started out such a good night. They'd had fun talking and counting and visiting. In the grocery bags on the other side of the coffee table from the cans was two thousand, four hundred fifteen dollars and fifty cents that they'd sorted, rolled and counted. Then Lee and Matt had left and he'd gotten the brilliant idea to call an old flame.

It had been Lee's idea, of course. It had to have been. It wasn't something he would likely think of all by himself. Damn Lee. I'll never ever do that again. I'll never ever do anything like that again. I'll never listen to Lee again. I knew it would be a disaster, and I did it anyway, and I should know better. Those kind of wild, take it as it come things just don't work for people like me. Well, for me. There are no "people like me". If I ever get the idea to do anything risky again, I'll just remind myself of the tone of Fred Ogg's voice when he said "who the hell is this?" That will put a stop to it forthwith. It was, as it turns out, a very appropriate question. Who the hell am I, thinking I want to start my own theatre? I hope Lee isn't really serious. I hope I didn't get his hopes up. I hope I can drag these cans and bags back into the closet where they belong and can't do much harm.

Under the coffee table, next to the pile of stray stuff picked free of the coins, was the box of tissue that Peter had brought out for Jim and that Roz had used for him. He got it and pulled several out, then slumped back onto the couch and blew his nose.

Cliche came into the room looking for Matt. He missed that guy. He had nice thighs.

The air in Lee's living room the next night was chilly around the edges, but he had a fire going which pushed the chill further back with every pop and crackle. A log fell from the pile with a satisfying hiss and flurry of sparks and ash. Abby snuggled closer to Lee on the couch. They were watching an old rerun of Death Valley Days, brought to you by 20 Mule Team Borax. It looked hot and sticky. Abby had resigned herself early on that this was about as romantic as anything they would watch together would get. That or A Clockwork Orange. Or Hud. Or Birth of a Nation. Or Love Story. Lee had been unusually quiet since she had gotten there at eight-thirty. When the closing credits began running at eleven-thirty, they both wordlessly went into the bedroom.

Lee lay on his back with his hands under his head on the pillow. His eyes seemed focused on something, but it didn't seem to be anything in the room. Abby watched him for a while, wondering what was wrong.

"You're awfully quiet tonight," she said.

279

He shrugged, then sighed.

"I don't know," he said, when he realized she had been lying on her side staring at him for some time. "I've been thinking about it all day. Counting all those coins made it really real."

"What really real? Oh, the theatre," Abby said and shifted so she could prop her head up on her hand and look down at him. "I thought you were really excited about the possibility."

He had to think about that for a moment. He was excited by the possibility. The reality was a different story.

"I'm flying by the seat of my pants, here, and I don't like it," he said. "I'm trying to like it because that's the guy you like, but I don't like it at all, and I don't like that."

Abby didn't know what to say to that. Neither did Lee, it seemed.

"Are you going to stay tonight?" he said instead.

"Come on, Lee, it's a school night," she said, then saw the look on his face and put her head back down on the pillow to settle in. He would have to get up at six anyway, to get to the diner, and she could get up a little before that so she could get back home to shower. And douche. (*That's pretty sophomoric, Steve.* **And shave**? *That's freshmanoric.* **And eat her Cream of Wheat®**? *That's soporific.*)

Lee snuggled closer to her and closed his eyes. And douched.

"I was half hoping you would try to talk me out of it and think it was really impractical," Lee said sleepily.

"Look, Lee, I love you and I want you to do whatever you want to do," Abby said, then heard what had just come out of her mouth, unbidden, and tried to breathe in so it would snap back and she could swallow it up whole and pretend it hadn't popped out so ignominiously.

The word sort of hung in the air between them, floating just above the blanket, waiting for room on one of the pillows so it could settle in for the rest of their lives. It almost sounded like a dog sneezing as it hung there. Abby hoped that at least Lee hadn't heard it, but thought he probably had. Then she hoped he thought she was spelling it "L-U-V". But she knew he knew she was too good a speller for that. Lee was glad he had already closed his eyes so he could pretend he was a cowboy riding across an arid plain on a bedraggled horse named America. Then the pillow between them sank as Gable curled up and nestled in under the word, and Lee knew Abby knew he had heard what she had said, so he got up to go pee. He didn't really have to pee, but he really had to get up, so he went into the bathroom and washed his hands for five minutes, hoping the word had dissipated so he could go back to bed in peace. When he got back, Abby was asleep. Or pretending to be, which was just as good.

Lee got to the diner at six-thirteen and his stomach was upset. He wasn't used to his stomach being upset first thing in the morning. Except, of course, on mornings after a night of drinking, which he'd had far too many of in this stupid town, but last night hadn't been one of them. Except for those mornings, he wasn't used to his stomach being upset much at all. Except, of course, when he'd found out about Beverly and the Jerk. Damn her. But that was long becoming something of the past. There was a general nauseating gentle wave that churned when he thought about getting to the diner thirteen minutes late and swelled when he thought about that word that was still hovering around the headboard when Abby left that morning and crested when he thought about theatres. Any theatre. A brief image of the local Bijou he'd seen a revival of Godzilla 1985 in with Beverly floated past the insides of his eyes and the wave broke. A sensation of sitting in the dressing room of The Willow Lane Theater sidled up to his nerves, and the wave crashed against the shore.

He prepared the morning coffee, then went back to get the kitchen ready for breakfast, but a stray vision of his name in lights caused a swell that was indescribable. He needed something to calm his gut. Baking soda was supposed to do that. Unbleached flour wasn't. (*That's it? Your joke about flour? That you can't use it for antacid? That's pretty lame, Steve.* **You gave me permission. How do you expect me to work under those conditions**? *So it's my fault*? **Always. Unless it's funny. And besides, it went over big in the Holy See.**) Twain must have baking soda somewhere, it was a diner. Where else would you find baking soda? Besides a bakery. Or a fire extinguisher. Lee opened cabinets and looked in cupboards and looked on shelves behind pots and pans in the dark kitchen. He looked in drawers, behind the recipe box and under the egg poaching form thing. He opened the refrigerator, and there was an open box of baking soda in there, but it looked like it had been there since 1985 soaking up stray food odor and the thought of using that to calm his upset stomach caused a strange numbing sensation to flow up his torso and tickle his throat and the back of his neck.

Finally, in a cupboard next to the stove, he found a rectangular tin of Arm and Hammer™ baking soda, popped the oval lid, shoveled a spoonful into a glass of water and swallowed it in three gulps. After a moment, the numbing wave settled back down and he put the tin back. As he set it on the shelf, he noticed, behind where it belonged, an unopened can of Durkee's French Fried Onion Rings. He took it out and looked at it, wondering how old the thing was. They changed their name to French's in 1995. Who am I , he thought, then put it back just as the front door opened and Twain came in.

Lee went behind the counter and poured coffee for them both. Twain looked at him for a long time without picking up the cup.

"Something happened last night," he said, then drank.

The breakfast rush was a lull, which suited Lee fine. It gave his stomach time to settle into a dull grumble. The lunch lull was a rush and Lee didn't have much time to think about stomachs or stray words or theatres or anything. Abby and Kim came in, but it was so busy he only had a brief moment to come out and say "hi" when they sat, and another brief moment to say "bye" as they left. It was almost two-thirty by the time he and Twain had the place cleaned up after lunch. It was almost two-thirty three when the phone rang.

"It's for you," Twain said. He seemed too tired to be bothered by personal calls.

"Hi," Peter said when Lee answered.

"Hey, Peter," Lee said. "Everything okay?"

There was a long pause, during which Lee was aware that Twain was gathering up the energy to give him a look. Luckily, Peter started talking before the full force of it hit him.

"Um... " Peter said. "How serious were you about that theatre thing?"

"Why?" His gut was beginning to rumble again at the mention of that word. At least Peter hadn't said "luv".

"Well, uh... " Peter said. "I've been thinking about it all day, and... um... Would you be really upset if... "

"You don't want to do it?"

"Well," Peter said. "Um... I... Well... Um... Kind of... No."

"Oh," Lee said. He was really disappointed, and wanted to get angry at Peter. "What's going on?"

"Nothing, really," Peter said, sensing Lee's reaction. "It's just... I don't think I can... I don't know... take the risk... right now."

Lee started thinking of all the horrible things he wanted to shout at Peter, not the least of which was "quitter" but suddenly realized his stomach wasn't churning. At all. He thought about working up a good snit, but he felt calm for the first time all morning. He was surprised at his reaction. It made sense, though. The theatre was a stupid idea. Acting was a stupid idea. He could quit theatre for good. No one at the Willow Lane would miss him, no one there liked him anyway. Quitting would be better than eating worms. He was the guy who had never rushed into anything in his life until the moment he got in his SUV and left Chicago. Abby liked the guy who lived on the edge, but she was going to have to get used to the fact that Lee was just a guy and that's all he would ever be.

"Okay," Lee said. "If you really don't want to."

(**Geoff**? *What*? **Never mind.** *What, Steve*? **Nothing.**)

"Good," Peter said. He was really relieved, even if he had disappointed Lee. He would just go back to life the way it's supposed to be. He liked his life. Mostly. No waves. Except Stella. Nothing unexpected. Except Stella. And he could deal with her. "I'll talk to you soon. Luv."

When Lee hung up, Twain's look of disapproval hung in the air just inches from the back of his head. He was too relieved to care. And anyway, looks and words can't really hang in the air. Except in cartoons from the forties. And in the minds of schizophrenics. Sheesh.

The cast and crew of Odd Couple had settled into a general routine of ignoring Lee and he tried to ignore them back, but at the run through that night, he was very aware that other people were having conversations with each other and it bothered him more than he wanted it to. Before they got started, Kim had a long chat with the prop lady. During a break, the prop lady had a tête-à-tête with the actor who played Oscar. Before notes, the guy who played Oscar casually talked with one of the Pigeon Sisters, and after notes, the other Pigeon Sister briefly spoke with Agnes. But no one chatted, talked, tête-à-têted, spoke or conversed with Lee. After the rehearsal, he went home glad that this would be his last production ever. Charlie ignored him, which suited him fine.

Monday morning, Peter came in to the office, took off his coat and hung it up, then slumped into his chair. He looked around the cramped room. There were two desks back to back in a space that should only have one. There were filing cabinets behind and to the side of him. There was chaos everywhere, although the chaos on his side of the room was distinct from the chaos on Stella's. Hers was more feminine somehow, covered with a thin patina of her perfume. His was just honest chaos. He breathed in, sat up and started organizing his day. This is my life, he thought. This is what it will always be. He felt content. Or resigned. Or flatulent. He would come in to this room every weekday for the rest of his life, except for one week a year, when he would stay home. And every morning, when he came in, he would remind himself that this was his life. He had done it on Friday morning and he would do it again on Tuesday morning. (**Geoff**? *What*? **Nothing**. *Steve*! **Okay, are you afraid of dying**? *Wow, existentialism. I'm impressed.* **No, execution**. *I should have guessed. Whose*? **Guess**. *That hurts.* **Not yet.**)

Stella came in and looked at him oddly. He ignored it. That, also, was his life. She hung her coat on the back of the door, flipped her hair and sat, the whole time looking at him.

"What?" he asked after a long bout, no longer able to ignore her with any conviction.

She just shook her head and opened a ledger book. It was chilly in the room, and that didn't seem to have anything to do with the weather. It seemed to be radiating from Stella's brow. Chilly air made Peter need to pee, so he left to relieve himself. When he came back down the hallway from the men's room he noticed the office door was open and several people seemed to be stuffed into the tiny room like a scene from A Day at the Races. Or was that A Night at the Opera? Or Duck Soup? (**Geoff, why do you always have to do things in threes**? *Because it's funny. And I don't, always. And people like it.*) Two people who were squeezed into the doorway turned when they heard him. Peter stopped short. One was Adrienne Gomez, the owner of Comma, Colon and Dickens and treasurer of the board of directors of the Willow Lane Theater. The other was her husband, Phil, a man who didn't seem to have any profession besides prominent citizen and who was also on the board.

"Hi, Adrienne," Peter said, confused by their presence. "Phil."

"Peter," Adrienne said. Phil just nodded. Once.

They parted a little to let Peter by and in doing so revealed two other people crammed into the office; Reginald Vanderding, a particularly snooty man who owned an insurance agency and was also on the board, and Hal Smith, a banker and the chairman of the board of directors of the Willow Lane Theater. He didn't need a fancy name. People called him Mr. Smith, and meant it. Unless they were married to him. Then they'd call him "Snookums."

"Snookums," Peter said.

"Yes, Luv?" Mr. Smith cooed.

(*Are you through, Steve?* **That was you.** *Ah. Carry on, then. Continue. Proceed. Move ahead.* **That's four.** *So are you.* **No, I'm thirteen.**)

"Mr. Smith," Peter said and they parted a bit so he could squeeze between them toward his desk. "Reggie."

Reginald Vanderding actually had to partially exit in order to give Peter room to get by, and he didn't look like he liked it. One bit.

Peter sat and turned to look at them inquiringly. They all looked at him strangely, so he looked over at Stella to see if she knew what was going on. She, also, was staring at them, uncomfortably trying to look like it was normal for four members of the board to squeeze into the office unannounced. She obviously didn't know what was going on, either.

"What can I do for you?" Peter asked as nonchalantly as he could.

"Well, Peter," Mr. Smith said. It was getting warm in there with all those power brokers. And Phil. "We've heard some disturbing news."

At that, Stella seemed to look surprised, then buried her head in the ledger book. Mr. Smith looked like he wanted to take off his overcoat, but there wasn't room. Peter had no idea what the fuck Mr. Smith was talking about. Maybe they figured out I'm gay somehow, he thought. I'll kill that Andrew.

"What news?"

"It has been brought to our attention," Mr. Smith said, "that you are entertaining the notion of starting your own theatre in direct competition to the Willow Lane."

Peter's head spun to the right and his chest spun to the left. **(Damn. That sounds painful. Especially for a robust gay man. Geoff? Why are you spinning?)** He shook his head to try to clear his focus and get a grip on his brain.

"No," he said. "We were just... Where did you hear... No."

"Yes?" Mr. Smith said.

The single word hung in the air and forced Peter to focus. His head and chest were no longer spinning, but his vision collapsed in until the only person he could see was Mr. Smith.

"We talked about it," Peter said with a slightly off key, nervous laugh that sounded like a cross between Mel Torme and Marcel Marceau. "You know, over a beer. It all started because of coins and Charles Chips© cans. I found an old phone number, too. Lee thought..."

"Lee?" Reginald asked. "Harris?"

"Yes, I mean..."

Peter wasn't sure why this was such a big deal that no less than four board members would show up to talk about it. Usually, the board members didn't come to the theatre unless they were trying to impress an out of town client or get free tickets, and if they did come on business it was never more than two and it was brief and any conversation was casually distant. And he had just brought Lee into it. Shit. I just ratted out my friend. I'm a fink. I'm a stool pigeon. A tattle tale. An informer. I squealed like a little piggy. Loose lips sink friendships. I should have taken the heat for this. Whatever the heat ends up being. Unless the heat was firing. Damn. I hate having a conscience. He had a brief image of Mr. Cogswell and Mr. Slate shouting at him in unison, but quickly shook his head to get rid of it and focused on the discussion at hand.

"So it's true, then," Adrienne interjected, tired of his ruminations. "You are starting your own theatre."

Phil nodded. It's what he did. That and service Adrienne. Peter was going to reiterate that they had just talked about it in passing and that they had both decided it wasn't a good idea for any number of reasons and that people talk all the time about things that they aren't going to do and that Lee was really a good guy who had just let a good review go to his head a little which was no reason for everyone to be so mad at him all of a sudden. He wondered if Matt had said something to someone. You can't trust kids. He would have to have a talk with that young tattle tale about keeping secrets. The board members suddenly looked like they were about to strip him of his ribbons and break his sword in two, and he would have to travel the country begging for food. He blinked his eyes to get Chuck Connors out of his head.

"No," he reiterated. "Who told you that?"

"Agnes," Mr. Smith said.

Peter still wasn't sure why it was such a big deal, but it obviously was. He knew Agnes went into the diner sometimes. How could Matt have such loose lips? Especially after he gave him a three-legged buffalo nickel that was worth a whole lot more than a four-legged buffalo nickel. A small spark of guilt ignited on the extreme tip of his sternum, which confused him, but he was used to feeling guilt about stuff that he hadn't done or that he hadn't thought was wrong or that wasn't wrong or just feeling generally remorseful. Damn gay guilt.

"Where did she get it?" Peter asked, his voice sounding a little pinched.

"One of the ladies playing a Pigeon Sister," Reginald informed him.

Okay, so neither of the actresses playing Pigeon Sisters frequented Twain's. Twain. Maybe Matt had told Twain and Twain was dating one of the Pigeon Sisters. Now part of his brain, the part that was confused by the glimmer of contrition that flickered for no earthly reason in his clavicle, was beginning to wonder why his sin was so fascinating to so many people. He felt like what Pvt. Slovik must have felt like in front of all those rifles. A shot rang out and he was about to clutch his chest, but it was only Reginald clearing his throat. He clutched the edge of his desk instead.

"How did she hear about it?" Peter asked, his throat constricting, making his pinched voice squeak a bit.

"The other lady playing a Pigeon Sister, I imagine," Adrienne advised him.

Maybe Twain was dating both Pigeon Sisters. He would have to stop eating at Twain's, that stool pigeon sister dater. Peter tried to deduce whether, by virtue of so many people talking about his evil wrongdoing, it really was an offensive wickedness or not, but his deduction mechanism was beginning to be overwhelmed by penitent embers spreading across his rib cage. His guilt would be tattooed to his chest like Hester and all potential future employers would point and laugh, sure that he would steal all their trade secrets and start competitive enterprises.

"Who told her?" Peter asked, his mouth dry, making his squeaky voice rasp.

"The guy playing Oscar," Phil revealed.

It was the first time Peter ever remembered Phil actually speaking. His voice sounded like cotton candy. Okay, so Twain couldn't be dating Oscar and he doubted Matt was, so how the hell did he know? Maybe Matt had told Jan and she was dating him. The little fink. His deduction mechanism was beginning to whimper. He could feel a couple of tears fall from behind his eyes, past the conflagration of culpability in his upper body. They fell silently down to the inside of his feet. He was about to become homeless, like Philip Nolan. And then who would feed Cliche?

"How the hell did he know?" Peter asked, his lungs tightening, making his raspy voice frail.

"The prop lady," Mr. Smith enlightened him. "Kim told her."

"Abby," Peter said, defeated, all trains of thought cascading down into an unusual moment of clarity. He couldn't believe Lee had ratted him out.

"Jim told me," Stella said, looking at him sadly. "I was really shocked. I'm hurt, Peter. I feel really betrayed."

That woke another part of Peter's mind, which told the wienie part to shut the fuck up and get off its knees. How the hell dare she feel betrayed?

"How the hell dare you feel betrayed?" he snapped at Stella and the embers in his chest started burning a completely different color.

Stella was really surprised at the vehemence of Peter's reaction. So was Peter, actually. Mr. Smith's pants tented.

"You feel hurt and betrayed?" Peter sputtered at her through clenched teeth. "You? I've given my life to this place and you feel betrayed?" He tried to unclench his teeth, but they refused, so he spoke louder. "I have to pick up after you all the time," he spat. "I have to fix your mistakes," he bellowed and his teeth finally unclenched. "I have to put up with your prima donna attitude, and you get a fucking raise and I don't and YOU feel betrayed?" he roared.

He was breathing hard, as if he had just run up a long set of stairs. Or even walked. Or even a short set. Or had bad sex.

"I don't have to listen to this," Stella said primly.

She got up and left. It was easier for her to squeeze out of the room than it had been for Peter to squeeze in. Damn her.

"Go ahead. Leave," Peter shouted after her. "You got them all fooled, but I know better."

"That's quite enough, Mr. Principal," Mr. Smith said.

"Don't tell me what enough is. Hal. I've given my life to this place," he shot back. "I keep it running. I got a car with no lock on the trunk that leaks when it rains."

"What's that got to do with the theatre?" Mr. Smith, said, nonplused. "It's not our problem that you can't manage your money."

"If you paid me a fucking living wage, I could manage to manage it. I mean I'd have something to manage. Fuck."

"Watch your language, Peter," Phil said.

"You're on thin ice as it is," Adrienne added.

"Thin ice? Thin ice?" Peter was beside himself. "I'm on thin ice?" the other one said.

"Mr. Principal," Hal said. "You're not irreplaceable."

"This place would fall apart without me," Peter laughed. It was one of those angry laughs that people too angry to have a sense of humor laughed. He could feel the heat pour from his chest and roll up his neck and out his face. It felt good. Really good. "You think Stella can do anything? You have no idea what goes on around here, do you? What fools these mortals are."

"We can always find out," Reginald said snidely. "What it's like. Without you."

"Yes," Peter said, fully straightening his back for the first time in many years and puffing out his already robust chest. "You can." He inhaled a little bit more. "I quit."

All the air in the room was gone. Peter grabbed his coat and forced his way through them out into the hallway. Bear walked by and nodded.

"What's up, Peter?"

Peter walked right by him and left the building. When he got outside, he filled his lungs with the rejuvenating, cold February air. He hadn't breathed so deeply in years. He felt like dancing. He felt like shouting for joy. He felt like running a marathon. He had never noticed how beautiful a gray sky could be. He had never realized the elegance of the of the willow branches, swaying slightly in a cascading ballet in the late-winter breeze. He had never noticed his feet. He floated all the way to his car. But not in a gay way. In a purposeful, determined, masculine way like Michael Jordan taking off for a dunk from the free throw line. He was on his way. A new life. A new beginning. He was free. At last. Even his car seemed to gleam and looked bigger and stronger and new. He opened the door and floated into the seat. He put the key in the ignition and the car started with a satisfying roar. As he pulled out of the theatre parking lot it started to rain. Cold, pounding February afternoon rain that fell in big drops at an unnatural angle. It was a weird rain. It shouldn't be raining, it should be snowing. And it shouldn't be snowing. Within ten seconds, water was trickling through the hole in his roof that was somehow still there. The branches of a the willow trees slapped at the car in the bitter wind and clung to his windshield, dragging slimy water across it as he drove under them, and the ugly, dank sky laughed at him, reminding him of who he really was. And his feet felt fat.

"Oh, my God," he said as he unsuccessfully tried to twist away from the rain pouring in. "What did I just do?"

Oh, my God, what did Peter just do?
Will he be reduced to government cheese?
Does government cheese even melt?
Has he just forced himself to start taking risks again?
Will he spend a night calling old flames?
Are there any other old flames?
Besides Henry Kissinger?
Will he remember the thousands of dollars worth of coins in the closet?
Will Old Paint make it back to the fescue grass?
Will Phil service Adrienne?
Was it in A Night at the Opera?
Or A Day at the Races?

Or Duck Soup?
Or A Clockwork Orange?
Will that word hover in the air forever above Lee's pillow?
Will he retreat further from the edge?
Will Abby still luv him if he does?
Will he become beige again?
Will heebie jeebie?
And who did shoot J.R.?

To find the answers to these and other bucolic esoterica,
tune into our next installment:
"Intermission"

(**Geoff?** *What, Steve?* **Nothing.** *Steve, is there going to be a payoff to this?* **Probably not.** *Then why are you doing it?* **'Cuz you're so cute when you're annoyed. Hey! I would never say that.** *Then shut up.*)

This installment first published July 11, 2004

Geoff Hoff and Steve Mancini

Appendix

Geoff Hoff and Steve Mancini

(I thought we lost this installment. **We did.** *I found it.* *Well, stop finding stuff. We lost it for a reason.)*

Installment Thirteen
"The Lost Installment"

Agnes (**why are we starting with Agnes, Geoff**? *I don't know, she didn't come to the party and I miss her.* **You miss her**? *Yeah, she's hot.* **That doesn't sound like you.** *That's why I said it.* **Oh. You're complicated, aren't you?** *Yup.* *What's going to happen to her, anyway?* **I don't know, she dies?** *No.* **Eventually, everyone dies.** *Even Twain?* **No.** *Okay, let's figure out what we're doing in this installment.* **I'm tired. Maybe we should just take a long hiatus.** *If we do that, we'll lose fans.* **Are we going to continue to write this forever?** *It sort of has to end sometime.* **Yeah, when I die. You don't look very well, Geoff.** *Thanks a ton.* **No, I'm serious. We should talk about taking a break, we don't have any fans anyway.** *Sure we do.* **Then why are only six people posting on the discussion board?** *They're all shy?* **I'm not.** *You're not people. I'm not even sure you're Steve, come to think of it.*

(Okay, so where are we going with this? **How come you put a parenthesis there?** *Well, with quotes, you don't close the previous paragraph but you open each paragraph with a quotation mark.* **I don't believe you. Give me three examples.** *Steve, I hate that game.* **Okay, give me one. Hand me your Blue Boy.** *They don't even make that any more, and anyway, any stories in that wouldn't have quotes that go over two or three words, much less more than a paragraph.* **Note even one by Pat Robertson?** *Okay, that issue was an exception. And how do you know about that, anyway?* **Hey, I'm cultured. I'm worldly. And it was reprinted in Look.** *Okay, I'll show you about the quote thing. Give me your Strunk and White.* **Get your own Strunk and White. You can order one from our site. Nobody**

295

orders books from our site. *My sister-in-law did once.* **Oh, yeah. What did she order?** *Blue Boy.*

(Where were we? Oh, yeah, Agnes. What's going to happen? **We have to move this thing forward, we're on Installment Thirteen and we've only gone a month and a half.** *That doesn't matter, it's been a pithy month and a half.* **Pithy, Geoff?** *Okay piquant.* **So, Agnes wasn't at the party. Will we ever meet her husband?** *He's dead.* **Really?** *Yeah, she wore him out. Would you want to live with Agnes?* **Well, maybe until I was weak. Or needed glasses.**

(What about Matt? *What about Matt?* **Should we give him a girlfriend?** *Sure. What should her name be?* **How about Jan?** *No, too common.* **How about Gladys.** *No, that sounds like an old woman.* **I think it's sexy.** *You would, you think Agnes is sexy.* **Not her name. Just her ample bosom. Should we give Twain a girlfriend?** *We already did.* **When?** *She came with him to Look Homeward Angel.* **We never said she was his girlfriend.** *Oh, yeah. Is she?* **Nice pants.** *Thanks. Did you just change the subject?* **Do you think I should shout everything I say for the rest of my life?** *Sure.* **LIKE THIS?** *Sure, Steve.* **AND THIS?** *You're scaring Cat.* **By the way, your neighbors called. THEY HATE YOU.**

(Okay, this is hard. It usually just flows. Where are our notes? **I lost them. Can we work in a Mr. Microphone?** *We've never really dealt with just passers-by, have we? You know, the people who pass by and say "Howdy" and Lee is confused that people are so friendly.* **You're not going to comment on the Mr. Microphone thing, are you?** *We already have Wheaties and Twister, that should be enough.* **Wanna take a writing class?** *What?* **They're offering one in this magazine.** *How much is it?* **Eighty bucks.** *And it's for on-line serials?* **No, stupid.** *Which magazine?* **Blue Boy.** *You've been waiting a long time for that, haven't you?* **What?** *Focus, Steve.* **I'm bored. This isn't going anywhere. There's no conflict. It's not funny. There's nothing happening. It's inconsistent.** *You always say that.* **We're interrupting it too much.** *We've only interrupted it once.* **Can we just skip to fourteen?** *That's just stupid, people will just think we're superstitious.* **Don't call me stupid.** *You called me stupid.* **I get to. Those are the rules.** *I never agreed to those rules.* **That's why they're rules. You don't get to agree.** *Huh?* **Focus,**

Geoff. Hey, what's this stuff in your refrigerator? *Which stuff?*
On the second shelf. *From the top or bottom?* **Bottom.** *What color
is it?* **I don't know, sort of greenish gray.** *Salsa.* **Got any chips?**
On the first shelf. **From the top or the bottom?** *Focus Steve. And
it's spelled "grey".* **Not in my story.** *I suppose that's a rule?* **It is
now.**

(*What about Agnes?* **She's boring.** *I thought you liked Agnes.*
Let's do one all about Headline. *Oh, a whole installment on a guy
whose only attribute is that he's incredibly handsome. That'll be
interesting.* **You have a problem with that?** *Hey, I'm a bad fag,
okay? I want a story with my titillation.* **You're just a bad male.**
What is this music we're listening to? **It's called "Mondo Exotica".**
*Put something on with a little umph, I'm having trouble writing, here.
Where are you going now? Steve, put that down, you're going to
break it.* **Have you talked to your sister lately?** *Yeah, she called this
morning.* **Tell her I said "poop".** *Okay.* **What happened to my
Spam® ball?** *It's under your chair.* **How did it get there?** *You
threw it at Cat.* **Oh. Sorry, Cat. How old is this coffee?** *I don't
know, I think I brewed it Sunday. Were there any flies in it?* **No.** *Then
quitchyerbitchen and focus.*

(**Ancient American secret, Mr. Lee.** *What, now?* **You know,
that old Tide™ commercial, "How do you get your whites so
clean?"** *Yeah, yeah, yeah, I know the commercial, Steve.* **How come
it's always ancient Chinese or Japanese or Greek or something?
Why aren't there any ancient American secrets?** *Think about it,
Steve. It's America.* **Oh. Yeah. Sorry. Okay, let's do a whole
installment on just Matt. It'll be really simple. You know, Matt
walked down the street. Matt went home and said "hi" to his
mother. Matt went out back and read Blue Boy. Then we could
interrupt it for the whole installment. And call it "The Lost
Installment".** *Okay, sure. And then we do a whole installment where
everyone just sleds down a hill.* **Okay, never mind.**

(*Where were we?* **Agnes.** *Oh, yeah.* **I'm bored.** *Okay, fine.
Sheesh. If I just agree to skip thirteen and go straight to fourteen, will
you focus?* **Sure.** *Now, I'm getting hungry, damn you.* **Salsa?** *Um...
No, thanks*) needed to get drunk.

Will Steve and Geoff ever write another installment?

Will Geoff eat the salsa?
Will Steve focus?
Will Geoff stop saying focus?
Will power?

To find the answers to these and other stupid stuff,
tune in to our next installment:
"A Day in the Life of Matt and Headline"

(**Oh, look, two beers fell in my hand and opened.** *I guess that means we're done, then, huh*? **I guess so, Mr. Microphone.**)

This installment first published August 8, 2003

Coming Soon:

Weeping Willow
The On-Line Satirical Serial
Volume Three: Intermission

About the Authors

Geoff Hoff acted at the Spokane Civic Theatre, then studied acting under Bob and Joan Welch at the Interplayer Ensemble. He moved to Northern California, planning on finding a small, serious theatre company where he could do important work in relative obscurity for the rest of his life. Then he saw the movie China Syndrome, decided he wanted to be part of an industry that could produce something so powerful and a month later was living in Los Angeles. Where he wrote a book. He is nothing like Peter.

Steve Mancini spent his youth in Michigan, playing sports, shooting things and doing what every red-blooded, Midwestern boy did: Not much productive. He studied "Communications" in college, got fired from two radio DJ gigs, canned from a job as a draw-bridge operator, laid off from a brass and copper factory, then decided he could be just as successful in Los Angeles. He is nothing like Lee.